ROGORIA: VOYAGE OF TEARS

KOTA KAI LOVETT

First Print Edition: May 2021

Editing: Write Your Best Book
Formatting: Ashley Munoz
Cover: Redbird Designs

❀ Created with Vellum

~PRONUNCIATION GUIDE~

Characters:
RoGoria: Roh-gOR-ia
Soen: Soh-in
Fristlyn: Frist-lin
Barrea: Bar-ray-uh
Galyn: Guh-lin
Sylvestra: Sil-ves-truh
Amilyana: Ah-mil-yah-nah
Tara: Tare-Uh
Lorraine: Ler-ayn
Theadalla: Thay-uh-Dahl-Luh
Places:
Sheol: Shay-ohl
Mazz'Ra: Mats-Rah
LinleCross: Lin-leh-cross
Shimslea: Shim-slay-uh
Yggdrasil: Ig-druh-sill
Que: Quay
Mang'Coal: Ming-cole

Dedicated to:
Jacob Holt, Breeanna Graham, and Riana Kaempen.
The trio who held my hand on this journey since it began.

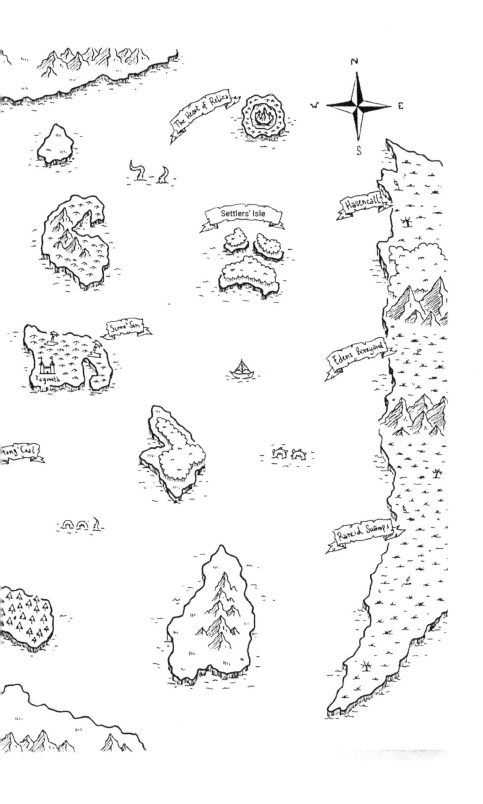

CHAPTER 1

THE HORSES' HOOVES CLICKED AND CLACKED AGAINST THE GABLED stonework of the streets as a royal carriage strolled through the city of Sheol. Rain danced on the rooftops of elegantly designed homes and shops, bursting into rivulets that gave the carriage a modest glimmer reflected in the moon's gaze. It was a setting fit for the four overly groomed horses that were chained to it, and the prince who infested the carriage.

I could see it from the turret outside my quarters, a gilded monstrosity strolling through the city I was unfortunate enough to call home. The rain signaled a coming storm, and its herald sat within the carriage. I grew hopeful as it passed through the market district; for the streets and alleyways were home to Fildra Fevral, a former noblewoman whose rapid devolving of her previous luxuries at the hands of my family had thrown her into a pit of insanity. "Do your worst, Guard Dog Fildra," I whispered on the wind, using the moniker I had given her, as I knew her for terrifying visitors, merchants, and even scared off the last two suitors who tried to court me.

That hope was quick to fade as I realized this one was unaffected. Fildra did appear, just as she always had when someone passed by during the evening hours. She screeched maniacally, with the harrowing wail of a banshee, fitting for a woman who lost everything and had gone mad. As would a starved wolf, she charged the carriage and slammed into it with the frantic persistence of a spider scrambling to subdue her prey. The coachman's ignorance of her abrasive actions only spurred her on, fueling her incomprehensible screams and bursts of rage as she railed against the carriage.

Her cries faded as the carriage made its way through the gates and up to the steps of Sheol Manor, home of the royal family; my family.

The prince stepped out into the rain and greeted my father, Lord Luke of Mazz'Ra, the continent where our city rested. From my turret, I still could not make out any notable features. I had to hope, unlike the last one whom I had met, that this suitor had more than three teeth.

No two suitors were the same, and they had a diverse spectrum in terms of personality; regardless, all were equally unpleasant. One was overly boastful, while another one was even a little handsy. Another wrote poetry, which would have wooed any other lady, I am sure. Not me, though. None of the suitors were right for me, but I was not *allowed* to have the man I wanted.

I entered my bedroom with a slight hunch due to my distaste of the evening's planned events, fluffed my burgundy dress, and brushed off lint from the matching-colored corset and sleeves. I had little interest in pleasing yet another narcissistic ass waiting in our foyer. Pleasing my father to avoid a beating, though, *that* was my end game.

My hair hung low with subtle curls, which cupped the peak of my breasts with each step I took. The level of upkeep required to maintain a "desirable appearance," as my mother would call it, was simply ridiculous. Though Mother and Father had both insisted it was essential when trying to impress a man. What a load of shit.

I made my way over to my powder desk, which contained the

menagerie of ingredients that I needed for the grueling hours of work that warped me into a powdered pastry. I slid open one of the drawers to pull out a pair of clippers, taking them to some wild, side-parted bangs that were dancing with every slight move I made. I then set the clippers back down and exited my room as I brushed remnants of hair off my apricot skin, and allowed the lavishly carved door to ease itself shut behind me.

I stomped deliberately through the corridors of the manor as my heels snapped against the hardwood, announcing my arrival. I hated wearing high heels. I much preferred my brown, flat-soled boots, but alas, I was to be auctioned off and had to maintain a sense of femininity. I wore tight, black slacks underneath my gown to at least be wearing *something* I enjoyed, something that neither the prince nor my father would be able to see.

I eventually made my way to the large balcony that married two luxurious staircases on either side leading down into the foyer. My mother, Lady Lilliane, waited as my father entered, unharmed by the rain's growing aggression, and thanked the suitor who followed as he held an umbrella over Father's head, allowing himself to get soaked in place of who he thought was a respected Lord of the Trade Circle. Of course, the prince was only doing this to kiss my father's ass, and of course, my father ate it up like a starved mutt. The prince looked up to see me and gave a wave so rigid; I had seen leaves fall with more enthusiasm.

I couldn't control certain parts of my body with him staring at me; my fingers battled one another, picking at already picked skin and chipping away at nails. When I noticed my own fidgeting, my hands retreated to playing with my hair in a sea of unnerved twitching.

The prince finally gave me an unsettling smile accompanied by another loveless wave.

I guessed that was my signal. Unimpressed, I walked down the steps, slowly, wanting to keep him waiting as long as I possibly could. That man made me instantly defensive; his gaze was more of a righteous glare as if he had just won a battle and all that was left was a trembling soldier from the opposing side. His hair was curly dark brown which, thanks to the rain, made him look like a matted, homeless dog. He shot me a smile that would light most rooms, I supposed, though it darkened mine. He was on the spectrum of handsome, but that usually came with a baneful attitude.

My mother took his coat, hung it, and then flipped her long, straight hair behind her shoulder. I got my ruby mane from her, but had yet to gain anything from my father, unless one counted my reserved, yet constantly angered state—which I did.

I approached the prince, who quickly straightened his posture and held out his right hand for me to take. I refused. I looked at his hand and then back at him with only my eyes, my head still hanging low.

"Good evening, M'La—"

"Don't," I interjected, holding up a hand. "Please, let us just skip the formalities. What is your name?"

Mother and Father looked at me with mild aggravation since they had had just about enough of me mouthing off to the average men they usually found and were stunned that I did the same to this one. It was like they knew that this was the first man they found who retained some solid looks.

"I am Prin—"

"Your name, not your title. I already know you are a prince; why else would you be here?" I cut him off again. My mother was about to scream at me. I saw it, the disgust in her eyes. But that moron held his hand up and kept his smile strong. I paid no attention to Father; I knew what his face looked like right about then.

Glare all you want, Father. I'm only single because of you.

"Darien Lockner," he continued. "I am from the City of Nien."

I lifted one brow, illustrating how unimpressed I was. The City of Nien. So he hailed from the continent of Mang'Coal, an island so poor from war they have never been able to recover economically. And yet he said it in a way that carried arrogance through the air. Oddly enough, Prince Teagan, the last prince to brave Guard Dog Fildra and pass, hailed from Que City off the continent of Que, the fierce little island that had devastated Mang'Coal in the war. In short, this man was below the Prince of Three Teeth.

Darien persisted with his hand. My previous hint did not take, it had seemed.

Instead of lightly grabbing it like the delicate flower I was expected to pose as, I firmly grasped his hand in mine and gave a good, strong shake. He even yipped a bit, and I was forced to hold back a laugh.

"RoGoria Sumner," I introduced. "My best friend is the town blacksmith." I winked at him before letting go.

He cleared his throat and went from looking slightly menacing to just a tad bit distressed. *He* was such a *damsel*.

I made a point to not look at either of my parents now.

"You are a brute of a woman…aren't you?" His voice cracked as he started off sounding pissy but changed it mid-sentence to make it sound more like a backhanded remark. Lucky for me, but unluckily for him, I was able to catch his shift in tone and see right through the facade. "It's no surprise to me that your previous attempts ran home with their tails between their legs." Again, he was trying to insult me.

By all means, Prince Darien Lockner of a dying country, I do not want you to like me.

There I stood, just grinning at my simple victory of exploiting his very fragile sense of masculinity.

He turned his attention toward my mother. "Shall we? I was told of a feast after introductions."

"Oh, of course, Darien!" she assured, trying to shake off the uncomfortable air the evening had already birthed. "Our cooks have been in the kitchens since dawn, preparing a feast of some of the most succulen—"

"No," I cut her off.

Mother stopped dead, and as she turned from the prince to me, I watched her face transform from that of a welcoming hostess to an enraged bear. My father's look never changed, but then he always looked at me with disapproval. Prince Lady Hands stood there, irate and flustered. Ah, yes, he was quite a catch, indeed.

"What was that?" Darien grabbed me, hard, by my upper arm and scowled. At long last, I was seeing the bastard's true colors. "Princess?"

I was appalled now. Never once did the previous suitors have the gall to put their *hands* on *me*.

"Unhand me." My tone never changed. I did not fear this 'prince' nor would I allow him to think he had dominance over me in my own home, at which he'd only just arrived.

"I will not! Your father gave me strict orders to keep you tame, lest you attempt to uphold your reputation with those before me."

Strict orders? In other words, prior to meeting him here, my father spoke with the twit and gave him permission to assert his dominance, or 'tame' me. Well, I was not a beast, and I refused to be treated as such. I sucked in a large gulp of air and phlegm and spat right on the poor prince's face.

He unhanded me in an instant and immediately started mouthing off. He then called me every name under the damned sun before storming out, being chased down by my mother.

I rubbed my arm for just a moment before my father approached me and slapped me down to the ground. I yelped as I keeled over, placing my hands on my cheek, where it had begun to burn.

"I have absolutely had it with your atrocities!" He bent down, grabbed me up by my hair, and stormed upstairs.

I tried slapping and wrestling free, but there was a clear winner in this fight.

He slammed me hard into a decorative table, the corner jamming into my hip and knocking me back down onto the ground. He gripped more of my hair and started to drag me across the floor as I screamed for him to let me go.

"If I cannot convince that man to stay, I will return, and you will be *nothing* but a freshly fluffed, black, and bloody pillow by the time I am done with you!" he threatened, growling the word "bloody." "You fiend, whore. You good-for-nothing heap of manure! You will be lucky if I do not kill you by accident!" He hoisted me to my feet and threw me into my bedroom door.

I slid down on my ass from the pain, and he opened the door, making me fall back. He stepped over me and dragged me fully into my room, once again by my hair, then stormed out, locking the door behind him. I attempted to get up but crumpled back down from the bruise on my hip. That kind of reaction had not happened before.

I finally got to my feet once the pain subsided, made my way to the turret, and watched as Prince Darien retreated to the carriage. My father was already halfway up the main walkway. I only had a short time to act. I ran to my powder desk and snatched up the clippers, my only weapon to defend myself with.

Gliding back to the turret, I noticed Father was already gone. He would be here any moment. I ran back inside, grabbed the chair by the desk, and propped it under the door *just* as he attempted to open it. He started to slam his entire body against it, and I knew that would not hold him for long. I jammed one clipper blade through my skirt, right where it met the corset and cut down. Then, I moved to the other side, now having a sizable piece of cloth and a train in the back of my outfit. I was glad that underneath my skirt were my black leather slacks, which I always wore, so I could be a princess around my parents, but an actual human being on the streets.

I limped toward the turret. On either side were sconces attached to the stone walls, a little offset from the turret itself. However, to the left, there was a roof only half a foot down from the lantern. I wrapped the fabric from my skirt around the sconce and lowered my feet until the tips of my toes were on the beam of the roof. The rain made everything slippery, which would only benefit me.

I slid down the roof and clutched onto the gutter right before the drop-off. Below me, slightly to the right, were soaked bushes and shrubbery. I was getting anxious. I was no soldier, nor was I an acrobat. I had to aim this perfectly. Otherwise, I would take the fun away from my father if I crippled myself. I pushed with my feet at an angle; I stupidly released on the first swing and plummeted right into the bushes with a mere stroke of luck. I rolled myself off and darted to and through the gate, my father's screams still roaring clear into the night.

I sprinted down dark streets, as well as back alleys while tying back my hair with the excess fabric. Eventually, I made my way into the market district just as Rolan, our blacksmith, was locking up. I shouted and waved him down.

Upon seeing my frantic state, he quickly unlocked the shop and swung the door open, allowing me to escape the rain for just a moment.

"I need your boat," I pleaded with him, not even saying "hello" or allowing him to greet me.

He looked at me, stuck in a confused state and a stuttering mess before he said, "Princess...It is just a rowboat, you can't possibly—"

"I either die at sea quickly or die by my father slowly," I choked between breaths. Since Rolan and I were best friends, he knew I was not joking. He busted back into a room behind the counter and came out with a map; he pointed out a small island on it.

"Here. The City Island of Metsa," he explained. "This was just added to the map, as they only recently revealed themselves to your father to join the Trade Circle. You would have no knowledge of it, and your father is going to assume you perished in the storm at sea, which is likely."

I ignored his pessimism, snatched the map, and gave a brief

goodbye, knowing I had minimal time for conversation, and was halfway out the door before he stopped me, shouting, "Wait!" I whipped around, and he was rummaging behind his counter, placing down two daggers, curved like hooks, and a crossbow, but in a style I had never seen before. I felt that would not help, considering I had no education or training in archery.

"These are base models sent from that very city," he informed me. "The bow is automatic; you load your bolts into this canister, like so." He halted his speech to demonstrate as he slid thirty bolts into the little holes on the short canister he mentioned and snapped it in place just behind the risers, typically where the arrow track would be.

Once more, I had to assume the way this weapon operated warranted no need for the arrow track. He provided me with a sling, and I grabbed both and slid it on my back. He held up the daggers, though he thankfully did not bother insulting my intelligence with another instructional speech for those. He sheathed them up and handed them to me, and I slid them into my belt.

"Arrow track is missing due to the rate of force at which they fire," he continued to explain, until I held up my hand in dismissal, having already noticed that.

"I think I would fare much better with a pistol," I said, not trying to overstep his generosity. He returned a solemn sigh, and I looked around, noticing there were no firearms to be seen in his entire shop. Father, that man drove this city to poverty and anticipated a revolution. I could only assume he took away the purchase of firearms from citizens. Smart, as there are hundreds here who would most definitely kill him had they gotten the chance.

The wave of shouting down the streets ensnared us into its web briefly before my friend pulled me around the counter into his back-supply room, filled with random materials for his craft. At the opposite side was a back door that led out into the alleys, which he swung open and motioned for me to exit.

"Don't worry about payment, it will not matter shortly, anyway," he informed me, cryptically, and shoved me out into the stormy night. I could hear the voices of Father's guards make their way over to the blacksmith, and I sprinted for safety as fast as I could.

Cutting through alleyways to avoid the main streets of Sheol, I found myself vaulting over storage barrels and makeshift homeless structures just to get through to the docks. I turned a corner and instantly heard the wailing cries of Guard Dog Fildra a couple of buildings over, charging the guards, followed by a loud gunshot which abruptly stopped her screaming. They killed her. They killed her and my heart broke for her, but I pushed myself to keep going. Death was nothing compared to what Father would do to me if I were caught. I stormed through the main road after hitting a dead-end in the alley. The docks were just across, and due to me having to scour for the rowboat I'd been gifted, I did not have time to sit and whine about it.

By chance, I found the rowboat instantly. It was docked right in front of the streets. I pulled out one of my daggers, cut the rope, and pushed the boat past the dock as I hurled myself into it, the force of my landing giving the boat a nice shove out to sea. I dropped my gear down and started rowing vigorously, putting as much distance between myself and Sheol as I could. As my arms began to ache and burn, all while feeling like jelly from battling the ripping tide, I decided I had put some decent distance between the city and me.

As the thought crossed my mind, another gunshot called to me in the distance, and I whipped my head around to see my father, his Guardsmen, and Rolan being held by his long hair, on his knees. He was the first to scream anything.

"Keep going, Princess!" his voice sliced through the waves, clear as day.

My eyes widened in horror. After Fildra, I knew what was

coming. However, aiding my escape in the first place, his fate would not change if I returned.

Father said nothing. He did not have to. I watched one of his guards hand him his gun, saving him the time to reload. He cocked it, his way of saying, "*One.*"

I could not turn away, no matter how much I wanted to. Rolan was sacrificing himself for me, for my freedom, and the price was having to watch and endure it. Father tilted the gun down to his head. *Two.*

"Don't!" I let loose a blood-curdling scream, horrified. I began to tear at the skin around my fingernails, trapped and unsure how to proceed.

"Then, return." Father's voice cut through the heavy rain. His tone, his rage. He was going to do it, anyway, I realized. People were expendable to him. He would find a new blacksmith who was loyal to him and not me. My father knew how close Rolan and I were; this was his last straw. So I had a choice; make Rolan's death be in vain, or give it meaning.

Tears teamed with rain, flowing down my cheeks, and I cringed at the feeling of snot dribbling down to my lips. Letting myself sob, I turned my back to them all, as I had during my life as Princess of Sheol. I continued to row, vision impaired, but I kept going. It wasn't long before the gunshot rattled my ears, dying as quickly as it came from the thundering waves. I let out a squeal, but refused to look back.

"Three," I whispered.

CHAPTER 2

IT HAD BEEN NINETY-SIX DAYS. I STARTED KEEPING TRACK OF HOW long I was hiding out at Metsa the second I arrived. Granted, I was away from Sheol for much longer than that, but I had lost count of how long I sailed. All the days I had spent on the boat felt as if they became one. It was a time so endless, working in tandem with my malnourishment that I remember thinking, *maybe I am dead, and this is my hell.*

It sure would be an eternity of torture to sail the endless seas while starving more and more each day.

By the Lord's will, that was not the case. I arrived at the Island City of Metsa, a town known for its excessive production of unique styled weapons and gear. It is what placed them in the Trade Circle, along with my home country of Ma'Zarra, the twin islands of Que and Mang'Coal, and lastly the Farmers Country of LinleCross. Smoke filled the air from the numerous blacksmiths and metalworker facilities, which left the sky above the island in constant overcast. There were extreme adjustments in terms of living, as within those ninety-six days I learned to sleep with the constant music of metal clanking and men shouting as my lullaby.

The layout of the city was difficult to manage, especially since

I had to avoid being seen. The main way to enter the city was through the docks, as one could only arrive at the city by sea. The docks were surrounded by a skinny beach, but large and poorly managed wooden stairs took you up a very steep hill to a plateau where the actual city stood. This was the only way in for most, yet I remained an exception.

I knew I made it because of the smoke, rowing from behind the island made me fortunate enough to remain unseen. A wall of houses blocked any sight of me, which made my only concern being whether someone saw me through a window of their sea view. I did not have a plan of where I would go or what I was going to do, but as it turned out, I need not have worried about it. On the backside of the island, there was a small plot of sand up against a jagged wall of rock that went straight up to the edge of the city. Out of sight from any inhabitants, it made a perfect spot to stay hidden during my stay. To make matters better, there was a faint indent in the wall of stone, where I could just barely fit. It provided shelter from light rain, but storms would leave me soaked. That was another thing I was forced to grow accustomed to.

I awoke that morning and followed my normal routine. I'd cringe at the aroma which emanated from me, that of saltwater and sweat. Of course, I bathed any way I could, but that consisted of me just soaking myself in the ocean and rinsing off any dirt or grime. It did not truly clean me, as my clothes retained the musk that had built over the ninety-six days. To add to the washing predicament, I could only bathe late at night as to not risk the very unlikely chance of being seen.

Next, I slid myself out of my little hole in the wall and stood up the second I was free to shake the stiffness from sleeping curled up in a ball all night long. That was followed by various stretches and shaking sand out from my train. I made my way to Rolan's boat, which I had beached so it would not drift away, and grabbed my satchel, which I had to steal from a vendor, as I did not think to grab money before my impromptu escape.

My satchel did not hold much. Inside were my two daggers, the hook-shaped prototypes that Rolan gave me, along with a single piece of parchment, rolled up and stuck shut by a tiny needle. I pinched the parchment and dragged it up, withdrawing the needle and unraveling the paper. I remember the first week, doing this made me anxious each time I had to since I am so terrified of needles. Days one through about eleven or twelve, my breathing would pick up and I would feel my stomach churn. By now, it had just become second nature.

I pricked the tip of my index finger on my left hand, giving the right hand a break. Blood peaked out instantly as though it was giving me a cheerful, "Good morning!" I held the parchment firmly and drew a smooth line with my own blood, then set the parchment into my little hole in the wall, blocking it from any unwelcome breeze while the ninety-sixth line dried.

Once I was confident the parchment was dry, I removed it and rolled it back up, carefully sliding the needle back into the same hole I pulled it from, then shoved the assembly back into my pack, trading them for my hook-shaped daggers. A girl needs to defend herself.

I then walked to the jagged wall of stone and rubbed my hand on it. It was as dry as a bone, which was exactly what I needed. The slightest bit of moisture would mean I'd have to wait like I normally did, but today I cracked. I could no longer just stare out into the empty sea for God only knows how many hours. I could not wait until hours after nightfall to see the empty city anymore. I needed a sense of reality and civilization, or I would go mad.

Before I got started, I hooked the daggers into my belt and crawled back into my hovel. Pushed far back were the only two items I had, other than the boat and my pack: my crossbow and a long piece of linen cloth that, unfortunately, I had also stolen. Ninety-six days and I was still not over my thievery. Stealing random pieces of bread, fruits, and vegetation should have gotten me used to it by now, but no—I just saw myself as a criminal.

I holstered my bow, slung it over my back, rolled the linen around my neck, and moved toward the jagged wall. I pushed myself up and started climbing up using the usual, accessible pieces. I did this with ease, but on my first day, it did not go nearly as well. My first day, I also tried climbing with my crossbow on my back from the get-go, making all those falls double in pain until I got the hang of it. Now, my growing upper body strength breezed through the process. It did not take extreme athleticism due to how the rocks jutted out. I just had to get the hang of where to grab, where to put my foot, and most importantly, I had to remember never, under any circumstances, look down.

Metsa's Upper City had no walls, which made that possible. When I reached the top, I was able to grab onto a ledge and hoist myself up, placing me between two houses. Within that small alley, I would unravel my cloak and drape it around me to hide my clothes. Though dirty, it was still similar to typical Metsa fashion. After I was safely covered, I left the safety of the alley and tried to blend in with society.

Making that climb put me in the Upper City, at least, that's what the locals called it. If this was Sheol, it would've just been known as the Residential District since this was where most of the homes were. The Upper City streets were just a massive circle, where about thirty large houses sat. In the middle of the circle was a giant hole, giving one a birds-eye view of the Lower City. Two long stone bridges connected one side of the Upper City to the other, and at the corner, where the bridges met the parallel street, were staircases that descended to the Lower City. It was clear the city came with a story. The Lower City did have walls, though it was just unkept bits that were carved out. Small apartments were built inside the stone.

I was about to make my way down the stairs when I noticed an abundance of guards roaming the lower depths of Metsa; they were accompanied by their captain, whom I had only seen once but worked my hardest to avoid.

The man was just scary-looking. He did not wear the normal Guardsman attire with the leather armor and odd brass goggles on the forehead. No, instead, he wore light steel armor, with a creepy leather mask hiding his face, and goggles were placed right over his eyes.

With no warning, the guards broke into a frenzy, charging through the lower streets. The change was random, so misplaced that I felt my stomach twist and my blood run cold, while I momentarily forgot how to breathe.

They saw me. I've been compromised.

I sighed in both relief and irritation when I saw what they were chasing. Everything about Metsa was so different from Sheol, but like the Sheol Guardsmen, those guards were after one thing: a woman.

A thief to be exact, and by far the strangest thief I had seen. She adorned a black corset, with a low-hanging skirt that barely kissed the ground as she ran. Her platinum hair was tied in an updo, and she wore similar-looking goggles to those of the guards. I had never quite figured out what the goggles were for, but I assumed they served some purpose if both soldiers and thieves were utilizing them.

She was quite evasive, dodging into alleyways in the Lower City, knocking over boxes and barrels to trip the guards. I even saw her grab a young boy by the arm and hurl him at the guards. The thief was an absolute menace.

I lost sight of her briefly as I got distracted. I was nudged as someone tripped into me for a moment, and I quickly turned my head to see a very well-dressed man walk right by me. He mouthed "sorry," and then kept moving.

I felt my blood chill, an inch closer and he would've felt the bulkiness of my bow, but he, thankfully, did not seem to notice. He made a slight turn toward a house and shoved his key in the lock. The realization of which house he lived in almost made me hyperventilate and robbed me of my ability to sit still; it was one of the houses that made the alley which I had just come from. Just before he crossed the threshold, he turned back and flashed a smile. Not a menacing or mischievous smile. It was genuine, and his perfect white teeth contrasted with his rich, dark sepia skin. He disappeared into the house, and I calmed down within seconds and turned back to witness the commotion the guards were dealing with.

Shit.

The thief was on the Upper Streets, and she was running in my direction. I moved into an alleyway. Not the one I came from, since I knew one of the owners was home. I picked an alley about three houses down, lying in wait.

With my back against the wall, I heard the thief's footsteps approach with rapid haste. She would be making her way to me in no time, and then what? She could hurt me, blow my cover and in turn, cause me to be shipped back to Sheol. I could not allow any of that.

I was not a fighter by any means. Three months ago, I was a princess. Now, I was some rogue hermit. However, this was survival of the fittest.

The footsteps approached faster and faster, and my linen shawl was damp with sweat. I was beyond nervous. Manic. Frantic. She was coming, and I had no plan in motion. My breathing unstable, I made a fist with my right hand and placed the palm of my left firmly against it. I was able to tell my mind to go blank, and in doing that I only focused on the stomping of her footsteps. She was so much closer, but not enough. Her boots smacked against the stone; she was almost here. Closer. Closer…

I took one step and shot my elbow into her throat, then dragged her into the alley the second she was on the floor.

Blood freed itself from her mouth, and I was horrified I may have smashed her jugular. Could she have lived through that if that was what happened? I was only so knowledgeable.

I acted fast and searched her. She did not have much on her, but I did see a gorgeous amethyst ring on her finger. That must have been what she stole, but since it had no worth to me, I threw it outside the alley and kept searching her pockets. The only other thing she had was a piece of parchment. Unfolding it, I sneered at the contents.

WANTED: PRINCESS ROGORIA L. SUMNER. WANTED FOR TREACHERY, THIEVERY, AND MURDER OF THE SHEOL BLACKSMITH. ANY INFORMATION WILL BE REWARDED WITH A MINIMAL SUM OF 100 GOLD, WHILE DELIVERING HER BACK ALIVE WILL ENSURE 5,000.

I tried to hold in my rage. I murdered no blacksmith. Rolan was the only friend I had in the city. Well, the only friend ever since…

"Stand." A voice came from above, and I was making strict eye contact with one of the Guardsmen; he was pointing his flintlock pistol right at me. He told me to stand, but it was really his malicious gaze that told me to do so right now. I jolted to my feet and thought I was complying by putting my hands up, but I must've triggered him. He fired his gun as a warning, the bullet just moving past my ear and the makeshift hood of my shawl falling back. Rain began to fall. I hadn't even noticed the sky due to the smoke Metsa pushed out into the air. It fell harshly, and my hair was matted within minutes.

"Sorry for that," the Guardsman said, though insincere. "But please try to only move when I tell you to."

I gulped, not knowing if that meant I should put my hands down or leave them there since he did not say.

This guard was incompetent. He turned away to face his comrades who were coming up from the street, paying no attention to me. "Captain, take a look," he called, but by the time he turned back he was faced with me, now armed with my crossbow and pointing it right at him. He scoffed. "Put that dow—"

I fired at his feet, missing, but it was close enough to cause him to yelp and jump back. I made my way to the ledge, where the alley faced the ocean and started to climb down the jagged rock wall, planning to just swim from where I was to my little hovel. My foot slipped, as the rain continued to fall, and I screamed, dropping my bow to the water in the process.

"Do not move again," a different voice ordered.

I looked up, struggling, and strained from the effort of not slipping to my death, to face the terrifying Captain of the Guard. His gun was pointed at me, as well, but the second we made eye contact, he slowly lowered it, took one step back, and cocked his head. "RoGoria?"

I went numb and fell to the crashing waves.

CHAPTER 3

I WAS SEEING DOUBLE WHEN I OPENED MY EYES. BLURRED IMAGES OF the ocean flashed away with each blink, and the flashing would sometimes show the beach for a split second. My head was pulsating with pain, and each blinking flash only made it worse. I was clearly on land, and I was able to calm down and focus on relieving the pain.

When I turned my head, another blinking flash revealed my home, my hole in the wall. I was back on my secluded beach. I turned over onto my back but quickly realized that was a bad idea because any sort of movement made my shoulders ache. I clamped my mouth shut to muffle any screams; I started to tear up, as doing so also hurt.

"That is going to hurt for quite some time, I'm assuming," a voice came, but I could not see from where due to my eyes being sealed shut to try to subdue the pain in my head. It was a feminine voice, and it sounded elegant. It hit my ears like falling silk, gently rippling as it traveled through the air. It was a voice that did not make me alarmed in a time when any voice should.

"I cannot see…" I started to cough vigorously, not able to get a word out.

"Easy," the voice said. "You just woke up; give yourself a minute. You owe at least that much to yourself."

I nodded, which was idiotic since I was not sure if she could see me at whatever angle I was to her and the pain shot through me again. The voice hit my right ear first, from behind. That was the most I could pinpoint in my state.

Several minutes went by, and my headache subsided in a minimal sense, but enough for me to crack my eyes open and be face to face with a darker, smoke-filled sky, and a black sea. It was night, and I started praying to myself that it was a night on the same day. My senses started to come back one by one. The visuals of the night sky were accompanied by the soft, tender kiss and chalky taste of the sand. Now I knew why I was coughing so viciously. The intense smell of fish curled over me, which was unusual. Living by the sea only gave me the smell of saltwater, but this was different. Like walking by fish markets on the docks of Sheol.

Please, Lord, don't let me be back in Sheol.

I wasn't, though. I already saw my hovel, and part of my mind kept reminding me I was just being far too paranoid.

I began to turn over to greet the voice once and for all, but I was chastised not to instead.

"Not yet," she said, causing me to panic and just slam myself back, so abruptly that it reminded me the rest of my body was in pain. I cringed and tried to breathe through the pain once more. "I'm sorry, but trust me; you're going to want to get used to my voice before you look at me."

What a weird thing to say, but I was in no place to argue right now. For all I knew, I could have been talking to a Metsa civilian. Not long after that thought, I realized there was no way this voice was coming from land. I started to lose slight control of my breathing, panicked about what on Earth I was talking to. My fingers, destroyed by my own fear, oozed blood as I scratched at them with vigor.

After spending a few minutes in my panicked state, I realized I had the power to stop it by just going with my gut and looking, anyway. I quickly turned my head, a mistake in itself since it was pounding and ached just as violently. Still, though, I gazed at the stranger and gasped at the horror that floated in front of me.

She did not look well. I only knew she was a "she" by the sound of her voice and her bare breasts. Her skin was grey and wet, the starlight reflecting off the rivulets of water on her shoulders. The lower half of her was submerged, and she was a little way out into the ocean, presumably where my beach dropped off into the sea so I could not get a strong look when those factors combined with the darkness of the water.

She held out her arms in surrender, showing that she truly meant no harm. Her hands were webbed, with pointed claws at the tips of each finger. She was truly terrifying to gaze upon, but knowing she had that smooth, silky voice and clearly meant no harm helped ease my discomfort.

"Can you move closer?" I asked.

She lowered her arms in hesitation but cooperated. She glided over to me through the water, as close as she could without being on land, and I was able to pick up on more details. Her eyes were wide and black, the moonlight reflected in a glossy haze. Her neck had gills, and the skin all over from what I could see was grayer than before and showed some signs of aging; it was wilted and deteriorated. Her nearness also revealed what I feared to see but was also excited to see at the same time. Her submerged lower half was a large, scaled, tail with two fins.

"Please, do not be alarmed," she pleaded in a frightened tone. "I know it's confusing to see me right now, but I promise you are not hallucinating and—"

"What's your name?" I did not want to be rude, but I hated that she had to fear my reaction due to what she was. Before me was a much scarier version than the child stories I read, but even I could not deny I was face-to-face with a mermaid, a Siren of the Sea, right before my eyes.

"Galyn," she introduced.

I cringed at a brief shock of pain which shot through me. "I am—"

"Princess RoGoria herself," she finished for me. "Your wanted posters flutter off into the water every now and then."

"Do you live here?" I asked.

She grinned widely and shook her head. "I'm sort of...around. I do not have a home, Princess."

I closed my eyes in irritation. I hated being called Princess. It brought back some sour memories, memories that should not have been sour.

"Please," I began to plead with her. "Do not call me Princess. My name is RoGoria, and sadly, Princess just does not apply to me any longer."

Galyn cocked her head, observing me. She smiled once more, this time showing a large row of fangs. She looked so terrifying I felt for just a split moment I should not trust her. She could pounce on me at any moment.

Her expressions told me she picked up on where my mind had gone, but she ignored it, which was both comforting and alarming. Despite her cheerful and polarizing persona, it was hard for me to match it with her physical aesthetic. I started to have a continuous pit feeling in my gut about her, but I chose to ignore it; she was the first real social interaction I had since arriving.

"Some words cut like a marvelous, well-crafted blade," she said. "'Princess does it to you. Your wounds are visible, as I say, I know when it reaches your ears. You are in pain by this word. Why?"

Now, I was offended. She was analyzing me, and I did not take kindly to it. "It is just because I am no longer a princess." I sneered at her, narrowing my eyes to try and tell her she crossed a line.

"Doubtful," she said. She glided closer to me and even went as far as to drag herself half out of the water. "It has nothing to do with whether you are a princess or not. No, it clearly goes deeper than that."

"I should get some sleep," I stated, ending the conversation right there and then.

Her eyes widened at the sudden change. It was not long before she shrugged it off and started to push herself back into the water. I had done nothing wrong, I felt. She waved at me before diving deep into the ocean without saying another word.

I turned to crawl to my hovel, and that was when I finally noticed it. My automatic crossbow. It was nestled into the sand, alone and unharmed. It fell before I did, and that was when it hit me. I had fallen quite a way from this small, random spot of land. The only reason I could have ended up here is if someone held me and carried me to the shore.

"Fuck," I muttered under my breath.

CHAPTER 4

I SLEPT ALL THROUGH THAT NIGHT, AS WELL AS MOST OF THE previous day.

I awoke the following morning, after speaking with the mermaid. I walked around the beach to stretch myself out, but it did not last long as I was still very sore from the fall. I could only imagine how many times the waves crashed my body against the rocks, yet at the same time, I surely would have died if the damage were extensive. I looked out to the sea and stared into what I could only describe as a watery abyss.

Galyn's head even made a brief appearance, and I know we made eye contact. She waved at me and dove back underwater as if she was just checking on me.

Since the jagged rocks protruding from the cliff's wall were still riddled with moisture, I had to wait. I was not going to fall like that a second time, so I crawled back into my little hole and drifted off back to sleep. In a constant battle between being awake and being asleep, I eventually woke up to a still, smoky night with the crashing waves being the only sound. I shoved my bow deep into my hovel. I did not have my linen cloth to cloak me anymore, and so I could not just openly carry it on my person, especially after having fired it at a guard, which was the first stupid thing I did since arriving.

I climbed up into the usual alleyway, this time being smart and avoiding any windows since I knew a man lived in one of those houses. The goal tonight was to steal some more food. It stressed me out having to do this without my linen cloth, but I had done so for the first month of being here, so I just had to be careful. The hardest part was sneaking down into the Lower City; it left me exposed.

Peeking out from behind the building, my eyes darted around to take everything in; two guards were patrolling the Upper City streets, one was making his way across one of the bridges, the other kept her eyes peeled in front as she mindlessly walked around the roundabout. It was near impossible to properly plan where to go, but as luck would have it, fate decided to throw me a bone here.

I heard the door to the house beside me open, and out came that well-dressed man again.

He exited, late in the wee hours of the night and took a deep breath. He stood still for a few moments, smiling at the sky before snapping his fingers and calling the two guards to attention.

There was not a lot of cover for me, so I laid flat on my stomach and waited. As the two guards approached, I heard him speak.

"I require an escort," he explained to them, his voice strong and deep, yet almost comforting. He was not demanding an escort; he was requesting one.

Both guards greeted him like old friends, and they walked him down the stairs to the Lower City, disappearing into the silence. This left no guards on the Upper Streets, so I had to hastily make my move. I shot up and tiptoed down the stairs into the Lower City.

Dashing behind the buildings of Lower Metsa was like riding a bike. With my linen cloth, I did not have a need to lurk in the shadows, so I was happy to see two months without being as sneaky did not make me lose my skill.

The Lower City buildings were only shops and factories, for the most part. The only homes were carved into the sides of the walls, with a bunch of skinny staircases leading up, around, and over other houses. I knew they had to be smaller and with windows looking out to see only into the city. I assumed they were for the poor people in Metsa, but I got a look into one, and they were actually cozy. However, with windows facing the city, I had to be careful.

I made my way to the Center, adorned with the large Faerie Fountain. I scanned everywhere I could before making my next move. Circling the fountain was various vendor stands; the reason for not having their own store was they sold goods traded from other Isles. For the most part, they remained closed at this time of night, except for one.

The vendor who oversaw produce, and had a large stock of vegetation and fruits, was the Metsa town drunk. His name was Lenstrid, and he lived in any one of the taverns most nights. On other nights, such as this one, he would be passed out on his chair at his stand.

I had only just started to approach when I heard voices coming from the left. I ducked down and peered from the corner of the house I was beside to see the two guards and well-dressed, dark-skinned man they were escorting enter City Hall. The fact he was clearly a man of importance rattled my insides. He had made eye contact with me just a day before and could easily turn me in.

The guards came out moments later and made their way to the large gate beside City Hall, entering the barracks.

The coast was officially clear. I made my way to Lenstrid's stand, where the lech had lain, snoring, causing all the sounds of Metsa's workers to fade away. I started shoveling carrots, apples, and peaches into my pockets before I filled my arms. I never stole a lot, but after the last day, I lost the few pieces of food I kept on my person, which was the last of what I had. I halted at Lenstrid shuffling in his chair, frozen in fear.

He let out an ear-shaking belch followed by a flood of drool.

I cringed at the site before going to grab more.

Then, the screaming started.

I jerked my head up to the apartments carved into the rock walls that surrounded Metsa. Blood-curdling screams and cries for help radiated from a single-lit window. The screams sounded as if they were coming from a young girl. My eyes were glued to an illuminated window, beyond worried that the screams would wake the city, or God forbid, Lenstrid, and I would get caught right in the act.

There was a loud crash, and a deeper, older voice yelled to shut up and stay still. The girl's screams were gone, or, at least, gone to me. There was clearly a child in there, and she was not safe. I had no control over my legs anymore as they charged through the city, carrying me as I worked to replace my fear with vigilance. I did not think about keeping cover and made no attempt to keep myself out of danger.

I charged to the Lower City living quarters and heaved myself up a narrow staircase till I reached the landing that met the front door. I turned the knob with violence, and successfully as I, thankfully, found it unlocked. I rammed into the door and swung it open and found myself in a skinny hall that led to a bigger opening, the leisure area, and gazed upon a horrifying scene. A girl with matted hair was pinned to the table by a taller and slimmer man. His hand was over her mouth for a second, but he whipped around at my entrance and withdrew his rapier.

The sight of me caused him to smile, while the sight of him almost brought up yesterday's breakfast. It was his familiar dark, curly hair, chiseled jawline, and deep stare.

"Darien," I said, through my teeth.

His smile never faded. "Ah, so you *are* hiding out here," he said.

I did not ask why he was here. It was obvious. Still doing Lord

Luke's dirty work, just as he did when he was conditioned to be my perfect suitor.

"What..." I broke off, still disgusted by the sight. The girl had all her clothes on still. That was relieving to see. "What the hell are you doing with her?"

He shrugged my question off as if what I caught was no big deal. His malicious smile faded to a bored, almost inconvenienced look.

"I almost called this place dry," he informed me.

Dry? What on Earth could that mean?

"Thought I would give myself a little reward for a thorough check." He taunted me by brushing the girl's hair. "Had I known that all it would take were the screams of little Marla here to lure you out of your," he sneered at me as he searched for the words, "nest, I would have acted sooner."

My blood burned with each word he spoke. I wanted nothing more than to gut him. I was not a fighter, though. He was.

"She—" I choked. Fear had started to remind me that I was out of my league in this. "She is a child, Darien." I had no words other than obvious ones. I felt the tears in my boots rattle as I shook. I had far too many thoughts running rampant at once.

Run. No, I cannot run. He will either catch me, or he will continue what he's doing. I could not run. *Fight. You can fight him. You will most likely lose, but you can.*

My hands moved slowly under my train, along the sides of my belt, allowing my fingers to dance with the hilts of my hook daggers. I moved slow enough to where he did not pick up on it, or at least did not find it worth commenting on.

"By all means, my lovely, spoiled princess," he taunted me once more. "You're more than welcome to attempt to do something about it."

I was too scared to even be angry over his words. He had me cornered. I could only focus on trivial details; left hand, holding a sword and pointed right at me, right hand had a firm grasp around Marla's throat.

He scoffed and spat toward me. "I knew you were all talk," he said. "Now, if you do not mind. I will get to you shortly." His right hand released Marla's throat and he grabbed her by her dark, thick hair and she screamed once more.

The small room cried with her, shaking the chandelier above their heads, rattling the pots and pans in the kitchen to the right. Her screams did not go to waste. As they entered my ears, the vibrations of her anguish filled my very core. I heard the sound that resembled a falling oak tree, and before any of us could continue, I lost it.

I darted through, unsheathing one of my daggers, and lunged toward him. His reflexes were sharp, and just as I had hoped, he raised his sword at me once more, and I was able to snag his skinny blade in the hook my dagger made. I slammed it into the table, forcing his arm down. He was stunned by my sudden burst of rage. Hell, I was stunned by it, too. It was as if everything that I had bottled up with my parents, living as a homeless hermit, having to keep the fact I had seen a mermaid a secret lest I blow my cover while ranting like a madwoman, and having my whole life robbed from me just broke. The glass pieces of my bottled emotions penetrated my brain as I looked at Darien and fueled my rage.

He was quick to release his sword from underneath my hook and raised it once more, and I prepared for him to attempt to skewer me alive. Instead, he slammed down, bashing the hand-guard on the crown of my head.

I screamed and fell to the floor, dropping my hook dagger in the process. I focused on the pain briefly. I had just gotten over the head trauma from the cliff, and Darien brought it right back. Pained, I lifted my leg and railed my entire foot into his. A loud snap followed, and he was down. Before I could react next, I heard sobbing behind me. I whirled around to see Marla back up against a wall, terrified. I scanned around her home, and tucked in a skinny hall were stairs—I turned back to Marla.

"Run," I said, out of breath. "Up the stairs, run." I remained calm speaking to her, and it seemed to have worked. She did not see me as an enemy, but she did not listen, either.

"This is my fault," she cried.

Distracted, Darien was soon on top of me with my dagger that had fallen, and he pushed me down. I was thankful that he had not thought to pin my arms, so when he came down with my dagger, I grasped his wrist and fought to live.

He's going to kill me.

At a steady rate, he came lower. He was much stronger than I, and I started to fear the inevitable.

There is no way out. Either I die...

He used a free hand to grab me by the neck of my corset and slam me into the stone flooring, and as we came down, his dagger fell inches from my eye.

I cringed at the pain that resonated throughout my body.

Either I die, or he dies.

My heart started to race, as I turned my head turned every which way and noticed his sword was less than an arm's length away. My hand fell from his wrist, and in an instant, I grabbed the hilt of his rapier and rammed it into his head.

His head hit the table, and he crippled to the floor.

I shot up, held the sword blade pointed down, and before he could utter anything else, I stabbed him through his eye. I kept going until I felt the blade reach the stone floor and then dropped to the floor myself.

Now, the part about murder on the wanted posters was true.

CHAPTER 5

SOUND DID NOT EXIST TO ME ANYMORE. THE BACK OF MY HEAD LAY back on the top of the dining table in Marla's home while my vision flashed; focusing on one point and then another, with no recollection of moving my eyes or head.

His body. Then a flash. His sword. Another Flash. His blood.

His blood was everywhere, oozing from the back of his head onto the stone floor.

This whole house is made of carved stone. This whole city is made of carved stone, with the exception of the brass rooftops on the standing buildings.

My mind expanded elsewhere, to everywhere except where I was. I had started to dissociate and wanted to focus on everything but the present. I knew that was wrong; I had to focus on the present, but I could not.

How did a small city afford so much stone? How much debt is this stupid city in?

I could not stop, no matter how hard I tried. I was stuck in an endless void where silence reigned supreme, and nothing I tried turned it off.

The Lower City is clearly carved in some sort of crater. How did it get there? Was it man-made? Add that to the city's debt.

I blinked and doing so caused sound to tiptoe into my ears.

What is that? Is that crying?

My eyes were glued straight ahead, facing the entrance and exit. Yet, the sound pulled my attention just beside me. I focused on it harder. It was muffled, but I could pinpoint it to my right. I was shaking, but I began to turn my head with a gentle swing, trying my hardest to keep it steady.

Marla was beside me now. I didn't notice her approach yet here she was sobbing into my sleeve. She looked up when I stopped turning, and her eyes which were at first relieved grew fearful. Her sobbing silenced, and she stared into the depths of my very being, her dark eyes wide with questions. It had only just hit me then; my current state painted a facial expression that would scare any child.

I blinked once more, and that second blink caused me to focus completely on Marla, and the void I was in seemed to collapse. A heavy sound of wind crashed into my ears, and my body finally relaxed. It was as if the blood that rushed to my head had subsided, and I had returned to the present.

"Is—is he dead?" Marla asked as each word quivered out of her mouth.

I just kept staring at her face, glossed by her tears, before I turned my head back and stared at the body, the sword, and the growing puddle of blood. With no control of my own, I felt my head nod in response as I stared at his punctured eye. I then saw the fourth element for my eyes to fixate on. The body laid crippled on the floor. The sword had dropped onto the floor, into the now large puddle of blood. However, down the sides of his head and moistening his hair was ocular fluid, from the eye that I had popped like a grape.

I killed someone. I'm a murderer.

My eyes began to flash once more, but only one image came to mind this time: the wanted flyer. I thought again about how it wrongly accused me of the murder of the Sheol blacksmith. While the victim remained a lie, the title rang true like a thousand thunderous bells.

"RoGoria?" Marla spoke again. My name this time.

I did not make eye contact with her, but I focused on my name coming from her innocent voice.

"That is your name, right?" She dug her fingers deeper into my arm, and I felt her head move up to where she was looking at the back of mine. "He is dead? He cannot hurt me anymore, right?" She must not have seen my desperate and slow nod when I confirmed.

I felt mucus building up in my throat and cleared it before I spoke. "Yes, Marla," I confirmed and gulped down nervous saliva. "He's dead. He cannot, and will not, hurt you."

"Good," she said, and I whipped around at that, thinking I should scold her, but her eyes filled with regret in an instant, and I could tell she did not mean it. She began to take some of her curly, matted, dirty hair to blot some of her tears away before I moved her hand down with my own. I started to look around for something clean to wipe her face, and I realized this home had nothing in arm's reach, and I was not in a place to get up. Beside my left hand, which I had placed with a firm clutch on the floor, was one of my hook-shaped daggers. My left sleeve was torn, and I did not even remember him tearing anything.

I picked up the dagger and transferred it to my right hand, puncturing right into the seam where the sleeve met the shoulder. As careful as I could, I dragged the dagger through the stitchwork until a complete circle had been made, divorcing the sleeve with the rest of my corset. I slid it down and off my arm, leaving it bare, and turned to wipe the tears, snot, and dirt off Marla's face. I unearthed that beautiful caramel skin of her, and she looked at me and actually smiled. I was not in the right mental state to smile back at her, but I cupped her cheek in my hand and she snuggled into it like a newborn puppy.

"He cannot hurt anyone anymore," she said, not asking this time.

"You are right," I chortled.

"I knew you weren't bad," she said. "The drawing of you, on the fliers; they told me you weren't bad."

I smiled. She was a young girl, naive at the crime I just committed. I kept staring at her, and I kept smiling until her face started to change. She grew fearful again. My look changed with her as I looked up to the entryway of the house, to see three Metsa Guardsmen and the Captain of the Guard standing in the hall.

They approached, and the guards started to look around and investigate. The captain, however, had his hidden face pointed right at me. My own reflection mocked me in his goggles.

My face morphed from concerned to stern, just done with the situation, and ready to make my next move.

"Metsa Captain and his understudies," I scoffed. "Am I too much for one man to handle?"

He stared at me, silent before he finally moved his head to the body. He studied it for mere seconds before facing me again.

"Yes, I killed him," I confirmed. I clutched onto my dagger, the only weapon I had left at that point, and challenged his glare. His hand slowly moved up to his holstered gun, so I reacted.

I shoved Marla to the side and dove down and rolled underneath the table just as a gunshot blasted and cracked the stone floor, though far from where I was sitting.

Marla screamed as I shot up from the other side of the table, and I lunged my dagger toward the captain.

I missed by an extreme distance, but I distracted him enough for an escape attempt. I charged up the stairs behind me and made my way up to a landing, where a second staircase ascended in the opposite direction. Making my way up, I found myself in a skinny hallway with two doors on both sides and a window at the end. Footsteps were following close behind me, so my time to think about my crazy plan ceased to exist. I sprinted toward the window and heaved myself through it. My eyes clamped shut, so I hadn't the faintest idea where to land. Not that I had much control over that, anyway.

I plummeted down into softness. Far too soft to be hay, but soft enough for me to barrel right through and be cushioned just enough to where the structure beneath broke and sent me rolling onto the ground.

"Shit," I groaned to myself. My back was quick to start aching, and I glanced at the broken wagon of sheep's wool that cushioned my blow. I was quite thankful for that, but I fell not far from the door of Marla's home and had no choice but to ignore the pain and get up, but I fell once more as I tripped in my train.

"Fuck!" I exclaimed before snapping it behind me. I sprinted through alleyways, which now seemed to be all I did since that last night in Sheol, and I was soon was back in the market. It was raining heavily, and the wind was relentless. Although, somehow, Lanstrid was still sound asleep, missing all the commotion that went on in just the past hour, and even sleeping through the guards shouting for me to halt behind me as well as the malevolent weather. I allowed myself to be impressed for just a moment before I kept running until I made my way to the stairs that led me to the Upper Streets of Metsa.

I thought I had lost them; I felt a little lighter with relief, but I kept running anyway until I was abruptly cut off.

The captain appeared like magic from behind one of the houses, a sword in each hand. I could not see his face, but his goggles seemed to glare for him.

He took a few steps toward me, and I started to back up. He was resourceful; one of the blades belonged to Darien. Everything about him screamed that he was going to kill me. An eye for an eye.

"I will get away," I yelled. "I always do."

"I'm confident you will, Princess RoGoria," he agreed, confusing me. What confused me more was that this man was the enemy, yet his voice provided a familiar warmth. This was not the first time I heard it, though. Just the day prior, the same captain said my name right before I fell to the water. Hell, it was the reason why I fell. He distracted me and I lost my concentration.

"You know me," I shouted as I wiped my soaked side bangs from my face. "I know you do."

He did not speak, he just kept stepping toward me, and I kept stepping back. "And I do not mean from the flyers, Captain. I heard it in your voice yesterday, just as I hear it now. You *know me,* and I have a right to know how." This was anything but the time for pleasantries, but my mind was a dancing maze of questions about this man.

He halted, as did I. He raised his arm, the one holding Darien's sword, and tossed it toward me; it slid just by my feet. "Arm yourself, please," he requested.

Arming his opponent? Was he mad?

I crouched down, my eyes fixated on him, and grabbed the sword with my left hand, my dominant hand, opposite of his.

"I know how to fight," I warned him. "I was taught by my first love." I regretted that statement the second I said it. Nothing about what I said was a lie, but not only did he have no right, nor a reason to know about my past, but I was not keen on thinking about it. However, now he knew, so I had to use what I could work with. I was not a fighter. I was a princess. However, unlike with Darien, I had a sword in my hand, and I was trained to use it.

"That is what I am counting in." His words hid a laugh. My right foot moved behind my left, and the second I was ready, he swung.

I parried with little effort.

He made a swipe toward my knees, but I backed away out of the blade's reach. He moved fast and made an immediate stab toward my neck, but I parried that, as well.

"Now I know for sure," he stated, cryptically. "I regret to inform you that I have no choice, but to send you back to Sheol."

My stomach sank, and my heart started to dance. I began to lose control of my breathing as his words shattered the core of my will. I could not go back. I could not bear to even think about the punishment my father would relinquish on me, let alone actually face it. I would not return, not quietly, anyway. I calmed myself, and looked up at him, and grasped the hilt of Darien's blade even tighter.

"Then, you will send me back in pieces," I declared. I jabbed at him with my sword, and he parried like I knew he would. I moved with my blade. As it moved his block, I twirled around and brought it down to his feet.

He leaped over, spun to face me, and brought his blade down to my head, but not before I rotated my wrist to have my blade face him by its flat side. I held it with my other hand, which stopped his attack. I lunged upward, knocking him back, and screamed. I went for his left, then right, his neck, then his feet.

He parried them all and flourished his blade around before he gashed me deep in my bare arm, which held the sword, causing me to drop it.

I cried in pain as I crippled to my knees, clutching the fresh wound as I felt my blood seep from underneath my hand.

"Do not feel bad," he said while he wiped the blood off with a gloved hand and jerked the sword to splash the rest off. "That flurry at the end is unblockable. Came up with that maneuver myself." He sheathed his rapier and gazed down at me, the goggles delivering the menace behind his stare for him.

"Is this the part where you cuff me up and send me home, then?" I sneered at him. The harshness of his gaze never left, and I found it odd I was so exhilarated by it.

He turned and looked down below, to the Lower City, where I looked to see his fellow Guardsmen standing down below by the stairs. "No," he said. He turned back to me, though it was brief before he began to leave. He offered me no explanation, as he just started to walk away.

"Wait!" I yelled as I rose to my feet, facing his back before he turned only his head, giving me a side glance as I stopped him. I searched for the words, before simply asking. "Why? Why spare me and let me be free? The flyers are true now. You could turn me in easily. My reward could make you rich!"

He laughed as he continued to walk toward the stairs, and descended below them. "Seeing you again, knowing that you're finally okay. That is my reward."

CHAPTER 6

I SPENT THAT EVENING WITH MARLA. AFTER MY QUARREL WITH THE
captain, I limped down to her house. There were several other
Guardsmen there, helping her clean up. They were ignorant of the
fact that I did it, that I killed Prince Darien. Odder than that, they
did not seem to care. They asked me a few questions, the main
point of them being how I ended up there and why I was involved.
I was honest with them about every detail. I explained how I
heard Marla's screams and stormed into a disturbing image.

The Guardsmen were quite rude to me, and I attempted to tell
them off by pulling the "You cannot talk to me that way, I'm a
princess" attitude. The guard just laughed and begged to differ,
which made me feel like nothing. My anger flared at his bold
statement, but considering I was off the hook and the Guardsmen
seemed to now ignore the warrant for my capture, I was not
going to argue.

I helped Marla put her dining room and living area back
together, which due to the small size of these homes, were the
same room. We went upstairs after we were done, and she led me
to the room furthest down the hall on the left, right next to the
window I threw myself out of. She opened it for me and the room

itself was pretty bare, unlit candles on two end tables, which were positioned right beside a spacious bed.

"This was my parents' room," she explained. "It's only for adults." She spoke much happier now, but I was fixated on the fact that she said this "was" her parents' room. She followed me in and watched me in excitement as I sat on the bed. It was definitely broken in, and it started to become clear why this little home needed four bedrooms.

I located matches in the end table drawers and lit the candles. Then, I laid down on the bed. For the first time in months, I was on a bed. It was comfortable, plush, and bouncy, and I felt like I could have amazing dreams on it.

I hated it. I hated that it was comfortable. I hated that it was not sand. I hated that a window gave a view from the outside and that it was not secluded in the least bit. I wanted to leave. I was going to leave, but that sweet, innocent voice chipped through once more.

"Is it okay if I sleep with you tonight?"

I looked over at Marla, who had the fingers of her hands inter-twined and pressed up against her chest in hope. I smiled and nodded for her to join me, and she did. I felt weird sharing a bed with a child, considering what I had just saved her from, but it warmed my heart knowing she felt safe with me.

"What happened to your parents?" I asked. Silence allowed the thought of me killing a man to creep in and I did not care what any girl or guard told me about how I did a good thing. I was in no position to take another's life. I tended to get lost in my own head, and right now that was dangerous territory.

"Oh," she said as if I just reminded her that they existed. "They're gone."

My heart sank for her. "Did they pass?"

"Nope. Just left."

I sat up in horror, now making deep eye contact. "What do you mean they 'left'? Where did they go?"

41

"I dunno. They packed up my big brother and sister and left."

"Without you?"

She giggled at the silliness of my question. "I'm here, aren't I?"

It was astounding how heartbreaking this talk was. She was abandoned, and what was worse is I did not think she knew it at the time. She seemed fine, but there was more than what scratched the surface, and I intended to find out what.

"So you just live here by yourself, then?"

"Only for another week or so," Marla said. "That's when I get 'evited'."

The horror only grew from there. The girl was going to get evicted, and she would end up on the streets, living as I did for the past three months. Though for her, it would last longer.

I GOT up the exact instant I awoke. I had fallen asleep still dressed, so I swung my legs off the bed and onto the floor. I rummaged around the home looking for parchment and some ink. All I found was parchment and a needle; I assumed it was for sewing. No ink, though. I shrugged and went to prick my finger before I stopped and yelled at myself about leaving a note for a child written in my own damn blood.

I grew frustrated and looked all around until I saw Darien's sword, hanging haphazardly manner from my belt. I withdrew it and marched back up the stairs and into the bedroom where I leaned it against a wall, and closed the door behind me, being very gentle.

I exited the home and stopped. It was daylight, and the city was alive and loud. People were going to see me, and I was not filled with confidence that it wouldn't be an issue. However, I had no linen wrap to hide myself anymore, so I had to think about what my options were.

Nothing. I had nothing else. With hesitance, I stepped down

the stairs onto the ground level and walked through the streets of Metsa.

When I made my way to the fountain, everyone was staring at me, whispering about me, and darting back and forth with their eyes.

Someone is going to turn me in.

"You reek!" a bystander yelled to me.

I turned to see a woman shouting from the other side of the fountain.

"You need a bath!"

I was quick to be offended. "You cannot talk to me that way, I am a…" I stopped. How many filthy princesses were in this town? Just one, and she had wanted flyers everywhere. It was evident the woman did not recognize me from them, so I had a chance to not blow my cover outright. "I am a squatter," I said instead, which was not a lie, really, by any means. "I do not have the privilege of bathing, so if you do not mind, piss off." I walked away with my filth and pride beside me.

I had no clue what I was going to do about climbing down the rock wall. No way in hell the rocks were dry, but I had to get there, regardless. After I climbed the stairs and passed through the alleyway, I made it to the cliff that I always climbed down and was worried the second I arrived. When I looked down, there was a long piece of rope that was nailed into the jagged rocks of the cliff, and it fell all the way down to the beach. I could see my boat was still there, and my satchel inside the boat, which had nothing in there since my daggers were not to be seen after the guards cleaned up Marla's house. That left only my crossbow.

I did not have time to sit and think. The rope was there, so I was going to use it. I lifted it to me and started to descend. My feet slipped a few times due to the moisture on the stone, but I had anticipated it as I had a firm death grip on the rope. Interestingly enough, with how many times I slipped and stopped to collect myself, climbing down with the rope took quite a bit longer than climbing up without the rope.

The second my feet hit the sand, I let go of the rope and dove down to the ground by my hovel, and for a moment I was relieved to see my crossbow was still safe and nestled inside. I reached through and dragged it out, along with its sling, and holstered it to my back once more. I checked my satchel and the boat next; the satchel remained empty and the boat untouched. The moment of relief subsided, and my head filled with questions about who put the rope there and why. Nothing was bothered, and granted I did not have a lot of value, but a free boat and weapon would have been worth stealing. Had the Captain of the Guard put it there?

"Oh, you are back," a smooth, sweet voice followed a faint splash in the sea behind me.

I grinned as I turned around to greet Galyn, who was peeping out of the water. "I am," I joked. "I'll be honest, I had hoped you were a hallucination from ingesting too much saltwater." The words came off rude, and maybe I half meant to do so, but she was the reason I came back in the first place.

She chuckled. "Fair enough," she said, taking no offense to my words, I guessed. I supposed anyone who looked like that would be used to others who are indifferent, considering what the general public thought mermaids looked like based on the children's stories.

"Regardless, I do need to speak with you. That is why I came in the first place."

"Anything for the 'princess'," she said and emphasized "princess." I could hear the mockery in her tone, and it heated me the way it mirrored the Guardsman from the night before. Still, it was evident Galyn was familiar with this spot, or maybe even this island in general.

"Firstly," I began as I gestured to the rope I had just climbed down, "Who put that there?" I did not even say it like a question, but more so demanded the information.

Galyn cocked her head to the side and examined that rope. "That was courtesy of Mayor Steamsin."

"Mayor?" I asked.

She responded with just a nod, followed by an awkward silence.

I tilted my head with wide, irritated eyes beckoning her to tell me more.

She appeared shocked by my expression, so instead of elaborating, she questioned me instead. "You've been here for months. Did you think this town was led by just the people?"

"Of course not," I said, rolling my eyes. "I had just never seen him or thought about him since avoiding the citizens was my main goal."

"How is that working for you?" she snapped back, matching my abrasive tone with a condescending one.

I leered at her question, as well as the mouth it came from.

She noticed that, as well, and rolled her eyes. "Not well from what I have heard, and that's only going to get worse if you try to coast through without knowing what you need to know. Now, I can help with that. But I'm not going to assist a self-righteous bitch who is consumed by arrogance and who thinks she can still play princess when it benefits her."

I was at a loss for words. Not once had anyone dared talk to me that way. What was more upsetting was the fact she was right. I pulled the princess card earlier and got shut down, and Galyn did the same before I even got the chance to use it with her. It was then I realized if I wanted to let go of my past responsibilities, I had to lose the perks, as well.

"I am sorry, Galyn. I—"

"Just sorry. Leave it there." She glared at me as she clenched her jaw and revealed her grotesque teeth, two rows of thin, pointed teeth that resembled exaggerated thorns. Images of me being torn to shreds by those teeth violated my mind and forced my skin to scurry like roaches.

"I'm sorry," I said once more and left it at that.

"Oh, well, all is forgiven," she chirped. Her tone had made a complete turnaround, and she was back to her happy self, which I thought added to how frightening I just realized she was. "Any more questions for me?"

"We were discussing the mayor," I said, still fearful of saying anything offensive.

"He runs this city," she explained. "Not much more to it than that. He put the rope there so he and his Captain of the Guard could find you, but you were not here."

"The captain..." my voice trailed off.

He did report me. I thought, *how I could be so stupid as to not think he would?*

Then, several questions infected my brain. Why did the guards not just arrest me last night? Even when I went back to Marla's house and they were there cleaning the mess. Nothing made sense to me at this point; I felt like there was a plot against me. However, one more question popped into my head, one that I needed to be answered right away. "What do you know about the captain?"

"Oh, Captain Elliot?" she asked, and I crippled to my knees.

Before I knew it, I was crying. I was crying a storm, and the few glimpses I caught of Galyn between tears indicated that I was making her quite alarmed. I knew it. From the end of our fight, it was clear, but I had no proof to back it up.

"RoGoria," Galyn's voice caught me between hiccups of snot and tears, and I looked up to see her close up, half her body out of the water. I was distracted, though briefly, by her gills and wondered how she was able to breathe. "Who is he to you?"

I sniffed and gagged as a clump of snot coated my throat. After I collected myself, I told her everything. "He was my first love. My only love. We met when I was barely a teen, and for a month we were inseparable," I explained. "He was training to be a soldier there, but we got caught by my parents who sentenced him to exile, I suppose."

I stopped to wipe away the fluids that were coming out of several holes in my face. "Only I had been told he was to be executed for 'violating' the princess. We fought last night...and he told me I was his reward, something he used to say back then."

Even though her eyes were solid black, I was able to tell, based on her expression alone, she was entranced by my story. I hadn't told her all the details, like how I would sneak off into the night to meet him at our courtyard and we would talk for hours and he would train me how to use a sword. I did not tell her how our first kiss, my first kiss, was in the courtyard by my mother's bed of roses, how it felt I was being constricted by a snake of passion. I also left out how he harmed me the night before, cutting me deep, which now burned when I thought about our past.

I rose to my feet and began to walk away without saying a word. I knelt back down to grab my crossbow from my hovel, forgetting I had already grabbed it when I first arrived this morning. I could feel my mental stability slipping from me as I stressed over the future while resentful of the past; my mind was everywhere but the present it seemed. I climbed the rope and when I made it to the top, I continued to cry as I made my way out of the alley.

I stopped at the edge of the Upper Streets and looked down to the lower ones as I questioned everything my life was at that point. I was no longer a princess; I was a sad shell of who I used to be, and I began to wonder if I had it so bad in Sheol. The pain of knowing Elliot was alive and had willingly hurt me last night made me think I wasted the last thirteen years being angry for his exile.

As I started to make my way down the staircase to the Lower Streets, I caught something moving out of the corner of my eye. I looked up, and it was gone for a moment. Though it was not long before I watched a brittle, old woman poke her head out from behind an alley on the opposite side of the Upper Streets. She moved her head around before moving out and sneaking into the house she was pressed up against, dragging a sack behind her. I would not have paid any mind to it had I not seen the sack, or the red fluid leaking from it.

CHAPTER 7

IT WAS EVIDENT THE HOUSE HAD BEEN ABANDONED FOR QUITE SOME time. I tried the door just maybe a minute beforehand, and it was locked. While I scoured through the windows to try and see if I could spot the woman with the bloody sack, I realized I was gazing into a complete dump of a home. The hag I had seen was squatting in there, that much was clear. From what I could see, the house was uninhabitable. While I couldn't tell exactly what they were as there was no candlelight at all, I saw toppled over pieces of furniture all over the place. The rest was masked by the overwhelming number of cobwebs on the windows.

I was sure I could break in, maybe by picking the lock. Not in broad daylight, though, when even the Upper Streets were riddled with people. I'd have to think of some kind of diversion. Several ideas streamed through my mind, and only one made sense but had a low probability of working. I stayed in the alleyway between that abandoned house and another, moving far back to the ledge where the cliff dropped down into the ocean. There was not anything to hide behind, but I was confident the guards would not come swarming in giving how they have been as of late. I crouched down, rolled my eyes, and began to yell.

"Hey!" I roared and my voice echoed throughout the city. "Princess RoGoria is trying to escape by the docks! Hurry, she's almost got a boat!" There was an instant thunder of indistinct murmuring, and I began to worry that the guards had decided to leave me alone.

Then, it happened. A loud, blaring alarm came from City Hall, and I heard the crowd make its way toward Metsa's docks. I guessed I wasn't as safe as I thought. No matter, though, I had just been given my one and only chance. Still crouched, I made my way to the front door of the house, my back turned to the Lower City. Even standing, I was sure I would have been out of view from the Lower Streets, but I had to be cautious.

I slung my rapid bow off my back and popped the canister where the bolts rested off and scoured for a way to open it. Loading them was just pushing through the holes in the back until they clicked, and, currently, the only method I had for getting them out was firing them. My bolts were the only thing I had on my person that could have worked as a potential lock pick, and even that had plenty of room for failure.

I continued to investigate the canister when I heard a *click* come from the door, and I shot my eyes up at it while the hairs on my neck stood to attention. Eyes wide, I reached up and placed my hand on the doorknob, and as gentle as I could, turned it all the way and pushed the door open. I was quick to pop my canister back into my crossbow. I had faced in front of me the entire time I entered the house and closed the door behind me.

It was disgusting. Every step I took, I heard the crunch of something dying under my boot. To my right was an entryway to the kitchen, which was infested with roaches as they scurried away when I entered. The toppled furniture included several chairs and end tables; the actual dining table was properly stood, but there were layers of grime and dirt caked on top. The only decor the house had was the cobwebs. The massive, hanging cobwebs were so thick they pulled my hair the one time I was stupid enough to get caught on them. I reached up to yank myself free, but those webs were firm and strong, and even getting my hair free meant I still had to struggle to get my hand free. I had never heard of anything that could make a web so strong and thick.

I jumped the second I was free. I yanked my hand free with a heavy pull, and something above me scattered. I made a small yip before I covered my mouth with my hand.

As it heard me, it made its way to the other side of the room and up some stairs.

The house was dark and decrepit, I could not see at all what it was, but my mind painted some grotesque pictures of the old hag I followed and a spider crawling on the ceiling like a possessed demon. I began to whine and step back, thinking I had bitten off more than I could chew. Then, there was a loud noise that came from upstairs, followed by a deep, raspy "Damn it!" My brain told me to keep moving back, but my feet started to move forward again.

It couldn't have been the hag. No old woman would have a voice as terrifying as that, yet despite its horrific sound, I eventually made my way to the stairs. I grasped the side of the wall to keep myself balanced as I went up. I thanked God that, like everything else in this city, the stairs were made of stone. No creaking wood to announce me snooping around.

I eventually made my way to the top, and I found myself in just one large room. The room did not have a lot in it, besides more knocked-over furniture and some fallen paintings. The only light came from a window on the other side facing the stairs, though it was faint. I heard breathing, so I knew I was not alone. I was uneasy, and my breathing was inconsistent. I may have realized I was no longer a princess, but I was still a scared young woman, and the deep darkness of this room did not help.

I began to have flashes of my past evils. I kept picturing Darien bolting out from the darkness and murdering me right there. Or my father, or the ghost of Rolan. The only thing that kept me sane from those thoughts was how the being was moving along the ceiling, which was followed by me being terrified of what could possibly thump in loud steps on a ceiling. I found myself in an endless, inner debate.

Say hello. No, don't say hello, are you mad?

I heard several scattered steps patter along the far end of the room, and I held my bow stiffly in that direction.

Stuttering, I eventually called out. "Who else is here with me?" That was a stupid and odd question. I did not even know what this thing was, let alone if it could speak. I groaned at my idiocy and took one step back before the heel of my boot bumped into something. I span around as whatever I backed into scurried away with the utmost haste, and that was my final straw. I made my way back toward the stairs and only stopped when a low croak of a voice grabbed hold of my ears; I froze.

"I'd be careful, lass," it spoke. The voice was evidently male, but bordering on inhuman. Every word was like a sore croak, and I could pinpoint the sound from coming just behind my head, at the same level as I stood. "She's got a temper."

Fuck. Fuck. Fuck!

My hands began to tremble, something I could normally hide, except, this time, it caused my crossbow to rattle. "She won't be happy with either one of us."

His last sentence brought me some ease, in the sense that I felt a little less in danger than before. "You..." I choked and cleared my throat before I tried again. "You unlocked the door."

"Aye, lass," he groaned. Moving as if I was sinking in sand, I made a complete turn and was facing the window. There was no one there as the light would've illuminated at least a silhouette. "I will just move with every attempt you make," he warned. "No human can stand the sight of me."

"Try me," I gulped. "I can handle more than the average man." This was a bold-faced lie, as anything during my time in Metsa would have proved. Galyn alone had the ability to give me night terrors, and I was sure she would have had I not have learned the fish had a personality. That was what kept me confident, though, knowing this being could also have a character of its own. He already revealed some signs. Even with his pitiful, raspy, croak of a voice, I could detect a slight Gaelic accent. I just wanted more to base my theory on.

He did not speak anymore; there was only silence, so I felt it was done. I turned to move down the stairs and escape this Hell House, but right as I took one step down, he spoke again.

"Wait," he said.

I stopped and turned around. I pinpointed the sound this time right to my left, above my head, but I did not look.

"Make your way to the window."

I turned back to see the window, which emanated the faint lighting for the room. I officially took my foot off the step and started to walk. I could not bear to think what would happen if I disobeyed.

Every few steps I took, I banged my leg, or my foot, on something; a dark chair, a wooden beam. As I got closer to the window, I even tripped over a rock that was on the floor in the house and cursed under my breath about the atrocity of the house. After what felt like a minefield, I made it to the window. I stood looking down toward the Upper Streets for what felt like a few minutes. I lowered my crossbow, thinking that would make anyone, or thing, hesitate to trust me. It seemed to work because the voice reappeared a moment later.

"I'm behind you now, lass," he informed. "Turn when you are ready, but please, do not scream."

That was an unsettling request to hear. I wish he would just tell me what he was so I could be prepared, but I appreciated how cautious he was being toward my feelings, regardless. I began to turn, though slow, and stopped halfway just to prepare myself to my fullest. This man could be anything since I knew of Galyn's existence. A swarm of possibilities devoured my mind, as I pictured him being a troll, a ghoul, a vampire, or I even comforted myself by thinking he was maybe a disfigured man.

I fully turned, shuddered, and gasped when I saw the large, hairy abdomen with eight thick, long legs coming from his sides while hanging from a thick strand of silk. His eight eyes black in the light as they all gazed at me. I felt that was a bit unfair, I was unsure where to make eye contact. He was of monstrous size. His legs would have no problem making a complete wrap around my torso.

"Oh, heavens," I squealed. I became a stuttering mess. "I'm not screaming," I reassured him.

"It's clear you want to, lass," I heard sadness coat his voice.

"Yes. You said nothing about *wanting* to scream. You just asked me not to." I heard a deep chuckle come from him. "Good Lord, are you *laughing?*"

"Of course. You are funny, lass."

I cleared my throat. "Well. How about an introduction, then? I'm—"

"Princess RoGoria Sumner of Sheol," he finished for me. "We've seen the posters."

"We?"

"Lorraine," he said. "She lets me live here as long as I don't disturb her work. I believe she's the reason you're here."

He knew far too much for a spider who hid away in darkness, yet I supposed knowing things was all he was able to do.

"What do I call you?" I asked.

"I no longer have a name. It was taken from me long ago."

"Well, I must call you something."

He started to groan and pull himself up with his silk, and my reflexes kicked in.

As gently as I could, I placed my hand on his furry abdomen. Despite what he was, I could tell he was shocked by what I assumed was the first human contact he had in ages. "No one can take away your name. Allow me to give it back."

All eight of his eyes watched me in awe, and he descended back to my eye level. "F…" he stopped, but I encouraged him to keep going. "Fristlyn. My old name was Fristlyn."

"Fristlyn," I repeated. "That should not be hard to remember."

We had a much lighter conversation from thereon. Fristlyn would not tell me anything at all about his past, and he was extra coarse if I brought up his name being taken from him. He had no problem telling Lorraine, though. How he talked about the old hag made it was crystal clear they were not friends. He said she was wanted by the Metsa Guards, as well, but no posters were up. I mentioned the bloody sack I saw her drag in, and he only told me he saw it before, but he never dared to look inside. It seemed my efforts were wasted.

He began to ascend to what I could now see was a large web that spanned across the entire ceiling. It was thick, and he had warned me to be careful from now on because me peeling myself out of the web downstairs was very lucky.

"You should be going, lass," Fristlyn said. "Lorraine does come up here every now and then."

"Oh, yes, I need to get home to Marla." I holstered my crossbow and made my way to the stairs. I turned back to look up at Fristlyn and maybe wave goodbye, but the darkness shrouded him, and he was nowhere to be seen. I turned back and headed down the stairs.

I stopped right on the floor of the living room and scanned the area. It bothered me how Lorraine was not insight, and I had seen every main part of the house; the roach-infested kitchen, the disoriented living room, the spider nest upstairs. I double-checked around and saw no back doors. There were some windows, big enough to fit a person, but they did not open, and none were broken. My head turned toward the fireplace as I started to walk through the house again—it was the nicest decor the house had, built into the house and beautifully carved out of stone. It was spacious, yet despite the beauty, there was something haunting about it.

I soon shrugged it off and headed toward the door. As I opened it, my ears alerted me of a slight clank. Metal on stone, unquestionable. I was careful, but I still made a move to grab my crossbow before I was smashed into the door. The door was closed on impact, and there was violent, maniacal screaming as the attacker shoved me into the door and wall. I screamed in pain as the attacker dug her nails into my arms before she pulled me back and slammed me into the door again. The doorknob jabbed right into my waist, and I screamed obscenities with each blow.

I did not need to look to know it was Lorraine. The shrieks of an old woman told me that much, and I could not think about how to defend myself because I was too confused about where she was hiding. My back was facing the kitchen, and it was darker than anything else in the house. She very well could have hidden in the shadows.

She slammed me against the wall once more, harder than the other times, and I had enough.

I threw my elbow back and hit something fragile and even heard a crack upon impact.

She roared in pain as she fell back, and I turned to see her, but she was soon up and ran upstairs howling like a wolf.

I could not see her face, but I saw her long, straw-like hair and ragged, patchy robes as she climbed up the stairs. I went to open the door as quick as I could but yelped from the furious cramp on my waist where the doorknob hit. I pushed through, swung the door open, and slid myself out of the house. One step out and I tripped down the few steps and landed onto the stone on my knees. I stopped to breathe through the pain and decided I should wait for it to subside before I carried on any further.

"Hello, hello, hello, Princess RoGoria," I heard a deep, authoritative voice come from above me. It was then when I remembered

I blew my cover so I could enter the house in the first place. Even though the guards were ignoring me, my blood stopped with anxiety the second I heard him speak. My life in Metsa flashed before me as I looked up to see the well-dressed man with the sepia skin. He smiled that beautiful smile he flashed at me before he said, "I think we are long overdue for a chat."

CHAPTER 8

THE MAYOR ESCORTED ME THROUGH THE UPPER STREETS, ACROSS the bridges to the house I witnessed the man enter just a few days prior. That alone had put several pieces of the puzzle together for me. Galyn told me he was the one to nail that rope into the stone cliff that allowed me to climb down to my hovel. His house was one of the parents to the alleyway I always climbed up to. He had to have known I was there since day one.

I checked my pockets for my parchment paper that had the days marked in my blood as we walked up the steps, only to remember since then I had been in a whirlwind of shit. Falling from the cliff to the crashing waves was probably when I lost it forever.

We stopped right outside the door, on the stone porch. I had finally gotten a phenomenal, not half-hidden behind a shawl wrapped around my face, view of the house. It had the same features as the rest of Metsa had, for the most part, stone walls and porch, with a golden brass roof. The most noticeable differ-ence was the big bay windows on either side of the door, and the brass-plated "*M*" above his front entrance. I hadn't noticed the *M*, which I was mad at myself for. However, the bay windows more than indicated that this was a house of importance, and I grew more displeased with myself that I did not pick up on these obvious hints.

He opened the front door and motioned for me to step inside.

I entered his home to see the first decorated home out of the now three houses I had been inside of in the entire city. My boots stepped on a large black and white embroidered rug. The large staircase greeted me second.

The mayor closed the door, locked it, and moved past me while motioning to follow. He led me past the staircase and down a hallway, where he stopped at a doorless entryway, and once again motioned for me to step into the room. In the room, there were various plants and furniture, and two loveseats, both an emerald green color, which guarded a glass and brass table. He allowed me to sit while he stepped away for a moment.

The hospitality made me a bit uneasy. I thought if he was going to turn me in, then this was just a cruel joke to rub his victory in my face.

He came back holding a tray, which itself held a steaming tea kettle and two teacups. The silence was starting to kill as there had not been an exchange since he saw me exit the abandoned house. I started to twitch and grit my teeth as he set the tray down with tenderness and care. That was succeeded by him pouring tea into the teacups, and I began to sweat.

"Good God. If you're going to turn me in, just do it," I snapped.

He jumped at my outburst and even spilled a splash of tea onto the glass tabletop before looking at me with wide eyes, accompanied not long after with a grin. "Please, do not tease me with pleasantries." He chuckled and scratched his head through his poofed, tightly curled hair. "Well, allow me to introduce myself first, Miss."

"You're Mayor Steamsin, I know."

His face scrunched with a smirk, and then he shook his head. "You can just call me Soen." Soen resumed pouring the tea into the cups, at last coming to a stop once they were filled. "I actually have a proposition for you, but I assume you have some questions for me, yes?"

"Only two," I answered. I was shocked with myself. After everything I had been through, I only had two questions for him. It was accurate as I could not think of anything else.

"Well, ask away."

"You know I've been here this whole time, yes? Why did you wait till now to confront me?"

Soen looked at me with pursed lips and a raised brow. "I'm confused. Does that count as both of your questions?" He ended his question with a wide, genuine grin.

I leered toward him. "No," I asserted as I gritted my teeth.

He mocked me with his eyes and mumbled under his breath along the lines of, "Okay, so more than two," before he reached down to the teacup and the tiny plate it rested on, closest to me. He extended it out toward me and nodded for me to take it.

"I had to wait for this to arrive," he said as I brought the teacup and plate to my chest.

I raised a brow and pointed at the set that I now noticed looked different than one he reserved for himself.

"Yes, that," he laughed. "It's not every day a princess shows up on my doorstep. Or you know, a needless chunk of land outside my island step." He laughed at his own words. "I had that specially made, came right from the town of Lovely, down in Farlara."

I examined the teacup and plate. They were a matching set, both a gorgeous marble with red veins. The cup and plate had a rose gold-plated rim that glimmered even in a room that lacked good lighting.

"It's beautiful," I whispered.

"Fitting for a princess, no?"

That was the second time he referred to me as Princess after I worked so hard to get that title out of my head. I even questioned if he was blind. The proof of me was painted right in front of him, depicting my matted, knotted ruby hair and dirty grime covering my face, some of which had even crusted.

I sat there and just stared at the tea set in my hands. The red vein marble was haunting me in the best way. Even in Sheol, I had never owned anything near as ostentatious as this teacup, which made it hard for me to believe that this was for me.

"What was your second-slash-third question?" Soen broke my concentration as he mocked my words, though I could tell it was playful.

I blinked back into reality to attend to him. "Marla," I said. Her name escaped from my mouth before I could even form any context around her predicament. It was like my mouth assumed Soen would know what or who I was talking about, and he did.

"Ah, yes," he sighed. "Poor thing. Her family jumped ship to Heratan on the other side of Relica with no warning, and—"

"I truly do not care about where they went if I am being honest." My voice turned cold. Heartbreaking as Marla's story was, her parents weren't my concern.

"We're going to have to get you used to speaking with contractions, I think," he chortled.

"This is not a joke!" I shot forward and leaned over to him, hoping my roar cooperating with my somewhat horrific appearance would make him open his ears. "You are about to throw that helpless girl on the streets!"

He grinned at me in lieu of responding to my accusation. His dark eyes whispered deep into mine, and they told me a story of compromise.

"It seems our interests are now aligned," he said. He leaned back into his seat and relaxed. "As I said, RoGoria, I have a proposition that just might put your mind at ease."

He had mentioned it earlier, but I was hoping to put that off as long as I could since I felt it was going to be more of a threat than a proposal. However, that perfect grin matched with his raised, dark brows made me feel more at ease. He reached inside of his outer shirt and pulled out a piece of parchment and handed it to me.

I was hesitant, but I did grab it and unfold it to read the contents. I looked back up to Soen. "'Confirmation of Enlistment,'" I read aloud. "You want me to join the Metsa Guard?"

He nodded, and his smile refused to fade away. "I could give you a new recruit bonus; this will give plenty of coin to buy fresh food from the market so you could stock Marla's house and reside there with her. In the meantime, after you leave today, I'll head to my office at City Hall, and reinstate the pipes to Marla's house so you both can bathe."

Everything I had heard about Soen knowing all that went on was proving to be true. He knew I spent the night with Marla, though I never told him that. He knew Marla had taken a liking to me, though I never told him that. The guards were his eyes and ears throughout the entire city.

"My answer is, of course, yes," I informed him. "But may I ask, why?"

Now, his smile faded. It was clear the next part made him a bit uncomfortable and seeing as how he had that damned grin during this entire conversation, I was almost concerned for him, despite me thinking he was just another corrupt leader.

"The, uh…The Captain of the Guard put in a good word, and that is all I will say about that."

As I burned at the thought of Elliot, who I had yet to actually see or talk to minus our previous altercation, Soen threw a sack onto the glass table. The noise of the impact on the glass forbade me from thinking much deeper into it.

"Go buy some food for you and the girl. By the time you return, you will both have running water once more."

I grabbed it, and the gold coins within raised a jingling alarm.

He stood to his feet, as did I, and he led me out of the room and down the hall, to his front door. He opened the door for me but stopped me as I went to leave.

"I need to tell you one other thing," he admitted. "I originally decided not to, upon his request, but I cannot blindside you like that." He looked at me with a sheepish gaze, and I had a feeling I knew where this was going. "I do regret to inform you that Elliot has promised to stop by your new home later tonight."

I was not happy to hear that, but if he were Captain, that would mean I would have to be taking orders from him. I stood at the doorway, one foot actually out of the house, and nodded. "An eye for an eye, then, as I also must admit something."

Soen cocked his head and slid his hands in his pockets; his curiosity was profound.

"You wasted tea. I hate tea. Fill my cup with gin next time, and we have ourselves a pleasant get-together." I left as he chuckled at my words and closed the door behind me.

<hr />

OUT OF ALL MY time in Metsa, I was never as stressed as I was the first time I had to buy food. I stood, dumbfounded, at Lanstrid's produce stand and was taunted by all the meats and vegetables and fruits as the drunk stared back at me. I was raised with staff who did all the cooking for me growing up, but I now found myself caring for a child.

"Listen, lady, shops are closing soon, and I would like to hit the pub," Lanstrid said. Every word left his mouth with a putrid stench of ale and what smelled like old fish.

"Pipe down, or I will reduce you to only two teeth instead of the six you have left."

He grumbled and sat back in his chair; I could not tell if he bought my fake threat or not.

I returned to Marla's house, struggling with the many bags of food, as well as the two pounds of ice I had purchased to place in the icebox in the kitchen. After a tug of war between the ground at the bottom of the steps and the stone landing up at the top, the landing won soon enough, as I made it to the front door after what felt like a struggle of life and death. I swung the door open and entered the home and slid myself down the narrow foyer as I juggled the paper bags of food. I made the turn and entered the tiny kitchen, setting the bags on the breakfast bar that overlooked the dining table.

"Marla?" I called out, but there was no answer. I figured she was out playing around the city, and I did not want to take away the independence she had just gotten after being alone all this time. I began to stress more about taking care of the girl, so I distracted myself with the chore of putting the food away.

Both iceboxes were full of melted water and rotted meat and vegetables, so I had to spend the next hour cleaning them both out and disposing of the decayed contents. I continued by filling both with ice and placing the food in their respective boxes. I felt I may have overbought, and shuddered at the thought of cooking meals every day, with my imaginary cooking skills, to make sure we'd eat it all so we would not waste any of it.

That settled the hunger, and next on my list was taking care of hygiene.

I made my way up the stairs into the narrow hall with the four doors I saw before. I had thought they were all bedrooms, but the one closest to the stairs was the lavatory. I entered and found myself nearly fainting at the sight of the tub. There was an assortment of soaps and shampoos along the wall on the vanity, up against the mirror. I was so excited, I felt like I blacked out because the next thing I knew I was submerged in water washing off over four months of dirt, grime, seawater, and sand. I sat in my own filth and had to drain the tub once and run the bath once more just to be happy in the clear water.

In Sheol, I would take bathing time for reflection, but I did not this time around. Even though there were ample changes to reflect on, I wanted to give myself a break and relax for the first time since leaving my home city. The bathwater welcomed me with open arms, and I sank to where my breasts were covered as I felt the water embrace and hold me tight.

My trance was broken at a knock on the door.

"RoGoria?" I heard Marla's voice from the other side.

"I'll be out in a moment," I responded. I was happy to hear that she was safe and sound, but her next words made my breathing heavy and my movements erratic.

"Okay, well, the captain walked me home since it was getting dark but won't leave."

"Again, I will be out in a moment."

She ran off with a chipper "Okay," and I heard a door on the same floor close. She either ran to her bedroom or the master suite.

I cut my bath time short, focusing only on cleaning myself and drying off as fast as I could. I remembered to grab a towel, but I had forgotten to grab a robe. I also forgot to check if there were any robes in the house at all.

Covering my breasts with one hand, I opened the door just a crack to call out to Marla but screamed at the sight of the leather mask and goggles staring down at me. I was about to yell the captain off, but he stuck a bathrobe through the door as he turned his head away. I groaned as I removed the robe from his hand and slipped it on over my shoulders and tied it shut. I then exited the lavatory, forcing him to step back.

I groaned once more; this time accompanied by an eye-roll. "Take that damned mask off, Elliot," I ordered as I brushed past him to move downstairs. He followed me, and I pulled a chair out from the dining table and motioned for him to sit, I noticed he had yet to listen. "I will not speak until that nightmarish mask comes off." I sat at the opposite side of the chair I pulled out for him, and he laughed as he made his way to the chair, untying the strings in the back of the leather and undoing the clip of the goggles, and revealed his aged face.

"It is actually a helmet," he said, setting them down.

For a moment, I was lost in his eyes again, just like when I was a teen. I gazed at his gray eyes and gorgeous blonde hair. I remembered being mesmerized by those traits, and the fact that he now had a scar that started from the corner of his faded pink lips through his ecru skin and ended at his jawline, did not deter my mind from that same fate of being infatuated with his beauty. I could not believe I was looking at him again.

"Not much of a helmet," I said as I folded my arms to hold the top part of the robe closed which I felt had begun to drift open. "Leather and goggles? Protective," I taunted.

"You seem mad," he said. He raised a brow, and I got heated again.

I slid the left part of my robe down and lifted my arm to reveal a nasty scab, a scab that covered a wound he had gifted me. "Do I? I'm surprised I'm not madder than I am."

"Ah, yes," he sighed. "That. Well, you had just murdered someone. Forgive me, I was merely protecting myself."

He was *merely* lying to me at that point. He knew who I was and that I meant no harm. What he did not know was the guilt I had, taking a man's life. Regardless of if the man was scum. I ignored it, though. During the brief exchange we had, I could tell he had changed. He was colder and did not speak to me in the honey-sweet tone he did when we were younger.

"Soen told you me you would stop by, so what is it you want?" I dismissed his previous statement and moved on to business.

"I just wanted to welcome you to the guard," he said. His lips were pursed, however, so I knew there was more to it than that. I must have been making a face, as well because he knew I saw right through that horseshit. "And I wanted to catch up. I have missed you."

I could not keep my anger up anymore. I was fresh, churned butter when it came to him. Keeping in mind his exile is what bittered me over the years, I had to make myself okay now that I knew he was safe and alive.

"I have missed you, too," I admitted. I could not lie to him. Not at all.

He chortled. "How long has it—"

"Thirteen years," I said. I interjected his thought because I had kept count of every year since I thought he was put to death. "Thirteen years since we got caught and my father told me you were to be executed."

He laughed again. "Your father is a lot of things if not merciful." He seemed to regret his words as soon as they made their way toward me because I felt my face change from calm to utter shock. "I'm—I'm just saying. He would not have the heart to actually kill or have someone killed."

I grew more daunted and had to stop him, even though I knew it would break his heart. "That is far from true. He killed Rolan."

Elliot dropped his jaw, and I saw tears form in his eyes. He had been training to be part of the guard back in Sheol, as well, and Rolan was a familiar face since he was the one who supplied the equipment. Rolan and Elliot had grown close and formed a student and mentor relationship.

"He had helped me escape," I explained. "An offense that was punishable by death, it would seem."

Elliot sat in silence to a point where it grew uncomfortable. He stared into space by the news, and I feared he began the process of resentment toward me.

"Tea?" I offered as I sat up and cringed at the idea of making the drink. I had bought some in the event Marla liked it since I hadn't gotten the chance to ask.

I entered the kitchen to retrieve the kettle but jumped as Elliot placed his hand on my shoulder. He followed me in without my knowledge. I looked up at him, into those overcast grey eyes.

He shook his head and stated, "I have to get back to my quarters." While he caressed my cheek with his other hand.

My stomach began to crawl as he just grazed my cheek, and I

had to decide right then and there if I was okay with where this was going.

He then started to lean in and moved only an inch closer before I jerked my head away.

"No, no, I'm sorry," I apologized as I brushed past him and walked toward the front door. "Thirteen years is too long to just continue like nothing happened. We have to reconnect, we need—"

"I understand, I get it," he said. He walked through the narrow foyer as I opened the door for him since he said he had to leave. "I got ahead of myself."

I nodded. "A little bit, yes." I did smile at him as he exited my new home, to tell him I had no hard feelings. I believed in time and place, and this was neither. I closed the door as he vanished into the smoke-filled night and decided it was time for myself to get to bed.

Before entering the master suite, I knocked on the other two bedroom doors to educate myself on which one was Marla's, and I asked her myself if I could take her parents' room. She said it was okay as long as her parents got it when they came back, breaking my heart a little bit. I entered the master and flopped myself onto the bed, giddy at the prospect of being cleansed from my bath, and drifted off into a deep sleep for the first time in months.

CHAPTER 9

GALYN'S JAW HUNG OPEN AS I TOLD HER ABOUT THE LAST EVENING which left butterflies nesting in my gut. I couldn't even stop myself from smiling. Though I stood firm on how I rejected him, my mind couldn't escape the fantasy of what would have happened had I welcomed his tender kiss. It would not have been our first, but the thirteen years of trauma and hard-living combined with how we found each other once again was an exhilarating feeling.

I had sat in silence with my legs stretched out and my hands pressed into the sand as Galyn went on and on about how my life had started to turn around, with being hired as a guard and reconnecting with a lost love. She continued on and on, and it got to the point where I laughed because I felt she was more excited than I was.

"So, what's next?" she asked, and I raised a brow. I didn't have time to think about that.

When I awoke this morning, I thought I would pay Galyn a visit, since she had been the only real friend I made here. However, when I left my house, my day was booked. Tacked to my front door was an order from Mayor Soen Steamsin, which instructed me to meet him at Doc's Docks, the Metsa tavern which sat facing the sea near the city entrance, at noon. It was already getting close to that time, and I was anxious about what my first day on the job meeting could be about.

With my mind only able to focus on that, Galyn's question caused a pause that, at the time, I did not have an answer for.

I looked at her and shrugged while pressing my lips tight together. She shrugged it off as well and told me that I had a lot to think about. I did, but it was not that.

I hadn't told Galyn about the notice Soen left, but he made it seem urgent and for my first day. It was hard to think about what he needed on such an adamant scale.

After another few minutes of Galyn ranting about how I better have a beach wedding, I had to cut her off and tell her I should be going so I wasn't late for my first day as a guard.

She nodded and gave a brief, "Oh, of course." Before diving down into the drop-off.

I rose to my feet and climbed the rope back to the city.

I assumed the guards in Metsa worked in shifts as they did in Sheol. Sheol had Day Guards, Evening Guards, and Overnight Watch. How Soen decided to handle this, though, made me think otherwise. I was a new hire, not a guard of status. I wondered if he met with all the guards on this level, and if that was the case, I thought maybe he wasn't the corrupt politician I labeled him as, despite threatening to throw Marla on the streets.

I made my way down to the Lower Streets before while an unsettling feeling took residence in my stomach. It was more than just being watched; it felt almost as if I was being followed. I stopped where I was and turned around to see the City of Metsa, awake and alive as ever. I watched as men wheeled sheets of metal across the roads and the women in an assorted color of outfits similar to mine with boots that clacked on the stone and trains dragged across the ground. Some trains hung straight down like mine; others were ruffled or frilled, but not a soul I could see was following me.

I looked toward the Metsa fountain, then I looked beyond it and there she was.

A woman with long, wavy brunette hair that flowed like wine in the slight breeze. She was light-skinned and held herself in an extreme stance from where I was standing. She stood several yards away and stared at me through the faerie statues that acted as the fountain's centerpiece. She was not glaring at me, but she stared straight at me.

She wasn't dressed in typical Metsa fashion, either—no train, no frills. I couldn't distinguish details with how far she was, but her clothes appeared to be skin tight, at least her shirt, anyway, since that was all I could see. A tight, white top with long sleeves that had long cuffs that draped around her wrists, and a mild V-neck shape that revealed just the top of her bosom. The V shape was rich gold, and it seemed to glimmer in the sunlight, despite how hidden the sun was in the Metsa smoke.

I decided I would approach her since I wasn't running late by any means, but I blinked once, and she was gone. A sharp but light gasp escaped my throat, as I was immediately concerned by the strange woman who just vanished into nothing. I darted my head around as I scanned the area and grew more frightened when I could not see anyone who matched her. After I made a full turn-around and faced the faerie fountain once more, I began to step backward toward the direction of Doc's Docks.

I made a quick turn and began to speed up to get to the tavern quicker, but just as I made a complete swing, I bumped into another and jumped back as I yipped in surprise.

"I am so…" I stopped.

It was her—with the long, bouncy brunette hair with the white shirt and the gold embroidery. Her eyes depicted a hazardous blizzard; a gorgeous, rich, stormy blue which complimented her fair, porcelain skin. They pierced right through me, and I was entranced by her ethereal-esque being.

The area around me faded to black. There was no stone, no fountain, no Metsa. It seemed like I stood in nothing as she transported me to a timeless and spaceless void where it was just her and I. I felt the weight of life itself dissipate into nothing in this world. Was this purgatory? There were no raging flames or pearly gates of gold. It was a void.

She lifted her hand and flicked a loose bang so it hung on the side of my face as it normally did and then lifted her other hand to cup my cheek. Her touch brought a sense of security as she leaned in close to where our noses just barely married.

"Hey, yeah so," she started in an odd manner of speech, "I really don't mean to sound cryptic here, but the Ani'Mas King is your key. Help him, and he'll help you."

The dark void vanished quicker than it manifested, and her with it.

I stood there, frozen, scared, and beyond confused. I had never seen nor heard of such an interaction. My mind raced through the hundreds of questions.

Who the hell was she? What the hell was she? What the hell did she want? Who the hell is the Ani'Mas King? What is an Ani'Mas King?

"Ah, Princess," the dark, smooth familiarity of Soen's voice called from behind me, and I snapped out my trance and blinked a thousand times a second as I turned to see the mayor run toward me. "So close. You would've beaten me if you weren't playing statue," he said and laughed at his own words. As he started to move past me, he placed his hand on my shoulder and turned me with him before locking his arm with mine as he pushed us through the crowded city.

He was talking the entire time we walked, but his words were muffled as my brain blocked out any sounds while I tried to recount what had just happened. I had no logical answer for it, but I started to think, maybe that woman meant more harm than good. She said she did not mean to be cryptic, but she was about as cryptic as one could get.

I stared into blank nothingness while Soen yammered on about whatever it was he was saying. I remember my train of thought going off course when I had considered the potential importance of his words.

Soen led me to the city gates, just before the docks, to take me into some hole-in-the-wall tavern and busted through the door. A large bearded man with peppered hair waved at us as Soen marched on through the dark bar.

The bar was lousy with drunkards, but the community seemed wholesome enough. Even the falling down drunks were friendly, and everyone seemed to know each other. Even Lanstrid, who was there and not at his stall, demonstrated he had been having a good time.

I was led to the very back of the bar to a corner booth which Elliot had already sat at. Soen motioned for me to get into the booth opposite Elliot, but I declined. I hated being against the wall. Soen sat first, and I followed. And within a second's notice, that large man with the peppered hair was by our table.

"Mayor Soen!" he exclaimed as he went in for a handshake.

Soen reached past me and grasped his hand back, as happy and excited as the man was. After they released each other, the man pointed a fat finger in my direction. I felt like I was being singled out by a large sausage with an unkept, jagged fingernail. "Is this her?"

"This is her," Soen confirmed with a firm nod.

"Wanted posters didn't do her justice, eh?" The man let out a dark, unpleasant laugh.

I just sat and thought about how he should have seen me just one day ago. Now, my clothes were washed, my hair was back to its ruby red, and there was no crusted dirt on my face. I wanted to make a joke about how he had probably seen me already but couldn't recognize me, I was still too shaken up about what just transpired right before I arrived at the tavern, though.

"Name's Doc. I own this tavern." He held out his hand, which was a lighter brown than the rest of him, and kept it there till I returned introductions.

I went to grab it and realized I was being dainty and then changed my response to a firm, hard grasp and shook his hand. He did not quiver from it as Prince Darien did when I first met him.

Doc smiled. "What shall I bring you, folks?"

"Just a glass of water for me, Doc," Soen ordered.

"Pint of ale," Elliot followed.

Doc looked at me with a crooked-toothed grin. I was unquestionably stressed still, and I went with my gut when placing my order. "Gin. One glass, and one bottle."

Doc laughed until he realized I was serious then moved right on to get our drinks.

I looked at Soen, who looked back with a shred of concern.

"You are an expensive date," he said. I debated whether or not to tell him about what happened, but I, then, thought about whether or not he would believe me over a woman who was able to entrance me in a lucid state.

"I told you: I like gin."

Soen smiled as Doc came back with our drinks carefully placed on a tray. He handed me Soen's water first, then placed Elliot's mug in front of him, and finally set down a small glass cup and a bottle of gin.

I was a little too quick to pour a shot of gin into the glass, down it, and then repeat it once more while the first shot burned my chest in the pleasant way gin always did.

"Are you all right, Princess?" Elliot asked as he leaned in.

"I will be in just a few minutes," I said. "Why are we here?"

Elliot shot his grey eyes in Soen's direction, who went from looking like a man enjoying a pleasant day out with his subordinates to uncomfortable and hesitant. Soen sat back and placed his arm along the beam of the booth while he sought the words.

"What was the biggest thing you hated most about your father, Lord Luke?"

I had never told Soen about my father, but between knowing I was the Princess of Sheol and having had Elliot as his Captain of the Guard, I quickly brushed my shock aside to focus on the logistics of his question.

"It's truly hard to pick just one thing…" I said, but I trailed off because I was not sure which reason to pick, as there were many. I loathed my father from the age of fourteen right after he sentenced Elliot. However, there was a concern even before that.

My father was a good man at one point, but as leader of the fastest-growing city, on an economical level of things, he was always looking for ways to improve his riches. When I was around the age of ten, he started to get lost over something I wasn't allowed to ever know about, and he was so secretive I was not convinced my mother, Lady Lilliane, even knew what it was he was after, either.

"I was always a princess first," I started. "Even at a young age, I wanted the best for my people. There was little I could do, though. My father taxed the rich to an extent of abolishing the rich in general, and when he couldn't tax them more, he would suck the poor dry."

I poured myself another shot and threw it back and then slammed the glass on the wooden table. "There was this noble, Lady Fildra. She was an heir to the Fevral Estate, Lady Fildra Fevral. By the time I left, she was reduced to a homeless and near rabid woman, all so my father could send scout party after scout party looking for," I stopped, trying to find the words but could only settle on, "Something."

Soen nodded and shot a glance at Elliot, who leaned back.

I had started to calm down and feel the happiness of being around Elliot once more, so my eyes were drawn to him, as well.

Elliot folded his arms and nodded for Soen to continue with his part.

Soen shuffled around in his seat, *still* trying to get comfortable. "What if…I have an actual lead on what your father was looking for?"

My eyes narrowed, and I was waiting for info, lest I began to think he was willing to shove his people into the dirt over the same nonsense.

He analyzed my gaze and put up a hand. "Small budget work, a small team of people; I would personally pay out of my own purse strings. But, yes, we have a lead on what your father was looking for."

I rolled my eyes and poured my fourth glass of gin, not sure if I was ready to hear it. I downed it, and as I was already feeling a little tipsy; I decided this fourth one would be my last.

"Tell me."

Soen reached into his suit and pulled up a rolled-up piece of parchment.

As he unrolled it, I saw a world map of Relica in a way I had never seen before. I saw Mazz'Ra, my home country, and Metsa, as well. I was able to recognize the Trade Circle, such as the southern counties of Mang'Coal and Que, and the western Isles of Farlara and LinleCross. In their proper places were the northern Frozen Wastes, and the east and west continents of Haven Call and Faeland. There were seven other countries I have never seen on the Relica map before, along with several unnamed islands.

"A true map of Relica," Elliot said. "Soen got his hands on it from an undiscussed visitor maybe three days before your arrival here."

Soen offered a slow nod. "The reasons why these are rare and unheard of is unknown," he explained, scratching his head through his curly hair. "Based on research, what your father is looking for is right here." He tapped on an island to the west of Metsa, labeled the Coven Isle.

"What is it?" I asked, as my eyes refused to peel themselves from a lie I had been fed since birth. I grew up learning about Relica and had been ordered to take classes on its history. Now, was I to believe everything I learned was either a lie or a simple bending of truth?

"Sylvestra's Tears," Soen said.

I scrunched my brows together. "So he was searching for someone's tears?"

That got a chuckle from Soen as he explained that was one of many names for it, but it was the most common. No one knew what it looked like, but according to Soen, it was a newer relic, only about four thousand years old.

"Why is it important?" I looked back at both the men, who exchanged awkward glances back and forth. They were not just hiding something from me, but instead, seemed to be working in tandem about how not to hide it. Elliot squirmed in his chair, and Soen wore a frozen face.

Finally, Soen leaned in close to me and lowered his voice. "Assuming it exists, it is said to hold the very soul of magic."

Both Soen and Elliot sat back, almost in defense, as if they were expecting a negative reaction from me. They would have gotten one had this conversation taken place a few days before. I'm sure I would have mouthed about some nonsense regarding my father chasing after fairy tales, but my time in Metsa had proven a fairy tale to be true already with Galyn, as well as Soen's explanation making what happened by the fountain make sense.

What this did was propel me to think about was what the woman by the fountain said. "What is an Ani'Mas King?"

Elliot's brow raised, but Soen grinned and flashed that too-perfect smile I had begun to associate him with. "I don't know what that is. Where did you hear about that, Princess?"

Liar. That smile told me he knew something, but he was busy playing safe, a game I was all too familiar with to not fall for the horseshit. But this was my chance to tell him everything.

However, it was fresh, and I did not know how to word it without seeming like a mad woman, let alone a mad woman who had now had a few. That was the last thing I wanted, considering I wanted to win Elliot over. Regardless, I made a mental note of Soen's reaction because it was clear he knew *something*.

"Never mind," I groaned. The alcohol began to hit me stronger, and I felt it get harder to keep my head up. "So, magic may exist."

Soen shook his head. "Existed. Legend states that magic is held prisoner, inside these 'tears'. I want you and Elliot to take a smaller ship and investigate."

I couldn't fathom the idea of a new guard being given such a task. Was *he* the mad one now? To hell with being a new guard, I was just a woman of royal blood. I was ill-equipped for a mission of this severity.

I did not want to argue, but I still had to stand my ground on concern. "I do not think this is what I signed up for," I said. None of this was. I did not even sign up to be a guard; that was done for me.

I watched Soen's gaze fall from a smile to a stern glare. "One: again, Princess, contractions—use them. Two: you signed up to care for Marla. If you want to do so, you'll do this."

Blackmail: I knew it. Just another corrupt politician giving subordinates a deceitful ultimatum. I returned his stare, disgusted that if I declined, Marla would pay the price for it.

There was something off about his glare, though. It started to...*fade* after I returned it. He began to look almost remorseful like he did not want to make that threat but felt he had to. "There is something you are not...sorry, *aren't* telling me." I got why my demeanor hit his ear wrong. Being raised in royalty, I was taught to not speak lazily. Soen had different tastes, and despite his ignorant threat, I could see now it was empty, and I began to retreat back to sympathizing with him.

The emptiness of his threat ordered me not to pry too much.

Soen had been more honest with me than I could tell he was comfortable with. So, for now, I decided to let it go.

After I eased up, Soen decided to move on from it and continue with business. "Elliot, do you think Barrea would be able to go along as the chef for this expedition?"

I turned my head to Elliot. "Barrea? Who is she?"

Elliot grew frightened at the mention of the name. His eyes darted in every which way as he stammered and tried to find the words.

I waited, irritated, just wanting him to spit it out. It took longer than I cared to admit but based on his reaction and the fact that he began to instantly sweat, I put it together. My eyes were hot to the stare as it formed, considering what had happened yesterday. "You have…a *fucking wife,* don't you?"

CHAPTER 10

ELLIOT WAS ON HIS ASS OUTSIDE OF THE TAVERN AS I STOOD over him.

Soen was trying hard to deescalate the situation and even had the gall to chastise me for my actions and explained how as a guard, I should show more composure. Fuck composure, fuck chastising me, and fuck this sad shell of a man. My blood boiled and I could feel my eyes beginning to match my hair in terms of color from how hard I rubbed them moments before.

Elliot was fucking *married.* Was I upset that he moved on, after all this time while I pined over his fake death? Or upset that the man I loved had a woman who coveted an undying commitment to him which he seemed to throw away the second we got to reconnect? I had to admit to myself, it was both, though, I was unhappy with myself that the first reason even existed.

He sat there on the stone ground with one hand pressed to his cheek.

I had hit him twice. The first was a slap, a slap that he felt was inferior to his manly being. I slapped him on his left cheek and felt the vibrations of impact ripple through my arm, and it burned around the lovely fresh scab that he himself put there.

Elliot had the audacity to joke about my attack, so I was swift in giving him a momentous right hook to the jaw, and I knocked him flat on his ego. He was the one who taught me how to throw a proper punch, so he should have known better.

Soen made his first attempt to intervene, but I raised that same fist, clenched tighter than freshly caught prey in a spider's web. It was a mistake on my part.

He grabbed my wrist and yanked me toward him, sticking a foot out for me to trip over, and threw me down to where I was eye level with Elliot.

I let out a cry as my knees crushed onto the stone before he released me.

He said, "Do *not* raise your hand at me." And left it alone, growling the word "not." Soen moved to help Elliot up to his feet and then helped me up as fast as he put me down. He gave a quick dart to Elliot and let him know that he did, in fact, deserve it, and that was all he was going to say on the matter; he ended it with a "you're dismissed." He wouldn't let me leave, though. He kept me there until Elliot was out of sight.

"I think I have a way for you to work out some of that anger," Soen said.

As my breathing grew more controlled, the amount of alcohol swam back to my brain. This brief moment of clarity entangled my memory of it all, as well. I stormed down the steps, away from Doc's Docks, and Elliot was quick to follow and said, as my captain, he ordered me to wait. That was when I snapped.

"I am—" I stopped to groan at Soen's eye roll. "*I'm* listening." It started to bother me with how much my speech bothered him.

He was back to smiling that smile again as if the last three minutes did not happen. "You're going to need a guide through the woods of the Coven Isle, someone who is knowledgeable, and someone who most likely won't come easily."

I was confused. Where would I find such a person?

"There's a resident here, a woman, who is actually wanted for practicing necromancy, despite magic being 'imprisoned'. This has led to her murdering people, and she squats around in the Upper Streets."

I already knew where this was going, and I did not like it at all.

"You wouldn't happen to know of where you can find a woman like that, would you?" He grinned.

I was annoyed by his grin. He knew damn well I knew.

THE DOOR to the abandoned house was once again locked, and I did not have time to hope Fristlyn would unlock it for me again, however, he did it before.

I stared at the door as if it was my opponent. I spread my legs apart and gave the wooden door a firm, hard kick. I heard the wood snap, but my still slightly drunken body could not withstand the impact, and I was knocked down the steps onto my back. I groaned at the aching pain and cursed myself for bringing a lot of that into my life as of late. I stumbled and struggled to get to my feet, but I eventually did and limped my way back up the steps.

At the very least, I had to be happy I was successful in kicking it open. There was a deep split where the door met the lock, and it hovered open just a crack. I pushed it open and let myself in.

The house looked the same as I had priorly left it. I guess keeping it nice was the last thing Lorraine was interested in doing. I left the door open this time and let the light pour into the house and light up the roach-infested kitchen. The kitchen was a completely closed-off room, unlike my own home now, which had a breakfast bar that allowed me to look out into the dining area. No one was hiding in there, which meant she had to have been upstairs.

I stumbled through the living room, the putrid scent and the ominous darkness combatted my drunk state, and the laziness of my eyelids was just the cherry on top of the shit day I was having.

I began cursing his name. *Damned Elliot. Fucking shit. That's what he is, just pure shit.*

I got lost in my feelings to an outrageous extent, and soon other toxic thoughts meandered into my mind.

I am no better. I am actually a murderer.

Prince Darien's face started to flash in and out of my mind, and then flashes of his body bleeding out in front of Marla soon followed.

I tripped as I groaned at the violent memories and threw my hands out as I fell to grab onto the nearest wall. I wasn't at the wall, though. My hands had fallen right onto the trim of the exquisite fireplace, the only nice thing inside the house.

I peered down to catch my breath.

My eyes were glued to the wide cavity of the fireplace, watching the iron rack where wood would typically be placed, and the pile of soot that surrounded it. Pile, of course, being a generous word. The soot was flattened and did not look as if it had fallen naturally.

A small thud from upstairs deterred my attention, and I was reminded of the task I had to complete.

As I approached the stairs, I began to grow saddened to think of what that mad woman would do to Fristlyn the poor, pathetic, and helpless spider, for letting me into her home the first time around. From what he said, the two of them weren't exactly friends.

I stumbled up the stairs. Even though I misplaced my footing a time or two, or three, I was able to make it up to the disastrous, empty loft.

Somehow, the place had become in more disarray than I found it before. The toppled-over chairs and tables were now broken, and fallen wooden frames were in pieces.

I looked up and feared my paranoia rang true. Fristlyn's webs were torn, ripped to sad, hanging drapes that stopped just before my head. It looked like I was right; Lorraine was not at all happy with him. I feared what she was able to do, now knowing what I knew she was wanted for: *necromancy*. A flash of her dragging that bloodied sack appeared in my mind.

I made my way to the window at the end of the loft, where I was gifted with seeing Fristlyn for the first time. The window was broken now with jagged pieces of glass threatening those who dared try to climb through it. On the top left corner, a sharp piece of glass was coated with a murky green liquid.

"Fristlyn…" I whispered, examining the green ooze carefully. "What did she do?"

I heard a tap. It was far from me, halfway down the stairs. It was the fact the stairs were made out of stone, and something was tapping on them. Seconds went by, and I heard another. My senses focused on just that tap, faint but noticeable. I continued to stare out the window as if I was still examining the glass and the ooze until the tapping stopped and turned into a closer creaking sound.

She was on the wood now. A whisper of cloth against the rough, splintered, wooden floor announced her presence. She made a gentle, hesitant maneuver as my hand flowed over to the hilt of my blade. A mistake.

Lorraine shrieked from behind me and started to charge, and I whirled around to see her run at me with a large, jagged knife.

I let out a shout, dove to the side, and swung my foot toward hers, causing her to stumble. She charged at me once more as I shot to my feet, and I withdrew my sword and pointed it at her, only for her to simply move aside and try to gut me from there. I backed up, but I found myself in a corner. I had no knowledge of how to actually fight a mad woman, a crazy hag; I had no training in that battle strategy.

She lunged herself at me with the blade held high, and it occurred to me she did not know how to fight, either. I hurled myself at her stomach and slammed us both down to the floor. Her brittle bones caused her to shout on impact, and I rolled up and kicked her knife away; I had my sword pointed right at her.

"Up," I slurred. I shook my head, but that only made me dizzier. I tried again. "Get. *Up*," I snarled that time through my teeth.

"Get up, hag," a voice came from behind me. Then, I heard the dark, accented croak that would've sent shivers down my spine had it not been familiar. I heard him crawl in through the window, across the wall, and down to the floor.

There would be time for pleasantries with Fristlyn later. No time now to talk about how glad I was that he was okay. Later.

Lorraine started to get up, but I was still heated from the altercation, let alone the scene I caused with Elliot. The moment she was up far enough, I grabbed her long hair between my fingers. It felt like straw; course, unkept, and tangled straw. I yanked her up, and she yelled as I dragged her down the stairs.

SOEN HAD INFORMED me he'd be in his office, in City Hall, all day to handle some busy work. So that's where I marched her. There were two guards positioned outside the door, and when they saw me with her, one guard opened the door, and the other took her off my hands and told me, "We're putting her right on the boat, Captain Elliot will tell you when it's time to set sail."

I nodded and bit the inside of my cheek at the mention of Elliot. Then, I entered the doors and stood in the lobby and was starstruck by the elegance of it all.

Brass was the recurring theme there; brass trims on desks, doors, and frames. The front desk was stone, as well as all along the walls. The floor was a dark, evergreen marble, and my boots announced my arrival.

There was a man at the desk. He was umber-skinned and bald, and he seemed to be arguing with a woman.

I went to step behind the woman at the desk, respecting my place in line, but there was a tug on my train. I looked down to see Fristlyn pulling on the fabric, and he looked up at me with pleading eyes.

"If it's not too much to ask, lass," he started, shuffling the other seven legs out of nervousness as if he was worried about my reaction to his question. "I'm weak enough as it is, and the cut under my abdomen isn't helping that all." I thought back to the green ooze on the long blade of glass and started to sympathize in an instant.

I turned my back toward him and slapped both of my shoulders twice. "Climb on." I felt the fabric of my clothes pull as the oversized spider climbed his way up to my back. I staggered a bit, underestimating his weight. He wasn't heavy by any means, but only after I got used to how heavy he was. He coiled his legs around my arms, and the rest around my back.

"Your corset is going to be a bit damp," he warned. "I'll only heal once I molt."

I shrugged, not caring too much. These clothes were ruined, anyway; it also wasn't his fault he was injured. It was the hag's. "You are fine, happy to help."

I started to move to wait behind the woman before he whispered, "I'm impressed how kind you are to me, lass. I appreciate you not treating me like any other bug."

I let out a brief laugh. What Fristlyn did not know was the fact that he could talk and even had a personality was what kept him safe from me. I was terrified of spiders. Lord Luke would have to come kill them when I was just a girl, but I bet they would not have been nearly as frightening back then if I could befriend them. The hairs on his legs were tickling my left arm, the one that had been left bare since my short duel with Elliot. Other than that, it was not a problem.

I stood behind the woman, her back turned to me so I could only see her short, curly brown hair. It was shaved and faded along the sides, but longer up top where the curls danced with every move she made.

I began to focus on the conversation she was having with the man at the front desk.

"There's only enough food for the trip *there*," the short-haired woman had stated. "I'm going to need supplies for while we're on the island, too." A woman who was stressing about the lack of rations while we'd be there, someone who would be in charge of the food.

Shit. It's her.

"You'll have to take that up with Mayor Steamsin," the man at the front desk said.

After some inspection, I did see a nameplate that stood on the desk: *Victor Banner, RECEPTIONIST.*

"So let me *see* him, then," the short-haired woman ordered.

The receptionist looked like his hands were tied and informed her that Mayor Steamsin had an urgent appointment that was waiting patiently. Then, he motioned in my direction.

She turned to look at me, and her eyes sparkled the second we made contact. "RoGoria?" she asked. I was getting tired of answering that question. There had been detailed warrants for my arrest only a few days ago. She extended a hand out to me, and I reached to grab it. She was quick to start introducing herself. "I'm—"

"Barrea," I finished, speaking soft but still cold.

"Ooh, bitter is not a good color on you, lass," Fristlyn whispered behind me.

I shot him a quick glare at his sarcasm and moved back to face Barrea.

Her face had turned from a happy greeting to pleading, and I could tell she was about to ask me something that I gathered I would not be happy to do.

"When you talk to the mayor, can you tell him rations are short? I have to get back to the ship and get things organized."

I asked myself how soon we were leaving. I had only heard about the job an hour ago, and people were already making preparations. I nodded and said, "Sure." The receptionist directed me to Soen's office.

SOEN'S OFFICE matched the rest of City Hall; stone walls, marble floors of a dark green, and grass trimmings throughout. The noticeable difference was his desk. Unlike the stone reception desk in the lobby, his was mahogany with a glass top, which the familiar brass trims decorated the lip of.

He motioned for me to sit in a wooden chair with a back, so I had to sit at the very edge so as to not kill Fristlyn in the process.

"Elliot's *wife* was in the lobby," I informed him, my sneering of the word "wife" accidental. I shook my head and continued but tried to be more pleasant. "She said there are not enough rations for when we actually are camping on the island."

He twisted his lips after saying, "Oh!" And made a note for it in his journal, assuring me he'd get it corrected. "The ship will be setting sail in a few hours, so I wanted to make sure you—"

"*Hours*," I repeated, astounded that he had everything prepared and ready to go within the same day he proposed this mission to me. "What about—"

"Marla will be cared for, but I'd take this extra time to say goodbye and let her know you'll be off."

That was a loaded statement. Marla had just been abandoned, and the last thing I wanted to do was contribute to an undoubtable pattern in her mind. She was just barely living by the time we found each other, and I did not want history to repeat itself.

My pause and silence grew to be uneasy, so Soen continued.

"Two other things, Princess. Firstly, please note that I will be personally looking after Marla, so she won't be left alone." That wasn't the least bit comforting. He had planned to throw her on the streets not too long ago, but I did not see another option, so I just nodded along.

"The other thing?" I asked.

"Yes, what the hell is that?" He pointed to just behind my shoulder, where eight eyes focused on Soen as he spoke. I let out a small chortle before explaining to him.

"This is Fristlyn, he—"

"Fristlyn?" Soen's eyes grew three times their normal size as his perfect smile did the same. His jaw began to drop in amazement, and I was confused as to what about this defenseless spider was so important. Of course, no one would give me a straight answer. All he said was, "Keep him close to you. He can bring great aid."

I raised a brow, but I knew asking him to elaborate would get me nowhere, so I left it alone, still not understanding how Fristlyn would be of much help in his current state.

Soen dismissed me, and I rose to my feet to exit his office. I stood at the threshold of the door when he called to me once more. "Oh, Princess, one last thing."

I gave a half turn, hoping what he had to say would shed some light on the cluttering of vast, vague information that had been left in my mind.

"You have a guide to get you through the island itself. Now, you need a guide to help you sail the seas."

I narrowed my eyes. "We have a map, is that not good enough?"

Soen shook his head. "No, the waters can be treacherous. You need someone who knows the ocean. I wonder where you could find someone who knows the sea like the back of her hand and is quick to react should you get into a pinch." He started to tap his finger to his chin, mockingly.

I groaned and let Fristlyn down from my back onto the chair as I got up. "Why must you pretend you don't know anything when you clearly do?" I said, cold and annoyed. "Watch him, or get him on the ship; he is coming with us," I demanded, pointing at the giant spider as I stormed out of his office and down the hall, ready to go ask that very guide if she'd be willing to come along.

CHAPTER 11

"I DON'T THINK YOU UNDERSTAND THE WEIGHT OF WHAT YOU ARE asking of me," Gallyn hissed. A long split tongue protruded from those grotesque teeth as she did so. That was new, I hadn't seen her do anything like that before.

"We have a map," I assured her, though that did not seem to convince her one bit. I knelt on my usual small plot of sand. The hovel I called my home for ninety-six days lost all essence of life. Its tight cavity that was my bedroom did not bother to reminisce about my time there, and it was a mutual feeling. The two days I got to sleep on a bed made me forget all about it, until now, as it sat uninhabited, save for a crab I saw walk right in when I arrived.

There was silence between Galyn and me. Only the song of the light ocean waves could be heard, so I added, "Soen did not tell..." his eye roll lingered in my absent mind, *"didn't* tell me why the map was not, ugh, *wasn't* sufficient. He was adamant on getting a guide through the sea."

"Well, I'll be damned," Galyn said, stroking her chin as she eyed me. "You've really become lower-class trash since we last spoke."

I smiled a playful smile. If I were to truly shed my title as Princess, I supposed I could, as well, get a handle on lazier speech.

Lord Luke would have flipped a table over it, but I had to admit it was…nice, not being bound by the fake laws of social status.

"So, will you help?" I asked to keep the subject from shifting too much, as well as to avoid talking to her. I was still a bit bitter from the interaction where she ripped into me. Granted, it was deserved, but still, I was bitter.

"Answer me this," she said, though I got the sense answering wouldn't be an option. "Why? Why is this so important to you?"

This answer was easy. Despite how hateful I had been groomed to be over the years, I tried my hardest not to be as heartless as Lord Luke and Lady Lilliane. "There's a little girl. Her wellbeing depends on me being compliant…I think." The face of Soen, looking regretful after he made the threat of throwing us on the streets flashed into my mind for less than a second.

Galyn's eyes, though black and lifeless, narrowed in remorse. I sensed she knew Soen also would not keep his threat, as well as something…more? I thought, perhaps, she had younglings or pups of her own at one point, though I felt as if I would have heard about them. She took a webbed hand and rubbed her claws down her cheek, stroking as if pondering my request.

I looked down, sensing defeat before continuing. "It's just to get us there. I'm sure after we discover Sylvestra's Tears, or at least discover they're a myth, we can find our own way back."

I gazed up at her, hopeful, but was soon scared by the look on her face. Those lifeless, black eyes doubled in size. Her teeth so bared at the mention of the Tears, it caused bulbous veins to emerge from underneath her skin.

My mouth began to fall. She was making me uncomfortable. "The *what?*"

"S-Sylvestra's Tears…" I stuttered, mortified by how terrifying her reaction became. I felt the situation escalating, and there was little to do about it as I did not know what I did wrong.

She winced at the name of the relic again and waved me off in an instant. "No. I will not help you."

I relaxed but fell, disheartened. I sank into the sand and fought to hold back my own tears as I was getting nowhere with her. I kept thinking about Marla; Marla playing outside, or Marla helping me with dinner, or Marla sleeping soundly in her bed. Those were things she would be robbed of, but I had no power over an actual mermaid to make her do my bidding.

One tear trickled down my cheek, and I wiped it away. "Then..." I stopped to breathe, to collect myself and pull away from my frustrations. I tried again. "Then, can you at least answer some questions for me? Can you do me that much?"

She stared, still stroking her cheek. After a moment of awkward silence, she nodded and allowed me to continue.

"Thank you," I said. "Firstly, what can I expect once we reach the Coven Isle?"

"Well, for starters, it's haunted," she informed me.

I chuckled at the statement. *Haunted.* I was about to make a snide remark, but her face stared deep into mine, her cold eyes narrowed and relentless. I cleared my throat and let her continue.

"Did Soen even tell you what Sylvestra's Tears were?"

I gave a slight nod. "He said they acted as a prison for the very essence of magic, blocked, so no one could use it." Repeating the sentence heated my cheeks. Lorraine was wanted for practicing necromancy, and that bloody sack, she killed someone to do it. I just knew she did, during a time when magic was supposedly inaccessible. She was just a murderer to me.

"That's..." Galyn trailed off, collecting her thoughts. "That's a brief way to put it. They don't just imprison *magic,* but anything *to do* with magic," she explained. "There are entire beings, like mermaids, who are magic-born creatures. The imprisonment of magic wiped out entire species and brought several others near extinction. I haven't seen another mermaid since then."

Galyn was actual living proof of the very ideology I had thought to be a fairy tale up until that point. She lived through this blight that was cast on the world, and while I still had my doubts, I now had less evidence to back them up compared to the evidence I had of everything being true.

"How are *you* still here, then?" If this catastrophic event were to have taken place, how was she even still breathing? I remembered how she said some species were brought close to extinction; what was the exception?

"Oh, honey, Sylvestra is just one person," she replied.

Good. I now knew that Sylvestra was, indeed, a person. She was a witch of sorts, I had guessed. I had read my fair share of books as a girl and was open to the idea that not all witches were terrible.

Galyn added, "Though she...was beyond powerful. Goodhearted, though my kind despised her. The only people more powerful than her were the Settlers of Old. That's why she was able to do such a catastrophic job."

My neck tightened at the mention of the Settlers of Old. They were beings of myth and legend. They were said to have been the ones, not to *create* magic, but to gift it to the ancient civilizations of Relica. They were worshipped as if they were God Himself. To think I was chatting with someone who personally knew of a woman to hold power of that stature was absolutely terrifying. If there was anything I *did not* want to believe, mermaids and witchers be damned, it was that the Settlers of Old actually existed. As a spiritualist myself, a follower of God, they were the last thing I would want to see.

Nervous mucus began to coat my throat. I coughed and decided to risk prying deeper. "So, this event. It caused the Coven Isle to be haunted?"

"I'm not sure what caused it to be haunted, though, that's plausible," Galyn said. She scratched behind her ear with a single claw, stalling to find the words. "But...I've *heard* it. The weeping spirits. The angry ones. I'm going to be honest. I don't think you're going to come back in one piece, if at all. There are far worse things there than ghosts."

I decided now was a chance to bring up my last lingering question, something that had been on my mind all day. I took a deep breath, looking up at the smokey sky, and silently prayed to myself that she'd have an answer.

"S..." I stopped. I did not want her to ask who, but I could think of no way around it. "*Someone* told me to locate the Ani'Mas King, told me he could help."

Again, Galyn looked at me, filled to her core with disbelief. Had I known more than I should have? It was not as if I *chose* to know these bits of information, they had all just happened to fall into my lap.

Soon enough, she just snorted at me. "Which one?"

My jaw dropped. "*Which one?*"

She put on a defensive smirk. "You asked. Did you not know there were four of them?"

I let out a loud, frustrated groan. "There are *four* of them?"

"Technically, there's ten. If you also count the Ani'Mas Queens."

"Fuck!" I exclaimed. I shot to my feet and kicked the sand, stomped the sand, and even knelt back down and punched it. It was everything short of digging my sword into the planet and stabbing it.

I had been going on, releasing an endless pool of anger before I heard Galyn shouting, trying to calm me down with as much as she was able to.

"Hey, Princess, breathe," she ordered. She wasn't gentle. She was stern, yet supportive. "I can tell you this, though this is probably not what you'll want to hear."

I leered at her. Not *at* her, but I leered, regardless. I might not want to hear it, but I knew I would have to, anyway, so there was very little choice. I waved her to get on with it, and she put her hands up in defense.

"The Ani'Mas King that resided in the woods of the Coven Isle...has been gone for quite some time. He was cursed, the effects of which I don't know. But safe to say, he did not survive after several thousands of years."

Well, shit.

I SAT at the dining table, patiently waiting for Marla to come back inside for the day. It was still light out, light enough for her to play, but I had told her I needed to speak with her and for her to take a break.

My eyes were drawn to the ticking clock, a clock I hadn't noticed before. It was on the rightmost wall of the foyer after it blended with the dining room. *Tick. Tick. Tick.* It was faint, but the dead silence of being alone in the dining room made it thunder. I ended up being happy with its ticking beat, as it seemed to keep me from picking at my nails which I really wanted to do at the moment.

I looked down at the cup trapped between my hands, hot tea that I made myself. Even though I hated tea, Soen claimed I would love sweet tea. I put in spoonful after spoonful, and just let it sit there, still too gun-shy to try it. After a little while longer, I lifted it to my lips and gave it a gentle blow. The whisper of rippling water lured me to take a sip, and as I pressed the glass to my lips and took a small one, I had to admit it was not *awful*. I could stomach my way through teatime with Soen again if sweet tea would be an option.

While I tolerated my beverage, I realized that I had not even begun to think about what I was going to tell Marla. The sweet child who invited me into her own home with open arms, and who was abandoned with no warning, would be on her own again for an undetermined amount of time. I had no reason not to believe Soen's promise of watching over her, but I had no reason to bet he'd keep it, either. I had grown attached to the girl during the few days I'd known her. This wasn't a bad thing to me, not minding her place in my life. Though, she was growing to be my responsibility, and I had to act properly. How was I going tell the girl she'd be alone again?

The door opened and closed shut in a way so ginger that only a little girl would have treated it with that much respect. Marla walked over and sat across from me at the table, flashing an innocent smile. I realized now she was missing a couple of teeth, all but adding playfulness to her exterior.

"Did you have fun today?" I asked her, still attempting to bide my time while I sought the words to tell her I was leaving.

She nodded her head with fierce joy, bobbing it up and down and bouncing those tight curls all over. She was filthy from playing. "Yep!"

I watched and offered her a cordial smile, which she was all too happy to return. I gripped the cup of tea tighter in my hands, preparing to break her heart.

I smacked my lips, deciding to end the small talk that had only just started. "Marla, honey, I need..." My voice broke. The tea began to ripple as I struggled to keep my hands steady. I felt my eyes start to well up.

"You're going with Captain Elliot to find a woman's tears," Marla said, and I felt my grief relinquish itself as she spoke the words. She already knew. "Mr. Mayor told me while you were swimming in the ocean." Further proof that Soen knew where to go to find a sea guide. He lied to Marla about what I was doing, because like me, he feared her childhood imagination would have put her in danger, seeing the nightmarish mermaid.

She shrugged. "He said it was easier to tell me himself."

It was even more impossible for me to get a read on Soen. Was he a corrupt Politician, or was it a facade? He had looked disheartened, threatening Marla and me. Was he truly a compassionate leader?

"I will come back, though," I assured her—promised her.

Marla bit her lip and nodded her head. If Soen had told her I was leaving, then he told her I was leaving that day. There was no question.

I took another sip of tea, not sure where to continue from there. We sat in silence, just enjoying one another's company. I was not ready to leave her, and despite her knowing, I could tell she wasn't ready, either.

All I could do was say it again. "I will come back."

She nodded still, making that same face. "I know."

I stood from my chair and went to dispose of the left-over tea. I entered the kitchen and dumped it into the sink, and my mind went blank as I focused on the tea filtering down against the brass. I set the cup down gently, and before I could return to her and tell her I was to be on my way, she asked another question. "When you come back, can I call you Mama?"

I stopped, fearing that I actually heard my heart crack like stone. *Can I call you Mama?* It went through one ear and stayed, lingering inside the depths of my mind. We assumed she did not understand that she was abandoned, but that question changed everything. It was also difficult to answer. I already told her I would return, but that wasn't all within my power.

I wiped tears from my eyes. "Only when I come back can you call me Mama."

BARREA WAS the one to show me around the ship when I arrived. I wasn't thrilled by that, but I told myself she wasn't the one I had a problem with, which was the honest truth. Despite that, though, she made it hard to enjoy her company.

While Barrea was not the issue between Elliot and me, the woman was just *annoying*. She led me beyond the main deck to some stairs that led to the forecastle deck, the platform just beyond the bowsprit, where she rattled off and told me what the bowsprit was. I wanted to yell at her, and say "I *know* what a God-damned bowsprit is." Yet I held my tongue and nodded; I did not want to anger the woman who was handling my food.

She walked me back down and through a door next to the stairs we had just used and then walked me to the lower deck. The steps ended just in front of a caged room, where I saw Lorraine shackled to the wall. Long chains allowed her to move freely in her cell, but she was a trapped animal.

Barrea led me past the cell and down a corridor, where a row of doors sat on just the left side of the hall. She stopped at the second one and swung the door open to reveal a tight bedroom.

"Elliot said he'd be more comfortable if you were closer to the prisoner," she stated, causing me to clench my fists. I had no doubt the hag would make sleeping difficult. "The first room is where Soen suggested keeping first aid." Soen had explained some of this to me as I had passed him when I first boarded the ship which she was present for, but she decided to repeat it, anyway. I had to keep myself from rolling my eyes, especially when she ended with, "This is your room." *Of. Fucking. Course. It's. My. Room. You just said that.*

She left me where I was, finally; I probably wouldn't have been able to mind my tongue much longer.

I stared into the room while I thought about everything and everyone. Barrea gave me the tour which led me past Lorraine, so those two were accounted for. I saw Elliot preparing to sail on the quarter-deck, so he was accounted for. My fists clenched tighter, as I realized someone was missing.

I stormed up the stairs and threw myself outside onto the main deck. I spun around as I walked, searching for the one person I really didn't mind being trapped on the boat with. It wasn't until I reached the main mast that I saw him, trapped in a tight cage just between the stairs to the quarter deck and the door to the Captain's cabin. His eight legs protruded from the little openings from the wire form. He looked miserable overall.

"Leave him be," Elliot's voice carved through the air above me as I approached Fristlyn. I stopped and glared up at him, and he shuffled his gaze around when he saw my anger. He stopped what he was doing, which to me looked like nothing, and waltzed down the stairs to meet me. My glare never receded when he was close. "We don't know him, Princess..." His voice became muffled as he justified the situation. My throat burned with bile when he called me Princess. He said it as endearing as he did when I was a girl, but times had changed. He had another woman now, which did not seem to matter to him.

"He's my friend, Elliot," I reminded him. It was not my only reminder, as I broke eye contact to look at the swelling on his cheek and pressed a hand against it. He knew my bitterness, and he knew I would have no problem trying it again.

His shoulders relaxed as he twisted his lips. "Is there a way I can offer a compromise?"

My glare shattered as I found myself blinking to help myself process what he had just said. A compromise? I hadn't expected him to work with me on this. I darted my sight over to Fristlyn, and they remained looking at him for the rest of the conversation. "What did you have in mind?"

Out of my peripheral view, I saw his hand go up and rub behind his neck while he sought the words for an agreement. "You know him, right? I don't."

I nodded, never breaking my gaze from Fristlyn.

"All I know of him is that he had lived with the actual prisoner, for quite some time. To me, that raises some questions, and as Captain, I need to keep everyone safe. Remember my wife is here, too. I have to keep her safe."

"Yes, your *wife*," I repeated. The tour of the ship and Barrea's insistent babbling lingered in the back of my head at the mention of her. Still, I grew to be offended on her behalf. "Your wife whose back you attempted to shove a knife into just the other day, that wife?"

I still wasn't making eye contact with Elliot. At some point, I began making it with Fristlyn, when all eight of his eyes met mine from several feet away. Still, I *heard* Elliot's eye roll. I heard his gut scramble from the kick of my words. I let out a grin.

"You may want to ask yourself why you're so bitter, RoGoria," Elliot sneered, though I could tell he had tried hard not to.

I twitched at the sound of being called bitter, and I guess I was out of line since Elliot was trying to work with me. Before he could go on about my demeanor, I did what was right. "You're right, I'm sorry," I apologized. "We're not talking about that; we're talking about him." I nodded toward Fristlyn, who had stopped looking over and went back to looking like a caged animal. "What do you propose?"

"Just…let me get to know him. I'll make an effort, and if he seems harmless to me, I'll release him to your custody."

Custody. So formal, even a bit arrogant, though knowing Elliot, he didn't mean it.

I scoffed. "Three days," I said. "I want him out in *three days.*"

Elliot nodded and before he could try conversing with me further, I dismissed myself.

After another hour or so, the ship began to depart from the Metsa docks. I stood on the forecastle and found myself staring at Metsa as it grew smaller and smaller in the distance. I said a silent goodbye to the city and those who made my time there worthwhile; Marla, Galyn, and even Soen now that I began to feel like he wasn't the corrupt leader I painted him to be in my mind.

As we began to sail out to sea and the ship began to turn to wrap around Metsa to sail past it, I noticed I was facing the direction of Mazz'Ra, of Sheol. I thought about my father; everything he ruined, and everyone he cast aside, like Fildra and Rolan, had been in vain. He was no closer to locating the Tears than when I left, and it left me with one thought as Metsa started to fade.

I'm winning, Father.

CHAPTER 12

MY PATIENCE WAS BEING TESTED ON A GRAND SCALE. IF IT WASN'T Elliot's need to boss me around or assert an intellectual dominance over me, then it would be his wife. Barrea, the woman whom I was expecting to handle our food, tended to get seasick, *often*. This only affected me directly when she would decide to vomit off the side of the ship, and it was always the side where I was relaxing nearby. If I were lucky, she'd pass out from blood rushing to her head and had about an hour of peace, after I carried or dragged her back to the captain's cabin. This depended on how charitable I was feeling at the time.

Fristlyn grew to be a bit of a problem, as well. He was going mad in that cage, and the closer we came to our destination, The Coven Isle, the more out of control he would act. Elliot could not talk to him without being snapped at. I even found myself defending Elliot, as Fristlyn's behavior was usually uncalled for. I'd remind Fristlyn that Elliot would keep him in that cage if he couldn't trust him, but the spider beast did not seem to care. Today, Elliot asked me to bring his cage down to the crew's quarters so he wouldn't have to listen to the rattling of the cage, which I agreed to because it was getting quite annoying.

I carried Fristlyn's cage from one end of the ship to the other and lugged him down the stairs to the lower deck. We walked past Lorraine, who had done nothing but scowl at me whenever I passed, and today was no different. I ignored the hag and brought the spider's cage into my room.

"All right," I shouted by accident as I slammed my door. I didn't realize how frustrated I was. "What the hell is going on with you?"

He gave an intent stare, which would have made me less uncomfortable if the damned thing could blink.

I took a deep breath and knelt beside his cage. "Allow me to try this." I unlatched his cage door and let it glide itself open. I stood and sat on my cot as he slowly crawled his way out of the cage, stopping only when he faced me.

"Thank you, lass, you are too kind," he said in the deep, grave voice. "At least, you are to me, anyway."

I tilted my head as my eyes narrowed. I didn't glare at him, at least I didn't intend to. I just wanted him to elaborate. "What do you mean by that?"

"Well..." He took a very long pause before spilling the thoughts on his mind. "I appreciate how compassionate you are toward me, but you are kind of a bitter hag to everyone else, except the mayor." His words stung like a scorpion; a quick jolt and it was over, but the pain lingered.

I bent my head down low, now with my ego bruised. I nodded in confirmation because I would be a fool to deny it. "That's been mentioned a few times now," I said. Elliot had said the same thing before we set sail, Prince Darien commented on it both times we crossed paths, and of course, my father had no problem telling me or everyone how I was a bitter bitch. I thanked Fristlyn to myself for not using that word, though.

"Oh, excellent. I was getting worried you didn't know."

I gave him a side-eyed grin as he picked on me.

"I wonder, is it justified?"

"Yes, of course," I said, though I second-guessed I may have answered too soon. "Elliot, he—well, there's a history. There he was, all too ready to get going again, despite a big change in his life. Barrea is—"

"Sweet as a freshly picked apple," Fristlyn interjected. "She's been nothing but kind." He was right. Our personalities did not match by any means, but that didn't mean I could not be civil. The woman knew her way around a kitchen, too. I thought of the dinner I had just had; garlic steamed potatoes and carrots, along with juicy pork. I ate my fill and was quite full, yet my tongue begged to taste it again.

"Princess?"

I looked back up at the spider and saw his fangs stretch farther to the ends of his face. I let out a giggle at the sight. "You're smiling," I said, examining the horrific, yet adorable, face.

"That's what it looks like to smile for you." He let out a bone-chilling chuckle, a laugh that would scar any sane person who didn't know him like I did. This was the first time I saw him happy. "Would it be too much trouble to keep me company a bit? The last two days I haven't been able to have a conversation with anyone."

I raised a brow. "Elliot tried."

"Yes, yes, he did. But I don't like him, not one bit, Princess. I would much rather talk to you."

"I'm a little tired. Can you make peace with a quick talk before I sleep? I wanted to ask you something."

"If I answer your question, will you keep me company tomorrow?" Fristlyn was the only person I felt I could talk to. He was observant, intuitive, and given his state, he would have no reason to do me harm.

"It's a deal."

"So kind."

"Well, I'm desperate for a friend, as well."

He let out that horrifying chuckle again. "Clearly, look how low you're setting your bar. What would you like to know, Princess?" He crawled up my lap and onto my bed with me.

"Your behavior," I said, restituting myself to face him but still smiling so he could still see I'm just being a concerned friend. "I hope you don't think me a complete fool and expect me to believe it was just because you've been caged. As we get closer to the island, your behavior escalates, and I want to know why."

His legs curled up underneath him. I've seen spiders do that before, usually, after they die but this was different. He was holding back.

I realized that maybe I was scowling, which I'd been doing a lot of as of late, but I made it a point to look more endearing. I extended out a hand and stroked his abdomen, and he fell loose and sprawled out once again.

"I hail from the Coven Woods," he admitted. "I come from a colony of spiders, like myself, who reside in the island's depths."

I kicked myself for going through the trouble of getting the hag. He would've been a well enough guide if he actually lived there at one point.

"Then, I can't tell if your behavior is due to excitement or nervousness."

"It is fear, lass."

I bent lower to face him, showing remorse. "Why do you fear going back to your family?"

"If I'm honest, I don't feel like explaining the chain of events that led me there. But I was on the island Metsa sits on long before the stone was carved and made into the city you know it as today. It wasn't until Henry Oliver, the last owner of the house you saw, died of plague that I made my way into the foreclosed house to have shelter, even if only for a little bit. Lorraine came not long after, though I don't know where from."

I tried to process Fristlyn's lonely life. I thought I was lonely, given my few months in Metsa. He would've been alone for years. Metsa was new to the Trade Circle, sure, but the city would've had to have been around for a long time before that. This spider lived several lifetimes on his own.

"Everyone, including me," I whispered, still in awe of his sad story. "We thought you and Lorraine were close."

"She treated me like a pet later on, but no, I was just an inconvenient roommate, when she was around, anyway. She'd often disappear."

"Disappear?"

Our conversation was interrupted by the door to the main deck slamming shut and several footsteps jolting down the stairs. My room door swung open, and Elliot rushed inside and tossed me a pistol.

"Grab your bow and your saber," he ordered me. "We're being followed."

CHAPTER 13

I DIDN'T SEE ANYTHING.

Elliot slammed his goggles into my chest when he sprinted to the captain's cabin to tell Barrea to stay inside. I realized those goggles were not just for show; I was able to spin the rim which resembled a gear on the left lens, which allowed me to view the sea as if through a telescope. More Metsa tech that they kept just for themselves.

I glanced all around the ship, running from side to side, scanning up, around, and even below. There was no other ship in sight, anywhere. I ran to the forecastle deck and found the same results. There was nothing new when I ran to the quarter-deck, either. How could Elliot have seen anything when there was nothing in sight?

My skin started to crawl when the sound of malevolent scraping against wood came from the port side of the ship. I raised my hand that held the pistol Elliot threw at me just a moment ago and quietly stepped my way over. The scraping persisted until I reached the other side and snapped myself over the railing, only to see nothing, except the claw marks.

Long, jagged scrapes in the wood wrapped all the way around

to the forecastle. I followed them around and up the stairs, to just below the bowsprit where they had stopped. None were going up, and none were going down.

I lost control of the rapid beating inside my chest. I was ill-prepared, but I felt the adrenaline pump as though through my own bones. I gripped harder on the hilt of my gun, to stop any shaking. I took in a long deep breath and readied to withdraw my crossbow should the gun fail me.

I stepped off the forecastle deck to be greeted with Fristlyn, who was peeking outside the door from the crew's quarters. I tried to motion for him to go inside, but he was insistent on staying out.

My body only truly relaxed when Elliot returned outside, asking if I saw anything. I nodded and pointed off the ship for him to inspect the deep scratches in the wood.

He said nothing, keeping as quiet as I was, and pulled out his pistol as he went to investigate.

I started to walk over to Fristlyn, to tell him to go back downstairs once more, but I stopped when my attention was forced to the floor. Before me, was a feather; a white feather with a scarlet tip. I knelt down to peer at it and set my gun down to pick it up. I was in no way knowledgeable when it came to birds, but I had never seen or heard of one with feathers such as this.

My heart wept as I pictured Rolan. His biggest hobby was birdwatching before he was forced to stop to keep his smith open for the long hours my father would demand from him. Rolan had taught me about the different finches and had shown me sketch after sketch. None of them, though, were as exotic as this feather. I would've remembered; it would've been my favorite.

Elliot began screaming my name. I dropped the feather and turned to him, panicked and shocked about his erratic behavior. Eventually, my brain picked up on what he was saying. "Get down!"

I reacted too slowly. As I began to crouch, my very soul shot into the air, followed by my physical body. I screeched in agony as something sharp clamped tight on both of my shoulders and delivered me to the clouds, my view of the boat quickly fading. It was the pressure that hurt, but now it was puncturing my skin.

I was carried away from the boat and over the sea. As I wailed, I made the mistake of looking up to my captor when I heard it roar with the call of a crow. It had short, dirty white hair with red streaks and bird wings with feathers resembling the one I had inspected on the boat. It squawked again, only to make me realize that while the face was relatively human, the mouth was a white beak. It dug its owl-like talons harder in, and I felt my skin open, inviting blood to leak out.

I cried out for help, looking back only to realize how far I was carried away from the ship. Two other winged beasts of different color patterns tormented Elliot and Fristlyn back on the main deck.

I reached down to the hilt of my sword and found I wasn't able to grasp it, as my arms were pinned higher from the grip of the winged man that held me. It would jerk me around and turn at random moments. Nausea swept my gut from the rapid movement, and I felt the talons dig deeper, causing me to vomit midair.

Life felt as if it was drifting, and memories started to seep through: meeting Galyn, my one kiss with Elliot when we were kids, Soen's too perfect smile, fighting off Darien for Marla, Marla's cheerful childhood innocence.

As I was hoisted away, I realized the thoughts of Marla were not the ones to break me free. One more memory crackled its way into my mind, one that made the nausea stop and my eyes focused, glaring out into the sea.

Father. His face. The hand he'd slap me with, beat me with, and the ringing gunshot that finished Rolan. I raised my scowl to the birdman and reached down once more to grab the hilt of my sword. I hooked the handguard with my index finger and anticipated relief as the song of the metal sang to the sheathe as it released. I fingered my hand down to grasp the hilt, and without a second thought, I shot my arm up with force. White blood decorated my face as my blade slid right through the beast's belly, followed by an ear-shattering caw as it released me.

Both of us plummeted down to the water, and the sea swallowed us whole.

I hadn't thought this through. The beast had carried me far from the ship, and the condition my shoulders were in, I would not be able to swim all the way to it. However, I refused to let myself sink regardless of my failure. The looming void of the ocean's depths terrified me more than anything on Relica, winged beasts be damned.

As I struggled to conserve my breath to reach the surface, impact struck my waist, hurling me through the depths. I tried to scream, only to fill my mouth with saltwater. I started to choke, started to *drown*. I began to pray whatever sea beast had a hold of me would eat me before I died a slow, watery death.

I felt myself being lifted; I penetrated the surface and allowed myself to cough up the water that left an unsavory sourness on my tongue. I was able to breathe, focusing on my surroundings. I opened my eyes to find myself right next to the ship. I held myself to it, pondering how on Earth I could have been all the way back there.

My eyes fell to the water, and I jumped at the sight of an onyx, scaled, serpent-like tail. My eyes followed it to the lifeless black eyes, the webbed hand with her claws. I smiled at the terrifying teeth that I was all too happy to see.

"You're here," I choked, coughing out excess water.

Galyn smiled at me and bounced her eyebrows to boast herself. "Want to fly, one more time?" She glided over to me and spooned me from the back. "Take a deep breath and hold. This won't take long."

I took several small breaths before taking one big one and held it there while she dove us both deep into the water. The night sky darkened the sea just below the surface, so when Galyn took me deeper, I began to panic. I started to squirm, but a soothing, warm melody melted my being. Singing enveloped us both, and I felt myself mold to the music. I was infatuated by it. Just a melody, no actual words of comfort. I relaxed to it and refocused on holding my breath.

The music never stopped. I felt warm. I felt safe. I felt *loved.*

Galyn shot up, bursting through the surface right next to the boat, and tossed me onto the main deck.

I grunted as my body rolled like a ragdoll from the impact and only snapped out of my trance when I heard a loud splash of water.

I memorized the feeling of the wood on my hands. My fingers brushed along the surface, deciphering any split, knot, or crack.

I'm back on the ship. I needn't worry anymore.

I allowed my body to lay there while I collected myself, re-establishing that I was on solid ground and not tearing the air or sinking into the ever-growing darkness of the sea.

I jolted to my side as another skin-crawling caw flourished at me. Another bird beast, a woman it seemed, by the large, feathered breasts. Her feathers were brown and beige, looking more natural. I attempted to roll away, but she was on me. She gnashed at me with those talons. Just when I had thought I'd been spared of drowning, I was now to be butchered to death.

The beast screeched as Fristlyn jumped on her back and chomped down, *hard.*

The two of them tumbled over me, and the woman bird beast started to shake and convulse before dying right there. I witnessed clotted blood ooze from her beak as Fristlyn rose up behind her.

Relieved, I started to crawl toward him when both of us were distracted by Elliot's screaming. He was grabbed just as I was but by a much bigger beast. Another woman, though her feathers were black and white, and she was twice the size of the other two, as tall as three men.

Elliot put up more of a fight, but as I saw him start to be carried away toward the forecastle, the memory of our good times broke through, just as they did when I thought I was going to die. I couldn't let him die. The memories; him training me to use a sword in the Sheol courtyard, our kiss in my mother's elegant rose garden, our endless talks while we sat on the fountain, where I told him I'd rather be a guard than a princess.

He wasn't mine anymore, but I only just found him. I wasn't going to let him experience the same fear or fate as I just had.

I rammed myself forward, just as Elliot was being carried off by the winged beast.

"Lass! Grab your bow!" Fristlyn's voice carried through the breeze of the night sky as I tried to remember where my bow even was. Elliot told me to grab it before I came up; what happened to it after that?

"I don't have time to look for it!" I insisted as I flew through the main deck. I heard Fristlyn call me, I swore he called me an idiot, but I told myself he must not get how severe the situation is.

I stormed up the stairs to the forecastle deck. Elliot and the beast were past the ship, but not too far out. I didn't think. I didn't have time to think, no time to stop to contemplate. I jumped past the railing of the forecastle onto the bowsprit and ran up it as balanced as I could. I threw myself off the end, and extended my arms, praying to God I would not miss. I kept my eyes on the beast, not Elliot, as I grabbed hold of the owl-like ankles, and not giving it a second thought, I twisted with all my strength. I felt the bones snap in my grasp, and she released with another blood-curdling roar. I dropped right after I saw Elliot get away, not wanting to be his replacement.

Galyn helped us back to the boat again, and Elliot was marveled by an actual mermaid. She kept dismissing him, but he wouldn't let it go.

Eventually, Fristlyn threw down a ladder made of web, and Elliot and I climbed back up to the main deck. Fristlyn's overcompensation in size meant the web was thicker and stickier, which allowed us not to fall back to the waters.

Once aboard, Elliot and I sat next to each other and tried to process the events that had just happened. Everything was so sudden, so quick, that when we finally calmed down, we laughed.

We laughed our asses off.

I even crippled over and leaned on him for support, starting to feel the pain in my abdomen from the excessive cackling. Tears streamed down my face as I fought to contain myself, to no avail.

We laughed for several minutes straight, taking no time to breathe, and we only stopped when we heard the pained call of the winged beast as it flew out in the night, no longer in view.

Elliot and I looked at each other and sputtered, falling back into laughter.

When we had finally collected ourselves, Fristlyn approached slowly. "Your crossbow, Princess."

I waved a hand. "Fristlyn, I told you I—"

"Your *bow*, Princess," he boomed, interjecting me., "has been holstered to your *back*, this entire time."

My head fell into my hand as I lifted the other one to feel the butt of the crossbow. I patted it several times and briefly wished it weren't true. But it was. Fristlyn *had* called me an idiot. I was an idiot; I was hilariously stupid. I looked at Elliot who was bright red, and we both wheezed as we fought back laughter, only to succumb to it again, anyway. To my surprise, Fristlyn joined in, too, with that ghastly croak of a laugh he had.

"I HADN'T GROWN HOPEFUL," I said. "Something told me you wouldn't stay long."

Galyn was readying herself for her leave. She explained to me she didn't intend to stay for the longevity of the trip, and I understood. I felt I had scared her off when I asked about the singing I heard, as she reacted defensively when I prodded her for an answer. It's not like I didn't have my own theories; children's tales depicted mermaids with a siren song. While Galyn certainly didn't perpetuate the folklore stereotype, the tales had to come from somewhere. Her awkward shuffling in regard to my inquiries made it clear that she used the same song her kind weaponized to lure prey. She had just used it to calm me down instead.

Galyn informed me that, after we left, she followed with the intent of going in the same direction, but southeast to an island called Sunne'Sun. I had heard of it; it was on the fake map that my generation, along with several before me, had been raised to believe was the true Relica. "One of the largest pods of my people resided just past the drop off of land there," she told me. She further backed her theory of more of her kind still being alive by referencing what she had told me, how Sylvestra was just one witch, and while she had made a dent in the number of magical lifeforms such as herself, Galyn found it unlikely that she was the only one left.

When I first met Galyn, I refused to trust her, to trust something with the grotesque features that she possessed could be a being worthy of trust. I still felt that way about her at times, but she saved my life and saved me from a fear I had no clue I had. So I supported her choice, unconditionally, despite how I felt about there being others of her stature.

She began to release the railing of which she held onto as we spoke before I stopped her. "What were those things?"

She gave me a blank stare as she twisted her lips and I could see her nibble at the inside of her cheek. "I am not entirely sure if I must be honest. I've seen them before, though, near Farlara."

She began to release again, but I placed my hands on hers. I cringed at the feel of her. Her texture reminded me of a moss-covered rock in a creek. A satisfying, slimy sensation engulfed my hand as I made contact.

"Is there any more helpful advice you can give me?" I was tired of being given vague answers from everyone but her, but I took advantage of her being there, anyway.

Galyn nodded toward the forecastle deck, or more so the door at its base, leading to the crew's quarters. "The spider...keep him safe."

"Fristlyn? I intend to, but why?"

"He..." she trailed off, but not from being distracted. It was almost like I could see her thoughts colliding with each other. She went to war with herself, debating how much information she could give. "He's significant in this quest of yours, Princess. It's definite that he is unaware, but without him, you won't succeed." She started to pull away from me, from the ship, and one hand even fell off the boat to signal she did not want to stay much longer. "Nothing prophetic or anything. But the condition he's in doesn't have to be permanent. If he breaks from it, he'll be your most valuable ally."

"Galyn, please, can you give me anything more?" I tried my hardest to beg for details, to ask and not demand like she yelled at me once for already.

"I simply don't want to. I hate that he's here, hate that he's with you. But listen closely to me, RoGoria."

I leaned farther than I probably should have over the railing. I hung hazardously, invested in Galyn's last bit of advice that she was going to give me.

"There are far worse things on the Coven Island than winged beasts, let me assure you. But if you play the game correctly, and keep that spider safe, then all of those things you'll cross paths with, will *fear him*."

CHAPTER 14

I SLEPT IN MUCH LATER THAN I SHOULD HAVE. THE ORDEAL WITH the winged beasts had happened late enough as it was, but the fear of the sea kept me up longer than I cared for.

I dreamt of the depths, the sinking, the darkness underneath the surface. When I first arrived at Metsa, I was on nothing but a rowboat; being on the ship itself was never cause for alarm, either. Yet when Galyn pulled me deep into the ocean, to a point where we were just cased in a casket of black void waiting to devour us both, I remembered thinking I actually wanted to die, anything to stop feeling the fear.

It was by no means a nightmare. Even in the dream, I heard that song. That lovely melody sang to me once more, and I welcomed the dream then. I wished I knew what it was, wished I knew where it had come from. My only theory was that it was a form of a siren's song, and she used it to entrance me just like the tales said. The only difference was she saved me with it, in lieu of luring me to my death.

The only reason I did finally wake was a knocking on my cabin door. Barrea's too cheerful for the morning voice sawed through the wood like timber as she called for me. My morning mood made me want to open the door and smack her, but I couldn't. Not while an eight-legged lap "cat" was asleep right on my stomach.

I found myself patting my body, confirming that I had worn modest undergarments. "It's unlocked," I called back. The door clicked open and Barrea walked in holding folded clothes, *my* clothes.

She let out a sigh as she closed the door behind her. "How can something so scary be so adorable?" Her voice squeaked by the end of the sentence. This woman was every girl to ever annoy in one package. However, for the moment Elliot and I shared, I played nice.

"It's only because he can talk," I said. I had said the same thing to Fristlyn himself, and that was a battle I was ready to die for. He would be dead if he couldn't.

Barrea set the clothes atop Fristlyn's cage, which proved to be a somewhat useful end table. "I patched up the holes the harpies left. I only had black fabric, but I covered them pretty nicely and—"

"What did you say?" I asked as I turned dumbfounded to her.

"Was black a bad choice? I'm sorry I didn't have any burgundy fabrics. I had red fabrics, but I felt they would have clashed."

"No, no, stu..." My hand flew to my mouth, stopping my sentence. I was about to insult the poor girl who stayed up all night doing patchwork on my clothes, and then the bitterness that Elliot and Fristlyn both mentioned would have been true. "No, Barrea...the holes that *what* left?"

A sparkle glimmered in her eyes and she picked up my clothes from the cage once more and sat herself on it instead. "The harpies! Did you not know what those were?"

Of course, I knew what a harpy was. I read the children's stories, heard the folklore, just as I had with mermaids. Now, the attack was even more shocking to me. Galyn was one mermaid who thought she was the last one, and just left on an uncredited lead to find others. Yet, three mystical beings, harpies, found each other and formed a pod of their own. Even in the stories, they weren't pleasant.

"Do you know much about them?"

"Nope, nope, nope! No one does. The few texts I read of the Before Ages even mentioned that due to their rarity it was hard to study them."

Her mention of the Before Ages turned my brain into a thunderstorm of questions. The Before Ages is what we referred to anything before our current Steam Age. Even then, teachings were limited.

The Steam Age had started not long before my adolescent years. History before then was clouded, fabricated, and any stories and books that dated any time before were outlawed. This clicked in my head with the maps. I and any other child in my continent were raised to believe that Relica consisted of just a few islands, but Soen revealed a whole other world yet to be talked about and discovered. I wondered if that was why the Trade Circle was formed. Each city was known for its own style of goods; Metsa had the technology, Farlara had novelties, Linlecross had meat, and Mazz'Ra had crops and money. Mang'Coal and Que were mining countries and crafted Relica's finest jewelry.

Nothing made sense to me anymore the further I moved in this quest. Everything I learned prior to arriving at Metsa was a lie, and now I had to throw harpies into the mix with mermaids and talking spiders. Of no control of my own, I began to seethe. My teeth clenched as the entire lie that was my life began to emerge from the murky fallacies.

Barrea picked up on my growing anger and shifted in her seat.

I found myself suddenly annoyed at anything she did. I glared at her. "Just get out," I said.

THE REST of the day moved on as normal. Elliot was upset with me; Barrea had told him about us talking and how I snapped at her out of nowhere. When I told him, I had no intention of apologizing, he glowered at me and sent me back down to attend to the prisoner.

An odd request. Aside from Elliot delivering stale crisps and warm water, he never requested anyone to have any interaction with her. It was clear he was just trying to get away from me, which hurt, considering the life or death struggle I had helped him with. There was also the moment of laughter we shared, the first positive exchange since I found out he was married.

Still, I had to treat him as Captain of the Guard on this expedition, so I made my way down to the crew's quarters.

When I reached Lorraine's cell, I was distracted by Fristlyn's voice coming from my quarters. He was cursing, and I heard his cage rattle as he batted at it from the outside. I took one step toward the corridor before the hag spoke to me, the first time I heard her speak since meeting her.

"Don't worry about him." Her voice made me jump. It wasn't what I expected to come from a brittle, old hag. It was youthful and motherly, and the words dripped from her lips like fresh syrup. I faced her, watching her kneel on the floor. She was hunched over, and her long gray and frayed hair hung down, covering her face. My attention was pulled to her feet, bare and caked with filth.

I heard Fristlyn thrash harder inside the room, his words barely comprehensible. "...helped...more do I need to do?" He was livid. My only friend was livid.

"Do you know what is wrong with him?" I asked Lorraine.

"Stupid, *stupid* girl," she muttered. "Leave the pest be!"

"If he's a pest, then what does that make you?"

Her head tilted up at my dig. One bloodshot eye revealed itself from the curtain of her hair, as I continued to insult her for how she was talking about Fristlyn. "The only pest here is *you*. You are

119

a sick, vile—" She lunged at the cage, her chains and shackles extending far enough for her to grab the bars of the cell's door.

I jumped and shouted, staggering back from her attack.

She let out a giggle, sounding as if she was a little girl again as she did.

I began to sweat and felt rising dampness where my clothes met my back.

I got a good look at her now, too good of a look. Her tawny skin was wrinkled and thin. She looked as if she had begun decaying already, just at a slower rate.

"You know nothing about what I am, *Princess*," she growled, giving me the sensation of a million tiny bugs fleeing up my back. "Ah, but I know everything about you."

I gulped, trying to find that fire that was usually in me. The fire of hate and anger that I always carried, but she snuffed it out and blew it away with her cold, dead breath. "Y-you don't know a d-damned thing about me."

My voice cracked as I stood back up, and I trembled as she placed her face up against the bars and rubbed her forehead back and forth. Her mouth hung open, but she wasn't smiling; it just stayed down as she moaned to the feeling of the bars on her skin.

"I know you are scared," she spoke again. "I know you are a rogue princess who is starting to feel like she bit off more than she can chew."

I had felt that way, but I never told anyone about it. I never fully admitted it to myself, but she knew. How did she know? She couldn't have picked it up off my body language. She hadn't interacted with me till just now.

"I know you hate your father. I know all about you and your endeavors. I know that the real reason you're scared to get close to the captain is only because you'll tarnish the opinion you have of yourself." The world around me started to fade from existence, as I stared horrified into her bloodshot eyes.

"That's really what it all comes to, isn't it, RoGoria?"

My name leaving her mouth punched me in the throat. I had begun to hate my name, the mention of it making me want to tear my skin from my body. Only from her mouth. I wanted to scream at her, to silence her from speaking my name ever again. But I couldn't move. I couldn't speak, and I couldn't act on any instinct I had.

"You care about you. You're a bitter shell of a woman to all those around, even the arachnid you call a friend. You lack compassion; you detest doing things for others. You're just as entitled as all royalty comes."

"M-M-Marla..."

"Ah, yes, the child."

My heart began to tighten, and I clutched my chest as the pain of Marla's name shook my insides.

"You cling to her, use her as justification that you're a good person. But if you use her for your own emotional gain, then does that hold true? To use a child like that?"

"Stop it, Lorraine," Fristlyn's voice shattered the trance I was in.

I snapped to attention and crippled down to the floor, weeping onto the wood. I heard the rhythmic beat of his eight footsteps approach, and one scraggly leg patted my back.

"I'm having fun, pest. Leave me be," she demanded, but Fristlyn refused to leave my side.

"You know where we are going; you know what opportunity awaits me. If I should achieve it, you will be *finished*."

As Lorraine backed away, retreating to one corner of her cell, I pulled my eyes up to Fristlyn as the eight of his did the same.

"Wh-what opportunity?" I choked.

"Shh, center yourself back to this plane, lass." Another leg moved up and tucked a wild lock of bangs to my side. "You are safe."

"Why were you angry? I-in the room, I mean."

"In due time, Princess. I owe you more, yes. But I think after this, it should be clear that you owe something to someone else." He pulled away and turned to face the door. "Go. Prove the old hag wrong."

Without a second thought, I darted up the stairs and busted through the door to the main deck. Night had arrived once more as I sprinted across the boat; the force of my run and sea breeze flapped my train behind me as I moved around barrels and various beams that held the sails. I was still crying, damn near sobbing as Lorraine's words echoed through me.

I stopped and fell to my knees, now wailing into the night as the events that just occurred combined with the bits of nonsense I had collected over the past week.

You're a bitter shell of a woman to all those around you. I knew. I always knew. I spent the last thirteen years being this way, and now I was becoming my own enemy because of it.

Find the Ani'Mas King. Who is it? What is it? Who was the woman who told me about him, and why does Galyn seem to think he isn't at the Coven Woods anymore?

You may want to ask yourself why you're so bitter, RoGoria. Elliot, I was bitter because of him. He was ripped from me just when things were beginning to be magical with us. I changed in vengeance for him, only to keep when I saw getting him was no longer an option.

The spider...Keep him safe. Galyn's words echoed and I screamed at them. "What is his significance? What's this opportunity of his?"

I cried and yelled till my throat felt as if it was being cooked from the fiery rage spewing out. I slammed my fist down, and only then did I see the brown boots standing before me. I looked up to Barrea, who stood there terrified of me, of how I was behaving. The sight of her burned my eyes. *I patched up the holes the harpies left.* I never thanked her. She fixed my clothes, fed me daily, and even answered the question about the winged beasts I never even had to ask. I scared her off, after seeing nothing but kindness.

She dropped to her knees, slamming down with ferocity and yanked me toward her. After processing it for a while I realized she pulled me into a hug. Her arms wrapped tight around me and she squeezed. Such love radiated from her.

"I'm so sorry, Barrea," I sobbed into her smock, she must have just finished dinner. "I'm sorry for how I treated you this morning, and I-thank you. Thank you for fixing my clothes. I can't...I don't deserve—"

"I forgive you, RoGoria," Barrea interjected my pity and held me tighter. "I know things moved very quickly for you." They did. My life moved far too fast for me to comprehend. "That tacked on with yesterday's attack...It's a lot for one person. But, please, breathe." She tightened even more. "Breathe, and everything will clear and make sense." She pulled herself away and looked at me endearingly. Her dark brown curls bounced in the wind as starlight danced on her glossed lips and she smiled. I smiled back, too.

"Why don't you have dinner with Elliot and me tonight?" She rose to her feet and held out a hand. On instinct, I wanted to slap it away, brush her off and retreat to my room. My first instinct was to be that bitter, entitled princess who I needed to let go of.

I grasped her hand, and she pulled me up. She was taller than me, a quality I hadn't noticed until now. She wrapped her arm around my shoulders and led me into the cabin as I leaned my head on her arm.

CHAPTER 15

BARREA WALKED ME INTO THE CAPTAIN'S CABIN AND MOTIONED FOR me to sit at the dark, round dining table.

Elliot was already seated, and Barrea assured me she was just wrapping up dinner and walked to the back room where she was preparing the food. I didn't sit right away; I was still collecting myself from my moment just outside the cabin. My eyes were irritated, and it took all of my strength not to rub them into oblivion. I tried to focus on the cabin itself, just to give me something to do.

Behind Elliot was a steep staircase I presumed led to the captain's suite. Where there was normally a bed on a ship seemed to be a kitchen, where his wife was. Other than the dining table, the room was bare, no decor or other pieces of furniture. It wasn't until my search centered back to Elliot, and I remembered this wasn't his ship, so there would've been no reason to customize it to his liking.

Elliot met my stare and motioned for me to sit next to him, but the warmth from Barrea's hug moments before told me not to. So as to avoid overstepping a line, I sat across him, instead.

"Still wrapping your head around what happened, too?" He

asked right when I was situated. I gave a dumbfounded blink, not knowing what he was talking about.

"Huh?"

"The harpies," he elaborated. "I was terrified...I never thought I would face anything like that."

"Yes," I lied. He did not know what my outburst was about, and I didn't want him to. I was happy about the moment we shared after the attack, but I wasn't comfortable opening up and being that vulnerable with him. It hurt my heart because I used to be able to feel that way around him a long time ago. I needed him to think it was obvious. "Galyn essentially told me this was practice, that the true test of what we could deal with would be in the forests of the Coven Isle."

Elliot sank in his chair at the thought of worse beings in his future. I felt bad mentioning it, but his reaction was good for me. It meant he bought my charade. "That's unsettling, to say the least."

I let out a chortle as my head fell down, and I found myself studying the table. Maybe it was to avoid eye contact with him, but I had little control over it. My body had a mind of its own, and I was submissive to it. Since Barrea found me outside, I acted like a dog with its tail between its legs. Shy, and needing to be coerced.

I sat there and traced the splintered wood of the table with my finger. It was oak, aged oak, and I disregarded it as a useless thought amongst a whirlwind of thoughts blowing in and out of my mind, not sure what point to focus on but also growing anxious at the thought of creating an uncomfortable silence between us.

"What are you thinking about?" Elliot asked me.

"Us." The word was devious, freeing itself from the cage of my teeth, and I lost the ability to pace my breathing. Why did I say that? It was an inappropriate thing to admit by far; my hand started to shake while I awaited his answer.

My eyes crept up to look at him. He was in much more casual

wear than his standard uniform and baldric. Instead, he wore a cotton, short-sleeved shirt that was white for the most part. Save for a few food stains.

Most alarming was his smile. Wide and mouth closed; it stretched up to his ears as his grey eyes gleamed, even in the dark provided by the cabin. I gulped, fighting back my fear of his reaction and the want to jump over the table and claim him.

"I think about us a lot, as well," he whispered. His being discreet set off a match inside me; he was married, and we *both* needed to learn to respect it. The flame died quickly, though. Even my heart knew that was what I wanted to hear. "Notably the first time we met."

I lost a battle with a grand smile as I recounted the memory. I remembered it like it just happened, one of the last good memories I had before my life turned to shit. I was fourteen years old, and I had just finished The Princesses Ball, a grand party and feast for a Princess of Sheol's fourteenth birthday, the day a prince was allowed to come court me.

I was wound up from the party and took to the courtyard. It was my favorite place to unwind, a perfect setting. When I exited the doors, I was greeted by beautiful masonry and two beds of tulips on either side. A fountain sat in the center, and past it was two beds of my mother's roses, the ones she always planted and tended to herself. A curb hugged the rose garden and led to a balcony that overlooked the sea. To the left and right of the fountain were two paths; one led to the servants' quarters, and the other to the basement, where the Guardsmen of the manor slept.

Elliot, nineteen at the time, walked out while I was playing on the fountain's border. When I looked at him, my eyes felt an instant attraction that could not be thwarted, no matter how hard I had tried.

"We became friends instantly that day," I said.

Elliot smiled at the memory, too, though we both shared a laugh when we realized the friendship didn't last long. I would sneak out to see him late at night, every night, just to get my fill of his company.

A week passed, and he asked if he could give me a hug before he left for the night, and I was all too happy to grant his request. He held me tighter than I clung to any doll or pillow, and he recounted how painful it was to let me go.

The next day was my first meeting with a suitor, a seventeen-year-old prince from Shimslea, Farlara. Tensions were high over the course of the day, and my mother was the most unbearable of all.

She would yank and pull at my hair while scolding me for how often I just tied it back. "Not at all ladylike," she would say as she curled it and threw it up into a ridiculous updo. "Not at all childlike," I wanted to say but never did. That was during the decline in my father's mentality. From respected leader to mad man, and talking back to my mother was more trouble than it was worth.

Before the prince had arrived, I rushed out to the courtyard to decompress. I sat on the stone fountain and looked up at the statuette of Victoriana Sheol, the first leader and founder of the city. She had put the asinine traditions in place, and as a child, I detested her for it. I had started to find pebbles in the fountain and heaved them at the statue as I cursed her name under my breath.

Elliot entered the courtyard and witnessed the frustration; he pulled me aside into the rose garden and hugged me, telling me it would be okay.

"Why couldn't you have been a prince?" I asked as I wept into his hardened chest.

He didn't respond; he just shushed me and held me tighter.

I pulled back to look at him and saw tears welling in his eyes. I tried to fight back my own and to give some statement about how we should just run off. But he wouldn't let me even start. He wished me luck, and afterward, he lifted my head by my chin. "There's not a chance he won't fall in love with you," he told me.

His head leaned to mine as my eyes forced themselves shut while he pressed his soft lips against mine. I fell into him; I couldn't help it. My feelings for him coiled around us both and pushed us closer as we kissed in the rose garden.

"My biggest regret was allowing you to kiss me," I said. Tears began to form as I said the words. "My father found us right in the middle of it, and—"

Elliot shushed me right there, just as he did all those years ago. "We know what happened, Princess," he whispered.

"You don't," I told him. "You know what happened on your end; you were ordered to be executed, but instead you were exiled and you had been in Metsa all these years. I...I was beaten, in front of the prince who had just arrived. My father *beat* me in front of him, and the prince ran off after seeing the ruthless torture I was put under. He didn't want to be a part of our family. My father blamed that on me, and he just beat me more. I was swollen, bruised, and a shell of a woman by the end."

Elliot looked at me from across the table, mouth gaping at the story he never knew. "I'm sorry. I hadn't known about that."

"It's not your fault, Elliot. It was an atrocious reaction on his part."

The conversation ceased when Barrea walked in with a plate of food. As she opened the kitchen doors, an aroma of brisket and spices kissed my nose while the heat from steaming tea and vegetables hugged me tightly.

"RoGoria, would you be so kind as to bring this down to Lorraine?"

"What about the bread we usually give her?" Elliot asked before I could answer. The endearing gaze he put upon me faded as he switched to his wife. Not cold or abrasive just...empty.

"We can't just feed her scraps. She needs an actual meal," Barrea argued, Though I disagreed with her on this, I had to grin at her kind heart toward even a murderer.

Elliot nodded. "Fair. But you are the cook and the server, love. You can bring it down."

The sweet conversation I just had with Elliot vanished. The

feelings, the nostalgia of our memories together, shot dead by his words. I leered at him at the order, at the disrespect to the woman who promised to give her life for him.

Barrea nodded with hesitance, and mouthed, "Okay" and started to walk to the door. I shoved myself up from my chair and blocked her path and took the plate from her as gently as I could.

"Go ahead and set the table, it's no trouble at all," I informed her. The last thing I wanted to do was put myself anywhere near the old hag, but this was no longer about me. Barrea smiled and retreated to the kitchen. Elliot watched me, astounded, and before I knew it, the feeling of wanting to punch him again resurfaced, and I was ready to do so.

Lorraine was 'asleep' in her cell, so I cracked open the door, slid the plate in, and locked it in just a second lest she decided to lunge at me again.

When I arrived back at the captain's cabin, Barrea was seated and changed into more casual wear, just a thin blouse with tight trousers. Elliot refused to make eye contact with me. Good. He should know how displeased I was that he ruined the beautiful conversation we were having.

I took my first bite of the meal Barrea prepared and lifted my hand to cover my mouth, as I felt myself beginning to drool at the bursts of flavor. Much of the taste came from her sense of care about those whom she cooked for rather than it just being a job like the servants back at Sheol Manor.

The three of us participated in casual small talk, and Barrea was extra careful to keep me included. It felt like she was hard at work to win my approval. She asked personal questions; where I came from, why I left, why I didn't just announce my presence to Soen when I arrived. All of those were questions I did not want to answer, but more importantly, all of those questions revealed one key piece of information; Barrea didn't *know*. She had no clue Elliot and I shared a past together, he kept it secret from her, and that only made my blood boil more.

I made it damn near impossible for Elliot to actually converse with me now. I ended up dismissing much of his statements directed toward me due to his uncalled-for attitude about Lorraine's damn food. I soon fell to silence, letting them talk as I just ate my meal.

I pondered if this was even the same man. We shared the same memories, the same beautiful moment from our pasts. But the Elliot back then was kind, nurturing, and went out of his way for others. Now, he was cold, dismissive to the woman he swore his years to, and all-around short and unpleasant. I hated myself for bringing up our kiss. I hated that I clung to that memory. As the dinner went on, I heard a snap in my head, and I started to not miss him at all. The more time I spent with him, the more I grew to loathe who he had become.

CHAPTER 16

I LEFT THE CAPTAIN'S CABIN DESPITE ELLIOT'S INSISTENT ATTEMPTS to engage in conversation. Maybe I was being too hard on him; I was just so irritated at his demeanor toward Barrea. It was the same dismissive attitude Prince Darien Lockner treated me with; as if she had to obey his every command.

I walked to the other side of the ship to the forecastle deck to enjoy the gorgeous night before I went to bed. The entire ship was alive with drama, so I hadn't gotten the chance to bask underneath the starry sky.

It was the first time I got to enjoy an evening like this since the night before I left Sheol. There was a storm when I left, and Metsa's smoke from the forgeries and production facilities made stargazing next to impossible. My hovel on the side of the island was no exception; smoke seemed to go on forever when I was in or anywhere near the city. I wished I paid attention to when the smoke stopped and the sky revealed itself once again, but being attentive to pleasantries was beyond my control.

I squinted at the distance, at a landmass several miles out. It was a large island, and the most notable feature was what looked to be a silhouette of a tree, though it was far too massive. *The Coven Isle...We are almost there.*

Barrea told me to be up early tomorrow as Elliot was going to sail the remainder of the evening in the hope of getting there by sunrise. Had they seen the landmass I saw? Was it within view, and I was only realizing it now?

The island was a pretty sight from here, though Galyn's words echoed through me every minute I looked to it, how there were far worse things on the island compared to the harpies, the winged beasts that carried me away.

That was what I wanted to think about. I sat with my back against the wood, now facing the stairs that led to the main deck, legs overlapping each other.

I could be dead right now. If it weren't for Galyn, I would be. It only just hit me now, how lucky I was to be alive. The harpy who carried me could have put just a bit more pressure and punctured my heart, or I could have drowned at sea. Something in the sea itself, like a shark or maybe a less friendly mermaid, could have devoured me as I sank. I shivered at the thought of teeth like Galyn's tearing me, shredding me to bits as my blood painted the ocean red.

Then, there was Elliot. He had gotten captured, too, and I was ready to die saving him. I had thrown myself off the boat at risk of missing the harpy who held him completely and plummeting to the sea as the birdwoman carried him away. Also, while saving him, I put his life in more danger, just as mine was when we crashed into the ocean. If mermaids existed, only God knew what else did.

My thumbs fidgeted together, and before I knew it, my palms pressed to one another and I held my hands up to my lips.

"Dear Lord," I whispered. "I haven't reached out to You in quite some time. In fact, I must admit for a while I began to question Your existence. Yet I feel that, because of You, I was able to break free. There have been more dramatic hardships since then, but I've always survived another day. I have to assume I have You to thank for this. Until next time, Lord."

It was years since I last prayed. A couple of years after Elliot's exile, I had given up. I thought I was a lost cause in God's eyes. I felt as if He didn't care about me. I was told most spiritualists, the title of those who walked the path of God, felt this way at some point in their lives. Mine lasted for eleven years.

"That was beautiful, lass," Fristlyn commended as he made his way up the stairs. He groaned with each step and then made a slow crawl to me. I patted my lap, inviting him to sit upon it. He did so gratefully and nestled his legs into mine.

I stroked the back of his abdomen, and he let out a whine of pleasure. Not a sexual moan, or a creepy gasp; just content with the feeling of my fingers combing his back.

"What kind of spider are you?" I asked him. I had always meant to ask.

"No specific family or breed," he said, "though I closely resemble a male black widow."

I let out a faint laugh. "You're a little brown to be a *black widow*, no?"

"Male black widows are actually a lighter color. The only thing missing to complete the look is the red spots, which replace the females' hourglass."

I nodded and resumed petting him as he sank farther into my lap until he couldn't anymore. "Are you going to tell me why you were so angry earlier?"

"Nope."

"Of course," I laughed. I made sure to sound friendly, and not upset by his secrecy. It wasn't any of my business, and the recurring theme of the past several months was I had to stop acting as if it was. "Just know, I only ask because I care about you. I consider you a friend."

"And I to you, lass," he said. I pursed my lips into a smile,

133

happy that there was at least one person, or spider, who enjoyed my company.

We sat in blissful silence, not talking for a bit and just enjoying the air. A night wind greeted us every so often, and it would push his tiny hairs as it did so.

I found myself comfortable, even with the weight of Fristlyn's body resting heavily on my legs. I was content with the scenery before us, with the crashing waves rocking the still boat and the occasional breeze that played with our hairs. The star-filled night seemed like it was its own ethereal being, blessing us with just one quiet evening. To tie it off was my friend, a friend I never dreamed of having, but a friend I needed more than anything. Fristlyn was like me in a lot of ways; lost, alone, and had lived with a horrid person who seemed to hurt him whenever she couldn't get him to do what she wanted. Two very different sides of the exact same coin.

It occurred to me that I would unload question after question onto Galyn, but I never thought to ask Fristlyn for any information. After all, we were going to his homeland, where he hailed from, and I wanted nothing more than to ask what "opportunity awaited him" there at the island, like what he threatened Lorraine with. But maybe it was a good thing I didn't pry him for anything, no need to open a closed wound. However, there was one question that might be fair game.

"Fristlyn," I whispered his name and waited for his bulbous eyes to look at me. "Can I trouble you for a question?"

He was silent for a while but came around with a deal. "May I ask you one first, Princess?" There was a satisfying roll of the "R" as he spoke. His croak of a voice made it hard to remember that there was an accent in there, a culture of sorts. "I'll answer yours to the best of my abilities if you'll let me."

"Of course." It wasn't even a question. I respected the eight-legged creature too much to not open to him about anything.

"You blindly agreed to this quest. Have you ever stopped to think why Soen wants the Tears?"

A wonderful question. A phenomenal one, actually, that I just lacked an answer for. I thought about it the best I could, but he was right. I did go along with this blindly; I never even stopped to think about what Soen had to gain from us bringing the Tears back. "No, if I'm being honest," I confirmed. "I was just so damn concerned about why my father ruined the lives of those who swore their loyalty to him that it never crossed my mind to ask. Another 'RoGoria, only thinking about how this benefits her' story, I guess."

Fristlyn let loose that laugh of his; though the more I heard it, the less terrifying it was. Not a single drop of malice came from him, that much was clear. I had no reason to cringe at his laugh anymore.

"I don't think that counts, lass. I think the opposite, actually. Even as an ex-princess, you still care about those you witnessed lose everything. *That* is what makes a leader." He removed himself from the crevasse of my lap and stood on six of his legs. His front two stretched up and rested on my chin. As if he were a human, cupping my face with his hands. It was, by all definitions of the word, odd. Though it was him; it was Fristlyn, and I found comfort in it. "You have a lot to work on, lass. That much is clear. But you know this, and realizing your own faults is the first step to fixing them." His mandibles stretched to either side of his face, and I fought back a cringe. I would never get over the damned spider *smiling* at me. It was horrifically adorable. "Give yourself more credit," he continued. "You're doing just fine."

It was my turn to be odd. My arms fluttered up and moved in between his legs and I pulled him in. The legs that were on my chin curled over my shoulders and the rest of his legs were around my waist. This lasted for about two seconds before we both started howling in laughter at a spider and a human girl hugging. We eased ourselves after a few moments when Elliot exited the captain's cabin and started to prepare to set sail farther out. He couldn't see us, it seemed, though, we could see him.

Fristlyn resituated himself back onto my lap. "What was your question for me, lass?"

I had several, but, again, did not want to reopen any scars. There was one that didn't apply to his life, though, one question he could answer without being reminded of his grand life with his family.

"What is an Ani'Mas King? Or Queen?"

The hairs on his abdomen shot up, and his eyes glistened in the moonlight for the first time in the entire night. "That is a title I have not heard in ages."

"So you know who they are, then?"

"Ah, yes of course. The Ani'Mas were men and women, who were on the brink of suicide, who felt as if they were incapable of living, and were visited by the Settlers of Old themselves. Those sad people were blessed with a fraction of their power, but that fraction was pure immense power, and it granted the user to speak, control, order, and revolutionize a colony of the animal they felt most connected to."

I sighed in relief, finally having an answer, as well as a detailed description of what I could be looking for. I found it hard to believe that the Coven Isle had a handful of animal-themed sorcerers.

I fought back tears of my own, receiving the answer to what was maybe the most mysterious question I had. "A woman..." I trailed off, not sure how to describe the weird lady that visited me next to Metsa's fountain. "A strange woman told me to locate the Ani'Mas King...and that he would help. But Galyn told me the last she had heard was he was gone and hasn't been around the Coven Isle for quite some time."

"I'm sure he's around," he said. "Good or bad, an Ani'Mas King or Queen loved their clan, would die for it. So he's either there, or he's dead."

A comforting thought, though a detail left me feeling defeated either way. "If he's alive, he wouldn't be much help. Not with magic being imprisoned in the Tears."

Fristlyn released a low, gravel-like chuckle. "Oh, oh, Princess. The witch's spell to imprison magic wouldn't apply to Ani'Mas. They were granted their power from the Settlers of Old themselves. There is no magic there, only celestial energy and ability. The Laws of Magic do not apply."

"How powerful were the Settlers that they could not only create powerful beings but also bypass the Laws of Magic itself?" The stories we read about the legends of the Settlers told of how ruthless and timeless they were, yet they went around blessing those who felt like they could not handle life anymore. How bad or evil could those beings be? How powerful were they to refute the guidelines of power such as magic?

Fristlyn was ready to answer my question, though I wasn't ready to hear it. "They didn't bypass the Laws of Magic, lass. They're the creators of magic and its entirety."

The Settlers of Old sounded benevolent, which was unlike any legend I had heard about them. I wasn't at all surprised by this, though; being lied to about the very world I lived on for the majority of my life made me numb, numb to the new information about the life I now knew little about.

I wanted to ask more. How did Sylvestra cast such a godlike spell? Who, or what, were the Settlers of Old, and what had they done to get the reputation they have today? I'm sure Father knew. If he were as adamant about finding the Tears all this time, driven by his thirst for power, he would've had to have looked up the Settlers and any literature he could find on them. My stomach turned at the thought of him knowing about the Ani'Mas and how they were an exception to the rule.

I looked down at Fristlyn as I pondered getting clarification, but his breathing had slowed, and he continued to sink deeper into my lap.

"Come, let's go to bed," I said.

He maneuvered off of me so I could stand, and crawled up my legs and back so I would carry him down.

I walked past Elliot on the main deck as he prepared to get the ship moving, and we shared an awkward glance.

"Goodnight," he said, shyly.

You have a lot to work on, lass, that much is clear. Fristlyn was so right about everything. Though a sad spider, he was able to read me so clearly, and I had to take his support of my own growth with a grain of salt.

"Goodnight," I said back to him, and even went as far as to give him a half-smile as I entered the crew's quarters.

CHAPTER 17

THE SUN'S RAYS WERE MERCILESS. A NIGHT OF NO SLEEP TAUNTED me in the form of sunlight as if it was giving me a final roar of victory, making my quarters shimmer with life while I contemplated throwing myself overboard and drowning myself, all for that extra bit of shut-eye. However, the sunlight wasn't the source of my misery.

It was the old hag in the room across from mine. She spent the entire night, from the moment Fristlyn and I entered the lower deck, all the way through till daybreak, crackling and screeching at nothing. She wasn't in anguish, more excited like she just inherited a fortune that could sustain her a lifetime. The only pause she would make was to sing; a dark poem though sung with her youthful, gorgeous voice, left a haunting pit in my gut. I remembered the words perfectly since it was the same lyric over and over again.

Soon, I will be whole, blessed by her Tears, and when I am complete, 'tis I they will fear. All the power, all the magic, will cripple my opponents, so tragic.

She sang this tune every hour in between cackling and wailing into the night. However, hearing the words come from that sweet, syrupy voice was disturbing enough that when she didn't sing it, it played in a constant loop in my head, so clearly, it felt as if she was in my room. This went on for the remainder of the night, so much I was almost certain that was what kept me awake instead of the maniacal noises coming from her cell. She hadn't acted this way during the entire trip. Hell, aside from yesterday, she had given us the silent treatment, even going as far as to not make eye contact with Elliot or Barrea when they brought her meals.

As I laid on my bed, practically lifeless, a terrifying yet exciting thought entered my mind.

I rose from my bed and scrunched my face in disgust when I felt the matted, tangled mess that was my hair. I couldn't worry about it at that moment, though. I did make the dreadful decision to try and run my fingers through the oily mane.

Disturbed by my appearance, I swung my bare feet over my bed and onto the floor. I felt the warmth of the sun-stained wood, soothing to the touch of my skin. I stood and yawned as I stretched to let my muscles once again feel at peace before I exited my quarters.

Fristlyn was nowhere to be seen, but if Lorraine's reason for acting so inhumanely was what I thought it was, then he might be outside gazing into the distance at the same thing. He once acted erratically as we sailed closer; it wasn't impossible he might be having an internal celebration now.

Before climbing up the stairs to the main deck, I stopped by Lorraine's cell to witness something that made me uneasy.

Lorraine, still shackled and secured, stood to the farthest right-hand corner and rubbed her head against the coarse wood with vigorous intent. I watched as she scraped her forehead with each brush, the spot of blood growing bigger and bigger each time she did so. She went back to singing that tune, "Soon, I will be whole, blessed by her Tears, and when I am complete, 'tis I they will fear. All the power, all the magic, will cripple my opponents, so tragic." She was mutilating herself, bloodying the ship's walls as she chanted and with each passing moment, she'd rub *harder*. I found myself feeling sympathy toward the prisoner, and I approached her door and was light to grasp a single bar, getting ready to ask if she was hungry.

She lunged herself at me. To my terrified surprise, she threw herself against the door and started laughing. The laugh didn't sound the same as her youthful vocals normally did; there was an overlay of echoes as she wheezed this dark, bone-breaking laugh. I stumbled and fell back, bashing my rear into the stairs right as she let out a high-pitched scream.

It felt as though it physically pierced my ears, causing a ringing that was faint at first but grew louder and more violent with the ringing escalating with it. It soon reached a high enough frequency to where I clamped my hands around my ears to muffle it out, to no avail. I curled into a ball, holding my ears closed as the howling spiked with force. I felt my brain throb, about to burst right from the inside. I started to cry; the pain was far too great, and then my crying turned into sobbing, and I couldn't bear it anymore. I started shouting; I begged her to stop, but she wouldn't have it. Little red drops fell to the floor from my face, and I felt my own blood stream from my eyes. My hands fell, covered in blood as it flooded my ears and poured down my cheeks, staining the wood.

I gasped as I shot from my bed, yelling in fear. Fristlyn was thrown to the wall, causing him to yelp in shock as I hurled myself up from the horrendous dream. My breathing accelerated as the events of the nightmare replayed in my head until Fristlyn crawled back up to the bed, talked me down, and ordered me to take slow, controlled breaths.

I asked him what was happening, why I couldn't calm down, no matter how hard I tried and how attentive I was to his orders.

"You're having an attack, Princess," he told me. He started to inhale and exhale with me, and I matched his breathing patterns until I was consistent, until I was steady. Once more, the sun beamed into my room, however, now it was welcomed. It felt friendly, and the heat was that of a hug from a dear friend.

"I need air," I said as I swung my bare feet over my bed and flung myself out of it. I stormed out of my quarters and made my way to the stairs but was stopped by an unseen force in front of Lorraine's cell.

She sat against the wall now, fidgeting with the chains on her shackles. She leered at me with a grin, but it was short-lived as she began to look confused at my unsettled stare.

I watched her for quite some time, before she retreated back to a glare and spat through the door, the saliva landing just by my feet.

"Where is my breakfast?"

I blinked once and told her to piss off as I retreated to the main deck.

———

THE REVEALING RAGS I used as sleepwear did not protect me from the chill of the morning, but I pushed through.

I stood at the forecastle deck, having to shuffle my feet constantly as the cold morning dew on the hardwood floor nibbled at my heels and toes. The chill quickened my awakening, and I was no longer groggy and dead-looking. I rubbed my bare arms for warmth; the scar Elliot left me was just that, scarred over. It was fresh and tickled the healed skin as my hand slid up and down it. All this time, I never got an answer as to why he inflicted me this way. He claimed he was protecting himself, but he knew who I was. That I posed no threat. I decided that, maybe, I didn't want to know; I didn't want to hear his reasoning, especially since he was still pining over me. The combatting for my attention, though, was something I'd have to discuss when the time was right.

The island was far out, but it was clear. It was lousy with dead trees; the branches jagged and absent of life itself. There was nothing magical about this place, and the trees warned me to turn back. One tree promised only riches if I kept going, though.

Farther out, deep into the forests was a behemoth of a tree. It still flourished with life as the leaves radiated a warm glow. Specks of gold shimmered brightly around them, so captivating and luminous, I could see them from here. There was something poetic about it being surrounded by its dead kin, like it was immune to fate.

"Yggdrasil..." Elliot's voice startled me from behind as he approached beside me, staring at the landmass. "Never in all my life..." he trailed off in awe of its emanating beauty, and I understood why. I was almost entranced by it, as well.

"That's...that's the Tree of Life itself, then?" I asked for confirmation, though I knew very well what "Yggdrasil" was.

"You've heard of it?"

"Every fairy tale I read was centered around this tree. The fact that it truly exists in our world. I cannot find the words to describe how happy that makes me."

Yggdrasil was always described as the Bridge between the gods' worlds in our stories, though it was rumored to be a portal to just one. Stories referred to it as "Otherworld", a place of consistent chaos. I couldn't imagine a life more chaotic than my own, though. Not anymore.

I was not too keen on sharing this morning with Elliot. Just thinking about his demeanor last night made my skin hot, and I went back and forth trying to forget the instance and just wanting to smack him upside his beautiful, blonde head. But his company was better than none, considering the start to my day. I wished Fristlyn was here; I longed for a conversation like the one we had last night, though I knew I could make use out of Elliot's time.

"Did Soen tell you why he wanted the Tears?" I probed him, expecting to be given the runaround once more.

Instead, he was blunt and honest with me, something I admired when he answered my question. "He wants to release magic back into the world," Elliot explained. "Honestly, I'm surprised you're only asking about this now."

I chuckled. "It wasn't until Fristlyn gingerly pointed out how naive I was for not asking him myself."

"I disagree. Watching your people suffer, lose everything they worked hard to obtain, and create the rich life Sheol once had over this exact…whatever it is; I understood why you were quick to accept."

Guard Dog Fildra came to mind. I was unable to remember how her family got their fortune, but the memory of how they lost everything was engraved, tax after tax, so my father could fund his excessive expeditions to push the richest families, aside from our own, to deteriorate into shells of who they once were.

I wasn't too happy about Soen's cause, either. Releasing magic back into the world seemed like a terrible idea, and I could only imagine what my father's intentions for that kind of power were. I didn't want to think Soen's were the same, but he was a leader, as well, and could benefit from a mystical power.

I would be a liar to say I wasn't curious at all. I just had the common sense to know that people would not be able to handle ethereal abilities.

"What does he intend to do with magic?" I asked.

Elliot shrugged. "He simply wants to fix Relica, restore it to what it once was."

"I feel like it was changed for a reason."

"Ah, but what if that reason was not a good one?"

Fair rebuttal, but doubtful. Based on the minimal information I heard about Sylvestra already, I doubted she had any ill intent with taking magic away. She seemed like someone who had a strong intuition and being the powerful witch she apparently was, locking up the source of her power didn't seem to benefit her in any way.

This inference on personality countered Lorraine's. As I gazed at that Tree, at Yggdrasil itself, one thing was for certain. I had assigned myself a task, and that task was not letting that old hag out of my sight.

CHAPTER 18

I WAS DRESSED AND BACK UP TO THE MAIN DECK BEFORE ELLIOT AND Barrea. Fristlyn helped me subdue Lorraine, which was difficult for both of us.

The witch trashed and jumped around, even going as far as to pin me down at one point. She tried to make a break for the main deck, which wouldn't have done her any good since we were still pretty far out from the isle's beach. While she cried about how she was going to retrieve what was hers, her magic, she tumbled back down the stairs, immobilized by thick, tar-like spider silk. To shut her up from screaming, I pulled my hair down and gagged her with old fabric from my dress that had been my hair tie for the past several months.

Now, we were back up on the main deck and waited for Elliot and Barrea to stop their love-making which we all heard clear as day.

My hair was tied back once more, now bound together, but with more of Fristlyn's silk. I didn't think he would be useful, but two times in one day he proved otherwise.

I was going to start the process of lowering the rowboats, but I realized I didn't know how. A few different ropes here and there and some of them had to be undone first after preparing one thing after another. So I decided to let Elliot handle that, when he was done pleasing his wife.

The symphony of moans heated me. How could he try to bond so hard with me but make tender love to another? I started to wonder if he cared about either one of us at all, or if we were just conquests. Thirteen years ago, I would've thrown my virtue off the balcony of Mother's garden for him. As I heard sounds of aggression, and the belted song of release, I realized I was smart to retain it. I shuddered and cringed as they walked out moments later, Barrea's short, curly hair wild from the frenzy.

I scoffed as they approached, and let out a "have fun?" at their expense. Barrea giggled a ghastly sound, and Elliot rolled his eyes and smirked.

I wanted to smack the grin off his face, but as Fristlyn's legs tightened around the arm that twitched I decided not to cause a scene.

ELLIOT and the hag took one rowboat, while Fristlyn, Barrea, and I took the other. Elliot made the point he would be strong enough to restrain her if she tried to throw herself into the bay, which was correct, not that she could do much wrapped in spider silk as strong as Fristlyn's, though. She would most likely sink and fall prey to the sharks, or Lord knows what else.

The three of us guarded the rations and food, which traveled with us. Barrea was making complaints about lugging this through the forest, but I assured her she wouldn't have to do it alone. It got a smile, and I fought hard not to smile back. A fight with myself I ended up losing. That same little voice in my mind reminded me that she had done nothing wrong, and therefore deserved no anger from me. I disagreed, as the sounds of pleasure she made were permanently burned into my mind.

I faced Barrea, whose back was turned to water and ship. This caused me to jump when Elliot grabbed the boat to drag us onto the sand. Barrea set the oar's down and departed, with Fristlyn and I behind her.

The trees looked worse up close. Not just scary, but straight out of a nightmare. Fristlyn had told me this was a place of peace, a place of balance. How could any place turn into a sight that would have me run with my tail between my legs? Wind echoed through the forests, and I began to feel like I bit off more than I could swallow. Internally, I cursed Soen's name for sending me, an ex-princess, out here with a less than qualified group.

I began to sympathize with Elliot. He was going to have to work harder than intended to keep us all alive. Galyn had told me beasts far greater than the harpies dwelled within. I believed her then, and the trees promised it.

Yggdrasil towered over everything; I could still see the speckles of gold, clear as day. The leaves sang with each breeze, and I knew that if we at least made our way there, we could rest soundly. It promised safety.

I felt a tug on my train and looked down to see Fristlyn begging me silently. I smiled at him and motioned for him to climb up. He had trouble adjusting around my crossbow, complaining more about the canister of bolts that allowed it to be automatic but found a position comfortable for us both.

Elliot approached after he and Barrea finished unpacking all the rations from the boat and handed me a set of goggles. Not brass like his, but ivory with brass sprockets.

"All guards have these," he said.

I took the goggles from his hand and equipped them around my forehead. I would have to get used to the pressure from them, but using his on the boat proved they could be useful.

"Why am I only getting these now? I've been a Guardswoman for quite some time."

His head fell, but he never broke eye contact with me. "I tried," he mumbled. "No time seemed good enough."

I would *proudly* take responsibility for that. He turned to walk away, and my silence refused to stay. I had to ask why he was the way he was, with both me and his wife. I spun around and started to call out to him, but he was frozen in place. He stared out to our boat, and I followed his gaze. I gasped at the sight of another ship, sailing just behind ours. An orange flag with a black S lousy with thorns signaled the arrival of a Sheol ship. I lowered the goggles and zoomed my sight closer and saw the green and gold trims along its walls. That style belonged to Sheol's battleships, equipped with the best firepower Father's money could buy.

I dropped to my knees as it came up, aligned with our ship, and my eyes began to well up, knowing the inevitable was going to happen.

"Calm, lass, calm," Fristlyn's croak whispered in my ears, and I shook my head in response. Calm? We were about to be stranded on this island with no vessel to get us back. We were about to witness our ship sink from an onslaught of cannon fire, and I was supposed to stay calm?

But there was no cannon fire. The Sheolian ship cruised right past, almost as if our ship did not exist. That was unlike Father. Another ship after a treasure? It would be at the bottom of the ocean already.

"Just wait, lass." Fristlyn pressured me to wait as Elliot screamed about how they had seen us already. The spider snapped toward him; not out of anger, just so he could be heard, and told him to trust that they hadn't. Fristlyn promised us all a miracle right after.

The ship never stopped. It was beyond the drop-off of the island now, and it kept going. My breath accelerated as I foresaw a ghastly crash was about to happen and noticed Barrea was right in its way. I yelled her name, and Elliot snapped to attention and charged her, barreling into her to push her out of the way. All for nothing.

I watched in utter amazement, as the ship passed through the island. The ground met the ship, turned to be transparent as it sailed seamlessly through the land, as though the island did not exist, and disappeared into the forest's dark hold. Elliot and Barrea soon swarmed us and prodded Fristlyn for answers. I didn't want to overwhelm him, but I couldn't hold it. I rattled off question after question.

"A veil, ladies and gent, a glamour," he said. Glamours showed up in many works of fiction. There were many tales told of witches casting a glamour spell to disguise something, to make things not as they seem.

"This..." I trailed off, not knowing how to organize my thoughts. "This isn't a disguise. This island just simply didn't exist to them!"

Fristlyn let out a chuckle. "Sylvestra wasn't renowned as the strongest witch for no reason, lass. In fact, we may stumble upon her Book of Shadows while we're here."

"I don't want to," Barrea chimed. "Sounds spooky."

For Lord's sake, are we twelve?

"A Book of Shadow's isn't dangerous," I told her. A fairy tale for beginners. The most basic information about witches was in their Book of Shadows. "It's the witch's work; her studies, her spells, her tweaks to already established spells."

"We still better hope we don't find it!" she exclaimed, and a nod of her head back by the boats told me she was right. Lorraine, mad or not, was fascinated by magic. The last thing we'd want is for her to get her hands on it.

"We're missing the point," Elliot said. "Why didn't the Glamour work on us?" A fair and obvious question.

We awaited Fristlyn's response, though I wish I never received it. His words sent a chill down my back I could have done without. "We've been expected, lad."

CHAPTER 19

I COULD TASTE DEATH. I COULD HEAR HIM, FEEL HIM, EVEN SMELL him. Entering the forest, finally, after several interruptions, was like walking into another realm. I could taste his presence. It was bland and chalky and made my lips chapped and cracked. The wind's wallowing roar was his voice, yelling for us to turn back. Even the chill the forest brought alerted us of the dangers around, the dangers Death would free us from. We just came from a sun-filled tropical beach, and the second we entered the forest, there was no sun. No warmth; there was only cold. However, just because his presence was pungent, rancid in my nose, it didn't mean I could not avoid him.

We walked single file and made sure to be as quiet as we were able to be. Lorraine in the front as our guide so she could properly lead us. Elliot was right behind her with his pistol pointed at her back. Behind Elliot stood his wife, whose breath had to be warming his back with how heavy each exhale was. She kept turning to face me, but I only noticed it every once and awhile due to her face being covered by a large pack on her back. We each held one, hers filled with cookware. I was too busy surveying behind and around us, making sure nothing would jump out to surprise us. Only God knew what breed of beast lurked in these woods, but I made a point to mouth, "We're okay," to her each time she looked.

I'd look up to the trees every so often; despite having no leaves, they destroyed any evidence that the sky ever existed. The long, scraggly branches made it easy for Fristlyn to transition from one tree to another. He had volunteered to climb above us. Firstly, because I now carried a pack holding tents and bedrolls. Secondly, so he could spot any potential dangers above and below. Forget harpies; I was sure they could not compare to any avail creatures that inhabited this Island of Nightmares.

Barrea's hand pressed into my gut, and I froze. This was a signal Elliot passed to her whenever he would stop moving so that she could pass it to me. He grabbed Lorraine by her shoulder to keep her from moving, and she yelped in pain. All three of us whispered a hateful, "Shut up," as Elliot attempted to listen.

Elliot was not a hunter. I wasn't a hunter. Barrea sure as hell wasn't one, either. The only experience we held was being prey. There was nothing, though, just the uneasy wind blowing right at us. Elliot jabbed his pistol in Lorraine's back to keep us moving forward.

None of us questioned whether or not Lorraine was leading us the right way. We knew she wanted to find the Tears more than any of us, and all believed she'd lead us right to them.

We walked for what felt like several miles, when in reality it was probably one or two. We kept our mouths shut the entire trek until Barrea nudged me and pointed outward. Following her finger, I could see she was pointing at a clearing in the trees, which included a pond of a decent size. It was a wonderful spot to set up camp for the remainder of the day, as we were all tired. I nodded at her, mouthing, "Good job," before I snapped my fingers for Elliot's attention. I pointed to the clearing and he nodded and shoved Lorraine over into that direction.

As we made our way over, Barrea stopped and made a small

yelp before I clasped her mouth shut, silencing her in an instant. I looked down after I noticed she was having a hard time balancing and noticed a large thorn bush peeking out, and three thorns stuck deep in her skin. The thorns were large on a grotesque scale, about the size of my finger, and I wanted to cry for her, as one was stuck halfway through. I knew removing it would cause a lot of pain, and it's not like I could have broken the branch off without mangling my own hand.

I looked up to see Elliot watching us, confused. I motioned for him to come by and he did so with swiftness, though still walking to our aide. He took a second to eyeball the situation before looking at his wife. He gave her a gentle kiss, which made me retch and whispered, so soft I was shocked I could hear, that he would help. But it was going to hurt.

He shifted his eyes to me and motioned for me to cover her mouth. We switched places, and I cupped her lips, making sure to be as gentle as I could.

Barrea was terrified, and I saw her eyes sparkle with tears. I found myself growing proud of her while I witnessed the effort she was making to keep quiet.

Elliot pinched the thorn and pulled with a firm, though careful, movement.

Barrea did not scream; she understood the risk.

I whispered she could bite my hand if she wanted, but she refused. I could feel warmth flow between mine and her cheek while she sobbed like a broken faucet, choking on her breath while she attempted to remain silent.

Even I shivered and winced in disgust, as I heard the thorn scraping and squishing through her skin. When Elliot finally removed them, I felt the moisture from her breath as she released a pained, warm exhale into my hand.

I entered the clearing to set my tent out, though I had to pause to stop a certain old woman from crawling away. A poor attempt; I grabbed her by her hair and shoved her against a tree beside Elliot and Barrea and removed her gag so that she could eat. I threatened her, saying another move like that and she wouldn't get food.

In response, she spat in my face.

I clenched my jaw in a violent haze. By the time I blinked once, my hand stung from the impact of my palm against her face. I didn't even think to do that, it just happened.

"You think that'll be good enough?" Elliot asked me as his eyes focused on my russet hand. His voice was still a whisper, and I figured that was the way we'd be talking the entire time we were here.

Still pissed, I snapped back at him, though I didn't intend to. "You of all people know I can throw a punch."

His hand floated up and the fingers brushed against his cheek. *That's right.*

"Throw more," he said. "Don't be shy." He turned back to his wife, who was in too much pain to even be attentive to the interaction.

Blood trickled down her leg, and once more, I felt sorry for the annoying chef. I walked over to Elliot and asked if he had a knife, and he unsheathed a dagger just beside his saber. He asked why, but I just asked him to set up my tent while I helped Barrea, as he was just finishing up with theres. His eyes darted between us, and he went to work on setting up my sleeping space.

I used the knife to cut off my other sleeve, leaving both my arms now bare. I slid it down my arm and cut it once more down the middle, then knelt to Barrea and began wiping the blood away.

Fristlyn approached as I did and asked if he could patch her wound.

Barrea said, "Of course," though she saw how he intended to do it, she was hesitant.

I got her to smile when I explained we'd be matching and showed her the tie he made to hold my hair back.

Barrea crawled over to start building a campfire with excess twigs and fallen branches. As much as I wanted to help, my attention was toward Fristlyn, who, after he'd tended to Barrea, sulked away and sat by the small pond in the clearing. I made my way to him, crossing paths with Elliot as he finished my tent. I gave a brief thanks but swiftly moved past him to sit next to Fristlyn. I didn't need to say anything.

"My silk used to have healing properties," he informed me. "Wrapped for a few hours and everything was good as new."

So he had magic at one point. He never talked about how Sylvestra's Tears affected him directly, but they did. He only just now showed how.

I wasn't sure what to tell him. Soen may have wanted magic back in the world, but that was a goal I didn't support.

"There's something new about you I never knew." I smiled, though he didn't return it. "Even spiders could use magic?"

"I used to be..." he trailed off and stopped himself, but it was too late. My curiosity had peaked as I turned my body to face him completely.

"Used to be what?"

"Doesn't matter," Fristlyn said. His voice sounded jaded, almost as if he was seen as a failure.

"I have only seen you upset twice, Fristlyn," I recalled. "You threw a fit on the ship, and now you're sad because your web doesn't have magic? Magic is gone, Fristlyn. It—"

"If it were truly gone, why am I still like this?" the spider snapped at me as if I should know the answer or even what he was talking about. He finally turned to me to make eye contact, which was hard with there being several, and I could see the pain in his bulbous eyes.

"I wasn't always a spider, lass."

I stiffened at his sentence. My jaw left a gaping hole as I froze at this newfound information.

"Fristlyn, please," I begged. "Tell me everything; you mustn't hold back anymore."

There was a long silence filled only by the crackling of the newborn campfire.

We stared one another down and for a moment, just a moment, I pictured him as not a spider. I saw him as a tall and regal man, happy, and maybe with a lost love of his own.

He finally cracked and broke the lingering quiet between us. "I was an Elf."

WE FEASTED on a delightful potato stew that Barrea cooked up with her kettle over the flame. I may not have favored her, but I would've been a fool to deny that she knew what to do with limited equipment. Granted, a lot of the taste came from not eating anything since the ship, but the chicken broth lingered on my tongue; the heat from the meal descended all the way down to my belly, and I felt at peace. Lorraine kept quiet, but she scoffed down the food, which told us all she enjoyed it just as much as we did.

Fristlyn didn't partake in dinner. He was up sulking in a tree somewhere; he retreated after he told me what he used to be, and I believed him. Once again, I would've been a fool if I didn't. More than enough proof came my way, and I began to rethink my opinion, the one about not wanting magic free once again. My best friend was miserable without it, and I couldn't ignore the thoughts of making him happy, making him *whole* once more.

I was an Elf. He didn't dodge around; he didn't hide it from me in any way. He was blatant, honest, and trusting of me to be able to tell me. I kept my mouth shut to respect his privacy, but didn't ignore the fact that he *wanted* me to know. He wanted me to be aware; he wanted me to help.

Many children's tales spoke of elves. The tales painted them to be high and mighty beings, though there were a few that talked about how they were no different than us. Human-looking people with pointed ears; the ears being the only difference. I longed to find out which one was true, but could I put the world at risk with magic over mundane curiosity?

After we all devoured any evidence of our dinner existing, Elliot and I worked together to unpack bedrolls to place in the tents. We agreed, after a satisfying meal, it'd be wise to rest and build up our energy. I laid on my side, and despite his sadness, Fristlyn used his silk to descend and curled up with me in my tent. He snapped at me, and it bothered me to my core, but I was not going to hold it against him. So, I wrapped my arm around him and snuggled with my friend.

I HAD ONLY JUST BLINKED, and something was wrong; I never actually fell asleep. Minutes turned to hours, and I still couldn't fall asleep. I shifted positions hundreds of times, all of which was precarious as to not squish my fragile bunkmate. I even pinched myself to make sure I was actually awake and not in the middle of another hyper-realistic nightmare like on the ship.

As the forest got darker and darker, kissed farewell by the day, I heard something rustle in the bushes. I turned to face out of my tent, and my hand flew to cover a faint scream from my mouth. There was a quick movement of emerald in the trees. Everybody else was sawing logs, and I feared we retrieved the intention of something because of it. I crawled from my tent, and just outside the entrance were my weapons. I grabbed all of them, though my bow was the only one to stay withdrawn in my hands.

I began to hear the cries of…a child? A girl to be specific, coming from behind a tree, near the thorn bush that struck Barrea. I tried my hardest to keep quiet, but the excess tree limbs on the ground broke like bones under my feet. This didn't halt the crying, however. It got louder as I stepped closer, and eventually, I peered around the tree to see a young girl. She was probably thirteen to fourteen years old, a few years older than Marla at least. She sat flat with her knees pulled to her chest as she sobbed into her arms, wearing what I'm sure was once a lovely emerald gown, now shredded and torn.

I took one step, and there was a loud crack. Another twig snapped between the pressure of my foot. The girl stopped crying and shot up to look at me, and my bow fell to my side as I began to tear up at the sight.

Her ruby red hair was curled up into an updo, and she had bright green eyes carved from gems themselves. She was me.

CHAPTER 20

"I tried," the younger me sobbed. "I tried to stop him, but I could not..." she continued to break down in front of me and kept asking for my help. I was unable to focus on her needs, though.

My bow was pointed right at her face; it bounced around as I began uncontrollably shaking at the sight of her. Why was she here? Why was I here? I stared at my sobbing past self, breathing heavy, and short as I contemplated pulling the trigger.

More off-putting was how she *smelled.* It was rancid, putrid odor that only escalated the closer she was to me, worse than anything in this entire damned forest. Her scent was almost rotten, though she looked perfectly fine, save for a tattered dress. Had she been following us this entire time? No, that didn't make sense.

Did Father summon her? Was he on the ship when it passed by, and he was able to do this? No, that didn't make sense, either. Summoning her would require magic, and if he had access to it, I wouldn't even be here.

"Help me!" She let loose a blood-curdling wail, causing me to drop my bow and clamp my ears shut. I let out a cry, but no sound came from my mouth. I put my hands up in defense, in submis-

sion. My only thought was to go wake everyone up so we could move on, just to get as far away from this girl as possible.

I turned to flee, but she was right there behind me, and I shouted at the sight of her. Her eyes were blistered and riddled with open sores where she rubbed away her tears. Blood oozed from under the eyeball itself, and she was marked with black and blue veins. She wasn't crying anymore. Now, she just forced a glare of daggers at me. "You need to help," she demanded, her voice hissed like a snake. "You did this, you need to make it stop." I was bartering for my own life now. I didn't know what this specter was capable of, but she was a supernatural being. That meant she had otherworldly abilities, and I was nothing in comparison.

I gulped. "Okay, okay, I'll help you." I didn't have to ask myself if I was honest or not. It was this or risk an unholy, gruesome death. What I couldn't tell was whether or not I'd see this all the way through, or make a break for it the first chance I got. This girl made it so that I wouldn't even trust myself. "You need to tell me what's going on, and whom it involves; otherwise, I cannot help you."

She sniffed and returned to looking normal right before me. The sores closed, and the veins receded to whatever hellish part of her they came from. She walked past me toward our campsite, to the thorn bush just beyond, to be exact. She plucked something from it and came back to me to reveal what she had just obtained. It was one of the thorns that punctured Barrea, still stained with her blood but dried up and crusted. She faced the large, dead tree we stood by and began to drag the bloodied thorn across the rotting wood.

She motioned for me to look at the tree, and I approached it, unable to hide my confusion. It was a perfect rectangle, marked with still-wet blood. I shot down to look at the dry, crusted blood on the thorn, but it looked as if there was never any there. *What sorcery...* I started to step back, but she shot me a quick image of those sore-filled eye sockets, and I stopped dead where I was.

She looked back at the tree and started a creepy chant, an incantation of sorts. "Blood is the lock, blood is the door." Her mouth moved with the words, but a much deeper, harrowing voice emanated from within. "Open the gate, show her more."

Nothing. There was nothing. I blinked and she was gone. Was it a message? What blood? What lock? My brain pulsed with the questions that ran rampant. Nothing changed. As I stared, helpless and confused, I started to hear a noise behind me, crashing waves on a nearby beach. We had come miles from the shore. I turned to face the noise and fell flat on my ass at the scene before me.

Before me was the courtyard of Sheol Manor; the fountain, the flower beds, everything. I was back home, the last place I wanted to be.

I shut my eyes as a brief ripple distorted the world for a second. When I opened them, I was looking at me and Elliot sharing a kiss near my mother's roses, our first kiss. I was just a fourteen-year-old girl, scared about signing my life away to another. The only thing that made me feel better was him, Elliot, whom I could hardly look in the eye now without being filled with rage.

The door to the manor swung open behind me. I jumped as my father stormed out, with my mother and guards following close behind him.

I knew what happened all too well. This memory—this was the one that changed everything. Or so I thought.

My father took one of the Guardsmen's swords and approached Elliot and I. *Wait...that didn't happen.* He grabbed me by the hair and threw younger me onto the stone ground and shoved Elliot down right after. I started to scream as I watched Father hack away at Elliot. Blood touched up the red roses and painted their stems as I shouted as loud as I could. "This didn't happen!"

I cried, but no one could hear me. No one paid any attention to me. I sobbed as Elliot was dismembered right before me, and I couldn't take it anymore. I got up and bolted to the doors behind me and slammed them shut as I sobbed my eyes out from the horrific scene.

I only calmed down when I heard a voice behind and above me. It sounded familiar with each word but was unlike anything I had ever heard. I spun around to find myself in my room, on the ceiling. My bed, desk, and powder table were above me, on the floor upside-down. Sitting at my powder table was a man, though I couldn't see his face. He had shiny blonde hair, and he wore something green.

"Hello?" I called. My voice sounded echoed, out of this world. I was about to take this silence to analyze the dreamland I had found myself in but couldn't; the sound of a violent wind rushed through my ears.

The next thing I knew, I was on the floor. Everything was right side up and back to normal. My old room, which despite the bad memories, filled me with some nostalgia, as I saw everything was exactly how I'd left it. I was right behind the blonde man who stood up to greet me. His green top stopped at the waist, where it became a matching train that hung down to the floor. It was a button-up garment with a black piece in the middle that the buttons connected to. He wore matching short pants, stopping just above his knee. Sandals that wrapped around his ankle and just under his knee pulled the look together. He was a witch if I ever saw one.

He was a completely and utterly gorgeous man and didn't look as if he posed a threat, but he also looked like he could if he wanted to. He gave me a smile that complimented an unusual feature of his deep, violet eyes. I saw those purple eyes that drew my attention toward the biggest detail; long, pointed ears. They were long enough they almost extended past his head, unlike any elf I had ever read about. When I thought about all that together, I feared for my life; the look, the ears, the eyes.

Is he one of the Settlers of Old?

"I mean no harm," he assured, with that heavy and familiar, while still different, accent.

I gave a shy nod. "Who are you, then?"

He tilted his head, still smiling. "Someone who wants to help you succeed."

"Help me succeed, how?" I asked, and his smile flipped into a frown. "What makes you think I need help?"

"Look at where you are, lass. This isn't normal, and you know it. You're trapped. I'm trapped. You need to let me help you; otherwise, you can't help me."

I wanted to ask what he meant and why and how he was trapped and why it was in my old room. But my ears focused on one thing, one word that blew past his lips. I stepped closer, and he started to grin again.

"*What* did you just call me?"

The doors to my bedroom swung open, and as they did, the blonde man faded into smoke with a pleasant laugh.

I whirled around to the doors to see Prince Darien Lockner enter my chambers.

Whatever was playing this cruel joke on me made the wrong call. I felt no remorse for what I did to him. Marla was becoming my world, and I was happy to save her. He strode through, looking as he did when we first met in this very mansion. His curly, side combed brunette hair; his regal clothes in Mang'Coal colors, blue and charcoal. In an instant, another ripple distorted my vision, and I damn near barfed when it stopped.

His eye was punctured, popped like a grape. And his skin was decayed with a greenish-yellow. I only killed him a couple of weeks ago, and this was accurate to how he'd probably look now.

He smiled and motioned behind me, and when I turned to face

my turret was when I felt complete pain and torment. Walking in through balcony doors was Rolan, the blacksmith and dear friend of mine, and Guard Dog Fildra followed. Both rotted, more decayed than Darien. Of course, they had been dead longer. Fildra's jaw wasn't fully connected, both her and Rolan's skin were infested with maggots.

I dropped and hurled vomit right onto the hardwood. Maggots and other vermin collided with the floor as they spewed out of me, and I started to weep onto them. I was being toyed with by some dark magic. Fuck if magic was imprisoned or not, this wasn't natural. There was no other explanation.

All three pointed and laughed as the insects continued to escape from my throat and crawl all around me.

I tried to get up and run from it all, but every time I made a change in direction, one of them would just appear in front of me; first Darien, then Rolan, then Darien again, then Fildra, and Fildra once more. There was no order, and I eventually keeled over and threw up more maggots and roaches.

The doors swung open once more, and a woman entered my room now. My head snapped toward her as she approached us, and I marveled at the sight of the girl from the Metsa fountain with the brown, bouncy hair and the white and gold outfit.

She spoke once again, but not to me this time. "It's time you all get the fuck outta here," she cursed.

I began to cower as her eyes rolled back into her head, leaving only white.

She extended her hand, and I was engulfed in a golden light so bright I actually felt blessed to witness it. The world around me began to shake; the floor, walls, and ceiling began to crack and fall in big pieces as I covered my head from the debris, praying none of it would crush me.

"WAKE UP!" My eyes shot open just in time to grab Barrea's wrist before her hand could come down with a ferocious slap. My face stung and was warm to the touch; she had already hit me at least once before. "Wake up!" she howled, and soon my vision adjusted to the darkness of the woods once more. I was back.

"I'm awake, I'm awake," I assured her. "Please, just stop beating me for at least a moment." I took this time to gather myself and realized I was standing upright. I wasn't on the ground or curled up in a ball. "Was I...sleepwalking?"

She scoffed and gave her toughest push on my shoulder. I moved maybe half an inch from the weak hit. My eyebrows raised in mockery of this, but she didn't seem to care.

"Have you any idea what you've done? How badly you've just fucked this all up for us?" She was yelling, and it only hit me just then how awful of an idea that was. I shushed her, fearful she'd already drawn too much attention to us.

"Listen, Barrea. What I've done, or ever did, has been a recurring theme all evening. I just want to go to bed and..." I gasped in horror when I realized I was nowhere near where I saw the younger version of me. We weren't anywhere near the campsite.

I tried to explain myself but became a stuttering mess. Eventually, all I could do was cry. I told Barrea everything that had happened, from seeing the girl up until now. I even gave her a free pass and told her I didn't expect her to believe me.

She told me she did and hugged me tightly.

I buried my head deep into her neck and cried about the whole ordeal. I felt useless as I told her about the gorgeous man with the pointed ears, how he needed my help but couldn't take it until I let him help me. As simple-minded as she was, she couldn't offer any advice. She just let me cry it out on her shirt.

I pulled away from her, looking down, and was reminded of her own issues with the forest. I wiped snot from my face and pointed at the blood-stained spider silk. "Did you limp all the way here?"

She shrugged it off. "Doesn't hurt as bad. Besides, you walked with such a stagger it wasn't hard to keep up." She smirked at me.

I sighed in relief that I caused her no pain but looked around to assess the situation. "So I got us lost, then?"

"Hmm? No, luckily, you didn't. We're actually not too far away."

I cocked my head to the side. "How did I 'fuck' us, then?"

"Well, who knows what is coming after us now? You were screaming and crying and shouting so loudly."

I had been so worried about everyone else keeping quiet that I gave us away myself. My head fell into my hand as I thought about what horrible creatures were already on their way.

We both jumped at the sound of Elliot screaming.

CHAPTER 21

THE CAMP WAS EMPTY WHEN WE ARRIVED. WE WERE FARTHER AWAY than Barrea had let on, which I mentioned as we were running. She didn't answer, though; it was only Elliot on her mind, more so when the shouting stopped.

It wasn't just empty; there had clearly been a struggle. The tents were in disarray, ripped, torn, and emptier than life on the island. There was no sign of Elliot, Fristlyn, or Lorraine. Whatever pulled my attention and cursed me with the dream had split us up, and I wondered if that was its intention.

Barrea began to rip through the tent and her belongings, searching for any sign of Elliot or at least a clue as to where he ran off to. I've been where she was, so I thought it best not to intervene.

I tried my hardest to think of a logical route. Elliot was a man of strategy, he would've had to be since he was a guard captain. How would he have reacted, and what steps would he have taken? Barrea was with me; did he run to find her? No. He wouldn't have put Lorraine or Fristlyn at that kind of risk. One knew the island, and the other was a hag whose lust for power would've led us right to our destination. The ship? No, he wouldn't have left either of us behind. There was no blood, and thankfully, no dismembered limbs. It was safe to assume everyone was alive, for now.

My thoughts began to fly in a disorganized fashion. My mentality began to match Barrea's, as I started pacing back and forth while stressing about how lost we were now. Realization struck as protecting Barrea was now my responsibility; a task that was more than I could handle. Not to mention Fristlyn, whom I began to feel like I had just seen during my hallucination. Was that him in my room? Full-fledged and elf-like once more?

Fristlyn's absence ate at me. He was the one with the answers and the only one who was willing to give them to me. I hoped he escaped through the trees from whatever attacked since it would be hard to get to him all the way up there, assuming that the attacker was a land beast.

I made my way to my own tent to see if there was any sign. It was torn and broken down, but I didn't see any claw marks, just rips. There was no sign of what kind of beast it was, but the lack of claw markings made me think it was possible that it was human. Did Lorraine break free? Was Father able to lift the veil that blocked him, leading him to find us?

I tore through the bedroll and found a clue that almost ended my world. Under my pillow was a large, hairy spider leg. Just one, broken clean off from his body, which was nowhere to be seen. Fluid began to leak and stream down my face as I started picturing the worst.

Barrea rushed to my side at the sound of my distress and didn't speak as I picked up the broken leg.

I begged for it not to be his, but the fact that I had to hold it with two hands made it clear.

"I'm sorry," Barrea whispered. Cordial, considerate, and the absolute last thing I wanted to hear. I couldn't be mad at her, though. Neither of us knew what kind of condition Elliot was in, which was the main thing on her mind.

"I don't have anything to hold it in," I choked as I tried to fight back a complete breakdown.

Barrea took it from me and slid it into my belt, next to the holster for my gun. She rubbed my back until I turned to pull her into a hug.

"We have my answer, but don't have yours," I told her. "We'll find him."

"What if he's—"

"Then, at least you'll have closure," I told her, which wasn't a great response, but she knew what I meant. She wiped away tears of her own and stood.

"We don't know what happened to your friend," Barrea said, trying to reassure me as I did her. "We know he's hurt; we don't know anything beyond that."

I almost didn't want to believe Fristlyn was alive. Despite being a spider, he didn't move like one. He wasn't frantic with strong agility. He was slow and moved at a turtle's pace. A big stroke of luck would've had to occur for him to get away, and it hurt to think he was limping around out there. Regardless, I nodded at her attempt to console me. We were all each other had right now, and despite how annoying I found Barrea to be, I had to give her credit for how much composure she tried to keep. I'd be horrible to even deny it.

"RoGoria," she called to me.

I turned back to see her shaking, facing beyond the pond. The bush right behind the pond hid it, but something was definitely behind it. Following it was a hissing noise. My skin crawled as I lunged my sword at Barrea's feet, and she snatched it up in less than a second. Why she hadn't been given anything to defend herself with at the start of this journey, and why I had only just realized it now were questions I would never receive answers for. In a blink, my crossbow was in my hand, and I was up on my feet.

Barrea looked at me and shouted as she stumbled back, unable to give me fair warning before something leaped at me from the side while I faced the bush near the pond. Another hissing noise slithered down my spine as it fell on top of me; only my crossbow kept it from gnawing at my face as I cried for my life.

There were few words to describe the creature; it looked like it could've been human *at some point*, but now it was a bloated, fleshy mess. Loose skin fell from its cheeks, and more rolled over its eyes. It bit at me with a dislocated jaw, broken completely to one side, and its teeth resembled that of a human's, rotten and misshapen. I felt the loose skin graze past my nose and had to hold back vomit as a wet, clay-like texture rubbed against my skin.

Barrea shoved the thing off me, and I stumbled to my feet, but more emerged from the bush, and several others appeared from the trees behind us. Most were in torn remnants of their clothes, and others were completely nude. Some just as loose-skinned as the first, others with tight, sunken skin, and some the flesh was completely intact, with others decayed and water-bloated.

I started firing my crossbow, not able to pay attention to Barrea who, last I saw, was swinging my sword like a mad woman.

They died like normal people. Nothing specific as long as I hit a fatal spot. One of my bolts hit a throat, and another punctured an eye. Both dropped dead in an instant. The ones with the loose skin proved to be more difficult, though, as the rubber-like flesh prevented my bolts from striking them.

I was soon overwhelmed and took a step back, only to trip over the one Barrea shoved off me, dropping my bow in the midst of it all. As I scrambled to get up, it found its way on top of me once more, now only my wrist blocking it while my other hand reached for my crossbow. Its low-hanging skin flopped all over my face with each ferocious chomp it made to bite me, and I eventually gave up on my bow and shoved both hands against its face; my fingers sank into its skin like mud, hardly holding it back at all. I reached down for my gun and wasted no time once I grabbed the butt of the firearm, and fired into the creature's head.

The gunshot shattered my ears as clumpy, curdled blood burst into the air, rendering the creature lifeless.

No time to reload, I lunged toward the crossbow to fire at the ones coming from the trees. A shriek of pain from Barrea spun me around to witness one bite her thigh as she fell back into the pond, bringing three of them with her. She tried clawing her way back up, but it was clear that there was a half-foot of space between the water's surface and the ground.

I watched her get dragged down as she tried to climb back up. I shouted her name as I tried to save her, but I was yanked back when one of them grabbed my train and threw me back on my ass. I whirled around to see one, probably a woman, though I couldn't tell by falling chunks of skin, crawl her way toward me. I lunged the butt of my bow back and smashed its face in with just one hit. It was clear I'd have to take the ones after me out first. Six were still alive, and the remainder of my bolts took out four of them.

I began to stress over the fact I was a girl who lacked proper combat training, now with no weapon. I rose to my feet as the last two approached, frozen, not sure what my move would be. I had no weapon. I couldn't make it to my spare bolts to reload my crossbow and reloading my gun was out of the question.

Before I could choose to fight or run, leaving everything behind, I heard Barrea gasp as she pulled herself to the pond's surface.

She shouted my name and threw the sword like a war hero. Albeit she threw it nowhere near me, but I was able to roll out of the creature's way as they tried to pile on my body.

I crawled to my saber, picking it up just in time to slide it through the head of one of the grotesque beings. It died in a puddle of green puss and blood, and I gagged at the putrid odor that followed. I moved away from it and noticed the last one was making its way toward Barrea. In a panic, I tried to charge it, but it was already at the rim of the pond.

Barrea sat there, watching it, and I could see her grow more distressed as she grabbed it by its torn clothes and yanked it into the pond with her.

I never stopped moving and helped her out of the pond and gasped at the sight of the creature dissolving in a stew of blood, puss, and sizzling skin until it was nothing. The pond remained a wicked mixture of yellow, green, and red until the damned thing was no more. The water killing these things in an instant was a note I would take with me to my golden years.

NEITHER OF US knew what they were, and the one person who could tell us was probably dead. Or, as Barrea put it with misguided optimism, "missing."

Her bite wound wasn't terrible; it could have been much worse with her falling into the pond. We were both thankful that there were no tears, just one bite mark that broke the skin a little bit. I cleaned the wound and bandaged it with the few supplies we had; it would've been nice to use the endless supply of thick spider silk we normally had, but that option was no longer available to us.

I was blessed to not sustain any wounds myself, though my own damage revealed itself when I sat to relax.

I fought to the ends of the Earth not to cry, but it was a battle I lost. I brought my knees to my chest and buried my head. I wept softly over everything; what had just happened, what we lost, *who* we lost, and why we lost them.

I thought Barrea would be the one to screw things for us, but it was me. I was lured away, and in the midst of it all, I missed an attack where I could've helped everyone. Elliot and I could've fought together, but I took that option away from us. Sleep-walking with a bad nightmare, and now an ex-princess and chef had to fend for themselves.

I, at least, succeeded in keeping my cries as quiet as I could, so as to not attract more attention. The most that hung on my head was having to continue on, not knowing what those gross, fleshy creatures were, or how many more we would run into.

After composing myself, I scanned the damaged remains of our camp; the tears in the tents, the broken spider leg in my belt, and the fact that Elliot was missing left me with a dry mouth and one thought. Those beings were deadly in groups, and two women were able to live through an attack; it was easy to kill if one was focused right and only attacked to devour us. Had Barrea not demonstrated what happened when they were submerged in water, I would've thought them to be zombies, the walking dead themselves. But the dead don't disintegrate like that.

Barrea was also a nicely proportioned woman. She wasn't chubby by any means, but had more mass than I. If she weren't so dense, she could probably take me in a fight. She was even brave enough to let one approach her and lure it into a trap. I was skilled enough to face several at once in basic combat...but Elliot had to *run*?

I never told Barrea, as my words would only bring her torment and fear. But I theorized that whatever attacked the rest of our group was something else entirely.

CHAPTER 22

BARREA AND I STOPPED DENYING THE INEVITABLE; WE HAD TO continue on our own.

We didn't have a map as Lorraine was our only means of navigation around the woods. Even that was a long shot since none of us knew if she actually knew where she was going. But I knew where I was going, the best chance to keep Barrea safe, and it was a plan she supported. We were going to Yggdrasil.

The Tree of Life itself; something told me that besides getting to safety, that would be where we would have to go, anyway. The gold speckles I saw floating around it indicated that magic was strong there, and if any place offered sanctuary to the Tears, it would be there.

Before we left the ruined camp, Barrea and I discussed our plan in depth. She presented some intelligent questions, the heaviest of which was asking how the Tree could still have magic since it was imprisoned. Well, I had a theory.

"Sylvestra was only one person," I echoed Fristlyn's words to Barrea, explaining how there were certain limits that prevented her from sealing all of it away. Galyn was a mermaid, a creature born from magic, as were harpies, and most likely talking spiders.

I told her about Fristlyn telling me he was once human, or at least humanoid, which meant that magic existed around him, as well. Those beings were almost hotspots of magical energy, and if they existed still, magic couldn't have been fully expelled from Relica. Barrea agreed Yggdrasil was our best bet.

I only took a few minutes to get ready, even though it was just me as I didn't want Barrea helping; I needed her to give her legs a rest as much as she could. I emptied the packs and decided we would only carry one with the absolute essentials. I had Barrea pick the two pieces of cookware she deemed most important, or the most helpful. When she pointed at the saucepan and the skillet, I slid them into the bag. She told me to pick the food we would bring, making sure I was fed to my liking. I appreciated her for that, but I made sure to ask what was perishable and nonperishable; I prepared us both for a trip of eating beans, rice, and potatoes and not much else.

Barrea assured me that there were several different recipes for just those items and that I shouldn't worry. "I could teach you how to cook someday," she told me after I closed up the backpack of supplies.

I turned my attention toward her, not sure what to say in response. I'd been a bit of an unsavory bitch to her, so the offer caught me off-guard.

She continued. "Elliot told me about the girl…Mara, that cute girl you're sharing a home with."

"Marla, but close enough," I joked. I hadn't thought about her a lot during this whole trip, even though she was the reason I went on it. It irritated me how empty Soen's threat likely was. I could've avoided all of this if I pushed back just a tad, despite how much I wanted to either prove my father wrong or find this relic before he did.

But I didn't think about her; I couldn't. Not after the harpies, and certainly not after what we had just faced.

"Marla, right," Barrea said. "I saw you in the market that day.

You bought a lot of food and didn't know what to do with it, but you have a good sense of flavor. I saw you pick up cabbage, carrots, peppers, and a lot of pork."

There was an unsettling pull in my hair, and I realized the altercation with the rotting creatures pulled Fristlyn's homemade hair tie down. I groaned, labeling it a distraction, and struggled to pull it out while I struggled to respond to her question.

"I...Pork is my favorite," I told her. Nothing made me happier as a child than seeing bacon on the breakfast table, or a glazed ham during celebratory meals. "I picked up things I liked, I never even asked her. I guess even when I'm caring for another life, I still only think about myself." I ended up just taking my sword and cutting the silk off; letting my long hair dance freely in the forest wasn't a smart idea, but it was better than being distracted. My hair hung over my face, thick and layered until I brushed it back and tucked one side behind my ears.

"Your hair is beautiful," Barrea noted and I turned to her quickly this time.

Ah, fuck. She's complimenting me, and I'm liking it.

"Thank you," I said, smiling.

"And I think you've more than proved you care about her," she continued. "Whether or not it was food you liked, you brought enough to feed you both. So make a note to ask her next time, but be proud that you thought about her, regardless." I didn't have the heart to tell her that didn't make me a good provider. Feeding Marla was the bare minimum, as both my parents made sure I was fed yet were far from being barely decent in the provider area. I thanked Barrea for her kind words, regardless, but brought our conversation to an end since we had to get moving.

We left the campsite the way we came, being careful to avoid the thorn bush as we did so, and continued en route in the direction we were already going.

On top of leading, protecting, and escorting Barrea, the

woman had two injuries that prevented her from carrying anything really. I carried the one pack of rations and her more important cookware; we had to leave everything else behind. I lent her my sword, but I had to carry my crossbow at all times, constantly ready for any attack.

As we walked, Barrea began asking questions about how we would find Elliot or Lorraine. I lacked the answers she needed but provided the ones she feared. It was likely that we wouldn't run into them, likely that we wouldn't see either of them again. It pained me to break the news to her, but instead of crying like I thought she would, she walked in silence. I think, on some level, she knew I was right.

HOURS WENT by and we continued to trek through the dark, decrepit forest with Barrea just inches behind me, almost breathing down my neck. I walked slower so she could keep up as she limped with her walking stick. I thought about picking up the pace since she proved to be keeping close just fine, but then I shook my head, realizing soon after she only kept up because I slowed down.

I stopped out of the blue, and she bumped into me and asked if I was well, but I wasn't. A sharp, shooting pain began to hit my head; I felt it trickle down my brain like a slow stream gliding over rocks. The lower it moved as I focused on it, the more agony it caused. I had to take a page out of Barrea's book like when she was struck by the thorn, trying my damned hardest not to take so much as a breath when it hit.

"You escaped my first two traps; let's see how you fare against the next," a woman's voice whispered from inside of me. I almost felt the words manifest within my soul and claw their way from my ears.

Lorraine. I recognized it, as familiar as crashing waves on an ocean. She could see us, and she was taunting us. But how? This was telepathy, which I could only assume required magic. How is she using it? How is she contacting me? And where on earth is Elliot if she's here, taunting me?

I began to loathe the pain, clenching my teeth and growling under each deep breath I took. "How are you doing this?" I snarled. How did she have power here? Unless…

Another voice from another woman started from within me once more but it was in response to Lorraine. *"She'll be fine. You'll be fine, RoGoria. Forget this bitch."* I recognized that voice, too, though I had no name to label it. It was the woman by the Metsa Fountain. I probably wouldn't have recognized it had she not pulled me from the nightmarish reality I was in just a few hours ago.

The familiar sound of violent wind overtook any noise that surrounded us and came to an abrupt end along with the headache. Everything was back to normal.

"Are you all right?" Barrea asked in a shaky voice.

It took a second for me to notice, but she was rubbing my back. I straightened myself off and cleared my throat, signaling for her to stop. I felt like a weight had been lifted off my shoulders, and I soon realized that was the case, quite literally.

Barrea held the rucksack of rations in her hand.

I offered my hand to take it from her, but she slid it over her shoulder.

"We can take turns," she said.

I gave her a smirk. I was thankful, but I began to detest that I became vulnerable in front of her so often.

"We have a problem," I said, trapping myself into telling her more if she asked me to elaborate. I'd kept so much from her, and I wanted to keep withholding information. This prevented me from doing so.

"Well…yeah?" She let loose an airheaded laugh. "We have several problems right now."

"No." *This damned twit, good Lord.* "I mean we have a new one. Lorraine…she's alone. And she's watching us."

"But that means Elliot is close by!" she exclaimed, and I tried to shush her but was too slow to stop her from screaming Elliot's name, the trees delivering it back with a menacing echo.

"Are you mad?" I scolded, still whispering. "Did you already forget what we just went through?" My blood ran cold as she yelled his name once more; I didn't even get the chance to tell her how Lorraine referenced traps and how she seemed to have power here.

Barrea inhaled to yell again, but I rushed her and slammed my hand over her mouth.

She fought me on it but calmed down when she realized I was strong enough to overpower her.

"Now, we need to go, and we need to move *with haste,*" I ordered. I turned to keep walking, but she grabbed my wrist and pulled me back.

"What about Elliot? He might be looking for me!"

I had to fight to keep myself from blabbing about the move Elliot tried to make toward me at Marla's house. Or his several attempts at getting close to me since leaving for the expedition. My options were to either break her heart or let us both get killed.

"We don't even know if they're together," I told her instead, trying to beat around the dangerous bush. "She is speaking to me telepathically. She's using *magic,* Barrea. Magic." It seemed like I had gotten through to her.

Her gorgeous, dark fawn skin became whiter than the dead. She stuttered to an extreme, trying to dig out the words to ask me how, but she couldn't get them out.

I put her out of her misery by adding, "I don't know. But she's doing it, and I doubt she'd be doing it around Elliot. We need to move."

I held her hand and pulled her through bushes and trees, straying from our path when Lorraine's voice hit again. *"For my next trick, something no fairy tale would dare submit your eyes to."*

We stopped dead in our steps when snarling came from the bushes behind us.

CHAPTER 23

B<small>ARREA RAN WITH NO WARNING</small>.

It took me a second to process it; to process everything. The snarling coming from behind got closer, and I was too afraid to so much as breathe, let alone move.

"You need to run to the left," the voice echoed once more, the woman from the fountain. She was telling me which way to go, telling me how to save myself. There was a problem with her order, though; Barrea had run to the right.

She was instinctive, unlike me, evidently. I stood frozen, combatting myself about what to do.

I can't...She's my responsibility.

I need to think of my own safety.

Elliot is counting on me to make sure his wife stays in one piece.

A possible death of one should not be a likely death of two.

No matter the argument I made, I always had a rebuttal for it. Rustling bushes a few feet behind me sang with the symphony of steps, and I turned to see three inhuman beasts charging on all fours. Their paws were just two long and thick claws. They ran like wolves, and barked like them, but were equipped with horns and three crimson eyes. Lorraine was right; no book from my childhood would've provided a beast so terrifying.

Corded with muscles, as they approached, they stood upright on two legs and charged at me in a human-like sprint which finally snapped me out of my frozen state. A decision had to be made, and while running to the left would somehow bring me to safety, I had to take Barrea's life into consideration.

So I bolted in the same direction she ran, hoping to catch up with her. I strayed from the path we were walking on and stumbled several times as my train attached to my waist snagged on bushes and hazardous twigs and I lost my footing with each step. I had to hold the train in one hand and keep my crossbow ready in the other as I darted through the woods, trying my hardest to control my breathing.

I sprinted in a straight line, and the growling of the horrid beasts ceased. I stopped to take a small break; my lungs felt like they had been made of fire and mercury as I tried my hardest to keep composure. My rapid heartbeat threw my body into chaos, and I became winded and a little nauseous. I was panting so heavy that it took me longer than I cared to admit to hear a whisper up in the trees.

"Pssst," she hissed. "Up here."

I looked up and behind me to see Barrea, high up in a tree gesturing for me to join her. I held up an index finger as I dry heaved, but the noise alerted the beasts. I heard the snarling and bone-snapping roar, and my body refused to give me more time to think. I blinked, and I was at the base of the tree she was in.

I grabbed the lowest branch; the wood was old and dry, I winced as splinters poked and stabbed my skin while I gripped to hoist myself up. Swinging my leg over to get myself upright, standing on the branch, I repeated this process until my eyes met with Barrea's. I leaned back against the trunk of the tree while examining the army of wooden shives stuck in my hands.

Barrea watched, disgusted, as I slid each and every one out of my hands and just wiped the blood on my corset until the bleeding was minimal.

"This is already ruined, it's not a big deal," I whispered, trying to choke out a joke during this nightmare. It didn't stick, probably because I had the delivery of a five-year-old boy when it came to punch lines.

It took me a second to notice she wasn't quiet because of my poor humor; instead, her eyes were focused up toward the tree-tops. I tried searching for what she was looking at, praying one of the beasts hadn't somehow made its way up there.

I saw nothing, though. Not at first. When I was about to ask her why she was entranced, there was a loud snap as some small branches fell, and something definitely scurried away. I almost screamed, but Barrea held *my* mouth this time—she had stopped breathing all together. I looked down, and there they were, sniffing us out, the three beasts.

They all looked the same; the horns, the claws, the corded muscles. The only differences were their sizes and the patchy fur. Two were about six feet tall, one was a reddish-brown color, the other was a shimmering silver. Then there was a big one: the pack leader, I assumed. Its fur was a mossy green, and a much bolder color. Everything about it symbolized its dominance, and I feared having to face it. Using magic to raise the fleshy dead was one thing, but those creatures...they indicated how much power Lorraine truly had here.

I turned to Barrea, whose hand was clasped around my lips still.

"What are those?" she mouthed.

I shook my head and shrugged. Damn if I knew. I had never seen or heard of something resembling anything close to those... those *things*. They weren't fully attuned to each other, either. If one got close, another would snap its jaw or nip it. Seeing that was trauma-inducing in itself; all three had jaws that unhinged as it opened, and they snapped shut with an otherworldly force. They had two rows of pointed teeth that looked pristine compared to the rest of their misshapen bodies.

After several minutes dragged by, they scurried off. Had we really survived this?

WE WAITED an extra hour before Barrea, who was braver than me right now, climbed down. The thought of returning to ground level made me twitch and twiddle my thumbs, and breathing became a foreign concept to me. I felt my stomach sink as I contemplated joining her, and when I decided to, so she wouldn't be alone, my body begged me to reconsider. I was severely slower than her; my hands wouldn't stop shaking, and I had to use what little strength I still had to not fall to my death.

All this time, I tried to be one of the strong ones, one of the reliable ones. I never let myself actually feel true, unfiltered horror, but this did it. I was terrified of every second, every minute that passed. In the span of what felt like one day, I had been seen as dinner to an unknown number of monstrosities. My breathing started to come back but picked up despite how much I fought to keep it silent, for fear that the pack was lurking around. It was clear they were hunters, for all we knew we just climbed down into a trap.

Barrea pulled me away from the tree and turned me toward herself. She felt my fear and could visibly see my distress. Her own eyes welled up as I'm sure she was missing Elliot; longing for her husband to save the day and protect her.

She moved even closer to me, hands firmly placed on my shoulders, and pulled me into a hug.

I collapsed.

She collapsed with me.

On our knees, I buried my face into her neck, weeping quietly; not wanting my emotions to get us killed. My hands clenched on the sleeves, the straps of her now torn sleeveless undershirt, and I felt it soak up my tears.

She rubbed my back as I wept, holding back her own tears.

After an uncomfortable amount of time, I pulled myself together and wiped away my tears. Her top was drenched in sweat and tears, but she told me not to worry about it. I rose to my feet and extended my hand to her and pulled her up once she took it.

"I don't know..." I gulped as mucus coated my throat, almost choking. "I don't know what that was, I'm sorry."

She presented me with a look of sympathy, something I've always hated but welcomed it this time around. "That's an anxiety attack," she informed me. "I get them, too. It's important to keep yourself grounded when it happens, and you'll pull yourself together. Sometimes we need help from others for this, and that's okay, too."

It made sense. The another recent time I felt like that was when I plummeted deep into the sea, and Galyn pulled me down lower into the darkness. I was closed off from the world as a princess; I never got to learn what my fears were, and now I was learning them all at once.

"Thank you," I told her, expressing all the gratitude I could. I worked hard to be the leader for her, but she reminded me how good it felt to just be human, to feel something other than bitter anger.

"Glad to help," she whispered, wiping her tears away. "Now," she started as she turned away from me, lifting her arm and pointing past me. "They took off that way, so we should be able to go back the way we came and continue the direction we originally were going." She headed back a few steps, past the tree, and stood in a small group of bushes. She was trying to figure out how far we ran off course, but I was entranced by the bushes she was standing in. One of them was full of black dead leaves. Untouched by life, looking the most natural in the forest, but the other two behind her looked uneven, lazy; like they didn't get the opportunity to grow the way the earth intended. Whatever was off about it was strong for me to notice. I looked down to see if the roots came up a bit. Then, I saw the fucking paw.

CHAPTER 24

I WAS FAR TOO LATE. I COULDN'T SO MUCH AS SPEAK LET ALONE scream before Barrea was slammed to the earth, caught in the silver beast's jaw. She was dragged deep into the woods, and I charged after her, breaking my silence and finally able to roar her name as I followed. I ran after the beast, damn near throwing myself in the direction it ran. I soon lost sight of it, but Barrea's cries of anguish were clear as day and painted the way for me. I forgot to focus on my breathing as I pushed and pushed to the point where I hit extreme nausea.

I finally collapsed. My energy completely depleted and, on top of it all, I didn't even know what direction she was in anymore. Her screams paired with an astronomical headache, and it was as if they came from every possible direction on an axis scale. I was drowning in her pain. So I sat there, on my knees, hands digging into the dirt.

"*RoGoria! RoGoria, please hel...RoGoria! RoGoria! It hurts, it hurts! RoGo...*"

I was knocked down in defeat at the sound of a bone-snapping crunch that echoed throughout the entire forest. Staggered breathing, I stared up at the treetops which covered the sky, absolutely petrified, and *alone*. I didn't need to keep going to know she was dead, devoured by the beast. I no longer had Elliot, Fristlyn, and now Barrea, all while Lorraine was seemingly pulling the strings behind everything that happened. In less than two days here, I lost my entire fellowship, and I was stranded.

I heaved, followed by a good ten minutes of vomiting. Once, twice, who knows how many times I gagged and choked on my own puke, creating a puddle of waste on the ground. My stomach was empty, but it didn't stop. I just dry heaved until I began to feel my very soul expel from my mouth. When it was all done, I fell to my side and lay there, near lifeless. Listening to the silence that surrounded me, not even a slight breeze to remind me that I was actually still alive in Relica.

"Barrea," I whispered. I whispered her name over and over again as I progressed to crying. I thought about my failure, and only *my failure* since I couldn't blame it on anyone else. At the same time, I selfishly hoped Elliot was dead, to avoid having to explain to him what happened in the event we crossed paths again. I heaved once more from the anxiety of having to look him in the eyes.

Snarling came from behind me. I weakly turned to see an auburn beast staring at me from between two trees.

Its eyes stared deep into mine, licking its razor-edged teeth and getting ready to feast. Its growl turned into a starved, malnourished exhale, wheezing in excitement. It charged me, moving at inhuman speed, faster than any animal in existence. It barked like a savage wolf, like the unholy beast it was. It ran like a deranged dog, but the rows of sharp, saw-like teeth promised me it was different; promised me it was going to rip me to shreds.

I began to cry again, horrified by the fact that this is what Barrea saw before she was presumably devoured. I had no energy. I had no strength. I had no *will*.

I closed my eyes and wished for my death to be painless as it placed its paw on my chest, pushing weight down to the extent where I thought my lungs would pop. I smelled rotten, molten flesh as it breathed its warm breath on me. It swam up my nose and instilled the mark of death in my brain. "Just fucking do it," I whispered.

Seconds, mere seconds passed, and I heard a violent squish, followed by my face getting soaked in a mysterious fluid. I felt it seep into my mouth, a bland and metallic taste complemented the suspicious liquid. Blood.

I opened my eyes to see the beast, jaw open and ready to feast on my flesh, with the bladed end of a staff coming out of its mouth. It was a gold spherical shape with two platinum angel wings on either side that were sharp enough to cut through the monster like butter.

The beast gagged in pain as the staff retracted back; it fell right on top of me, and its weight almost crushed me into dust. Dead. Its blood fell from its throat, down my neck, and pooled onto the ground.

I tried my hardest to move it, but I was too weak, on top of the thing being two damn heavy. However, luckily, it was removed for me. I saw well-manicured fingers curl up around its muscly arm and shove it off of me with ease. Staring down at me was the woman, the same one who saved me from my nightmare, who combated Lorraine's telepathy, who met me at the fountain. She donned the white, low-cut top embroidered with gold, white pants, and white boots with a gold buckle. She wasn't a vision this time. I was coherent, the world was unchanged like it was the first time I saw her; she was actually here. Her thick, wavy brunette hair hung down and tickled my nose while she stared down at me.

"Bitch," she said in a lazy accent and then started clapping her hands between words. "I said left. Left!" She squatted down as I started to come up and put her nose mere centimeters from mine. "Clean the shit out of your ears next time, okay?"

CHAPTER 25

"THIS IS JUST GOING TO KEEP FUCKIN' YOUR SHIT UP," SHE SCOLDED vulgarly as she used her bladed quarterstaff to cut the train clean off my attire. I enjoyed it for the aesthetic it added to me, but she was right; it was almost the death of me as it was caught on various forest debris.

Of course, I had to ask the obvious question that I'd been craving to know. "Who are you?"

She balled up the cut fabric and tossed it aside. Looking at me with her bright blue eyes, she flashed an angelic smile at me but didn't answer the question. Instead, she was firm in placing her hands flat against one another, with her quarterstaff balancing between her thumbs. I marveled as the staff itself began to dissipate into a silvery smoke until it was completely gone.

Magic. Right before my eyes. It was peaceful, elegant, and it flourished as it came to the end of the staff. I finally got to see it first-hand.

Her arms fell to her side as she walked toward the dead beast. "The name's Tara," she introduced, casually as if she didn't know how hungry I was to finally have a name for the face. She grabbed the beast by its hind legs and dragged it over to a patch with minimal plant life and held out her hand with the palm facing the wolf.

The same silver smoke emerged, and I couldn't help but smile in awe, with minimal fear, as the beast burned from inside out into fire before it was ash. She was just casually summoning weapons and fire like it was nothing, and I grew worried that those abilities were something Lorraine had, just being on the island. Tara was soon back and facing me after the beast's body had been taken care of.

"Quick question for ya." Her face was annoyed and irate. I started to wonder if she was my savior at all or just another being who was set to kill me whenever she wanted. "I told you to run left, so you can probably imagine my surprise watching you do anything *but* that. What happened?"

"Maybe next time, do not be so cryptic," I amazed myself at how fast I was to snap back at her condescending tone. I probably shouldn't have been so cold, seeing as how, at the flick of a wrist, she could end me; I just didn't feel like I was in danger yet. "Try courtesy. Let a lady know why—"

"Being courteous isn't my fucking job, RoGoria," she interrupted. She didn't care for pleasantries, or how rude she was being. She disarmed me easily, and I was submissive to her potential power. "It's to make sure you complete this stupid quest you're on. I told you left, and you stood frozen, processing the fact that your friend ran off in a different direction. While you were standing there, what do you think happened during that time?"

"I didn't think about that," I snapped back. "I just knew I could not leave her alone. What are you getting at, anyway?" I couldn't keep myself from fuming. My emotions were seeping out of me in a red haze, but what could I do? If I so much as breathed funny, Tara could write me a one-way ticket to hell if she wanted.

Her icy blue eyes were locked on me; she wasn't glaring or staring me down, but the gaze wasn't comforting, either. Blank, idle, almost as if she were void of emotion. There were no words, only silence, but during the silence, she was telling me to really think about what happened. Tara was controlling her anger, her annoyance, but not saying anything. I'd have to take notes.

Then, it hit me. Tara had just mentioned how I froze and struggled to process everything. At that time, the beasts ran closer as they approached and had locked onto me.

"My God..." I whispered as I sank to my knees. I felt sick again, this time mixed with a heightened sense of self-loathing. "She would've been okay."

"Oops, there it is!" Tara exclaimed as she snapped her fingers into guns toward me. "You both would've been." She shrugged and knelt down beside me. "Small word of advice, when an unknown being breaks all laws of science to speak to you telepathically," she paused to lean closer to me, "it might be best to just listen."

In my defense, Lorraine was talking to me the same way, too, threatening and toying with me. So trusting an unknown voice was easier said than done.

I still caused Barrea's death. That much was clear; if I had listened, things could have turned out different. That caused a sinking feeling in my gut and telling Elliot was going to be hell if I ever saw him again.

I sensed I was about to cry, again, and I didn't want to seem weak in front of Tara. So I sentenced myself to sit with this alone since I was going to be just that for the remainder of the mission. I changed the subject in the meantime. "Why are you assisting me? You have no prior relation to me, so I don't understand."

She grinned. "We have a mutual friend; he asked me to keep an eye on you guys."

I drew in a deep breath while I uttered his name. "Soen."

She nodded to confirm before actually saying, "Look at you, figurin' shit out." Followed by her snapping her fingers into pistols once more. I looked at her dumbfounded by how unusual she was. Was she a witch?

Tara stood up and brushed some dirt off her pants. She began to walk away from me, turning her back on me and I saw something interesting about her attire I didn't notice before; her blouse didn't have a back. Her back was bare and unprotected, with the actual fabric starting at her sides. Everything about her was out of this world, and now I had time to take her in completely, I was able to admit she made me look like a rat that crawled its way out of Sheol's sewers. Those icy blue eyes complimented her porcelain skin, which contrasted with her gorgeous brown mane.

"I have an important question for you," Tara informed me. She leaned against a tree with her arms folded, and a solemn expression morphed onto her face. "If I gave you an out, would you take it?"

"What does that mean?" I asked her. "'Give me an out'?"

"I could send you back, away from this island, and you could go back to living your normal life." She moved closer. "With a snap of these fabulous fingers, I could fix it."

I shook my head. "I wouldn't be able to look Soen in the eye if I abandoned everyone—"

"No, no, that's not what I meant." Tara squatted to eye level, and I thought it was silly that she just got up only to be right back by me. "I can send you back to Sheol, back to before you ran away, back in *time*. I know you weren't happy then, but are you happy now? Was it any harder than your life in the present?"

What would have happened if I never left? I had to think hard about that, which is all Tara liked to make me do—think. Had I never left, I would've kept thinking Elliot was dead. I wouldn't have gotten my heart broken seeing how he had moved on, and I wouldn't have grown to loathe him for the passes he made at me while being married to a woman I now respected. I could've been spared seeing Barrea's gruesome death. All of it sounded wonderful, but I couldn't. First of all, I couldn't leave Fristlyn's probable fate in vain. Nor could I let Barrea's. As well as…

I rose to my feet, Tara standing with me; my eyes met hers. I was maybe an inch taller than Tara was, which for some reason, I thought to be odd.

I held my hand out to her, and she smiled and firmly grasped it in her own.

"No," I told her. "I wouldn't take it. I have a girl, Marla, to look after. So I'm seeing this through."

She winced in pain at my statement before shrugging it off.

Higher being or not, I noticed it, and I would make a note of how the mention of me being a good guardian caused her distress.

"Bitchin'" she...said? Exclaimed? I wasn't sure what that expression meant. "You had the right idea going to Yggdrasil. You'll have a place to rest, and I'm sure there's a bunch of supplies for you, as well." She pointed me in the direction of the Tree of Life itself. "Ask for Amilyana—she'll help." She started to depart but I stopped her.

"Wait," I called. "I still have a lot of questions. You said your job was to make sure I succeed, so help me."

"Okay," Tara groaned. "Yes, Lorraine is able to use magic here. The aura emanating from the Tears still has power, but not a lot of it."

"No, I gathered that already."

"Yes, Amilyana is a witch, a necromancer, to be exact, and she has access to her power, as well."

I rolled my eyes. "Noted, but that is not—"

"Yes, Fristlyn is alive," she said, and my heart skipped a beat.

My hand fell to my belt on instinct and rubbed the broken spider leg holstered into it. Still wasn't a question I needed to ask, but it was good to know. I teared up and choked on my own emotions. "He is?"

Tara nodded. "I have to go, but I'll leave you with one more piece of info." Was it an answer to any of my questions? Like, what is she? How does she have such amazing power with magic's weakened state? What were those things? "Oh, those beasts, right," she said, and I blinked and twitched at how she pulled the subject right from my head. "Those are vuldoars, deranged beasts that inhabit the island. They're super-duper rare, so consider yourself unlucky that you ran into them." She gave me a deadpan stare as I was still debating whether or not she read my mind. "Oh, and even though you didn't ask," she continued, proving what I thought to be correct since I didn't ask about the vuldoars, either, "those gross walking boils you fought at your camp, those are flesh fiends. fleshers, for short. Necromancy for dummies and you have Lorraine to thank for that."

Noted. Sounds like Lorraine didn't arrange for the vuldoars, that was strictly an unfortunate coincidence.

"I'm guessing that was your last piece of information?" I asked.

She shook her head. "Nah. As I told you, Fristlyn is still alive. Not entirely in your control, but you should try to find him if you can help it."

"I already planned to keep an eye out," I told her. No shit, though, now that I knew my closest companion still lived.

"Good," Tara said. She patted my shoulder. "Very good. You'll need him."

"He's it, isn't he?" I asked her, knowing damn well she knew what I was talking about. It was the first thing she said to me. "He's the Ani'Mas King you mentioned at Metsa."

She flashed me a big, blinding smile. "You catch on quick," she said before being enveloped by a shimmering silver smoke and disappearing right before my eyes.

CHAPTER 26

BARREA'S BODY WAS SHREDDED. THE FAT IN HER LEGS WAS OUT IN ribbons as she bled pools onto the soil. Sharp, jagged pieces of bone jutted out of her neck which could barely hold onto the rest of her body. Her innards were spread across the earth, half-chewed and devoured. I prayed her neck had snapped first so she didn't feel the rest of the gruesome mutilating while she was alive; I prayed that the vuldoar had shown her some form of mercy.

I, however, had not. I followed the path of blood to where it stopped to feast upon her and wasted no time. I had one canister of bolts left, and I emptied it into the beast. While it was immobilized, I rushed toward Barrea's corpse and retrieved my saber, and hacked away at its arm until it was cut clean off. When it tried to wail in pain, I stomped on its face three times and broke its teeth right from its mouth; that was succeeded by me removing its bottom jaw and tongue, so it was no longer able to pose any threat.

Bleeding out from the shoulder, and no way to call for the leader, it just laid still and near lifeless before I unleashed a barrage of stabs. I didn't want it to be dead, yet. I wasn't *done*. I wanted it to feel let down, lost, and witness its own carnage just as Barrea most likely did.

Two days into the island and my mentality started to decline at a rapid pace. I was too scared to be focused, too enraged to be scared, and too focused to be enraged; this was the cycle my mind imprisoned itself in and it was safe to say, I was losing it.

The loop of emotions and lack of mental stability caused me to start losing what bit of humanity I had. I suppose it was just simple vengeance to any third-party view, but it was more than that. RoGoria the Princess was finally dying.

Barrea did nothing to deserve the fate she got. I didn't like her up until her final moments, but just as quickly as she became someone for me to rely on, she was taken away. It was a cruel, twisted joke. Everyone I knew referenced my bitter, hateful attitude over and over again, and the progress I made to stop it seemed to have vanished.

Why waste my time being the person others want me to be, if they're going to die, anyway?

Her final words rang in repetition through my ears, as if she were just next to me. *"RoGoria! RoGoria, please hel...RoGoria! RoGoria! It hurts, it hurts! RoGo..."*

My name. An honor for some, baggage for me. Blood-curdling screams called my name, and not only could I not save her, but Tara made it clear it was me who sentenced Barrea to this end. I started screaming as I plunged my sword into the now lifeless beast, livid that it was done and couldn't feel the pain I was causing it anymore. I wanted it to feel every innard I punctured, I wanted whatever hell it was in to be a punishment served by me.

I brought my terrorizing to an end and moved away to grab various stones and whatever wood I could find. I saw Barrea do it at the campsite; how hard could starting a fire be? I had a large pit lined with rocks and flooded with twigs and sticks and chipped two stones together until a spark ignited the pit. The flame kissed me with its heat with a mother's warmth, and I dragged what was left of Barrea into the fire. Wrapped around my neck was the fabric that Tara had cut off; I tore it down to my hands and gave my final words.

"Dear Lord, make sure she sees this. Barrea was a loving wife, a talented cook, and a close friend even to those who rejected her. Words will never describe how hard I'll push so that her sacrifice won't be in vain: day one of meeting you, I was unkind. As I was day two, day three, and so on. I had never been so thrilled to have a first impression be proven wrong. Your death wasn't painless, it wasn't quick. I'm sure you knew minutes before that this was the end for you, and I'm sorry. The beast didn't kill you, I did. My negligence, my stasis of fear, killed you. I'll find Elliot..." My voice began to tremble, and the fear of having to continue alone set in. Tears streamed down my face as I started to break.

"Thank you...for never leaving my side and holding my hand during the brief time we were alone. I wish you nothing but peace and tranquility in the afterlife. With love, Barrea. Amen."

Her body burned and melted in the flames, and with each minute, the flame grew brighter. The light illuminated the harsh severity of my situation; I was alone. Barrea was dead, Elliot was missing, and the fact that I held a piece of Firstlyn didn't give me much hope. The witch finally broke me.

CHAPTER 27

I WAS BEING HUNTED. TARA HAD KILLED THE REDDISH-BROWN vuldoar; I had slain the silver one. What was left was the bigger, disheveled, moss-colored pack leader. It was following me not in a way that I could see, but I could hear it, as well as smell it. It was the pungent odor of aged, shredded flesh between its teeth. The low purr of its growl followed me for miles but never attacked. It knew I was aware of its presence.

I found myself in a battle of wits with the beast. Its growl spoke of vengeance against its fallen pack members, however, each growl shuddered with each exhale, a signal of its hunger and desperation. Maybe it thought Tara was still around. The helpful witch took one of them out in seconds. Or, it saw what I did to the other vuldoar and labeled me as a formidable foe myself. I couldn't attack. Not yet.

I was no better off than it was. It knew I wasn't going to rush it; a much smaller, petite, ex-princess wasn't going to charge a beast of its stature. It could outrun me, overpower me, and worse, it knew I was afraid of it. It wasn't afraid of me, just that witch that may or may not be with me.

Marla hung in my thoughts, yet another reason why I couldn't act foolishly and just attack. I had to get back to her; I had to care for her. She was all the motivation I had left—not even Fristlyn being alive helped me push forward. Tara said he was the Ani'Mas King, but he was unable to do much. Not to mention, he confirmed he was in a cursed state and couldn't access the powers that were granted to him. He was of no help right now. He may have been a magic-wielding elf at one point, but he was just a decrepit spider now.

There was a rustle in the treetops, yet another being that was hunting me down. Unlike the vuldoar, though, I had no clue what it was. Barrea pointed it out first; when we were hiding in a tree ourselves. I couldn't see it, but it was large enough to where it couldn't move without making the trees shake and rumble with each step it took. Though, it was either small enough or dark enough that it blended in nicely. It moved with me and only me, not with the vuldoar. I'd make five paces ahead, and it would transition to another tree till it was directly placed above me.

Five more paces forward. Rustling branches above, and then it would stop, causing small twigs to fall to their doom and graze my arms. Five steps to the side, same thing. Of course, twigs didn't fall every time, but plucking the source of the sounds and movements wasn't difficult by any means.

Since it was all I could do, I carried on, unsure what my casual approach should be. I couldn't play dumb; the vuldoar was still aware I knew about its constant lurking. By how obvious my testing was, the creature above knew, as well.

As the minutes turned into hours or maybe more, I noticed the vuldoar was getting anxious. I could hear its breath. Not the growling, no, but the wisps of air that followed. It smelled like an unbathed, wet dog, and its aggressive scent stabbed my nose. I picked up my pace.

Don't let it smell your fear.

I was afraid, but I couldn't let it know that. It stalked me by matching my steps, picking up its speed as I did; slowing down as I did.

I couldn't take it anymore. I stopped dead in my tracks and calmed my frantic eyes and tried to scan the area. I unholstered my pistol and withdrew my blade, ready to fight if need be.

There it was, using the little lighting the forest provided to its advantage. Its dark, mossy green mane blended well with the bushes. The silhouette of its wild, tattered fur didn't look much different than the sporadic, restless sight of the branches and leaves surrounding it.

One bloodshot eye locked onto me.

I was terrified but kept my face still, now showing signs of stepping down. I could feel the dirt sink as my attempts of being strong pushed my feet into the ground. I wasn't ready to fight this beast, but I don't think I had much of a choice.

"She's still here," I lied, referencing Tara's merciless kill of its packmate. It took one step from the shrubs, and I pointed my gun directly at the vuldoar, my arm having a mind of its own. I watched as it licked its lips.

Next, in the lowest, deepest, most horrifying voice I thought to have only existed in nightmares, it responded. "No, she is *not.*" That was followed by maniacal, twisted breathing; my own breath stuttered at the noises and right there, he sensed it. My fear.

I bolted. I ran as fast as I could, but he was catching up with ease. Several times, the vuldoar tried to pounce, grab, or ensnare me in its jaw, but I darted around trees, ducked under logs, and hopped prickly bushes. I left the duty of hindering its speed to the earth. This wasn't the first time I ran away like this. I had to be cautious, though; as I stormed away from the beast, my ears reminded me of another issue.

The being in the trees jumped rapidly with each couple of steps I made. As I ran and dodged the vuldoar, it moved from tree to tree, still being stealthy enough not to let me see its form.

I turned a corner, and that was the end. I stepped clean off a dip in the ground and rolled ferociously down the slopes. Violating bushes as I tumbled and bruised my body with no control, alerting the growing list of dangerous inhabitants of the forest with my screams. I hit my head with force on a rock, and the forest swirled in my vision as dizziness took over. Falling down the slope seemed endless, and I was thrilled to be stable once I hit the bottom. My head pounded and leaked blood. Though, I had little time to focus on it.

The vuldoar emerged from the shrubbery. It removed itself from all fours and glared down at me with its bloodshot eyes.

I whipped around to run, but I crippled as I felt the skin of my back tear with one sweep of its claws. I shrieked in pain and fell to my stomach; the warmth of my own blood hugging me in what was sure to be my final moments.

I looked up at the beast, the vuldoar.

It licked its lips again and snarled at me. Though I knew he could talk, he chose to tell me he was hungry by other means. He taunted me, but I knew I was about to die.

Emerging from the treetops was an eight-legged monstrosity three times Fristlyn's size. Behind the vuldoar, other spiders of varying colors and sizes revealed themselves. None were as big as the black widow that descended; her fangs dripped with venom. Fristlyn's family, it had to be. He admitted he hailed from this island, and I must've stumbled into his territory.

Before it knew, the vuldoar was under attack. My vision blurred as it fended off the small unit of spiders that attacked it. I tried to live long enough to witness the vuldoar's death, but I kept blacking out in spurts and knew I wouldn't be able to handle it much longer.

I watched it throw the massive black widow with ease, and it tore the other smaller spiders into pieces. I wasn't saved, after all, it seemed.

"Lass," a voice called from behind me, but he knew I couldn't move, not with the gaping claw marks that gushed blood. He moved in front of me, and I saw the limping spider with a missing front leg. I didn't have to find him at all.

I choked on blood to say his name, but he shushed me. I reached down, trembling, going cold from blood loss but found the strength to push it aside and yank something of his from my belt. I offered his leg to him and coughed up blood in the process.

He didn't take it, though; he couldn't. He turned to face the vuldoar, which was now staring down at us both. Pieces of spider decorated the forest floor, and the massive black widow was nowhere to be seen after she was thrown.

"It's okay, lass," Fristlyn reassured me. "At least you won't die alone." He hunched back, and I hazily watched him spit a ball of web, *from his mouth*, onto one of the vuldoar's horns.

It cried in an instant, and the horn was melting into the consistency of a chunky, curdled porridge right away on contact. "We're going to die together, lass. I promise, I won't leave your side," he choked. The spider was actually starting to cry. He knew it was our end.

"Fristlyn..." my voice faded, but I was happy to have his name be my last words. I had to tell him about Marla; had to give him a message to give to Soen. One of us needed to live. At death's door, I lost the ability to speak, and his name was to be my last words. I shivered from the cold and the intense feeling of nausea. The world was spinning, and I was tempted to give up just to make the sickness stop.

"Shh," Fristlyn shushed me once more. "We're at our final moments, lass. Don't waste your strength."

The vuldoar roared in rage, and it began to charge at us both.

This was it. I wanted to yell for Fristlyn to leave, but all I could do was mumble and choke on my own blood.

He finally shut me up by adding, "I'm going to die with you, lass. Have faith, you will not be alone."

Everything seemed to move in slow motion. The vuldoar rushed us and wasn't too far away, to begin with, yet it seemed like years before it would finally reach Fristlyn and me. I watched the crazed look in its eye, acting out of pure pain from the melted horn caused by Fristlyn's silk. During the whole time I knew him, I had never seen, nor was made aware, he could do that. I misjudged his power in his current state, as still, he had quite a bit.

Seconds from blacking out for good, I heard Fristlyn's voice once more. "I don't...I feel strange..." I witnessed the spider start to glow with a green, shimmering mist. He started to screech in pain and crippled to the floor. The vuldoar attacked, but once his claws met the green smoke, it cried out, combusting with minor flames. Fristlyn was protected, despite the pain it seemed to bring him.

Fristlyn began to grow in size as the green mist started to whirl around him. His screams turned to laughter as his abdomen cracked open, almost as if he were beginning to molt.

CHAPTER 28

Fristlyn was desperate for air. The pain finally subsided, and the protective green smoke had vanished. The vuldoar was back against the line of bushes, shaken by the threat that now stood in front of its eyes.

As the green smoke swirled away, there was a feathery breeze. Pieces of Fristlyn's shell were revealed to be strewn about; a leg there, flakes of skin here. In his place was a man, a man I had seen, despite the different attire.

Fristlyn heaved and coughed as he dug fingers into the dirt. Though he arched on all fours, I could see the tips of his ears, which bore an excessive length. He had not realized it right away, that he had hands instead of hairy spider legs. When he did, the coughing ceased, and he examined himself by running fingers over chipped nails. He then ran his reborn hands through his ashy light hair while his ears twitched at the touch of his skin.

The laughing returned, a laugh of freedom and relief in lieu of the mania he demonstrated before.

Fristlyn stood upright, slamming a high-heeled boot into the soil, and towered over me. My vision still blurred as I continued to lose blood, and I was just as desperate as he while I clung to life.

He turned to face me, and his attitude changed, a mixture of fear and rage, dominated by sympathy.

The black widow of inhuman size approached, catching Fristlyn's eye.

Happy to see it, he nodded her in my direction.

It obeyed and moved to stand over me while Fristlyn winked a violet eye at me, turning back to the vuldoar.

Fristlyn blew a kiss toward the beast that hunted me, followed by eight, thick spider legs growing from nothing on his back. The legs were proportionate to his size, making them larger than any spider, besides the one that was guarding me.

"Placing bets, Rose," Fristlyn called, and his enormous companion shuffled its legs in response. "Three hits, two evades." His voice was smooth and light, rolling a pleasant *r* when he said "three." The croak I had gotten used to had ceased.

Rose shuffled her legs again, to which Fristlyn responded with "Okay, lass. Keep count." An indication she accepted.

The vuldoar snarled at him, and when Fristlyn took one step, the beast charged. Fristlyn shot his hand up, extending two fingers. Web shot out like a whip, hooking around a branch. He used it to flip up, used the silk like a trapeze, and landed behind the vuldoar. His other hand whipped the same attack, cracking into the beast's rib cage.

It yelled in pain as it tumbled down but was quick to get back up. It lunged once more, bringing down its fist on Fristlyn, only for the elf to catch it with his bare hands.

Fristlyn's jaw then unhinged and revealed large, grotesque fangs and mandibles. He bit down on the vuldoar's arm and yanked it clean off.

The beast crippled on its back, and blood pumped from the gaping tear in its arm.

Fristlyn stood over it, and spat webbing from his horrific mouth, covering the beast's face. I thought it was my vision from my blood loss, but smoke started to emanate from the vuldoar's head.

It roared and screamed, as the imprint of its face on the web started to deteriorate inside. It was as if the web was coated in acid, burning the beast alive.

Fristlyn did not waste a second. As soon as the beast stopped moving, he rushed toward me. Everything started to go black when he began ripping away at my corset.

CHAPTER 29

WATER. I AWOKE TO WATER NUZZLING MY BARE HEELS AS IT FLOWED back and forth in small waves. Its tender hug tickled my feet, and that was what truly woke me up, allowing me to open my eyes, allowing the sunlight to greet me with its familiar presence. It felt like it had been months since I had seen it, though it was only a couple of days.

I was lying down, flat on my back with my hands at my sides. Everything was sore, and my back ached and stung some if moved too much. Not enough to keep me down; I just had to push through the pain. I moved my arms up just a little bit and placed them flat on the ground, palm first. I hoisted myself up, grinding my teeth and groaning as little as possible so as to not alert any more predators. Vuldoars, harpies, or giant spiders that may or may not have been friendly. I'd seen enough.

I stayed in a sitting position for quite some time, due to the numbness that had taken over my legs. My ruby mane hung down to my stomach; I had not realized how much it grew since leaving Sheol. All my clothes had been removed, except for my bottom delicates. Spots on my arms and legs, where cuts and gashes were before, were now hiding behind wraps of spider silk. The entirety of my torso was bandaged by it; around my breasts, stomach, and I could assume my whole back, as well. Whenever I shifted or extended an arm, I could feel the webbing pull on my skin with its tough, sticky grip.

Finally, I noticed my surroundings. It took longer than I cared to admit to notice the sunlight meant I was no longer in the forest. In fact, I was lying on a riverbank which married a beautiful stream of water, large and peaceful as it flowed through. It was a calming sight, not a raging river by any means; it just moved and flowed majestically past the rocks and tickled my toes as I sat.

Across the river, past the opposing bank, was more of the Coven Forest, as well as Yggdrasil, now much closer than I had anticipated. The speckles of gold that hovered around it promised sanctuary; I was almost there.

I promptly turned around to the sound of humming. Male, clear as day, and though I was not a musician myself, I could tell it was off-key to the point I couldn't recognize any particular tune. Regardless, it was remarkably close. With a pained grunt, I looked around me and noticed my weapons were all missing and found an odd comfort in that. Between that and the spider silk, it was clear I was in no immediate danger, even with the unknown humming.

The 'music' was coming from behind me, up a small hill that led just outside the forest line. I attempted to stand, but my legs and feet were far too stiff, so walking was going to be a challenge. Dragging myself, however, proved to be much easier if I was okay with losing what little dignity I had left. One hand at a time, I pulled myself up to peer over at...an interesting sight.

First, the vuldoar's body had been stuck through a massive branch. From my angle, I could see it penetrated through a gaping hole where its head used to be, and I saw it protrude out its backside. It spun over a massive fire by the massive black widow I had seen before I passed out. She was *cooking* it.

As the spider cranked, I saw a man dancing with his arms

folded, bouncing his feet in the air. He hummed with a high pace, a tune I was not familiar with. After focusing my eyes, I damn near collapsed at the sight; his gorgeous blonde hair, fair complexion, and the long, pointed ears that went far above his head.

"Fr..." I started, but my voice was hoarse. It did not hurt; I had just not used it for only God knows how long and it was dry. I allowed my saliva to coat it and cleared out phlegm before trying again. "Fristlyn!" I called, and he stopped dancing immediately. He was several yards away from me, yet the sparkling in his eyes blinded me even there.

He sprinted toward me, ducking down once he was close enough, and held me. His triangular face pulled his features together, but his purple eyes with flakes of green really painted the magical being he was once again.

He pulled me onto his lap and pressed his forehead to mine while he spoke. "Top o' the morn, lass," he greeted, in a much richer, silk-like voice compared to the one of his previous state. His accent was not thick, but it wasn't subtle, either.

"I knew it was you," I sighed. The only difference about him here, compared to my dream state back at camp, was his attire. Instead of the regal, green buttoned top with a long train, he wore a tighter, more combatant style black top that had a frilled train instead; stopping just above his knees as opposed to touching the ground. Black pants in place of the mossy green shorts, and high-heeled boots in place of his sandals that wrapped up his leg. Interesting choice for a man, but I liked it. I felt silly for craving him during my hallucination; I began to get the feeling I wasn't exactly what he sought in a romantic partner. That didn't make his self-confidence any less desirable though. Most men wished they were like him.

"What tipped ye off, lass? The spider silk? The dead beast? The actual spider by my side?" Fristlyn was teasing me and I loved it.

My best friend teased me as he held me, and for a brief moment, I felt happiness in place of scorn and numbness.

"I was awake," I said. I saw his transformation from horrid beast to elf-born. His entire battle with the vuldoar, and the bet he made with his spider companion. I did not get into specifics, though. Instead, I just told him, "I saw all of it before falling unconscious."

"It means the world you got to see me protecting you, lass," Fristlyn said. He formed a loving smile as he spoke to me and tightened his grip around my shoulders. He was careful not to touch anything that was too tender from my wounds.

"There is someone I would like you to meet," he said as he gestured to the behemoth black widow to come over. I was amazed as she approached, morphing down and looking a bit more human with each stride she made.

By the time she reached us, she was no different than I, minus her wondrous beauty. Her flawless, ebony skin was complimented with a red hourglass mark right on her throat.

She extended her hand, and I fought to cringe at the sound of her 'clothes', which was just her body wrapped in webbing, stretch and give as she moved. Fristlyn helped me to an upright sitting position so that I might take it, which I did. She gave me a firm grasp that I returned.

"This is Rose, lass," Fristlyn introduced. "My second in command."

Rose's face was stone, void of emotion almost. Her voice was the same when she greeted me with "It's a pleasure to meet you. Thank you for saving my king." She said the bare minimum and wasn't as social as she retreated to the fire in full spider-form and continued cooking the vuldoar's body.

"Don't mind her, she hasn't had a lot of social interaction," Fristlyn told me. "I found her as a newborn hatchling and made her my queen. The human form is still new to her, especially since she hasn't had to use it in centuries."

So, she was a spider who could turn into a human, not the other way around. I questioned how unnatural that seemed, but she didn't seem to mind. Even with magic gone, the wonderous effects still lingered. I was fascinated by a lot of what I'd seen.

"What did she mean when she said I saved you?" I asked him. "You saved me."

Fristlyn let out a chortle. "You're right, I did. But you...you broke my curse, Princess."

I winced at the word "Princess" again. It was hard to work on shedding the identity when everyone kept referring to me as such. He cocked his head and widened his eyes as he remembered the boundary I had set.

Ignoring it, I moved on. Things had settled down, and now I could talk with the Ani'Mas King I was sent to find. "How? What were the terms of your curse?"

Fristlyn's smile faded; he wasn't ready to give me the full details, so all he told me was, "My curse was to be broken only when I was able to put my life before somebody else's."

That explained his tantrum on the ship after the harpies attacked. He barreled into one and pumped it full of venom when it was on me, and that must not have been good enough. "That... doesn't sound like a curse from a bad person..." I trailed off, thinking it over. What evil sorcerer would want Fristlyn to care about others?

"Aye," he responded. "It was Sylvestra herself who cursed me."

My eyes widened. Fristlyn only ever had good things to say about the powerful witch who was Sylvestra. How merciful she was, how pure. "I wasn't always a good person, lass. I screwed up once, and I hurt people who trusted me. I was filled with so much rage and hatred for myself... until I met you."

"Me?"

"Aye. You were so filled with hate and anger, and you lacked the will to live when our paths first crossed. I saw myself in you, and the weight of emotions I felt for the past four thousand years is something I would never wish upon my greatest enemy. When I was sure you no longer saw me for the beast I was, I allowed myself to get close to you, to help you let go."

Let go. If only it were that easy. I was still full of hate, but only at myself now. While talking with Fristlyn distracted me, the thought of my actions being Barrea's end lingered throughout my brain. I found my nails attacking each other, causing them to become chipped and jagged.

The option of talking to Fristlyn about why he had been cursed vanished, as I started to cry. All I could think about now was Barrea's innards strewn across the forest's floor and her blood that had stained a vuldoar's coat.

Fristlyn pulled me into his chest and held me as I did so; I soaked his shirt, but he never complained about it. He just sat there, brushing my hair.

Minutes later, another hand came and rubbed my shoulder. Rich dark skin with perfectly manicured nails was all I could see as Rose herself was also comforting me. I heard her whisper to Fristlyn, "Dinner is done," to which the Spider King whispered, "Ooh," in excitement.

FRISTLYN WOULDN'T LET me continue our venture until I had one more night of rest. He informed me I was unconscious for the remainder of that night when I was attacked, and well into the evening sunset of the day I woke up.

After we finished eating, which was hard to stomach despite how many times Fristlyn assured me it was okay to eat vuldoar meat, we decided it was time to see what the damage was and unraveled my bandages. The cuts and scrapes were healed, and no scarring had been done, it seemed; that was before he pointed out my back. Though I couldn't see it, he informed me there were long, deep purple scars from the vuldoar's claws. With my corset being completely unusable, Fristlyn used some of his own spider silk to wrap me in a sleeveless 'shirt' that covered everything I needed to be hidden. He did the same thing for a new hair tie, bounding my hair back once again.

We talked about nothing important for the remainder of the night. I still wanted to ask why Sylvestra had cursed him but he just said it was not his question to answer when I asked. Whatever the hell that meant. "Something the High Priestess of Yggdrasil can provide for you. Maybe a new wardrobe, as well," he joked. I didn't laugh, though. I was happy I was reunited with him, but this voyage had devolved so quickly I couldn't keep my thoughts stable. My focus was that our group was still incomplete.

Even though Barrea was dead, all but one of our original group was accounted for. I worried for Elliot, but I also worried for myself. Occasionally, a thought would come in, something along the lines of, *Now, we can be together*, thoughts that made me want to puke for being so disrespectful toward Barrea's memory. It didn't help that Elliot had lost the chivalry he had when we first met, so there was no reason to keep pining over him.

Fristlyn couldn't promise he was okay, but said if he was alive, he might be waiting at Yggdrasil for us.

"What can I expect from Yggdrasil?" I asked no one in particular.

"Elves. A lot of elves," Rose answered, the first input she gave us all night. "The humans that were part of the coven passed away thousands of years ago, as none of the witches cared for immortality. Four thousand years for elves, though? They're barely hitting fifty in human years."

I analyzed Rose, looking her up and down. Aside from the spider inside of her, she looked relatively human. She noticed my gaze, and I shot a glance at nothing out of fear.

"I *am* immortal," she continued. "I was just a spider at one point; my human form was due to the Magic of the Faer Folk; Stygian Knight—"

"Stop," Fristlyn ordered. His voice cracked, and with the crack came the birth of a pool in his eyes. He was so bubbly and quirky seconds before, but the mention of this name changed him. He stood after a soft whimper escaped his lips, choosing solitude in a mere instance.

I disrespected his wishes once he was out of earshot and turned to probe Rose for more, but she stopped me.

She watched as he walked farther and farther away and gestured to her ears, mouthing something about his.

I understood; ears as big as his had to mean heightened hearing, something I got mad at myself for not thinking of.

Once he disappeared out of sight, Rose scooched closer to me and whispered as light and clear as she could.

"Don't mind him," she pleaded. "He's pretty stressed about going to Yggdrasil." Rose was hard to read. Her voice was monotone as if she couldn't express emotion verbally. Her face was blank, cold, and a bit frightening; like Galyn, she had glossy, onyx eyes, but at least the mermaid had expressions.

"Any particular reason he's uneasy?" I asked, testing the waters with how much information she'd give.

Rose's stare was blank. Luckily, I was learning that this meant nothing from her. This was just her natural face. She didn't scoff, didn't grin. She just stared right through me before she spoke. "A couple. For one, he is not looking forward to seeing Amilyana, the High Priestess. They never got along. Two, I was insensitive... mentioning that name."

Too late now, though. I wouldn't forget a name like that. *Stygian Knight*. Rose had called him Faer-Folk, which was a term I had never heard of before. On top of that, I finally had a name for the High Priestess we would be meeting—Amilyana. Both names represented power, furthering my fear of the new world I was discovering.

Everyone I had spoken with was great at keeping secrets from me. Rose lacked the ability to think before she spoke, so I had more information now than I knew what to do with.

"What about you?" I asked her. "Where do you hail from?"

"Nowhere," she informed me. "Here, you could say. Like Fristlyn told you, I was just a typical eight-legged critter when we met. I didn't have a story until Stygian gave me one."

I was not dense, either. It was this immense power blessed by the Faer-Folk that kept her alive all this time, kept her strong. I began to question what their magic was compared to the Settlers of Old, the ones who blessed Fristlyn with *his power.*

"Who is this Stygian Knight?"

"I apologize, Princess, but that's not my question to answer."

A fair response. It was nice to see that, for a woman who was born a bug, she learned enough to respect the ones she cared about. Upon getting to know her better, I'd pry at how having a human form had altered her mind. Blending in with society as a completely blank canvas made Rose one of the most interesting people I'd ever met.

I thought about locating Fristlyn and apologizing, but Rose urged me to reconsider, which I did. She said the king hated feeling vulnerable, and now that he was back to his old self, he may not be comfortable looking weak or sad in front of me anymore. I disagreed since that didn't fall in line with how I knew him, but I let it go.

Rose used spider silk to create a cushion of sorts for me to rest my head. She covered it with moss and various leaves she found, sticking it to the webbing so my hair wouldn't get stuck. As she did this, she started to explain how she lacked the ability Fristlyn did in terms of magic; her webbing was just her webbing, coming from orifices on her fingertips, throat, and toes. Whereas Fristlyn could manipulate whether it was thin, thick, poisonous, acidic, and so on, as well as not being limited to where it comes from so long as he channeled his power.

She transformed back into the massive spider she truly was

and curled up, acting as a guard dog of sorts. It was sweet, but I worried if Elliot were to see it, he'd stay away. He'd need to find his way to us if he were still lost, which would be hard given the new group I had found myself. Fristlyn wouldn't be as he'd remembered, and he never met Rose. Not to mention, not seeing Barrea with us...

I silenced my thoughts as best I could. I needed a good rest after the past few days I'd had, so I tried to focus on happy things. Things like Marla, whom I hadn't failed yet. I would fulfill her hope that I would come home to her. I didn't promise her I would. After everything I had gone through, and what I survived, I made a promise now. A promise to myself that I would see her again.

CHAPTER 30

Morning came, and Fristlyn was still off on his own. Rose had reverted to her human form when I awoke, an act I was silently thankful for. Waking up to a Golem-sized arachnid would've given my day quite a sour start. She confirmed she had seen him this morning, and that he was fine, just still in a pissy mood after last night. I hurt for him; the mention of one name made it clear his curse wasn't the only part of his past that left a hole in his heart. Of course, I knew he'd probably never tell me, but I still hoped he'd confide in me at some point.

I took the time to really organize my thoughts. Yggdrasil was bound to have answers for several of my questions; I had to prioritize what was most important. For starters, there was information on Sylvestra's Tears. What were they? If they were truly Tears, how would we bring it back?

Then, there was the matter of Sylvestra as a whole. I wanted to have a face to match with the name, but of course, that may be impossible since it was clear she was dead now.

Fristlyn's Curse—why was he cursed? Both he and Rose had admitted that he wasn't a standup civilian in the past, so what could have possibly done to acquire such a punishment?

Finally, Lorraine: our main enemy. I wasn't sure what I expected to find on her, but she showed great power, even with the limited magic the island offered. I had suffered several hiccups along the way, and I knew she had a clear head start on us.

Those were the top four. Other questions, such as who lifted the veil for us? Who were the Faer-Folk versus the Settlers of Old? These questions were big contenders, but they weren't applicable to what we were trying to accomplish.

All the while, we'd have to find Elliot. He deserved to know the fate of his wife, and what my role was in her demise.

Fristlyn eventually returned, but we didn't push on right away. Hell, we didn't even speak; it was almost as if he were barred from looking me in the eye, which irritated me. I hadn't mentioned Stygian, Rose did. So what in Lord's name was his problem with me?

He sat at the riverbank and just gazed at the running water. I watched as his hands curled into the soil, feeling the earth mush between his fingers. I got it; across the bank was just more darkened forest, and I wasn't ready to return to it, either. No offense to Fristlyn at all, but his triumph over the vuldoar pack leader left a shameful feeling in my gut. I had taken out one of them myself, as well, the smaller white one, but it was an effort. Fristlyn showed no signs of injury or scarring from his battle, and I felt useless because of the fact. Granted, I could only assume an immense amount of magic came from an Ani'Mas King; the King of Spiders. Comparing myself to him was truly apples and oranges.

There it was again. Focusing on how someone's accomplishments negatively affected me; I hadn't changed even a fraction in my eyes.

With a fresh dose of insecurities, I walked over to Fristlyn and sat on the grass right next to him. I wasn't sure what to say or what to do, but he took the initiative.

He wrapped one of his arms around me and dragged me close

to him, and soon his other arm followed. It was instinct to return his hug and hold him as he held me.

We sat there for just a moment in the grass with a gentle wind playing with our hair.

"I needed to give you a proper hug, lass," Fristlyn said. "Because I have a strong feeling you won't want another from me once we arrive at Yggdrasil." The high heels of his boots stabbed the soil as he stood prominently; all the while I was trying to decipher what he meant. "We should get a move on," he ordered.

NEITHER FRISTLYN nor Rose were keen on me walking. While my wounds had recovered, I was still quite stiff from the two-day slumber I had partaken in. Rose offered herself as a mount, which made me feel like some ancient, tribal queen. My imagination was alive with the thought of storming into battle against my father while riding a black widow spider.

Fristlyn returned my weapons to me, and we continued our journey from there. With a quick flick of his wrist, his fingernails began to glow with a golden light, and I was amazed as he flourished spider silk from them; he created a bridge to connect the two riverbanks.

As we walked across, and, therefore, got closer to Yggdrasil, an unsettling feeling grew at an accelerated rate. Fristlyn was worried I would grow to loathe him, and I was frightened to figure out why, frightened that his prediction would be true. Despite the brief moment of attraction I had the other day, he truly did become that of a brother to me. The last thing I wanted was for that to change.

Memories soon came into my mind; the first time I met him in the abandoned house, the first time I worried for his safety after I saw his blood on the broken window glass, the first time I hugged him, still a spider, while he wrapped all eight of his legs around me, how I carried him physically while he carried me emotionally. He became my rock throughout all of this, and he acted as if I had become the same.

Please, God, let me forgive.

Those memories faded when I thought about what it was he could've done. Lorraine, *she* was unforgivable; making me hallucinate, summoning the fleshers, which led to Barrea getting injured. She may not have had anything to do with the vuldoars, but we would've better off if she hadn't split us up.

Fristlyn, though, I just couldn't see him doing anything nearly that heinous. I wouldn't go as far as to say he didn't have a violent bone in his body; I don't even want to know where the head of the vuldoar was when I awoke from my coma-like state. He sure was on more of a chaotic side, but it was a good kind of chaos, chaos with a purpose. Plus, he had only just gotten his powers back, so he might've just gone overboard. But I didn't think of him as malicious, or as someone with ill intentions.

Even now, as we neared the Tree of Life, he was cold, different. Above all, though, Fristlyn was scared. The only reason I could get mad is if he were to hide it from me, lie about who he was. He wasn't lying, though. He wasn't trying to hide it from me at all. He just didn't have the backbone to tell me himself; he wanted me to see it, or learn about it.

A blood-curdling scream cut through the silence like softened butter, and both Fristlyn and Rose halted.

Fristlyn put a hand up and started to slowly approach the anguished call. His long, pointed ears twitched as if he was trying to pinpoint it; the sound filled the world around us, and Lord knew I had no idea where it was coming from. I was just happy that, for once, I wasn't the only one experiencing something.

The screams faded in and out, and each time the words became clearer and clearer. It wasn't long before I heard my name, as well as Barrea's.

My heart sank as I dismounted Rose and sprinted down the

riverbank, with Fristlyn shouting for me to stop. I couldn't, though. Elliot was alive, alone, and in danger. I sprinted and charged through, running along the forest line as I started to shout his name.

I stopped as a headache ensued; brief, but it dazed my vision. When it passed and everything was vivid again, I could see Elliot in the distance. He was beaten, battered, and bloodied as he crawled to me. I cried his name out again and picked up the running again, but I was grabbed from behind a tree along the forest line and pulled back into the forest.

I yelped as I was spun around, with an unknown hand covering my mouth. I struggled to break free, but when I gazed upon my captor, I realized how stupid I was. I stared into his grey eyes while his platinum hair fell, unkempt, over his brow. His hand rose from my lips to his, ushering me to be quiet. "That's not me," Elliot whispered.

CHAPTER 31

ELLIOT'S EYES LOCKED WITH MINE WHILE HIS FINGER WAS STILL pressed against his pursed, chapped lips.

He looked horrible, riddled with cuts and bruises. A black eye decorated his face while his fingernails were chipped, crusted, and filled to the brim with dirt. Of course, I didn't look much better myself. I was wrapped in spider silk to keep me from being topless.

"What is it?" I mouthed, but he shook his head and shrugged. Whatever it was undoubtedly saw me get pulled in here, but it was still out there, wailing.

"Who is your friend?" His whisper was almost inaudible, but I was able to make it out if I focused on his mouth. "Are we able to trust them? When did Fristlyn get so big?"

Given how serious the situation was, I couldn't so much as let out a silent giggle. Otherwise, I would've found it hilarious. "The blonde man *is* Fristlyn," I said, though I made it clear he'd have to be filled in on that another time. "The spider is a friend of his." I was shocked by how unmoved he was by finding out Fristlyn was human, or elven, once more. Then again, after the shitshow I had seen during the past few days, I wouldn't be surprised by what I thought was good news, either.

I fought to hold back tears when it came to the bad news I had to deliver. I had no idea how to even start talking about what happened to Barrea and was thankful that now wasn't the time. I kept picturing her shredded corpse, mutilated to where she was almost unrecognizable. Now, she was nothing more than a pile of ashes, and I grew to be angry with myself that I didn't stick around to collect those for him.

I jumped as Fristlyn appeared behind me. I, a woman, couldn't walk silently in heels, yet Fristlyn did so with ease. I didn't have a chance to say anything as Elliot spoke first with a, "You're looking better, Spider."

Fristlyn gave a slight glare in his direction. "Aye, I've always looked better when I'm not forced into a cage." His words jabbed at Elliot, opening a wound so that Elliot could bleed guilt.

A sudden tension arose that could be cut with a knife, and I soon realized it had a lot more to do with me in lieu of with each other. I was being held by the man who craved me in front of the man who didn't want me to be with the other. I pulled back from Elliot and stepped toward Fristlyn, who threw an arm around my shoulder once I was close enough.

Elliot looked confused, maybe even a little hurt, but Fristlyn became the protective big brother to me ever since he changed into his true self, and Elliot was the last man any brother would want for his sister.

After a long, uncomfortable silence, I decided to maybe get back to the issue at hand. "So," I gulped and cleared my throat, still taken aback by the seething going on between the two. "What is that out there, then? The other Elliot?"

"A banshee," Fristlyn informed us, but his eyes stayed on Elliot, drawing a line between the captain and I. "Typically believed to be a product of necromancy, as stories have painted them to be ghosts."

"I'm guessing they're something more, like every other blasted thing I've seen so far?" I started to think about Galyn, and how she was a hard-hitting reality check of what a mermaid truly was.

"Aye," Fristlyn confirmed. "They're demons. So they wouldn't be a necromancer's spell, they'd fall under Demonology, lass." It was only now that I noticed Elliot's stance in comparison to Fristlyn's. More aggressive; his hand was stretched open over his sword, and I almost begged him to act the way he clearly wanted to. I would protect Fristlyn just as hard as he would protect me.

"It's evidently another one of Lorraine's parlor tricks. The closer we get to the Tears, the more magic she has access to."

"Parlor tricks?" Elliot gritted his teeth as he spoke. "Was it parlor tricks when she conjured those...those *things* at our camp?"

"Ah, yes, the flesh fiends," Fristlyn taunted, "a beginner level raise of the undead, yet you couldn't handle them. The princess, on the other hand, was able to take them out. Even your wife, for that matter..." he trailed off, and his glare was replaced by a look of sincere fear. It was too late, he realized what he had just done.

My breathing picked up, and my heartbeat was erratic as Elliot asked the one question I was dreading.

"Where *is* Barrea?"

For a fraction of a moment, I was trapped in darkness. Dark space ambushed me, and tears streamed down my cheeks, providing an unwelcome warmth. For a fraction of a moment, though, it felt like unending minutes. I found myself unable to breathe, gasping for air.

"Where *is* she?" Elliot repeated and took one step toward me before Fristlyn stepped in front, cutting him off.

"Open your eyes. The lass here is having an attack; can you not see the trauma in her eyes?"

Elliot watched me with a newfound sincerity, and he choked up as he fought to hold back his own tears. "Inform me later," he advised. "Right now, let's just take care of that...that *demon* out there." He walked past us out into the fields, where we saw he was greeted by a now human Rose. Her voice was emotionless enough that she could probably communicate with him more than I.

Fristlyn wrapped himself around me and provided me with a tight embrace and then ushered me to cry into his garment, but now wasn't the time.

I pulled away and grabbed his arm, leading him past the forest line.

Elliot informed us the banshee was the only thing in our way, saying it was positioned in front of the path toward Yggdrasil. He pointed it out, indicating that amongst the dead, barren trees were a line of lush leaf-filled ones. Kept alive by the magic of Yggdrasil, no doubt. The green was a pleasant sight, but Fristlyn ruined it with the truth.

"That's not good, lad. That means the hag is far ahead of us."

"Not too far," Elliot countered. "I've been tailing her since the camp attack. She had no knowledge that I've still been using her as a guide."

Rose let out a scoff, and Fristlyn a chuckle. "Trust me, lad; she knew."

I knew that would only insult Elliot, but a witch who could wield magic at Lorraine's level had to require a level of wisdom that wasn't easily attainable. I'm sure she was aware he was following her the whole time, so there was nothing for Elliot to boast about. Hell, it was probably why the banshee was there in the first place.

A bright flash of purple and black fed off our attention, and we witnessed the battered, bloodied version of Elliot snarl and scream as it began to hatch as something else. Its skin broke and cracked like a cocoon, flesh fell in chunks, and the eyes even rolled down and exploded like grapes. Emerging from the gore was a creature unfathomable to the human eye. Gray, decayed skin complemented the lipless mouth, so no matter what, we could see its large, rotting teeth. It was hunched over on all fours, but both front and back were arms and hands and no feet at all. It dug at the dirt with long fingernails, and the only noises it made sounded like a mother weeping.

"I'm guessing this is still a parlor trick?" Elliot beamed at Fristlyn, whose ears twitched from irritation.

"Banshees change forms depending on who it's trying to entice," he whispered as the banshee collected itself from its transformation. "But it can't if the victim is looking at it. If it does, its transformation fails and can only show its true form." He took a step past us and assured us he'd handle it.

Fristlyn was at a disadvantage, however. He took one step in a sprint, but the banshee lived up to its reputation, throwing its neck back till the head touched its bony back. It let out a wailing cry that vibrated through our ears. Elliot, Rose, and I took a knee as we covered them, blocking out as much sound as we could. Fristlyn was ill-prepared, and was crippled down and went into a seizure. The most dangerous person on our side had fallen.

Rose rushed to him, trying to subdue him from shaking; excess saliva spewed from his mouth and soaked his clothes as it flailed everywhere, splashing Rose herself in the process.

The banshee gave a quieter, sniffling cry before charging us; all four hands acting like a dog's feet, picking up momentum.

Elliot and I presented our blades, ready to die right there. I felt sure my luck had run out, but Rose proved me wrong. With a swift and effortless wave of her hand, a shield of thick spider silk blocked the banshee from us, giving us an extra minute to think of our options.

I started looking around for an escape route as soon as the barrier was up, and I was filled with a boiling rage when I saw her across the riverbank. The white, frayed hair and the ragged robes. I seethed at the hag; she finally made an appearance.

I noted the swirling, purple mist around her hands; she was definitely accessing magic. Her mouth was moving, but I couldn't hear anything over the ferocious sobbing from the banshee as well as with how far away she was.

I whipped around to Elliot. "Do you have any ammo left for your gun?" I asked him. My pistol didn't even stand a chance; I used the little firepower I had left with the other mass of shit I had to deal with.

He shook his head. "No, but I made sure I always had one of these on hand," he said as he reached around his waist and unclipped a canister of my crossbow bolts from his belt. Tossing it to me, I handed him my sword and unholstered my bow from my back. I'd have to really aim now, unlike the fleshers who were never more than a foot away from me. I tried my best to steady my breathing and aim right at Lorraine. My finger courted the trigger for a bit while I tried to find my courage to fire.

"Hurry up!" Elliot rushed me, and I had half a mind to kick him for it, but I had to focus. I pushed on the trigger, and as I heard the satisfying *phht* as four bolts flew from my bow. I groaned at the inaccuracy of all of them.

"Damn it," I groaned before resituating and trying again. Five came out this time, none of which actually hit Lorraine, though some did come close. My breathing began to pick up as I wasted bolts. I shot six more, nothing. Though as I started to stress, I was blessed with an idea.

"Rose, tear the barrier down," I ordered, pointing my crossbow in the banshee's direction. I couldn't exactly see it, but I prayed I was close enough.

"A crossbow is not going to work on a demon, Princess," she sneered. I made an effort to take no offense. Fristlyn's ears were leaking with a mixture of blood and puss, and Rose was rightfully scared for him. I thought the screech hurt us. I could only imagine what it would do to an elf.

A deep, menacing inhale came from the other side of the barrier, and I knew it was getting ready to do it again.

"Cover your ears!" Rose roared as she covered Fristlyn's.

Elliot and I braced ourselves as it let out another vibrating shriek, paired with Rose's agonizing wail while her ears remained defenseless.

"Rose, take down the barrier!" I ordered once more. "You and I, we can handle this. But you're going to have to trust me."

Rose looked at me with worried eyes, moving between Fristlyn and me. I nodded, and as she wiped her own saliva and a small amount of vomit from her chin; she outstretched her hand, and the barrier dissipated as if it never existed.

I didn't hesitate, I pointed my crossbow and emptied the rest of the canister into the banshee, not doing much damage but enough to stagger it. "Now, Rose, now!"

She left Fristlyn's body as a human but was on the banshee as the Spider Queen I knew she was.

The two rustled around before her long fangs buried into the demon, and I saw her pump it with her potent venom. The banshee was gone within seconds after the bite, sizzling into smoke and erased from history.

I turned to see Lorraine already escaping to the forest on the other side. Finally, we were ahead.

I rushed to Fristlyn and turned him over onto his back. He wasn't shaking anymore, and it looked like he remained conscious through the whole ordeal.

What a hellish time to be awake.

He choked on spit and hacked up mucus onto his shirt and finally found the means to take deep, controlled breaths.

"That was," he stopped to choke again, but kept going, "that was phenomenal thinking, lass. Good job."

I had to admit, I was quite pleased with myself. "Couldn't hit the ol' bitch, so try focusing on something you knew you could. I'm impressed. No, I'm proud."

I gave him a gentle kiss on his forehead, and Elliot extended a hand to help him to his feet. To hell with Elliot and me; I just needed those two to learn to get along.

"Come on," Elliot said as he also started to control his breathing. He was scared, and he would admit that, as well. I'm not sure what horrors he had to face, but the banshee was the lesser of evils I had witnessed so far. "Let's get to Yggdrasil."

CHAPTER 32

Y ET ANOTHER PURE EXAMPLE OF MAGIC WAS BEFORE US. T HE banshee had blocked our only route to Yggdrasil; Fristlyn explained there was one path in and one path out from the grounds of the sacred tree. The trail stood out from the rest of the forest, mainly because the rest of the isle didn't have any paths or trails that you could just follow. But the trees that lined it were… something out of a storybook.

They were full of leaves, but not dead like the rest of the forest. To me, they were pink and white, and very reminiscent of spring. Friendly bees swayed around and bounced off the flowers that grew along the branches, and they stayed far away from us and minded their business.

To Elliot and Rose, they were red, orange, and brown. I knew Elliot loved autumn more than anything. I remembered him telling me when we were young, how he loved to play in the leaves as a child. Or how he would climb an autumnal tree just to be surrounded by the color. Both Elliot and Rose bonded over it, and they talked to each other for most of the walk down. So much so, they were quite ahead of Fristlyn and me, gushing over the beauty visible to only them.

I wanted to ask Fristlyn what he saw, what season the island blessed him with. However, a mere five minutes away from the Tree of Life, he was more unsettled than he was before. I grew solemn over it. He was never going to be his true self until I figured out what story his past told and found forgiveness in it. I wanted to reassure him the past is just that; the past, and that it wouldn't matter. However, that was a promise I wasn't sure I could keep. All of that depended on what he did, who he was aligned with, and how much it impacted the outcome. I continued to pray that he was overreacting, but the more anxious he got, the more I felt that I was going to be quite livid.

Though most of it was blocked by Elliot and Rose, I could see the exit where two trees married one another by an arch of their branches, allowing a pleasant doorway onto the sacred grounds. Finally, we were all almost there. Finally, I was going to get some answers.

Fristlyn grabbed my arm, not in any way firm, and told me to hold wait for a second. He then ran to Rose and Elliot to say the same before running farther ahead.

I met up with both, and of course, Elliot was the one to ask me what was wrong. I shrugged, but still said, "Probably wanted to make sure the coast was clear," given the trials we had faced. The issues Fristlyn and I faced, at least. Any hardships Elliot had were still in the dark.

I watched Fristlyn as he stopped right at the arch and put his arm through while waving it around. He then poked his head through and looked around the grounds for a brief moment. He turned back and waved us over, so we continued.

When we were close enough, he walked completely through, and we followed, and Elliot and I both let out a gasp in awe of the beauty.

Yggdrasil wasn't just a tree; staircases wrapped around the massive trunk and lead up to small huts in the branches. Another arched opening was carved right in the trunk to the base, leading into what looked like a library. It was dark inside, but I could see the bookshelves and tables inside. This was a home, a sanctuary for those who lived there.

The gold speckles I saw in the distance weren't just around the leaves; they decorated the space throughout the entire grounds. I was so sick of the continuous dark, dying woods; this whole area filled me with life.

Off to the side of the tree was a gorgeous, wooden gazebo up on a slight hill. It was lousy with vines paired with blue star flowers ensnared in the vines themselves.

I looked over at Elliot; his face was the brightest I had ever seen. The gold speckles reflected off his grey eyes as he was filled with what I assumed was the same happiness. He was ready to lay into me over Barrea's absence just a bit ago and this place, the aura that it birthed, brought him peace and cleared his mind, which pissed me the *fuck* off.

I was ready to smack him, but I caught movement out of the corner of my eye. I broke from my trance the beauty of the grounds cast me under, and I looked all around to try and see it again. Gone. Yet, out of the corner of my eye, I sensed movement again. No matter where I looked, it was always *just* out of view.

My breathing stuttered as I realized, while this place is beautiful, magic held a presence here. We could be up against something completely out of our scope.

I withdrew my saber and took a few steps forward past everyone, toward the large group of picnic tables that perfectly lined up in the open area just before the tree itself. Fristlyn urged me to play dumb and to sheathe my sword; I refused. For once, I would be prepared to fight whatever was coming.

I took one more step, and within the span of seconds, the world disappeared, leaving me in blackness with a specter that roared in livid aggression. I shouted and fell back but was caught by Fristlyn's arms.

"Please, lass. Sheathe your blade. The High Priestess is going to prefer we submit rather than challenge her," he whispered softly, and I could hear in his voice he wasn't trying to order me. He was begging me. Something about this High Priestess scared him, and I could see why.

The ghost I saw wasn't even there. Just for a split second, I was taken to some empty nether realm, just to be screamed at by a spirit of sorts. Theatrical, Fristlyn called it.

"Because you know what I do and do not like," a voice echoed from within the tree. No one was visible yet, but it was a woman's deep voice. It was the sort of tone that demanded respect and attention to any that heard it. "Is that right, Mr. Everleef?"

I looked at Fristlyn and mouthed, "Everleef?" and he made me feel silly by just informing me that was his surname.

From the shadows of the large cut archway of the tree emerged a woman, the High Priestess, though she wasn't dressed as someone I'd expect to hold that title. Tight black and blue pants and a faded blue, sleeveless tunic paired with boots not much different than mine; she looked like your typical adventurer. She held something as she approached, a staff of some kind. It was a color that was in between brass and gold, with a small blade at the tip shaped like three leaves.

Fristlyn sneered at the sight of it.

She stopped after stepping up onto one of the picnic tables, staring us down, all of us, from a high stature.

"Who is the head of this little group?" she demanded. Her voice shattered the elegant silence of the grounds like a fragile porcelain doll. A woman of power, and despite her casual attire, she looked the part. "Surely it's not you, Everleef."

Her skin was a lighter brown, rich in vibrance. The priestess's hair hung down just above her breast on one side; burnt orange dreads bounced along with each step she took.

"Aye, Lo'Ren, I am not," Fristlyn confirmed, and nodded to me. *I beg-to-fucking differ.*

"That would be me," Elliot chimed in.

I rolled my eyes as he lowered his own voice; he made himself appear to be gruffer than he truly was. *Fuckin' twit.* "I was to lead this expedition for Sylvestra's Tears. We hail from Metsa—"

"I don't recall asking your damned life story, *boy*," the High Priestess snapped, and I watched as Elliot shut up and backed off. Tail between his legs. "I asked who the leader was, and you tell me lies?"

"He isn't lying," I snapped back.

Fristlyn let off a groan behind me, I even heard him mutter a, "Shut up, lass," but it was too late.

The High Priestess glowered at me, stepping down from the picnic table she used as a pedestal. Her brown eyes reflected the golden speckles that filled the air, paired with a blue-winged eyeliner.

"Stand."

Fristlyn helped, lifting me as I used one of the table benches to stand.

"Turn," she ordered. "Face your fellowship."

I did so, though with hesitance, as I did not trust having my back turned to her.

She stepped aside from me, stepping onto another picnic table. I was not sure why, she was taller than all of us, but I guess she needed that extra bit of dominance. "When the harpies attacked, did you fight for your comrades? Or did you fend for yourself? The princess here could've died leaping off the ship, yet she did so to save *you*."

Breathing was no longer an option for me; the fight she referenced happened a few days from docking, yet she knew about it. I feared Elliot would grow to resent me if his lack of leadership were fully brought to light; hell, I didn't even consider he wasn't caring about us.

"I called after her, I helped her with—"

"I am talking; you will not speak until I say otherwise," the High Priestess roared, though her voice was different, almost a manifested echo that rustled the leaves surrounding the Tree of Life itself. "When the flesh fiends summoned by Lorraine attacked, did you fight, or did you run after the hag? No need to answer. I already know. Running after a brittle old woman was easier, right? Leaving them for the princess to handle. You weren't even there when the vuldoars attacked. You weren't there to see your wife get ripped to ribbons. You weren't there when the princess had to burn her corpse, to give her something of a proper memorial. You were absent."

I was on the verge of tears. Elliot hadn't known. I hadn't gotten the chance to tell him about Barrea.

His face lost what little color it had; he looked identical to the ghost I had seen minutes before.

He tried to stutter out words, but the priestess held up a hand. "By the Hourglass, do not make me yell again."

Elliot stopped, but tears flowed down his face. Maybe he didn't love Barrea the way she loved him, but he still cared for her. Barrea had been his best friend all this time, someone he could come home and talk about his day to. The High Priestess was harsh, and I was harsh toward him, too, but the man didn't deserve to find out that way.

"Lastly, my banshee," she continued. "Banshees aren't easy to conjure, but under the control of that old hag, I could see you had no choice but to eliminate it. You were frozen. Stiff. *Useless.* Princess over here used quick thinking, risked her life, and came up with a plan that involved teamwork, and not one that would've painted her to be a hero."

She stepped down and stopped behind me. She set the staff she held down, which Fristlyn never took his eyes off of, and cupped both my shoulders. "My name is Amilyana Lo'Ren, and I dub this woman to be your leader. What do you think of that, *Captain?*" She hissed his title, and Elliot took the bait, resorting to defense. His fists clenched as his feet pressed harsher into the dirt. Before he could speak, though, Amilyana interjected. "Exactly my point."

AMILYANA INFORMED me that we were supposed to stop at Yggdrasil, anyway. In fact, there was no way to avoid the Tree of Life during our expedition for the Tears, as they were kept in Sylvestra's tomb.

The High Priestess was quite helpful in terms of information; she explained that to end the Witches' War, Sylvestra siphoned magic from the Hourglass, the heart of magic itself, to lock it away until the "world was ready for it once more."

I scoffed as I planned on trying my hardest to convince Soen to rethink his intentions. My father was more than enough proof that man couldn't handle power.

Amilyana was blunt about who she was; she claimed keeping secrets benefited no one, something I wish she could teach literally everyone else I'd spoken to up until now.

She was the adoptive daughter of Sylvestra Winwill herself, making Amilyana a couple of thousand years old. Again, no secrets as she explained she accepted the gift of immortality from the Nethren, as a reward for mastering both Necromancy and Demonology. This granted her the title of warlock, by the Faer-Folk's definition. Finally, I was starting to understand how Relica functioned thousands of years prior to my own existence.

I never had to ask her who the Nethren were; they were the keepers of the supernatural. Necromancers had to form a bond with them in order to call upon the dead and rule supreme in the spirit world. She opened my eyes, nearly confirming my own religious beliefs, saying that Necromancy did not allow her to call from Heaven or Hell; she could only call on spirits that were trapped in the spectral plane and had to tame them from angry ghosts to comrades of combat.

In her time being the Guardian of Yggdrasil, alone seemingly, as no one else was here, she studied Demonology to a harsh extent. I nearly fell back when she told me she had to speak to the

Devil himself and form a bond with him, as well. She assured me, though, I had nothing to fear of her, nor him, a theory I planned on talking to her about later.

It only seemed fair that I would be as open as she was and explained that while Yggdrasil was a required stop, I had a list of things to research while I was here.

The warlock led me into the main entrance carved in the tree's trunk, and I was right; it was a massive library. She gave a stroke of her hand while she sang a brief, lyricless melody, and light was birthed within the dark book stacks and desks. She told me to help myself, but to also be quick, as there were things that needed to be done before she could allow us to retrieve the Tears. I asked why she was so willing to let us attempt it in the first place, but all she said was, "If you don't find the answer in here, ask me again."

Amilyana waved her hand once more, though with no song this time.

I watched as a candle on a desk crammed between two bookcases lit itself, and she ushered me to sit down. I sat at the desk and was quite pleased with the workspace. Closed off in my own little nook, the only thing unsettling was a large painting over my head, covered by a thick cloth.

"Don't find this rude, but I'm not keen on letting a girl I just met rummage through nearly nine thousand years of research," she informed me. Understandable enough. Hell, she was so terrifying I didn't even trust *her*. "What subjects were you hoping to gain insight on?"

I wasn't sure how to answer as I wanted to make sure she could understand my curiosities clear enough to find the proper texts. "The most important would be Sylvestra's Tears. What are they? What do they do? I know they were used to imprison magic, but why her tears? And why are..." I stopped to put a hand out, "and I mean this with no offense, but why are you so considerate in letting us attempt to retrieve them?"

She nodded. "All fair questions, however, you must remember

Sylvestra died creating the Tears. She wouldn't have been able to document it. Her biological daughter, Alsyn, wrote extensively on the subject. I think those records are still in her hut, but I'll have to look. Anything else?"

I stopped to think about how to word everything else. If I mentioned Fristlyn's curse, it could have seemed like I was trying to gain access to the recipe and incantation used to turn him into the dreadful spider he was. That was far from my intent; I wanted nothing to do with magic for me personally. Asking about Fristlyn would be too specific I felt. "Are there any records of the Ani'Mas Kings and Queens?"

The High Priestess scoffed. "Plenty. I'll fetch her main volume."

"Is there anything regarding Sylvestra herself? Perhaps an image of some sort? Who she was? What her specialty was in terms of magic?"

She shook her head. "All of that would be listed in her personal volumes of craft; her Book of Shadows. Every witch has one. In terms of pictures, there are detailed oil paintings that you can't quite see from your current view. Perhaps, once you're done, I can show you around. Or the elf can."

Fristlyn went off on his own when Amilyana led me through the study. He sat on the gazebo and just stared off; I was doubtful he'd be any help.

Amilyana then added, "I'm sensing a theme with your questions. I'll pull some other helpful texts along with records of the Ani'Mas Kings and Queens. Just sit tight for me." The priestess vanished behind several different shelves and bookcases, pulling some big tomes until she eventually had a nice stack. As she walked back, she levitated them out of her grasp and dropped them down, harshly.

I jumped at the crack they made; all hardcovers and probably a few thousand pages of detail made for a hefty weight on the wooden desk.

"My apologies," she said. "Being gentle was never within my

grasp. I'm going to see if I can find my sister's records on the Tears. For now, happy reading."

Amilyana exited Yggdrasil, and I opened the first book I considered to be a priority. *"The Ani'Mas: Hand-Picked Druids of the Faer."*

CHAPTER 33

THERE WAS BARELY A MENTION OF FRISTLYN IN THIS RECORD, ASIDE from his brief blurb, of course. After reading the whole book, I could write an analytic biography on all the other Ani'Mas Royals, the general term for them as a group, but not Fristlyn.

His section was a mere half a page,

Fristlyn Everleef, The Spider King. Age at time of record: Unknown, subject is Immortal. Born during the Age of the Hourglass. Status: Alive. Hometown: Rinlock Port, River Shores. Family: Unknown, Parents were murdered during an Elven Genocide of his country when he was just a teen. Granted the title of Ani'Mas King of Spiders not more than a week after. Known Allies: Rose, his self-proclaimed Queen. Islabella, Guardian and close friend of Stygian Knight. Stygian Knight, lover. Fristlyn is the one of the first ten Ani'Mas Royals ever created, ranking at number six. He's the last of the originals presently and is currently the second most dangerous, in my own opinion. Alignment: Sadly, none. It typically costs a great deal of funds to get him to side with us. Overall, the High Court sees him as high risk.

While not useless, it didn't give a recording of his past, his faults, or his accomplishments. He was almost described as a mercenary of sorts, which did not fit how I knew him in the present. I had a clue about his issue with Stygian, at least. *Lover.* I wondered if it was just a bad breakup, or if Stygian was no longer with us.

I flipped through one of the other tomes Amilyana brought me. She collected four texts in total, and this next one, while large, just dragged on about the Settlers of Old and the Faer-Folk; same species, according to this text. The "Settlers" was what the humans dubbed them, recognizing them as the first beings to settle on Relica's soil. The standing theory was that they were God's first creations. A mixture of angel and human, with a few enhancements done to the latter. It was believed that God was the One Who dubbed these beings faeries, or Faer-Folk. Of course, there were no images, though I counted my blessings with that one. Probably a horrific-looking creature if anything I had seen so far was anything to compare to.

We were taught that God created man to be His greatest creation and that there had been no other. I loved and believed in God but didn't doubt the theory He created the Faer-Folk first. I thought about the map I saw in Soen's chambers; I had been lied to so much as a child, therefore, it wasn't as if this wasn't plausible.

The next book talked about the Hourglass. It wasn't written by Sylvestra but instead was written by a healer and elemental witch known as Eden RaVelle. His writing wasn't as consistent or precise as the former High Priestess, but the overall takeaway was that the Hourglass *provided* magic. It created the life of the mystics and was an ancient relic believed to belong to one of the Settlers themselves. This was what Sylvestra had to siphon magic from to lock it away, but even she couldn't withstand all of it at once.

I was angered and saddened; there was such a rich history to our world it seemed. elves, mermaids, faeries…none of what I was doing would be possible if it weren't for the existence of these elements, and I grew more and more disheartened about how much was hidden from the world. The longer I thought about it, the more rage built up inside me.

I took a couple of deep breaths and decided to take a break. I stood from the desk and faced the gorgeous interior that was the Tree of Life. It almost seemed disrespectful to hollow out a tree and fill it with archives, yet it was a clear symbol to the witches that rested their research here. The witches here wished Yggdrasil would keep their studies safe, and it did so with pride. I left my little nook and observed the area a bit. Unlike my desk, the other workstations and study tables were neatly lined and positioned throughout the main foyer. To my side was an upper level, one which had even more stacks and a few art pieces scattered throughout. Like my home at Sheol, a turret that married two staircases overlooked the bottom floor. Against Amilyana's wishes, I started to wander up the stairs, though I made a point to not search through the texts, to respect the High Priestess to an extent.

I believe what I found most tasteful was, though these were ancient studies, they weren't just forgotten texts piled with dust and debris. Amilyana must have made it a point to clean those on a frequent basis, though I was sure all she had to do was wave her hand and hum an incantation. Still, the priestess respected the research enough to make it a regular point of her day.

The corner of a framed painting caught my eye, while most of the frames were a gorgeous, earthy brown. This one was a gentle ecru. I approached it and gasped at the beautiful art of two women.

One was an elf. Her ears weren't as dramatic as Fristlyn's, but the defined point of her them gave her away. Her silver hair was a bed of bouncy curls that hung down over one shoulder, and she wore a blue dress with a long train flowing from her neck; the color made her lifeless, pale skin a thing of beauty.

The other woman was quite the opposite; dark, golden russet skin with a black dress. Her hair was black and came down in a long, thick braid embroidered with chains and a few gems. She had an open-mouth smile, which showed off her crooked teeth, some of which displayed some tooth rot. Her hand was placed on the elven woman's chest; right over her heart, as they both looked out to anyone who viewed the painting; their eyes promised sanctuary.

I turned and jumped at Amilyana standing right behind me, terrified that the warlock was going to be enraged at my snooping around.

"I-I didn't. I left the books alone, I prom—"

"They're beautiful, aren't they?" She moved next to me, enticed by the painting. I nodded after letting out a sigh of relief. I did not want to anger the woman. I agreed with her, though. Both women were flawed and had distinctions that society would deem unpleasant. The elf looked sickly due to her complexion, and the other had some unfortunate dental hygiene. Yet both were still gorgeous, irresistible in their own right. They wouldn't let minor blemishes hinder them from being what they knew they were, powerful. I could never...

"The elf," I whispered, now enticed by the painting along with Amilyana, "That's Sylvestra, isn't it?"

Amilyana nodded. "She was wonderful. I miss her, dreadfully. Both my parents were war heroes, you see. My mama died in combat, and Father died after giving his life for the wounded. She took me in the second she heard my story about running through the streets as an orphan. There will never be a heart as pure as hers."

A deep speech, and one that brought me a feeling of unease. What could Fristlyn do to cause someone as merciful as this witch to curse him? I was about to find out, as Amilyana held two books in her arm. One for the Tears, and the other that had his name on it.

I shook my head, wanting to put it off as long as I could. "And the other woman? Is that her wife?"

Amilyana chuckled. "No, no. Both were married to men. Sylvestra imprinted on her, though, the act of tying an Hourglass Born to a Relica Born. They shared a bond unlike any other until..." Her words faded, damn near dying as they slipped through her lips, and just stopped there. She shook her head, and refocused her attention to the books she carried, handing them to me. As I reached for them, she pulled back and put out a hand.

"RoGoria, I need you to understand something before you read this," she started, staring deep into me. "The Spider King and me...Well let me just say, we're not fans of one another. In fact, even now neither of us are each other's favorites, but I always give credit where it's due."

I nodded in agreement, admiring how humble she was. I was too stubborn for a trait like that. Fool me once, you're dead to me.

"You're going to read about a person who made a monstrous choice on top of several smaller ones. Keep it in your head that him sitting outside right now is proof that not only did he correct his mistake but... is far from the same elf I knew." She extended the books out to me once more, and I made sure to be gentle in taking them, as now I was all too eager.

"I won't tell you what to think," she continued. "Just...try to keep an open mind?"

I READ the book on Sylvestra's Tears first, written by Amilyana's stepsister, Alsyn. It was a small journal, detailing what Alsyn saw as Sylvestra performed the Ritual. To watch her own mother decay and be ripped by magic, all so that she could protect the world as much as she could, would've traumatized me beyond repair. That is, assuming I had a healthy relationship with my mother, which was not my reality.

Alsyn recorded the results of some tests she ran. Magic still existed in small frequent hotspots scattered around, with the

Coven Isle being the biggest source. Alsyn had drawn a small, detailed map of Relica, and marked Xs on where magic was on its last legs but still existed. All of those places were islands or countries missing from the map I had grown up with, including Metsa. Metsa had a small source of magic, which shed some light as to how Lorraine was practicing some Necromancy of her own while she squatted in the abandoned house.

Alsyn also recorded what was needed to release it:

When the world needs it the most, it will return under these specific guidelines: One: A human of no Magical background must be the one to open mother's tomb. Non-practicing humans loathed Magic, so for one to willingly step into it, will prove the world needs it again. Two: The human needs to go through a Ritual of Imprintation with an Hourglass-Born being of their choosing. Hourglass-Born meaning not human but doesn't have to be a Witch. This could be Elven-Folk, Orcish-Folk, should they be found again, Mer-folk, and so on. Lastly, the human to retrieve the tears must bear no motive to release Magic for their own power; any human described as such will not even gain access to the Isle.

The veil. No one lifted it like I was led to believe. I had no interest in using magic of my own right; I even felt the Tears should be destroyed, but that is exactly why I was still granted passage through the Isle. If I had no motive to take it for myself, the Isle itself allowed me to infect it with my presence.

I closed Alsyn's journal and picked up the one titled *The Treachery of Fristlyn Everleef.* "The Treachery" terrified me. I opened the book and read up on my closest friend; my breathing staggered as I flipped through the pages.

The book was reliant on info from the Witches War. He had been in the army that opposed Sylvestra; difference in political opinion, so I thought. According to Sylvestra, he joined the army out of spite against her for banishing him from the Coven Isle. *"Fristlyn wasn't the same after Stygian... left. He was careless, and was becoming quite the problem."* Nothing out of the ordinary so far; Sylvestra wasn't understanding how Fristlyn was coping, and I was sure Stygian did more than just "leave" given her use of writing. There was trauma there, clear as day. Not that it excused whatever his actions were, but as the poster child for acting off of trauma myself, I was relating.

As I read through, I was relieved. His joining a less tasteful army of a cruel war was wrong, sure, but nothing I could hate him over; the war was nearly four thousand years before my time.

It all came crashing down when I learned that wasn't why he was cursed,

As of today, Month Nine, AHG 5,999, I've perfected the Ani'Mas curse, and Lord Everleef has been sentenced. I hated to do it, but he had to be stopped. Eden planned to wipe the native Orcs of Mang'Coal from the face of the planet, and the High Court and I learned this was Fristlyn's doing. Though he was friends and allied with Orcs up until this point... he sold them out regardless. My heart hurts for the Orcs; their hiding place took months perfecting, only for the one they trust to turn them in to the one who wanted them dead. This attempted genocide will not go unpunished.

Genocide. The Orcs of Mang'Coal were in danger. Orcs, who were perceived as savages in all tales made available to the world, were quite the opposite. Sure, they were described in the book as brutes, but none were bred for good or evil. They were people, and they died due to the audacity of the one who treated me like a sister.

"Lass?" His voice came from the entrance of the Yggdrasil Archives, and it scraped against me like a fork on a plate. Piercing, unpleasant, the last thing I'd ever want to hear. Without even looking upon him, I saw him for the monster everyone else thought him to be.

"They begged you for help," I seethed. My skin was hot to the touch; my fist was clenched on the page. The only thing that held me back was how he could cripple me in seconds. "They were your allies, your friends, and you sentenced them to extinction for...what, exactly?" I turned to face him, but I couldn't bear to look him in the eye. I couldn't look at him at all. His stature was almost god-like; gorgeous, with that odd mixture of mossy green and purple eyes. He didn't *deserve* to look like that. Saving me was not enough. "Over some petty feud with Sylvestra?"

"You don't understand, Princess, pleas—"

"Then, help me *fucking* understand," I roared then threw the book at him.

He caught it and gazed on the page I had just read.

"Try to justify this to me. I fucking *dare* you!" The words seethed out in a raspy whisper, menacing and confrontational.

Rose stomped in along with Elliot, both demanding what was going on. I marched to Fristlyn's side, and only then did I muster up the courage to look into his tear-filled eyes. I broke his heart, but I didn't care. *He* didn't care back then, why the hell should I care now? "You told me I was just naïve, that I needed to learn how things worked before," I continued. "Was this how the world worked with magic around? Was betraying those closest to you and causing the deaths of Lord knows how many people part of witchcraft curriculum? Sylvestra and Amilyana surely didn't think so!"

Fristlyn's lip trembled, and I shot a glance over to Elliot, who stared confused, wide-eyed, longing to know what was happening. Why the person he saw me bond with so closely was being treated as an enemy. "I should've left you in that *fucking* cage," I whispered.

I stormed past the elf and grabbed Elliot's hand, dragging him with me to as far away as I could get from the Spider King.

I refused to have no one; Elliot would have to do.

CHAPTER 34

ELLIOT AND I SAT AT THE GAZEBO JUST OFF TO THE SIDE OF Yggdrasil. Overlooking a small pond, I felt a sliver of peace in the mass of rippling truth that had just revealed itself.

Elliot, of course, probed me for answers, and I was stunned I didn't receive any, "I told you so's" of the sort. In fact, I was irritated when Elliot took Fristlyn's side. Going on about how if he was cursed, and the only way to break his curse was to change, then that must've meant he was filled to his limit with remorse. The joke was on me for telling Elliot the whole story. Broken curse or not, though, it didn't matter. Fristlyn's allegiance to the opposing side of the war didn't matter; what mattered was his crime.

Fristlyn's betrayal, though, was only the surface of a sea of mind-crippling truth. I started ranting to Elliot about being raised with no dates, no days, and the only years I got to keep track of were my own. I told him how Sylvestra's journal mentioned, *Month nine of the year 5,999*, a specific date that I never got. What year were we in? What was the time? I lived in what was known as the Steam Age of Relica, a name it received due to the worker colonies such as Metsa tinkering with materials that filled the air with smoke. That was all I had. Between the end of the Witches War to some time when my parents' elders were babies was a black mass of unanswered questions; anything before this time left in darkness, never to be touched by mankind. I hated it all.

"The seventeenth day of month seven, 9,854," Elliot whispered into my ear as he wrapped an arm around me. "Mayor Steamsin taught me how to read calendars when I first arrived in Metsa. This is actually the norm! It appears your father didn't want people knowing how to read time."

A meaningless gesture that put a smile on my face. I didn't get angry at Elliot's words about my father; I'm honestly not shocked at this point. Elliot took the time to explain it all to me, which I appreciated. Twelve months in a year, each one containing forty days, and the years counted from when Yggdrasil was first discovered. How did society live without this reference? I would never learn. I felt crippled without it. Crippled without Fristlyn, as well.

"Did she die peacefully?" Elliot asked me; no need to request further information, I would be stupid to do so.

"No," I admitted. Lying wouldn't benefit either of us, why bother? "She died fighting, though. She stepped up when you weren't there to protect her. I couldn't protect her, so she did what she could to protect herself. She started this voyage as a housewife but went down a soldier. Her specialty was keeping me grounded. She held me and comforted me more times than I did for her. Then she...was mutilated. Torn to ribbons by a beast you should be lucky to have missed. Her last words..." I trailed off. The subject was tender, and my own wounds were fresh still. It was better than talking about *the king*, though. "Her last words were my name, begging me to help. By the time I got to her, there was little left. I burned her corpse and left a memorial."

Elliot began to sob. I suppose in my dark state of mind, I gave a little too much detail, but he deserved to know. It was clear he didn't love Barrea the way she loved him, but he still *did* love her.

She was there when he came home from a long day; there for him when he woke up.

"She was my best friend," he said between sniffs. "I should've treated her better."

"You should've been honest with her," I interjected. He treated her...sure, not the best. But it wasn't awful. I'd seen awful, and that wasn't it. Not superb, but not terrible. Not even mediocre— more than I ever received.

"You should've told her how you felt when you learned I had arrived. She would've been heartbroken, but she had a lover's mind."

"You didn't know her like I did," Elliot managed a laugh. "She would've rooted for us, I promise that."

"How did you two meet?" I asked, ignoring his mention of "us." I had been wanting to know for a while, but I wanted to know more. "Start from when you were sentenced to exile."

Elliot scoffed. "Not sure we have enough time."

"We've more than enough," I confirmed.

Elliot sat back, leaning his back on the wall of the gazebo, and stared off at the lake.

"I was to be beheaded. Lord Sumner just...just couldn't do it. This was near the beginning of his decline; he hadn't become the complete monster you described. So, instead, he imprisoned me upon a ship and asked them to ship me off to the closest island to fend for myself."

My eyes rolled to the side as I tried to process that. "The closest country was Linlecross, not Metsa?"

"Linlecross is close only to Mazz'Ra as a whole; Metsa was much closer to Sheol. It's how Metsa was discovered for the Trade Circle. Soen kept it to himself before all that. Metsa's advancement in weapon technology—think of your crossbow—put them on the map."

I nodded and tried to ignore my own idiocy. Some princess I was.

"So, they dropped me at Metsa," he continued. "I lived a similar lifestyle as your girl did. Marla, I think? Soen found me by accident, and just conversed with me and asked how my day was. He's really a different leader than your dad, that I can assure you. I told him my story, and he got me a job at the Metsa Guard. I was given a dorm, warm food, and one day at Doc's Docks...I want to say maybe three years after I arrived, I met Doc's chef."

I grinned, loving the beginning of any good love story. "Barrea," I whispered.

"Yep. She and I married a year later. I was so content until..." he trailed off.

My fingers twitched, curling in my hand as I knew what the end of that sentence was going to be. I wanted to say it, but I waited. Patient as I could be, I wanted him to say the words.

Elliot hid his face in his hands, letting out a sigh before showing his face once more. "Then you came back and I realized I didn't love her the way I should have."

This was the first time Elliot said something like that to me that didn't boil my blood. He mourned over his wife, recognized that Barrea held significance in his life. I never truly hated Elliot for his passes at me, though I almost did. I just hated he wasn't respectful; he never sat down and had the conversation with Barrea she deserved. I liked to think he did through me just now, as he poured his feelings out and finally opened up about his past.

It brought me happiness to know Elliot's life wasn't hardship after hardship for too long, as joyful as I could be. Fristlyn was carved into my thoughts, and whenever his face popped into my mind, I just wanted to kick and scream. I thought what I felt with Elliot back in Metsa was betrayal, but nothing compared to the secrets Fristlyn hid from me.

Elliot was looking at me as I was deep in thought. I hadn't noticed, but those overcast grey eyes were staring into my own; a shimmer of light reflected off of them as he locked on. A faint gust seeped through his hair as he inched closer to me. I did and

I didn't want it, but I had to feel something. I felt numb as if what I had just learned about Fristlyn manifested into a haunting being. I was isolated and alone; Amilyana didn't know me well enough to care, and Rose was Fristlyn's right hand. Elliot was all I had.

So I inched closer, as well. I studied his face as he leaned in, noting every blemish, every scrape, every prominent cheekbone. The closer he got, those characteristics started to phase, until he was just the boy I remembered, the boy I fell in love with all those years ago.

I didn't even notice, but I was leaning, too. I slouched over until I felt the soft, tenderness of his chapped lips pressed against my own. My first kiss in thirteen years.

And I felt *nothing*. No sparks, no binding passion like the first time we kissed. *Numb.*

I opened my mouth with his and grabbed his cheeks in the process. I was desperate to feel something, so I tried to force it; suck whatever indication of hope, of love, but there was nothing. My fingers were no longer tight, and my gut didn't feel fluttery with a thousand butterflies. No emotion, no love, no fiery passion constricting us as one. I wanted to cry yet again; what happened?

He pulled away, and once I opened my eyes, he was the full-grown man I had known him as after all this time. He wasn't the boy in the rose bed. He was the man I couldn't trust with my heart.

A deep feeling of concern flooded me as his face lit up; happy, smiling as he showed his crooked teeth, and stuttered breathing. Elliot was absolutely floored with emotion, yet I was numb.

I found myself silent, unsure what to say. Was I supposed to mimic his reaction to appease his ego? No, then, I could easily find myself in a relationship that I didn't want.

God granted me a blessing in the form of Amilyana as she approached the gazebo. Her orange dreads swayed from left to right as she glided effortlessly toward us, stopping at the entrance.

"I hope I'm not intruding," she said as she stared down at us with judgmental eyes.

You most certainly are, but I'm thankful for it.

"But I need to speak with the princess."

I looked back and forth between her and Elliot and was all too happy to stand and walk toward her. She was my savior in what was about to be a heart-breaking, awkward conversation.

I told Elliot I would get back to him later, which was a lie. I was already planning what I was going to do in terms of avoiding having to reject him. Then, I damn near ran out with the High Priestess.

I HADN'T REALIZED how much I was picking at my fingers before Amilyana pointed it out. From the time I left Elliot at the gazebo to now walking up the stairs that wrapped around Yggdrasil, I chipped away at the nails and the skin around until it was torn and frayed. I just wanted to feel something, to give myself any indication that I was human.

Elliot and I bonded, reestablishing our connection once again. Why didn't I feel anything? Why did I lean in to kiss the nineteen-year-old boy but opened my eyes to the thirty-two-year-old man? What changed?

Amilyana begged me to stop, and I did. However, I found myself scratching the skin of my neck till it was raw instead; she noticed that, too. When she noticed my fingers, she was stern in asking me to stop. When I transitioned to itching my neck for seemingly no reason, she just looked concerned and kept quiet.

Instead, she talked lightly to me about other things. First, she chastised me for throwing the book about Fristlyn at him; gave me a minimal lecture about how she didn't give me texts dated back nearly four thousand years ago just for me to disrespect them. I apologized, though that only made me scratch harder.

She then gave me a rundown on the Ritual of Imprintation; a dance she called it, and one I'd have to do if I wanted to gain entry into the tomb. She said I'd have to do it with an Hourglass-Born being or with someone of magical practice, though she made it clear it couldn't be her, telling me the story of how she imprinted on her wife during their wedding.

This left Fristlyn, as Rose was *technically* just a spider, which disgusted me. My hand fell to my side as we continued up the stairs, passing huts built into the branches and leaves. Amilyana gave a grin and stopped us both for just a moment.

"Have you spoken to a doctor about that?"

"About what?" I asked, not paying complete attention. My eyes were drawn to lavishly carved huts. Far more than just wood and nails, I could tell the elves had taken extra care in shaping the wood, creating a sense of coziness and magic in what was to be their homes.

"You pick at your nails when you're deep in thought, or stressed, I have noticed. If that is stopped, you then scratch at a phantom itch on your skin. In times of great stress, you can't control your breathing, and your hand twitches maniacally in the process. Fristlyn told me that last bit; said he saw it quite a few times."

Of course, Fristlyn noticed. All he ever did was show concern about me. It mattered to me a great deal; even amid my anger toward his atrocities, I couldn't deny that.

"What are you getting at?" I asked, with a slight snap. I feared disrespecting a witch who specialized in dead things and demons, so I added a "M'lady," at the end.

Amilyana noticed and gave a brief chortle. "'M'lady' is right. Remember whose home you're in." She started to walk again and nodded for me to follow. "I meant your anxiety. You clearly suffer from it, and I was merely asking if it had ever been addressed by a professional."

"No," I told her. "It hasn't." My parents were far too busy to ever take me to the doctor, which made little sense considering we had one living in Sheol Manor—Dr. Roak, I think the name was. I never met him, sadly. My parents couldn't have cared less about my health growing up; mental or physical.

"Shame," Amilyana responded. "Should my wife, Theadalla, return, I can have her attempt a test or two. She is a healer and a damn good one. She was in charge of the medics during the Witches War. She won't cure it as she believes that sort of healing violates the mind, but she can help you cope."

"Where is your wife now?"

"Oh, in the tomb, actually. She guards my mother's Tears; I guard the tomb. She's sealed away in there, waiting for the door to be opened." That explained why she was so prepared to let me waltz in there; the poor woman just wanted to see her wife again. "You'll meet her soon if this ritual bodes well for us." Her eyes rolled to me again, and darted up and down, focusing on my hands which were now at my side. "You've stopped."

I didn't even realize it, but indeed I had. "Yes...I guess you kept me briefly distracted from my thoughts."

So that's what she continued to do as she told me the love story of how she met her wife as we climbed stairs. Amilyana had just begun studying necromancy, her first chosen school of magic. But both were apprenticing under another witch, the name of which she decided to keep from me. They started being together in early adulthood and married during the war. In a time of death and carnage, Amilyana and Theadalla made time for each other still. True love at its finest.

I was at a point in my life where I wondered if I'd ever have that.

We finally stopped climbing up the stairs and walked along a branch guarded by railings. At the end was a smaller hut with an open door. I got a small peak, and there was just a bunch of glass and vases, no bed or anything of the sort. It was dark inside, and it didn't offer the same cozy feel as the other huts did.

"Your hut is down there," she pointed down to the hut I focused on before while she probed me on my mental health. "But first I'd like you to spend some time here. Random little pots, vases, and various objects I bought for maybe three gold. Cheap, nothing special. When you're done, get some rest. We're doing your Ritual first thing in the morning."

"What am I to do here?"

Amilyana took a deep breath, letting it seep through her closed mouth which bloated her cheeks in the process. "Just let go?" She flashed a big smile and started to leave me with no actual answer but stared at me until I entered the small hut.

Closing the door behind me, I looked at all the cheap pottery and glassware. A small, yet gorgeous chandelier hung from the ceiling. Fake crystals, clearly, but still beautiful.

What I was to do only hit me when I looked in the corner and saw a thick branch propped against the wall. I picked it up, and a few spiders scattered around to the floor, disappearing through small cracks in the wood. The branch was heavy but not much more than my sword. Nice heft to it, I went to give a swing in the air until I noticed another spider, blending in perfectly with the brown wood. I examined it closer, no longer fearing the eight-legged creatures. Brown, hairy, with a thick thorax. It looked to be a more realistic version of Fristlyn when I had first met him.

"Fristlyn," I whispered. An emotionless void crashed down, obliterating my mind as I uttered his name. I was numb, again. No, I was always numb. I was numbed by what I had learned of my friend; numbed from Elliot's passion, numbed from the assortment of beasts that complicated my mission, my father, my mother, everyone who had ever lied to me, mistreated me, kept secrets from me. I couldn't feel anything.

My upper lip curled, and I felt my chapped lips stretch and tear as it did so. I would rather continue to feel nothing but rage rather than this emptiness. I wanted to feel *something*.

I shouted a hellish war cry as I swung the branch against a row of vases, perfectly lined on a vanity counter. The shattering was a satisfying symphony to my ears, so I roared and slammed it down on the broken pieces, crushing them down to nearly nothing. I lost control at that moment. A cluster of cracked pots and bowls were shoved back into the corner, dusty and untouched for years, it seemed. Some were large, others were smaller though bigger than the vases I had just brutally beaten. As tears started to stream down my cheeks, I groaned into a wail as I smashed them all with the branch. Broken pieces of ceramic and glass littered the floor as I broke literally everything that this hut had to offer.

Finally, I looked up at the gorgeous chandelier. Still beautiful, still fake. A lie, not what it was at first glance. I could feel my livid being seep through my eyes, through every scrape, every cut. I gripped the branch harder, feeling the wood poke into my hand, which only spurred me on.

A blink and it was over. The chandelier was in pieces. Completely unfastened from the ceiling, and not a single fake gem remained intact. I wasn't ignorant as to what was wrong; having a meltdown was long overdue. No, my ignorance was toward why I hated the gorgeous chandelier. Fake but beautiful. It was him to me, *Fristlyn Everleef*, the definition of fake and beautiful.

Now, as I examined the remnants, I realized I was wrong. Fake and broken, and the shards of glass reflected my face. Fake. Broken. Destroyed. *Numb.* I wanted it to stop, and I damn near begged it, too. I wanted to feel something. I had felt anger, but it was gone. A few minutes of feeling angry and I was numb once more.

I tried to cry. This whole trip I had refuted the idea of being vulnerable, but anything was better than this dark, empty void of numbness. I dropped to my knees, defeated by myself. To me, I had doomed myself to a life of this feeling, of this mentality.

A knock on the door didn't snap me out of it, either. This wasn't a trance; this wasn't a spell. This was just me.

"L-Lass?" I heard from the other side. He was lucky I couldn't feel anything. Hate, anger, resentment, all of it had been put on temporary hold. I rose to my feet and opened the door, my fingers tightly wrapped around the knob as I swung it open.

There he stood, holding a green robe of some kind. Fristlyn started to speak, but he saw the chaotic aftermath behind me, and those ethereal green and purple eyes filled with fright as the branch swayed in my other hand.

"Believe it or not," I started, "this actually had very little to do with you."

"I..." He didn't even know where to start. "Um..." He kept making noises but couldn't speak. He didn't believe me; he thought this mess was all for him, but it wasn't. I was in no mood to ease his mind, though. Let him sweat.

"These are my royal garments," he explained, handing me the green robes. "It might be a bit big, but I figured you'd find more comfort sleeping in this than a shirt made of spider silk." His voice was soft and pained. He didn't believe me. He was hurt by the thought of this breakdown having everything to do with him.

I took the robes from his hand and let them unfold so I could take a look. I remembered those clothes from my dream state that Lorraine used to separate everyone. It was mossy green with a black centerpiece that buttoned to both sides of the green robe, a long train started at the waist and flowed down to the ground, just as mine had done.

I bounced my brow once. "Thank you," I told him, wrapping the robes around my arm.

"Ami left you dinner and a small journal that details the Ritual of Imprintation," he continued. "I thought I would still...explain." His eyes never left the broken shambles behind me.

I scoffed. "I can read just fine. Thank you for the robes," I sneered. "Maybe find something more constructive to do with your time. I have an idea; find a map and look up where Mazz'Ra is. Travel to Sheol and sell us out. You are a powerful being, I'm sure you can make it back in time."

Fristlyn's lips trembled at the words. I wished I never said them, but I had zero control over my speech at that point. Feeling like that, feeling the numbness, allowed me to speak without a filter. My words hurt, and while I was disgusted with him, he was still always on my mind. Hurting him wasn't my job, that was to be left for his guilt.

"I..." he started.

"Let's just...I'm going to get some sleep." I brushed past the elf, closing the door behind me. "See you at the Ritual, *Everleef.*"

I left him to wallow on his own.

CHAPTER 35

I WAS CAST INTO SUCH A DEEP SLEEP, ANYONE WOULD'VE THOUGHT I was dead. For the first time since being on the ship, I was able to sleep without anything weird happening; no ghostly version of me, no beasts attacking, no hallucinations. I did have a dream and I remember it vividly. I was playing out in the Sheol Courtyard; Mother and Father were both out there with me, drinking a blended drink and laughing at the odd stuff I did as I fluttered about.

The only thing odd was a woman, a woman whom I didn't recognize, but did at the same time. Her thick black braid was flowing down the entire length of her back. Adorned in the braid were some various pieces of gems and jewelry. I recognized her not-so-perfect teeth as she smiled at me while I played.

I didn't know the woman, but I somehow recognized her. She was the woman from the painting, the witch who stood next to Sylvestra. According to Amilyana, Sylvestra had imprinted on the woman, and I dreamt about her the night before my own Ritual of Imprintation. I liked to think she was watching me, wishing me luck for my big day. Whenever I had some coronation I had to go through, or some rite of passage any Prince or Princess of Sheol had to do, they would sit out in the courtyard watching me play. I dreamt of the best versions I knew of them, watching me and smiling.

The woman, though—while her long, black, sleeveless dress whispered against the ocean breeze, she herself didn't move. She wouldn't approach or be near my parents. She stood by herself and flashed a motherly smile at me as I played around the fountain. I wondered why she was there instead of Sylvestra herself.

She blew a kiss in my direction and that's when I woke up. No gasp of fear, no sudden jerk as I broke free from a nightmare. My eyes opened at a slow, consistent pace. Minimum effort, but they took their time. I had forgotten what feeling well-rested was like, and it was a feeling I never wanted to leave.

The previous night was a haze; Fristlyn gave me his robes, and I left him where he was, but that was the extent of my memory. Luckily, I made such a mess of the cabin I slept in and was provided with clues.

First was the grand helping of food on the end table just beside my bed. Not a crumb remained; I devoured the ham, assortment of fruit, and roasted carrots a little quicker than I was proud to admit. It reminded me of Barrea's cooking, each ingredient handled with care to make the one eating it feel safe.

The spider silk that made the temporary shirt was torn to shreds, which was the main kick my memory needed. It was a bitch to get off; my sword almost snapped in two when I tried cutting it from my body. The robes Fristlyn provided were more comfortable. Soft but thin, so I didn't sweat in my sleep.

Lastly was a book. It was in the hut when I arrived as was my supper. Barely a book, it was more of a pamphlet detailing the Ritual of Imprintation. The sight of it rushed everything back I had learned from its contents, and, with it, dread followed.

I was to share a bond with Fristlyn otherwise unattainable by natural means. The Ritual was just a dance, a dance I would have to perform with Fristlyn to a ceremonial song with a kiss near the end. It could be any kiss; lips, forehead, cheek, hand. The Ritual didn't have a preference, just that a kiss was needed. Not that it mattered, I could barely stand the thought of Fristlyn talking to me, let alone giving me a smooch *anywhere*. Whatever was needed to get the Tears, though, I would do. To return home to Marla, it would be done.

The pamphlet was written by Amilyana herself, and I learned why I didn't see a lot of texts by herself in the Library of Yggdrasil. Her handwriting was damn near incomprehensible, probably because of how fast she had to slap it together just so I would be prepared.

Amilyana had said my Ritual was to happen first thing in the morning, so I didn't waste time getting up. Though it was just us, I wanted to make sure I was presentable for an actual Ritual. The mirror on the dresser sufficed. I fixed any issues my bangs had and re-parted them with a comb that the hut provided. My hair, for once, was not a complete rat's nest, so I just tightened the spider silk hairband, and I looked good...enough. I picked up everything in the room that wasn't to stay; the plate with no evidence of food ever having touched it, the book, and the remnants of Rose's spider silk. I exited the hut and closed the door behind me, just as Elliot was approaching. His eyes sparkled at the sight of me, and I was left with an unsettling feeling in my gut.

Oh...that's right. Poor guy.

There was a time and place for everything and now was neither in terms of me rejecting him. He approached me with haste to take the things off my hands.

"It's a plate, silk, and a booklet," I argued as I held firm to the items. "I think I can manage."

Elliot let out a laugh and continued to pull, removing them completely from my grasp. "I don't mind," he declared.

I'm sure, but I do.

"Amilyana and Fr..." he stopped of his own accord and

reworded it to, "They're down there, waiting for you." Absurd. The mention of Fristlyn's name didn't bother me, just his existence, currently.

I let out a sigh. "Guess I should head down, then."

THE LONG DINING tables were placed in a circle with Fristlyn standing in the center. Everyone was there; Rose and Amilyana. I remembered this from the booklet: as though it was a wedding, witnesses needed to be present.

The High Priestess held out her hand as I walked toward the site. Once I took it, she ushered me to walk up on the picnic tables and back down into the circle. She really wasn't kidding when she said "first thing". I had only just woken up.

"We can't waste any time," she ordered. "So I shall give a brief rundown: neither of you has experienced the Ritual of Imprintation. This is good, as you can only imprint or be imprinted on *once*. So, in other words, I kindly ask you not to fuck this up." Amilyana's eyes were glued to me, and I was already failing with my thoughts being elsewhere.

Fristlyn called her Ami. Can I call her that? No, those two never got along, according to her. Fristlyn could be saying it to annoy her.

With my mind elsewhere, I had no time to be offended as she alluded to me causing everything to go south.

"Princess," she called me, and I snapped my attention toward her. "I know the Spider King can dance as he demonstrated..." she turned to Fristlyn and sneered, "at my wedding."

Rose let out a soft chuckle, and Fristlyn shrugged. There was a story there, and I made a mental note to ask her about it when this was over. "Can you, though?"

"Hmm?" I asked, still thinking about anything but this Ritual.

"Dance, Princess. Can you dance?"

I nodded. I was a princess, of course I knew how to dance.

Balls, preparing for suitors, and coronations; most of my child-hood was dancing.

"Good," Amilyana said. She began to circle us both. "You had no time to learn this dance, but neither did my wife when we performed it. I learned, as long as you feel a connection, the imprint will grow regardless. Just try your best. Now, let me explain what is going to happen to you, just so you can be prepared."

She was by me now, still walking. She patted my shoulder as she passed by and then continued. "You are going to share an otherwise unattainable bond. No mother and child, no brother and sister, no twin, no lover can hope to feel this close to some-one. When the Ritual is over, you will feel when the other is happy; you will feel when the other is sick, when they're hurt, or when they're broken." She stopped and shot us both side glances. "I'd be lying if I said I wasn't excited for the drama that is undoubtedly going to ensue with the two of you."

I couldn't help but let out a chuckle. I was a mess, I was numb. Fristlyn might go mad with such a bond. Let alone, he'll feel how I truly felt about him. I doubted he was ready for that.

"Now, approach each other," Amilyana ordered.

We did so, not even a whole arm's length apart when we stopped.

"Princess, repeat everything he says."

I looked into Fristlyn's sad, broken eyes. He wasn't looking forward to this. My current state of loathing toward him was something he would feel, and I started to grow somber at the thought. I may not like him the way I did, but I would never want to sentence him to this life of torture. He must've been thinking about what I said the evening before when I suggested he sell us out.

"This is a bond I seek," he said.

"This is a bond I seek," I repeated.

"I open myself to you, and I agree to let you in."

I repeated, but not after noticing his voice starting to shake. *Hold it together, elf.*

"Now, I ask you for this dance, so that our souls may be one."

I remembered this from the booklet; this was the only line I wasn't to repeat completely. "I accept this dance, so that our souls may be one."

A gentle stroke of a violin began to emanate from the world around us. I heard it, even though there was nothing there. No quartet, no instruments in sight. The music just began to happen. He placed his hand on my waist, still shaking. *Hold it to-fucking-gether, elf.* Last thing I needed was to get spun right into one of the tables and bruise my hip. His other hand interlocked with mine, while my other rested on his shoulder. The ethereal violin grew louder as Amilyana left the circle, and Fristlyn's grasp tightened everywhere it could.

A delicate piano chimed in; the music was beautiful, and I began to move with it as Fristlyn and I started to step. The longer we danced, the more intense the music became. What started as a slow, gentle ditty on the instruments slowly transitioned to an epic song of coronation; it engulfed my very being.

At a certain point, I no longer moved with the music, I began to flow to it, became part of it. Fristlyn would spin me, dip me, and at one questionable point, he slid me between his legs and shot me back up.

A high-pitched note of the violin vibrated my ears, and I closed my eyes to deeply appreciate the noise. Just me and the music. The song took form as it hugged me from behind, and I felt connected to everything the song was telling me. A tune of love, pain, and heartbreak all at once compressed me like a mother from the back. I missed this feeling, so much that I had to turn around and reciprocate.

At the open of my eyes, however, Fristlyn was gone. I was now dancing with a woman, another woman whom I recognized.

Sickly pale skin that made it easy to see her blue veins. Her long, semi-curly white hair…I was dancing with Sylvestra herself.

Despite her near-death-looking features, she was gorgeous. Elegant. Her hair flowed like wine with every sway we took. She dipped me and rotated me before bringing me back up.

Then she was gone, too. Now, I gazed upon the woman she stood with in the painting, the woman from my dream just before the morning. I was feeling connected to her, as well, and it started to kill me that I didn't have a name with the face. She was a stranger, and she danced with me as if I couldn't be a bigger part of her world. She whirled around me, and I felt her long, braided hair coil around my leg. She spun me to her, but she was gone. Fristlyn was back.

He lifted me by my waist and held me high up from the ground. At the sudden stop of my ascendence, I felt a searing feeling I could never describe. It was like being branded by hot iron, but it didn't hurt; it left a tingling sensation as it carved a magical mark on my face. A small circle. Then a big circle. Four lines on either side.

I started to come back down as Fristlyn carefully placed me in front of him. I was mesmerized. I had become a cesspool of emotion after feeling numb for so long. No longer empty, I was almost fulfilled.

Fristlyn started to lean into me, his eyes shutting as he was about to place his lips on my forehead. I knew him well enough; the kiss was going to be tender, and he was going to show how much he cared for me, even after the horrible things I had said to him.

I didn't want tender, though. I didn't want passion. A pit of numbness remained on my lips; the first kiss I had in thirteen years, and it left me with a void. I craved feelings, damn near praying for the pit to be filled.

When Fristlyn leaned close enough, I shot my head up and

smashed my lips into his, right when a beat of a drum dropped from the ethereal melody.

He was nothing if not aware, picking up on what I wanted from him. He tightly wrapped his arms around me and pulled me in closer to him, crushing my body against his as our mouths opened. I was taken aback by the absence of sexual tension; there was no deep-rooted passion there. Though our lips moved together ferociously, I didn't want him to undress me. I didn't want to feel that sense of love. I just wanted to feel grounded, and this kiss provided this to me for just a second.

I pulled away as the music started to fade, and we let go of each other completely. The Ritual was complete, and I didn't need to have any verification that it worked. I felt him; his mind, his body, his spirit. So, I screamed.

CHAPTER 36

A POOL OF MY OWN TEARS COLLECTED BELOW ME, DROWNING THE trimmed grass. "Wh-why do I *hate myself?*" I wailed, to no one in particular. Everything hurt; my heart, my chest, my mind. I felt my actual soul rip itself to shreds as I pulled at my hair, begging for it to stop.

Elliot jumped the tables and rushed to help me up before I smacked his hand away.

"Don't *fucking* touch me! I don't want you to touch me, I don't want you near me! *You,*" I gritted through my teeth. "You are the *last* person I want to touch me!"

I went mad, crying at the strands of ruby hair that fell from my hands as I tugged and pulled and ripped the locks from my scalp.

Amilyana stepped in and pulled Elliot away, who stood, dumbfounded, by my focused rage. "Don't take it personally. This... there is a price," she said to Elliot, leading him out of the circle of tables.

He should take it personally! I don't want him; I don't ever want him!

But in a way, I did. I wanted Elliot to kiss me again, so I could feel nothing. I missed the numbness he brought. It was beyond better than what I was feeling now.

I turned to Fristlyn, and his reaction to the ordeal drove a blade of fear into my belly. He was stiff, frozen in place as he looked down at me. His face leaked with despair, as well. Did he feel the numbness I had been feeling? Or was he terrified he did something to me?

Amilyana's eyes locked onto mine for a split second, in which I watched as the pupils in her eyes grew to past the iris, making them look almost pitch black. She turned to Fristlyn and ordered him to tell me something. "Tell her the truth now," she said. She didn't yell, nor was her voice aggressive by any means. Just stern. "Save her from this."

Fristlyn hesitated but started to finally step back. Seconds passed, and he vaulted over the tables and fled the scene with Rose tailing closely behind him. Both were soon out of sight, curving around the other side of Yggdrasil.

Beaten. Flustered. Hurt. I soon lost the ability to speak, so I just fell to the ground completely and let out scream after scream after scream. Each shout was rough, rasped, and powerful. I could feel my throat give in, as it had nothing left to offer. Soon, the screams were mere breathless squeaks.

Amilyana rushed back and knelt to help me up. "Let's get you to bed," she suggested, but I slapped her hand away, as well.

"I do not want to go to fucking bed," I rasped. "I...everything hurts, and I brought it on myself! I've only ever felt numb for months, and even more so this past day. It started to drive me mad and I just wanted to *fucking feel again.* I begged to feel anything to remind me that I was human, but I just couldn't feel. I couldn't *care.* And now... I'm feeling too much! It's too much! Please, this hurts too much; I want to be numb again. I don't want to hate myself. I've never hated myself this much! Why do I wish I were dead? Please, Priestess, take this from me, I've changed my mind. I see that I was wrong now!"

Amilyana began to well up as I spoke. A high priestess, attuned with feelings so she can harness magic, could sense what I was going through. She brushed hair out of my face and held up my chin.

"Princess...you are feeling *him.*"

Relica itself went still, went numb at the sound of her words.

"Y-you-you mean..."

"Yes," Amilyana interjected, putting me out of my misery from speaking. "By the Hourglass, RoGoria, what did you think it meant when the book said you would feel an empathic bond? That no lover, no twin, no family could hope to achieve?"

"This...is how he feels?"

"Every second of every minute. Every minute of every day. Therefore, I warned you to read about his treachery while keeping an open mind."

I shook my head. "An entire race is extinct because of him."

Amilyana shook her head. "No one died, RoGoria. My mother, sister, and I saw to that. He came to us. He told us his mistake. That's why Sylvestra cursed him instead of executing him; he proved he could do the right thing. We arrived at Mang'Coal just before Eden's army did; we packed them up and moved them somewhere safe. Her journal didn't mention that, did it? I never read it. It's hard to touch anything of hers."

That rang true to me, a necromancer with ties to all things dead. Touching anything of her mother's would be Hell, I bet. She'd feel how I felt now, at this moment.

Sylvestra's journal mentioned nothing about saving the orcs. Only about what Fristlyn had done and his betrayal. No word on how, last minute, he fixed his mistake. That must've been what Amilyana meant just a minute ago, when she ordered Fristlyn to tell me the truth. He couldn't though; he was so busy holding himself accountable for his actions that, in that moment, he was focusing on the deserved consequences. The Ani'Mas King refused to seek validation of any sort.

271

Plus, I had said a handful of nasty things to him.

"You need a dose," Amilyana continued. "A dose of happiness, something to bring you joy. Think of anything or anyone, and I can make it happen."

I coughed up dirt and mucus, they splattered into droplets on the ground. "H-how… how can you do that?"

She faced past me now, gazing up. "Because we can, right? You can. You can allow her to talk to anyone she wishes?" Amilyana was no longer talking to me; someone was here. I saw Fristlyn leave, and Rose with him. I forced Elliot to leave. Who else was there? I twisted my body to see the white and gold clothes. The icy eyes. Tara stood with her arms folded, putting on a tough front, but I knew…she empathized with me. The only meaning for darkness with eyes so bright would mean she knew.

"Anyone," Tara reassured. "You give me the word, honey. You can talk, truly, to anyone."

What I needed most was a reminder. A reminder that I could feel love. Compassion. Something worth fighting for.

"Marla. I need to see Marla."

***

I WAS BACK IN BED. At the wave of Tara's hand, I was hugged by a few blankets, the weight of which pushed me down into a never-ending realm of warmth. I screamed every so often still, but as it subsided, I was able to pinpoint why. While I felt Fristlyn's everything; the screaming was from the pain I had caused him, the gaping wounds of my words.

I was bound to him, and I had to tell him it was okay. I had to give him credit where it was due, just like Amilyana did.

He never told me Amilyana and her family stopped it before it was too late. He never made any excuses; he focused on the topic at hand. Not once was there a justification. An admirable trait.

The more I forgave Fristlyn, the less it would hurt. The urge to drive my blade through my neck, to watch myself bleed out from the throat, subsided. It was like I had told him already, even though we hadn't spoken yet. We were bound; connected by an ethereal line forever keeping us close no matter how far. So he felt me forgive him, and he was able to feel better.

After managing about an hour without lashing out from the pain, Tara and Amilyana both entered the hut to check on me. They needed me to calm down before allowing me to speak to Marla; a rule I was all in favor of. Marla didn't need to see me in that condition; she had to be assured I was well enough to come back. I was told Soen would be joining the conversation, too. Which was fine, I needed to ask him a question or two, anyway.

"Could you give us a moment?" Tara asked Amilyana, to which the priestess scowled back at the mysterious witch. If looks could kill, Tara would be a goner.

"I am not letting you walk around unsupervised. You aren't particularly welcome here." Amilyana sneered at the witch in white and gold.

Tara rolled her eyes and waved her hand, the priestess vanished in a veil of shimmery, silver mist. She looked at me and flashed a face of slight regret. "Oof, *she's going to be pissed,*" she pushed, grunting the words.

Tara was trying to make me laugh, but I was terrified of the warlock's response, should she find her way back up here. Tara didn't care, though. Seemed like she knew she could hold her own if it came down to it.

"Anywho, I was asked to bring you these," Tara explained, and that same silver mist formed on the ground, revealing a large box when it dissipated. Nothing fancy, just standard cardboard with nothing fragile, demonstrated when she kicked the box toward me. It slid with grace across the smooth, wooden floor, and I peeled myself from underneath my covers to open its contents.

I sighed in relief at the sight of a new uniform; shirt, long coat, boots, and new pants.

"Soen bought those for you," she explained as she turned her back to give me some privacy. "Special ordered the coat, so, I'd say thanks when you talk to him."

I was quick to undress from Fristlyn's clothes. No disrespect toward the elf anymore, but it felt weird wearing his robes. I threw on the black collared button-up first; loose, thin fabric that allowed my body to breathe and give a bit. I never wanted to wear a corset of any kind again.

"I'll make a point to do so," I told her, as I grabbed the dark, chocolate-colored leather pants from the box. "Did you know I had been wearing makeshift shirts out of spider silk?"

Tara gave a laugh before she confirmed. "Hence the new wardrobe."

She was watching me then, even when I didn't know it. I felt better knowing that between her and Fristlyn, my chances of death were decreasing. I only wished that applied to everyone else.

I slipped on the black boots and pulled out the coat; it was a long leather coat with a gorgeous burgundy color and sprocket-styled buttons. It felt as if I was officially considered a Metsa resident, and the clothes made it hard to be away from my new city. I looked for a full-length mirror of some kind and was bummed to see there wasn't one in the hut. Tara told me not to worry and created an illusionary mirror for a bit so I could see myself in my new attire. I looked like a citizen again.

"One last thing," Tara said as she approached me, causing the magical mirror to vanish. She extended all her fingers out and pressed them together. Her hand was low, just past her waist, but the fingers radiated her smoky magic. She raised her hand, and a new sword appeared out of the mist. I gasped at the beauty of it. "This is a gift from yours truly, not the mayor," she explained. "Using the sword that almost killed that little girl is a 'nah' for me." She handed me the sword, and I was speechless at its beauty. The blade was thin but sharp, and the handguard replicated silver vines with tiny, rose gold flowers. Tara performed the same maneuver, and a black leather sheath appeared.

"Don't forget the belt," she said, pointing at the box. I didn't notice a belt but upon further inspection, it was in there, along with three full bolt canisters for my crossbow, and a new flintlock pistol.

"Are these from you, as well?" I asked.

"Nope, just the sword. Seems the mayor has taken a liking to you, that or he's overcompensating for something." I was doubtful Soen had taken a liking to me. No, if anything, these were an apology for threatening Marla's home life if I hadn't gone on this expedition of his. Still, it was a lot for just some off-color orders.

"I hope you like them," a low, smooth voice startled me from behind. I jumped and spun around, and there was that blasted perfect smile that made my own crooked teeth hide in embarrassment. "Well, you better. They were a lot of coin," Soen joked.

"I do," I said as I walked toward him. "I really, really do." I threw my arms up to give him a hug to show my appreciation; I passed right through him, though, and face planted onto my bed. I let out a yelp that was higher than I cared to admit as I plummeted onto the mattress.

"Oh, right," Soen said. "Sorry about that, I'm not really here you see." He stepped forward to stand next to Tara, though he asked her to give us some privacy.

Tara nodded and exited the hut without a second thought.

"Let me know next time," I grunted, pushing myself back up to my feet.

Soen gave a laugh and extended an arm out, looking in the same direction, and motioned for...something. Tears began to form as Marla entered the frame of view; I guess Tara could only keep a certain area open for them to talk.

"Mama!" she exclaimed in her cheerful, wonderful voice. She looked positively beautiful. Her hair was no longer matted and hung down past her shoulders in loose, tight curls.

We agreed she could call me "Mama" when I returned, but it was welcomed now. I needed to hear it, the reminder of why I was here. Even if Soen's threat was empty, it was a reminder of why I needed to succeed now. The only failure was death.

So I fought back yet another cry and just greeted her with a, "Hello there, sweetheart." The words stung my throat; I had never really called someone sweetheart before.

"Are—are you okay?" Marla asked, and though I hadn't been for the majority for the trip, I was now. Amilyana was right; I needed this. Marla was my dose of happiness. With her, there was no pain, no numbness—just a happy trust and compassion that kicked my heart into overdrive.

"I'm fine, Marla. I promise. We're almost done here," I told her. It was not exactly a lie. Being imprinted by Fristlyn made me a key to the tomb; we were, in fact, almost done. I just didn't know how many more creatures would be in our way, how many more tricks Lorraine had up her sleeve. "I'll be home soon."

Soen ushered Marla out of frame, telling her to go play. He reached over and grabbed a chair which I recognized; the cracked and knotted wood on the back indicated he was watching Marla in his office. I'm sure he was a busy man, so as long as she was cared for, it didn't matter to me.

"I didn't think we'd be seeing each other again so soon," he said then flashed me a grin. "So any reports or questions while I'm here?"

I began to chuckle. I was pissed about the several turns this voyage took, but I directed my anger toward anything but him. He couldn't have known. "Well, let's see. Barrea is dead. Died after taking charge while I was breaking down. Fristlyn is no longer a spider; turns out he was the Ani'Mas King I was supposed to be looking for. Galyn is gone, so sailing home might get tricky. Oh, and Lorraine has escaped. Oh! And she's able to use magic since the isles are a hotspot for magic. There's a lot of information you withheld, so might I ask why?"

Soen's face grew solemn at the mention of Barrea. He had to have known; Tara was acting as his errand girl this whole time. Surely, she told him. "Ignorance, Miss. I didn't think about the possibility that the Tears would radiate the essence, let alone be strong enough for the witch to bend it! I heard about the flesh fiends she sent after you, nasty fuckers. As well as controlling the ban—"

"How do you know what flesh fiends are?" I interjected. Now, he could've easily said Tara showed him what happened. If she can show us each other now, she could replicate the scene or play it as it was happening. Had he fed me that shit, I would've eaten it up. However, he became a stammering fool, unable to organize his thoughts.

A lingering silence emerged, followed by several uneasy shifts in his seat. His eyes blinked to their own beat, and they refused to meet my own. His hand switched between playing with his curly goatee and picking at the skin of his thumb, signs I was all too familiar with, a reaction I wouldn't wish upon my worst enemy.

"When I return, when I succeed," I started. "I need you to tell me everything. I'll say something I never thought I'd say: I didn't mean to trap you just now, and I doubt the information would benefit me, anyway. So calm down, and—"

"The only reason you all are there instead of me is strictly because I'm busy."

I shook my head. "You wouldn't be able to find it, anyway. While your intentions are to release magic back into the world *for* the world, Elliot had told me, it's still seen as a selfish act. Selfish acts repel humans from the Isle unless..." I stopped, killed by my own words. Our eyes met now, but he was no longer the anxious mess he was just a minute ago. There was that trademark smile, but there was mischief mixed within. "Unless you either are accustomed to magic...or an Hourglass-Born being."

"Because I'm busy. Because I'm busy. Because I'm busy." Soen's choice of words echoed through the hut around me. In my own

mind, they were bouncing off the walls inside the glorified tree-house. Aside from being the Mayor of Metsa, he was babysitting Marla for me. He was, indeed, busy, so is that all that kept him from coming here on his own? If so, what is he? Or what does he know how to do?

"I'll tell you what, Princess," he continued, standing and pushing the chair away. "When you return home, allow me to take you out for a drink." He paused and shot me a wink. Politician of secrecy or not, I was not about to deny the fact his wink made my heart skip a beat. "I'll tell you my own story. We need to talk when you return, anyway. Seeing what I've seen of you handling things out there, I think Guardswoman is a bit...beneath you."

So much flattery in such a small speech. My cheeks were hot and my breath shook between a possible job offer as well as...

I shook my head. I couldn't get distracted. "Yes, to both of those." I was blasted with a fluttering feeling in my gut. I was already getting distracted. I stood up and shook the butterflies away. "Now, I'm sure you have more work to do," I continued. I only just then realized I had a big, dumb smile on my face that refused to fuck off. "And I have a rather uncomfortable conversation to have. Some shit to eat, if you will." Fristlyn's face never left my thoughts, and it was time I got this over with.

"Of course, of course. I'll tell Marla you send your love. See you soon, Prin—RoGoria."

He vanished with a slow dissipation of smoke, and I grinned at his quick change of words. Soen had just become the only person to put a stop to my former title.

The grin faded with utmost haste, however. We had to be off, but I refused to leave before I tied up all loose ends here. I had an apology to make.

CHAPTER 37

FRISTLYN WAS OVERWHELMED WITH NEGATIVE FEELINGS. I DIDN'T need to find him or chat with him about it to know; I was cursed with feeling it. As I hunted the grounds for the Spider King, I found myself playing with my bangs and picking at my finger-nails, even though I was not feeling anxious in any way. It was all him.

I started with the gazebo around the lake, but only Amilyana was there. She hadn't seen him since the Ritual, so I continued my search. I would've asked why she was so cold to Tara, but that was truly none of my business; the last thing I wanted to do was to disrespect a high priestess, especially one who demanded respect the second you made eye contact with her.

Shortly after, the picking at my nails, the twirling of my hair, it all stopped. I was washed over with a sense of feeling blue and found myself fighting the urge to cry. Had I done this? Had my hurtful words cut so deep that I was punished by feeling the consequences?

This feeling didn't last as long. Soon, my blood began to boil; I clenched my fist and wanted to hit something. *Someone.* Did Fristlyn want to hurt me? My last words to him were cruel, sharper than a blade belonging to a renowned war hero. I sliced him deep, but I didn't know. I didn't know he tried to correct his heinous crime because he neglected to tell me. Now, I was feeling his rage; his urge to hit someone.

I'm sorry, Fristlyn. I'm sorry.

I apologized in my head over and over again, hoping he'd feel it. I fell to my ass, sitting behind Yggdrasil entirely where I saw him run to originally. He felt me get over my hatred toward him before, I could sense that, so I begged for him to feel my sincerity as I apologized.

I'm sorry. I'm sorry. I'm sorry. I'm sorry. I didn't know...I'm sorry.

"Do you want me to stay away from you, lass?" Fristlyn's voice punched me from the inside. My breathing staggered, taken aback by his ability to communicate. Could I do it, too? Had I already done it? Did I just have to think?

No, I'm looking for you.

No answer, so I tried again. *No, I'm looking for you.*

Still no answer.

"Your boyfriend's a bit of a dick, isn't he?"

He was with Elliot, but I still had no idea where. I started to hear shouting, and I slammed my eyes shut as Elliot's voice ripped through my ears. He was yelling at Fristlyn to stay away from me, and my war drum heartbeat overpowered the one I felt from Fristlyn. Just when I thought Imprintation was more of a curse, it hit me that this wasn't part of the telepathy; I was hearing Elliot.

The debate was faint but happening right behind me. Both were inside the Library of Yggdrasil, so I flew up to my feet and sprinted around the massive tree.

The two squabbling men were the first thing I saw when I entered the dark, well-kept archives, standing by the desk I read all my books at, shoved between two bookcases. I noticed the only thing that was out of place; the cloth that hid the painting above the desk was in Fristlyn's hand and hung down to the ground as he gripped it tightly. He was the first to notice me.

I didn't have to look at him to know he saw me; the second I was within sight, I felt a brief rush of happiness as if I was pleased to see myself. He knew why I was there, why I was looking for him.

Elliot turned to see me, too, and as upset with him as I wanted to be, I had to realize he was looking out for me.

"Let's ask her then, shall we?" Elliot's words packed a hit; the ferocious tone didn't sit right with me at all, but I allowed him to approach me, anyway. "You want him to stay as far away from you as humanly possible, yes?"

I shook my head.

His mouth filled with his own shit when he realized the line he crossed. He knew I didn't like to be a damsel in distress, a woman to fight for, regardless of how true that had been before.

Elliot looked back at Fristlyn, who just fired back with a displeased raise of his brow. "I'm sor—"

"Apologize later," I interjected. I reminded myself to give the slightest of slight smiles. Minimal effort to relay that there were no hard feelings. "We need to get a move on here soon. May I speak with the spi...Fristlyn, I mean, alone?"

Elliot's focus swayed between the two of us before he nodded with a sheepish movement. His ear twitched, and I saw his actions for what they truly were. Our kiss was dead, void of any love that he hoped I would feel. Then to watch me kiss Fristlyn during the Ritual. I could feel the black hole of envy even as I stood a few feet away from him.

Jealousy. Elliot was damn near green. I really couldn't put off my talk with him any longer; he deserved to know how I felt. Now wasn't the time, however, and he exited Yggdrasil with his head hung low.

I walked over to Fristlyn, who I could now see was choking the life out of the cloth. His hand shook, his eyes were bloodshot and puffed, so I turned and gazed at the painting the cloth hid for my answer as to why, and my heart shattered.

An oil painting, in which Fristlyn was depicted wearing white robes. Same cut and style to his green ones, with a buttoned chest piece that married the two sides of the robe together, and a long train. This train however was bordered by a flowery lace, similar to the train on his current shirt now, just minus the ruffles. Donned with jewelry, specifically a necklace that replicated a star and a crescent moon. His feet were bare and his hands interlocked with another.

The man beside him was quite the different-looking specimen. A hooded shawl wrapped around his neck and hung down, but his chest was shown, though covered in bandage wraps. As were his wrists, ankles, and hands. Arms and legs bare, as were certain parts of his chest. His most notable feature, however, was the mask he wore: silver with what looked like the bottom half of a skull. One tarnished sprocket was welded to the side of it, and a chain moved from the center of the gear and was hooked to one of the mask's teeth.

"Stygian," I finally said. I didn't ask, just stated. It was clear as day. I turned to Fristlyn, whose lip was quivering at the very mention of the name. "Sylvestra's book said you were lovers, but it was deeper than that, wasn't it? He was your husband, wasn't he?"

Fristlyn gave a single nod and choked as he tried to speak.

I couldn't put this off anymore; I pulled him into an embrace. Not formal, but not casual. I hugged him just as a sister would.

"He's the reason..." Fristlyn started, stopping just for a moment to truly collect himself. "He's the reason I reported my wrongdoings to Sylvestra and the High Court."

"Did...did he die during the genocide?"

Fristlyn gave a slight chuckle. "He can't die. He's not necessarily alive now, but he can't die, he...he goes where death happens. Ascended into a primordial entity, as was his calling. Lass, have you ever wanted to see someone so bad, and when you finally do, they're the last thing you ever hoped to see?"

"No. Typically when someone is the last one I want to see, there isn't a desire to see them at all."

"Try to picture this as best you can, then you sell out your allies, and it risks the death of hundreds, as I did. You are in the middle of planning the assault as you were commissioned to do; creating cages for children, sharpening swords for soldiers to butcher fathers, even mothers. Amidst the commotion, you see the purest love of your life after not seeing him for nearly fifty years. Your heart is missing a piece, and you know he was the piece that was obliterated.

"So, while you're planning this assault...this slaughter, you finally see him. You make eye contact with him. And he looks at you like you're a *monster*. Like you're the pure filth of Relica, a glitch from the Hourglass itself. The one you love, the one you promised to love be it while he's sick, or hurting, and so on. And he looks at you like he hates you. He looks at you like he wishes he could drive a scythe right through you, gutting you right where you stand.

"Stygian looked at me that way. Fifty years after he had to leave, I finally got to see him again, and he just wanted me to be butchered. No, he wanted to *be the one* to butcher me. I couldn't take it, so I defected, and went to Sylvestra and told her what I had done. Ami wanted to kill me, Alysn said I should be executed, but not Sylvestra.

"Sylvestra saw my face for what it was, fearful of death. Not because I didn't want to die, lass, no. Because that would mean I would have to see that face again. His face, gazing upon me with hate and the urge to damn me to Hell just out of spite and disappointment, regardless of if it was I deserved. I couldn't do it, lass. I couldn't see that face again."

Fristlyn and I were both crying at this point. Not even due to the empathic bond we shared; I could never imagine the brutality of how that felt, to miss someone so much only to see them again, after several decades of waiting, and only feel hate from the person that used to radiate love.

"That's why you were cursed to live life as a spider. Sylvestra wouldn't kill you; she was far too merciful to put you through that kind of torture?" I asked though the answer was obvious. I had heard so much about Sylvestra, the most powerful witch to exist, someone who could have that power and still be renowned for her decency was the true definition of a leader.

All Fristlyn gave was a nod as I pulled him in for another hug. I squeezed him gently as he began to weep, burying his face into my shoulder. He wouldn't say it, but I know he experienced that pain a second time through me. Neither of us had said we loved each other, but we did in a familiar way. He really became the brother I never knew I wanted, and he didn't keep it a secret that he felt the same way about me. Fristlyn had to watch someone he loved look at him with hate a second time, and I was the one to deliver that blow.

"I forgive you for keeping this secret, but sadly I not able to forgive you for your choices. That isn't my place," I finally said as he cried onto my new coat. "I get why you didn't tell me; I wouldn't have been able to admit it out loud, either. I hope you can..." I started to tear up *again* as his grip on me tightened. "I hope you can one day find the orcs who were saved and do what needs to be done."

We were in that position for a while, but I didn't keep track of the time. I rubbed my hand through his blonde locks and scratched the back of his head with my nails, which he seemed to enjoy, as he almost stopped crying immediately and let out small little moans blended with a few giggles. He pulled away, and I gazed at what was once a chiseled, annoyingly near-perfect face turned into a red, puffy mess.

"I love you," I promised him.

Fristlyn gave me a smile again, which I hadn't seen since I awoke at the riverbank. "I love you, too, lass." He pressed his forehead against my own, and I was engulfed in a tornado of happiness, mine with his own. Our bond strengthened just now, and I could feel the warmth wiggle its way back to his chest. I wanted to preserve this feeling, and I would fight for it just as I knew he would fight for my own.

We pulled back once more, and he straightened the collar of my coat and flattened it so it looked proper once again. "This was uncomfortable to cry on," he joked. "Next time I have a breakdown, maybe take it off."

I laughed as I noticed the imprints from the leather on his face, and replied with, "I'll try to remember."

He wrapped his arm around my shoulders and began to walk me out of Yggdrasil. The moment we just shared was nice, and I knew I was going to treasure it for a lifetime. But we had more work to do, and little time to do it.

CHAPTER 38

THE HIGH PRIESTESS RELINQUISHED THE STAFF SHE CARRIED TO Fristlyn, the one he couldn't stop staring at when she held it before. It was his, I learned. His weapon of choice. A beautiful brass staff with a blade cut into the shape of leaves. She also returned finger armor to him, which he jumped with glee to see again. Five rings that came out to sharp points, giving him another deadly weapon not centered around magic before we left.

Amilyana led all of us; all of us being myself, Fristlyn, Elliot, and Rose, past the gazebo to a dirt road that wrapped around the entire grounds of Yggdrasil. The path cut through two trees and was then lined by breathtaking lush woods on both sides; similar to the path that entered Yggdrasil but lacked the customized seasonal setting. She didn't trust us to walk right into Sylvestra's tomb, with good reason, I supposed.

Both Fristlyn and Elliot walked close beside me on either side; one in the hope of professing his love, and the other to make sure that wouldn't happen. Now wasn't the time. I had filled Fristlyn in on my kiss with Elliot and how it fucked with my mind. He still feels it every once in a while; a random shot of feeling numb. Odd, because ever since the Ritual I didn't feel numb anymore.

I was swimming in emotions, really. I could feel the self-loathing that Fristlyn feels toward himself, having yet to let go of his past atrocities. The orcs of his past were saved, but, of course, some were butchered before it was stopped. He may never forgive himself for it.

His self-loathing was no longer the dominant feeling, though. For the most part, I felt his warmth. The happiness he gained after I reaccepted him into my life. I had only been mad at him for about a day, but to him, it felt like forever. I curled my arm around his and leaned my head on his shoulder, but he uncoiled his arm and instead pulled me in entirely, which got quite the heated reaction out of Elliot.

Elliot hated how close Fristlyn and I had become; he hated seeing even it more since we exited the archives of Yggdrasil, closer than ever. Fristlyn held me then, too, and Elliot looked like a sad mutt whose chew toy was taken away. Of course, I knew that wasn't the case. I had yet to talk to Elliot about our own moment. I'd have to eventually, but as our mission was beginning to near its end, we had to stay focused.

"Princess, up here if you don't mind," Amilyana's voice shattered the awkward silence.

I looked up at Fristlyn who just nodded and slid his hand down to my back and nudged me up toward the high priestess. I hadn't realized how far ahead she and Rose were; I had to run a slight jog to catch up.

"Yes, Priestess?" I asked.

"Oh, no," she chortled. "None of that. Just Amilyana is fine. Ami, even."

"We thought you could use a break," Rose chimed in as she twisted her neck back to the boys that followed, "from the silent battle for your affection."

I let out a singular "ha" and looked back myself. "More like a slaughter. Fristlyn and I share a bond deeper than anything Elliot and I could've felt. I need to talk to the poor captain soon, though."

"Agreed," Rose said. Her monotone voice was stiller than the silence between the men. Surely, Fristlyn was able to get her to laugh every once in a while.

Rose looked back to Fristlyn and then to me; straight forward eye contact between the two of us. She blessed me with a smile, and I found it unfair how straight her human teeth were despite Rose not being an actual human herself.

But she was happy; happy that I had reconciled with Fristlyn in the end. Despite her lack of emotion, she grew fond of me. It was clear, and the feeling was mutual. She was the one who carried me to the riverbank after I was wounded by the vuldoar, so I knew she cared on some level.

"Rose," Amilyana began. "Would you mind giving me a moment with the princess? I'd like to speak with her as privately as I could."

"Of course, Pries...erm, Ami." Rose retreated and moved back to Fristlyn and Elliot, who shared a looming side glance to one another. Best Rose be there; someone had to mediate the never-ending cesspool of testosterone. I could feel the tension brewing from here, and I hoped Elliot was smart enough to know he didn't stand a chance against the Spider King.

"Is everything all right?" I asked Amilyana.

"You want to keep magic locked away."

My pace slowed, and I gasped at the words as they crept their way into my head.

"By the Hourglass; keep up, please." Her words were cold; lacking the tinge of hate.

I felt comfortable approaching her. Amilyana and I had only partaken in pleasant conversation until now, so I worried if I offended her.

"How did you know?"

"Reading minds is a simple flick of the wrist; I don't even need to recite an incantation for it. I just think the words and it happens. I just want to know why."

I shrugged. "Call it human ignorance," I answered, honestly. "I don't even know how magic works, just that it's dangerous if in the wrong hands."

Amilyana nodded. Her head turned to face mine, and through her burnt orange dreads I could see the eyes of the warlock; deep pools of honey irises lined with a mystical blue-winged liner. Colors that I would've said didn't work with her light brown skin tone, but they did, regardless.

"You're quite right," she continued. "It is dangerous if in the wrong hands. Bending the powers blessed by the Faer-Folk, you could easily cause harm by it."

"I hope my decision doesn't offend you," I told her, nearly begging for a forgiveness that wasn't even requested yet.

"No," she scoffed. "Imprisoned magic or free, I still have access to my power. Just as Lorraine had access to her own. Your decision barely affects me. No matter what you choose, I'll be able to bring my wife, Theadalla, home."

"Is she trapped?"

"In a sense. She was to guard the Tears until a human such as yourself came along to open the tomb. You see, magic only has one chance. If the human decides not to release it, it never can be. No exceptions. So, if you leave the tomb after rejecting it, magic will stay imprisoned for all eternity, and Theadalla can finally come home."

I knew that Amilyana just wanted to see her wife again. However, her words cast a sudden pressure on my shoulders. All fine and good that Amilyana considered it a win in her favor, regardless, but I was making a decision for the rest of Relica's eternity.

It wasn't long before I started to bite at my lip and pick at the skin that lined my nails.

Ami's hand fell onto mine; pulling them apart from one

another. Following this act was a gentle pat on my shoulder then a slight rub.

Everything ended with a sudden halt, as Amilyana stopped dead in her tracks. "By the Hourgl—" her own words, murdered by the confusion that struck deep into her skin.

I saw it, as well.

In front of us was a wall of stone, and two carved, rock doors were carved into it. To Amilyana's shock, and my annoyance, the doors were already open.

AMILYANA WENT ON AHEAD, whimpering Theadalla's name as she sprinted into the tomb, and disappeared after she descended a long set of stairs.

Fristlyn, Elliot, and Rose stood just as dumbfounded as the high priestess, but I just stared at the open doors and fought back a fit of rage.

I was happy to be bound to Fristlyn, happy that he had imprinted on me. But the sheer pain I felt right after, the stomach-turning fire that brewed when I learned I had to undergo this Ritual with someone I, at the time, detested, it was all for nothing. The tomb doors mocked me with the draft that birthed from inside, and I wanted nothing more than to shout at God Himself for playing such a cruel trick.

Elliot began shouting at Fristlyn; the questionable bridge that was his mental state finally snapped under the weight of all he had endured; finding me again, the death of his wife, being on his own while I was always with someone, watching the woman he truly wanted pull away from him. Now this, the mission he was put in charge of possibly compromised beyond repair.

"You *fucking* did this," Elliot roared. "I just know you fucking did."

"Did what, lad?" Fristlyn fired back. "Opened a pair of doors?" The elf provided a mockery of a gasp. "The sheer gall!"

I groaned. "Boys—"

"You're up to something," Elliot leered at him. "You want the Tears for yourself!"

"What fuckin' sense does that make, lad? You've seen I already have my abilities, I'm back in fighting shape. What use would I—"

"Don't play fucking dumb with me," Elliot interjected.

"Boys!" I yelled again but was once again ignored.

"You need to back off," Rose stepped in now, and I was watching the group I trusted my life with begin to crumble.

Elliot fired slurs at her, only referring to her as an insect, which was quite an uneducated insult, and then proceeded to clock Fristlyn right in the mouth, knocking the Spider King back down to his ass.

Rose blew a fuse, and reformed back to her true self, the massive black widow spider; she stomped over Fristlyn and hissed at Elliot.

"Elliot, that is *enough!*" I screamed, but he still paid no mind to me. "You are after him because you're jealous; it's time to admit it! It's asinine, really!" Fristlyn was just a close friend, nothing more. That wasn't Elliot's business, though. Regardless of my feelings or Fristlyn's sexuality, Elliot had no entitlement to me.

I marched over to Elliot and went to shove him back, but to my dismay, I fell right *through* him. More like a ghost of Amilyana's conjuring, I passed through and showed no corporeal form.

They couldn't hear me, and they couldn't see me.

I watched, as Fristlyn got to his feet and punched Elliot in the nose. Elliot did more than fall on his ass, he was thrown right back into one of the trees that lined the dirt path we were on.

I started screaming their names, all of their names. But they couldn't hear me, see me, or *feel* me. All too wrapped up in their damn drama to notice I was missing from the group.

I scratched at my hands, not sure what to do, but as my eyes leveled back to the tomb entrance, I saw her. That woman again. With the thick black braided hair. The black and green dress. The bare feet, the gorgeous russet skin.

The woman who stood beside Sylvestra in the oil painting, who I had a dream of, stood at the entrance of the tomb, and was only able to offer the most astounding advice, "Illusions fail under your own awareness."

She vanished into nothing. A riddle, no, not just a riddle. A hint with the undertones of a warning.

This was a trap. *Lorraine's* trap. The woman told me I was under a spell, and then it hit me; that's why they were fighting. I just vanished into nothing in their eyes, and Elliot thought Fristlyn had gotten rid of me.

As Elliot collected himself from the ground, he withdrew his sword and went to charge both spider beings. *Illusions only work if you fall for them. It's an illusion; my being gone is an illusion.*

It all was a spell, another Illusion like the one I had back at our campsite. I wouldn't fall for it again, though. Not this time.

Even the context of their fight was wrong. As I started to notice, become aware of the illusion that was placed onto us, keywords began to change.

Elliot shouted, "You just want the Tears," but that wasn't what he really said. "You just want RoGoria." The spell was cast on all of us. Their illusion was that I was missing, but my illusion was them fighting about something completely different. She almost had us.

As Elliot charged, I withdrew my blade. My hand fit perfectly into the vine-styled, rose gold hilt as it might the satisfying song of metal whispering against the sheath.

"I'm right. Fucking. Here!" As Elliot's blade began to come down on Fristlyn, I heard the clash of metal against metal as Elliot's blade met my own. A crack in the air shattered everything, and I was once again revealed to them all.

Elliot's grey eyes damn near rolled back into his head out of fear, as I seemingly appeared from nothing.

"Lass," Fristlyn breathed.

Elliot shot back and dropped his saber, then fell to his ass once again.

We both heaved, gasping for air as the situation finally started to calm down.

Elliot's already pale skin became void of any color, any hue. Fristlyn's did, as well, when I looked back, just as Rose was reverting to human form. I returned my rapier to its sheath and extended a hand to Elliot. I had never seen the man as drunk in confusion before, drowning in a tide of his own embarrassment.

"It's okay," I assured him. "We're all fools."

He grabbed onto my hand and pulled himself up, picking up his sword.

I patted his shoulder just as Fristlyn patted mine, and Rose followed suit.

"I'm so sorry," that same silky, youthful voice addressed all of us, and we turned to see the unnamed woman standing at the tomb's entrance. "I'm so, so sorry."

She dissipated once more, just as Amilyana's screams shook the tomb's interior.

CHAPTER 39

WE WOULD HAVE TO SAVE APOLOGIES FOR LATER, AS WE ALL DECIDED to disobey the high priestess and storm the tomb.

As we charged down the stone stairs into the crypt, we were greeted by a stale, eerie draft that partnered with the fiery sconces which lined the walls to create a forbidden feel for any who stepped through. Our steps were on beat with one another; our march into battle as a group.

I wanted this all to be over. More questions sparked against the flint that was my skull, but I had no appropriate time to ask them. Who was that mysterious woman I keep seeing? Why help us then apologize for helping us? If you had to be imprinted on to enter the tomb, how on Earth was Lorraine able to enter? Who would've imprinted with her?

I told myself the answers would be wherever Amilyana was; my own motivation to run faster, push harder down the chilly corridor of Sylvestra's Tomb.

We ran till we saw a wall, and the corridor split off in two directions. We didn't need to worry about which way to go; one side flashed with lights of blue, green, and red, and the colors were preceded by the haunting melody of Amilyana's songful voice.

No specific lyrics, but a different tune beckoned a different color, and I knew Amilyana was using some powerful magic against Lorraine.

We whipped around the corner and were greeted by another set of stone stairs, we descended as quickly as we could. I tripped about after making the mistake of not lifting my foot high enough, only for both Elliot and Fristlyn to grab a hand and keep me stable. A small hiccup, and one that didn't stop us.

We eventually reached the end of the stairs and found ourselves in a massive hall that housed a battle between two witches.

Lorraine was levitated high in the air, and the hag combatted the necromancer in an equal battle. With the flick of the old woman's wrist, a whirling blast of wind knocked Amilyana hard against a wall.

Lorraine dropped, stopping on the rim of a fountain. Every-thing happened at once; I wasn't quite sure what I was looking at until I stopped to focus.

As Lorraine stood on the fountain, I noticed a gorgeous mural of Sylvestra painted on the wall behind her. The famous witch's eyes were hollowed out, and water poured from the cavities and flowed like syrupy honey into the fountain. The water glistened with flecks of blue and radiated cyan aura.

The Tears were not something we could simply *retrieve.*

"Shit," I heard Fristlyn gasp as he ran to a woman collapsed on the ground. I followed just as he knelt down and placed two fingers on her neck. "She's alive," he confirmed and proceeded to inform me that she was just knocked out.

Amilyana didn't go into detail about her, but I knew this was Theadalla. She wore a beautiful maroon dress, and her black hair was nearly shaved. Her face was aged but was carved with the innocence and love of a mother; Amilyana had said her wife was a healer, and she looked as if she loved to bring good health to all.

He stroked the healer's buzzed head and insisted Rose carry her off somewhere where she wouldn't be in the line of fire.

Elliot and I were prepared. My hands shook with no way to tame them as I realized that our turn to fight was now, but Elliot armed himself with his gun and fired two shots toward the old hag while I collected myself.

It would've been a direct hit, but they bounced off seemingly nothing when she put her hand up.

My jaw tightened, and my hands wouldn't stop shaking. I clenched them into fists and took one breath, trying to find my inner strength that seemingly escaped me.

"I love you, lass. You can do this." Fristlyn's telepathic words did more than boost my confidence, I felt a sudden rush of adrenaline fill my veins as my hand threw itself back and removed my automatic crossbow from its holster.

I took maybe two seconds to aim and fired what, again, would've been direct hits had the witch not deflected them once more. Attacking with range was not the way to go it seemed.

I withdrew my sword and charged the old hag but was suddenly frozen and couldn't move.

She was pointing at me with one, chipped, boney finger and flashed a grin with the grotesque, rotted teeth she flaunted before on the ship.

My body proceeded to lift at an accelerated rate as the witch levitated me off the ground, then released me. I began to plummet to the stone floor, only for Fristlyn to jump and gracefully grab me, spinning us around as he transformed one of his arms, corded with muscle, into a massive whip of spider silk the size of a tree trunk. He launched it at the witch, but the barrier that surrounded her blocked it from colliding against the brittle body she bore.

We landed and Fristlyn set me down and began to heave. No, began to grunt. He was hunched over and began to convulse as drool dripped down his lip. I called to him, even went as far as to approach him, but he pushed me back and assured me he was fine.

Fristlyn was right; I had seen this before, though I was playing with the line of consciousness when I saw it the first time; his iconic purple and green irises were overshadowed by the pupil, as the black expanded throughout his entire eye. Two eyes appeared off to the sides of his face, bulbous, and just as black as the ones before. Four more lined his forehead, two above each brow. Then the legs; eight dark brown spider legs emerged from his back, thus completing his full transformation.

I asked if he was okay again as he started to gag and choke. Rather than answering me, he heaved a massive sphere of web from his mouth toward the old hag, confident his power was greater than her own.

Fristlyn's attack was deflected, anyway, at the raise of another hand, but the Spider King just laughed at the blocking of his magic.

The silk fell flat to the ground and burned into a green-tinted smoke as it faded. I recognized this acidic spider silk; he used that to melt the vuldoar's face before. I was shocked he took such a gruesome approach to the old lady.

"Not a chance in Hell you would've blocked that, hag," he accused her. "You may be strong, but you don't have the power to ward off an Ani'Mas King."

Another spell was at work here, but it wasn't Lorraine's. It was Sylvestra's. A protection spell of sorts, hovering over the fountain that was Sylvestra's Tears, and it blocked any attack from breaking through.

It became hauntingly clear how intelligent Lorraine was; she knew about the barrier in place and used it to fool us into thinking she couldn't be hurt when she was hiding.

"I can't enter the barrier, lass," Fristlyn informed me, telepathically, as to keep his words hidden from the old witch. Our own upper hand; strategizing without her knowledge. *"A barrier that*

strong, to deflect mundane attacks such as yours and the captain's; it's not going to let an Hourglass-Born creature anywhere near the Tears."

I thought the words, *"Say no more,"* but wasn't sure he heard them; telepathy might be something I'd need to take the time to learn later.

I handed Fristlyn my bow and withdrew my sword and began to work up the courage to charge Lorraine. She was silent; refusing to say anything but mocked me with her rotted grin. I'd been mocked by many things since leaving Sheol; I was 'fed up with it. I took the time to learn what I could, to understand how this new world worked, and I was still treated as some naive and useless *princess.*

I roared as I charged her, jumping onto the rim of the fountain where the witch stood; I felt a draft as I broke through the barrier, entering a magically safe space granted by magic itself. I raised my arm and slammed my sword down, but to my surprise that didn't faze her, either.

Lorraine laughed as she caught my wrist and grabbed onto the hair on my head and pulled me till our noses touched. Her breath reeked of rancid meat; it tortured my nose as she breathed heavily into my face.

"You demonstrated a fear of water; a fear of drowning when the winged beasts attacked," she continued to taunt me. She was locked away in her cell, how was she so aware of all of this? "Well, seems only fitting then..." she growled as I whipped my neck to face the fountain.

She slammed my head into the water, holding me under by my hair.

I slapped into the water and felt my feet kick at the stone floor, but it was no use. The brittle old woman was overpowering me, and I heard her laugh as I screamed into the Tears.

I was running out of air, and my chest pulsed and tightened as the ability to breathe escaped me. I started to flashback to recent trauma, when I fell into the dark ocean water, only to be saved by Galyn.

But Galyn wasn't coming this time. I couldn't breathe. Couldn't fight. Couldn't win.

Blackness engulfed my vision as I started to run out of air, and I thought I knew I was dying. But something else was at work here, as breath returned to my lungs and I felt my entire world rotate and shift. I opened my eyes to an unlikely sight as I stared at the gabled stone streets, the extravagant homes, and the signs that hung from some buildings, announcing what kind of goods were sold within.

Most notable was Sheol Manor, off in the distance, looming with light and riches, and promising royalty.

I heard footsteps behind me, a clear high-heel clacking against the gabled stonework with a rhythmic persistence. I turned to face the noise and was greeted by a woman, the last woman I would've thought to have seen.

Her long, wavy silver hair. Her sickly completion. Her pointed ears.

Sylvestra approached me, and though I was drowning just a moment ago, her presence made me feel the safest I had ever been.

CHAPTER 40

IT WAS STILL NIGHT IN THIS FAKE VERSION OF SHEOL. IT WAS FAKE because I saw no boarded-up windows of old shops, and the roofs of the buildings weren't in disarray; no battered shingles, no broken windows. It was old Sheol; it was back to how it looked when I was just a child, before Lord Sumner drove it into the ground.

Fabricated by the most renowned witch in existence, who stood a mere five feet from me. Sylvestra's face promised love and kindness, but her attire demanded my respect. A sapphire dress with one slit off the side and a laced collar that went up and curled at the frills. White opened-toed heels to add to her already tall stature. She stared at me with a mother's smile, no, a *compassionate leader's* smile as she offered an elegant wave to greet me.

I was beyond terrified. I knew she wasn't a bad person, but everything I heard about her screamed supremacy. At the snap of her finger, I could be a stew of cartilage and blood.

"You have a choice to make," she informed me, and the sheer sound of her voice filled me with the happiness of a child on their celebration of birth. She tucked one side of her silver mane behind her ear; the other side was braided back and banished from ever hanging in her face. The former High Priestess of Yggdrasil strutted past me and looked upon the light that radiated from Sheol Manor. It was only then I noticed a train of blue lace start at a point on her neck and whispering against the slightest breeze as it extended out to the ground.

"You have had the misfortune to have had to make several choices already," she continued. "Some good. Some bad. But you're just a person; no one is perfect, so don't feel discouraged."

I was too fearful to say anything; Sylvestra's presence worried me into feeling like any kind of communication from myself would be disrespectful. Even if she wanted me to speak, I would be too scared of offending the woman everyone talked so highly of.

She looked back at me, nodding for me to stand by her. "Come."

I wasn't about to disregard an order from her, so I marched to stand next to her.

"It looks to be a lovely home," she said.

I grew solemn at the words. Sure, it looked like a lavish place to live, but I was hardly living when I was there.

"It's not home," I finally spoke. "Not anymore."

"No," she agreed. "That would be a good choice on your part. Living in the shadows, not trusting anyone during your first days in Metsa, also a good choice."

I tilted my head and offered a small grin, and she raised the bar by giving me a wide side smirk.

"You know about that?"

Sylvestra laughed. "A princess sheds her title and lives as a rogue hermit? Even in death, word spreads. I knew instantly you'd be the one to locate my Tears; it was just the simple matter of when."

"You're saying my arrival to Metsa was a prophecy?"

She snorted at the words. "Prophecy. RoGoria, there is no such thing as prophecy. No chosen hero. There isn't a single man, woman, or anything in between that has the power to dictate someone else's story. No, RoGoria. You are here because of your choices, and now you have to make yet another." The witch turned to face me, and her sapphire eyes buried themselves deep within my own. "So what will it be, RoGoria?"

I took a deep breath. Not sure what my answer should be. She wrote this spell, sealed her Tears specifically for someone like me to come release it. "I wanted to leave it imprisoned."

"So be it," she said as she lifted her hands, and began to concentrate.

"Wait," I stopped her, and then she gasped at me ordering her. However, she listened and lowered her arms. "I...I can't make this choice. I'm just a girl, a mere speck in a world far bigger than I could ever comprehend. I can barely follow orders without cringing at the idiocy."

"That's because you are not a follower, RoGoria," Sylvestra explained. "You're a leader, and a damned good one, too. I've watched you; the whole time you've been on the Isle, I've watched you. I've witnessed your refusal to give yourself credit where it's earned. You may not have noticed, but I have; you took charge when you were separated from your captain. And when you felt lost, you relinquished control, though briefly, to a woman who was in a more stable headspace than you. When that woman died, you honored her and then pushed on knowing you had a job to do. You went through an intense Ritual with someone you detested, for the sake of getting your job over and done with so your fellowship might return home.

"Your refusal to recognize your growth always irritated me. You aren't the hateful, dismissive, entitled princess you were when you left; you apologized when you were wrong, you forgave when it was deserved, and you assumed the role of a guardian for a poor little girl you didn't know. I did the same when I adopted Amilyana; it's no different from that sweet, precious life you have waiting for you back at home. The choices you have made are far greater than any princess. I would've assumed you were a princess."

Tears of my own appeared, and while I didn't fully cry in front of the high priestess, they managed to stream their way down my cheeks. Kind words coming from a now ascended being; it was the validation I didn't know I needed.

Sylvestra turned back to Sheol Manor; the light illuminated her sapphire eyes with a radiant glow. I noted her ears and how different they were from Fristlyn's. While his ascended high above his scalp, hers were much shorter; ending just below the curvature of her head. With every slight breeze, they twitched and perked as if the winds were speaking to her.

"So as queen, in my eyes," she continued. "What is your first order?"

I wanted it imprisoned, thinking no good could come from it. Lorraine was proof enough for that. However, she wasn't the only witch I had met thus far. Amilyana made deals with Nether Masters, beings of the spirit world, and even went as far as to make a deal with Hell beings, demons. Yet she continued to fight along the side of good. Ami's realm of magic was sourced through what was said to be the embodiment of evil, yet she bends her magic for the greater good. To fight for those she cared for, or for the people she had only just met.

Sylvestra, the most powerful witch in existence, stood next to me. A woman who mastered power, and knew what to use it for. If the world had magic now, people would rise to power. Rules would be made, laws placed to keep it from getting out of hand. It was basic politics, really. Rogue princess or not, I was able to see that.

I placed a hand on Sylvestra's shoulder and turned her to face me.

She cocked her head and gave me a grin.

"Release it," I answered. "Restore Relica to how it should have always been."

The witch's hand floated up and cupped my cheek; her thumb caressed the skin while she stared endearingly. "Growth," she said. "It's there."

The world around us began to shake as the sky started to crack like glass. Water seeped through, crashing onto the stone streets of Sheol. Soon, pieces fell which granted more water to pour through. The breeze that protected us turned into an unforgiving wind, and I felt myself start to fade from consciousness. Though blurry, I saw Sylvestra lean into me, and right before I blacked out, I heard one more request from the witch. "Try not to kill her if it can be helped."

CHAPTER 41

THE WATER FROM THE FOUNTAIN BURNED MY EYES AS THEY SHOT open underwater.

My lungs were filled with air once more, and though I was living out my worst fear, I refused to let it hinder me. Sylvestra herself believed in what I could do; she validated me more than anyone else had.

I swung my arms back and placed my hands firmly onto the rock rim of the fountain. I felt the sudden will to live stew inside me. I realized how much I hated losing, and I wasn't about to be defeated by the brittle, old hag.

Sylvestra's last words echoed, almost as if it came from the fountain and wasn't just a figment in my head. *"Try not to kill her."*

I would try my hardest, but hurting her was still on the table.

I lunged myself up and took a deep gasp as I was surrounded by air once again. No time to think, I had to act. I rammed my elbow back and felt it connect into a pocket of sorts; a cavity.

Lorraine let out a thundering cry of pain and fell back off the fountain.

I whirled around to see her screaming as she pressed on her eye, twitching on the ground as she did so.

I looked to the fountain and saw my sword propped up against the rim and clutched it in my hand once more. I proceeded toward the witch and grabbed her hair, pulling her to her feet. As her screams subsided, it turned into a ferocious cackle. As Lorraine's hands fell from her eye, I was met with a questionable sight.

Her wrinkly, near decayed skin started to flow like water; it melted down and soaked her ragged robes, which then also started to melt themselves.

As every detail, every trait that made the old witch who she was washed away, I could see that magic had been restored officially. Once her skin finished dripping onto the ground, I saw a woman rich in youth. Her wrinkled skin was smooth with some light blemishes. A freckle here and there. Her hair turned from her brittle, gray, straw-like hair to a luscious natural black, and it floated up as it tied itself into a long, thick braid. Her rags morphed as well into the signature black and green sleeveless dress that I had grown to be fond of when I saw it.

It was *her*; the woman from the painting who stood by Sylvestra, the woman who appeared in a dream but didn't speak, the woman who helped me break the illusion that *she* cast on us.

At the snap of her fingers, her braid was decorated with chains and jewelry, appearing from nothing. Most notable was her anklet, wrapping twice around her ankle and one singular strand that came down and looped around her middle toe. Lorraine looked almost god-like compared to us.

I stepped back, raising my blade not sure what was going to happen next. As her lifeless, bloodshot eyes reformed into a more human state, besides the unnatural gold color of her irises, she jerked her hands out toward me and chanted, *"Black Lightning, of the Faer."*

The words rang true, as her hands started to crackle with quite literal black sparks. As the roaring thunder she conjured plummeted toward me, I yelped and threw my arms up, tensing, and shutting my eyes, fearful of the pain that was about to be inflicted on me, though I accepted it was going to happen, anyway. I couldn't dodge it, not with how fast it came. After seeing the powerful witch she had been reborn as, I accepted my fate.

Though, seconds passed. Which then turned into what felt like a minute, maybe two. My eyes opened to a marvelous sight. Though her electric-based spell was wide and hurling toward me from a few directions, every strand of lightning stopped and curved and fed directly into my sword. My blade had become a conduit of sorts, and no matter how much power she would add to the spell, my sword lapped it up like a dog. Lorraine finally gave up and put her hands down, stopping the magic in an instant, though remnants of it remained on my blade.

The sword as a whole began to crackle and spark, emanating a black lightning of its own. I turned to Fristlyn, who was dumb-founded by the scene that just occurred. Then Elliot, who had less of a clue than the Spider King.

Then back at Lorraine.

"I see you're going to be quite the bother," she insulted. "Doesn't matter." She extended an arm toward me again, curling her fingers which then clenched and tightened around my neck. Pressure followed, causing me to gag and choke as I was lifted from the ground. Lorraine's other hand did the same, gripping around my wrist tighter than she could ever hope to do with her bare hands. After I was forced to let go of my sword, she spun around, dragging me through the air with her. I cut through the air and the velocity of it all was made apparent by the rushing wind as I spun around in circles.

"Lass!" I heard Fristlyn shout, but not long after the grip on me was released and I was sent hurling back to the ground, though I made impact right into Fristlyn's chest, knocking us both down to the ground.

As I choked for air, Elliot charged Lorraine, and while I tried to yell for him not to do so, he couldn't hear my croak as the pain in my throat ached to an extreme.

"*Infera, Faer of Flames. Corethias, Faer of Wind, work in tandem, the Faer Folk Way,*" Lorraine chanted, and a powerful whirlwind of fire emanated around her, and she launched the feathery magic toward the captain. With an impressive barrel roll, he dodged the attack but was picked up by another gust of wind. A trap and he fell for it. Any one of us would have.

Lorraine crossed her arms, and the next call of a spell would haunt me for the rest of my life. "*Corethias: Tomb.*"

Elliot was then put in a sphere of wind, which rotated like Relica itself though at top speed. Lorraine proceeded to yank her arms away from each other, tearing the ball of wind apart. The change in pressure was something we could all feel, as we heard several of Elliot's bones snap and jut out from his arms and legs.

I shouted his name, but I only hurt myself in the process due to the pain my throat had been through. Elliot's blood traveled great lengths, some of which splattered onto my face. He fell from a steep height, though Rose came from what felt like nowhere, turning into a spider and catching him midair, so as to not let him fall to the stone ground and crush what little intact bones were left.

Rose didn't waste any time. The second she landed, she fled the tomb and brought Elliot away from any further immediate danger.

Lorraine faced Fristlyn and me and mocked us with a clap. The Spider King was curled up in pain from the force of my bashing into his chest.

"A quick tidbit of combat," Lorraine said, though her words held hands with an unsettling giggle. "Enemies provide you all the information you need to win. The captain; hot-headed, and desperate to be the strong man attacked blindly with no thought...not a single strategy set; no plan. Simple." She nodded back behind us, to where Amilyana held her unconscious wife.

"High Priestess could've taken me down; she's strong. But too in her emotions. A surprise attack on her wife caused her to be erratic, and thus disrupting her magic, as well."

Lorraine fluttered toward me, kneeling on one knee at eye level with me. Her smile faded, and she stared me down with those menacing, gold eyes.

"Then there's you two. Princess, you were so ready to be the leader. I saw it; the burning determination. Yet because you're so naïve, no, *ignorant* to magic, you choked. You feared magic the second you saw it. Beautiful, really, as you're the one who freed it. You share a bond unlike any other with the elf, a bond I know all too well. You see, you're so new to this world; that the revered Spider King lost his strength over you. He didn't matter to himself, only you. So he took the pain that was assigned instead of yourself. Don't be hard on yourself; these weren't things you couldn't help. Traits you couldn't hide. This is just how you are. As a witch, I'm to take traits for what they are, and bend them to my will."

She gave me a small tap on the cheek with her hand, and I was so fearful of death I couldn't move. Couldn't retaliate.

"One piece of advice, RoGoria," she continued. "You cannot defeat me because you do not *know me.*"

Lorraine noted my breath. Not just uneasy by the chokehold she still had me in, but stuttering out of the same fear she exploited. "Not to worry," she assured. "Killing you, *any of you*, is not in my best interest. Should the aggressive man get some much-needed medical attention, he'll live. Just head the warning his injuries speak of; do not, under any circumstances, stand in my way. I have work to do." Lorraine whipped around and lunged her arm toward the fountain, and the water began to ripple out of control before it lifted from the fountain itself. The water took the shape of a totem pole of sorts, creeping up from the surface. As Lorraine released it, and the water fell back down, a deteriorated, beyond decayed corpse was all that remained.

The clothes the carcass bore were the only recognizable indication; a blue dress, with a train made from blue lace that descended from the neck.

"No," I managed to choke out. My voice rasped and burned with intense agony; I sounded as Fristlyn did for the first several weeks of knowing him. I couldn't remain silent, not when I was blessed with meeting the legendary witch herself. She deserved peace. I was unable to stop Lorraine though; the "no" I pushed out was the only word I could speak as the pain in my throat carried on torturing me.

"Put her down," Amilyana's voice shook the tomb, and was equipped with an unsettling, manifested echo. Upon looking back at her, I saw her dreaded hair float up as a cyan light swirled around her. Her attention was turned toward us, no, it was turned to Fristlyn, as if waiting for his input on what she was about to do.

He granted it, coughing up the words, "Do it, lass," which was all the high priestess needed to hear. As she moved her hands and hummed a tune, the blue light bent into the shape of a weapon, a scythe. She grasped the weapon and lunged at Lorraine from the other side of the crypt and almost sliced the witch in half, but Lorraine just chuckled, and became enveloped in a cloud of crackling white mist, and vanished, causing Amilyana to slam the blade onto the stone floor.

Fristlyn was quick to help me to my feet, and it bothered me for just a moment. He was the one who had a whole person slam into his chest, which not only brought him down but kept him there. Still, he saw me as a priority which is exactly what Lorraine used to her advantage.

I couldn't go on with that mindset, though. I wasn't going to push Fristlyn, or anyone, away. Not after I just started letting people in. So when he put my arm around his shoulder to hold me up, I let him and rested my head on him in the process.

Amilyana began to whimper at our failure. I heard her mutter under her breath, "How did she get in? How did she get in?" Over and over, she repeated the question, not clearing her mind enough to realize she gave me the answer days ago.

The only person who could unlock the tomb was a human, who was imprinted on by an Hourglass-Born being. The answer of which Amilyana told me when I first gazed upon the oil painting in the Yggdrasil Archives.

"Sylvestra imprinted on her; they shared a bond unlike any other."

CHAPTER 42

"I'LL KILL HER!" AMILYANA ROARED AS HER CONJURED SCYTHE disappeared, right before I could get a look at it. Its disappearance caused Fristlyn to relax a bit, so I took that for what it was. I needed him to be sharp and focused, not tense.

"We…" I tried to speak, though my throat burned. I coughed to try and clear it and croaked the words I needed to say. "We mustn't. Or, at least we must try not to."

"Well, what fucking sense does that make, *Princess,*" she sneered back, but I was not in the mood to be talked down to any longer.

"Mind your tone, *Priestess,*" I retaliated. A tone so abrasive even Fristlyn flinched a bit. "This was your mother's wish, from the great fucking beyond. I'd recommend we adhere to it." The growl of my voice only worsened the pain in my neck, but it was no match for the pride I felt in finally standing up for myself.

"You…you saw her?" The great warlock's voice quivered; her lips trembled as the very utterance of my words caused her to fight back a few tears.

I nodded, now putting my hand to my throat and applying pressure to try to ease some of the pain. "When she-Lorraine, tried to drown me. Your mother spoke to me, asked if it can be helped, not to kill her."

The high priestess covered her face, only to drag her hands down and wipe away the welling tears that were beginning to appear. "The two of them were very close. Damn, that's how she got in..."

"I'm confused, Ami," Fristlyn chimed in, his grip on me getting a bit tighter to ensure full security. "I thought a witch couldn't get in?"

"Sylvestra was oddly specific," I informed him. "She was so specific that she was vague. While her notes said a magic-user couldn't enter, it said nothing about a magic user who had already been imprinted, just that a human who had gone through the Ritual with an Hourglass-Born being could open the tomb. This applies to Lorraine, as well." I hoped they understood based on that description; there wasn't an actual *spell* that could be done to open it, but Lorraine didn't need one.

I felt a sudden wave of guilt that caused a whisper of uneasiness in my chest—it wasn't my own, though. I rubbed Fristlyn's chest, where his heart would be, with my only free hand; I made a note to ensure him that my own Ritual wasn't a waste later.

"Does anyone have any idea where she could've gone?" Amilyana finally asked.

"Metsa," I confirmed, without even a single thought. "She was accused of Necromancy there. The island sits on what was a confirmed magical hotspot before the release. It's safe to assume what she intends to do with Sylvestra's body."

"We better be off, then," the priestess concurred. "Bringing someone back from the dead...it will take hours. Even if she went straight there, we have a chance of getting there in time."

"You can't teleport, lass," Fristlyn reminded the priestess. "You said it was something a lazy witch practiced; that was always your opinion. We can't sail. We'd be dumb to think the hag would leave our ship intact."

313

"I have a ship."

"What then, lass? It took us a week to sail here, and she only needs a few hours."

A lingering silence was birthed in the air, only interrupted by the groans of Theadalla as she awoke in the corner, where Rose had placed her out of harms way. I watched her rise; she didn't put her hands out to lift off the ground but instead floated up to her feet. I observed how graceful the lift was, using nothing but her mind to do so.

Amilyana rushed to her, and between asking if her wife was all right and sneaking in a few long-awaited kisses, I thought about just how strong a witch's mind was. Or, rather, anyone with any sort of power was.

"What are you brewin' up in that head of yours, lass?" I turned to face Fristlyn; his grin knew I was up to something. The example of magic skidded against my brain like flint, sparking the only way I knew we could reach Metsa in time.

"You and Amilyana both know how to use Telekinesis, yes?"

"Yes…that's fairly basic."

"Tell Ami to get the boat ready," I ordered. "I'm going to go make sure Elliot is alive."

LORRAINE'S PROMISE that Elliot survived the injuries he endured wasn't exactly swimming in truth, only seeing it for myself would ring true.

I scaled up the steps and raced through the tomb, leaving Fristlyn and Amilyana to both tend to Theadalla and get Ami's boat ready. Elliot's status would be just a quick confirmation and wouldn't eat up our tight schedule. I just had to know, and it wasn't even for his sake; it was for Lorraine's.

If I didn't witness my companion be murdered in cold blood, then there was room for forgiveness. For redemption. Just like

Fristlyn's past mistake, he was quick to alter the outcome. It was all possible if he was alive.

I escaped the dark memories I now associated with the tomb as I found myself back on the dirt path hugged by woods. I was met by Rose once I exited the open doors to the crypt, who was relieved to see me alive, but I saw the fear in her eyes when Fristlyn didn't accompany me.

"He's fine," I assured her then filled her in on the small details of my plan that I was still working on. I was happy when she told me she'd accompany me; we'd need all the hands we can get. "What of Elliot? Is...I mean, is he..."

"They're tending to him right now," Rose confirmed.

I cocked my head. "They?"

"The elves. The whole *coven* is back because of the release of magic, restored to their former glory."

I nodded, forgetting the fact that Hourglass-Born beings were also imprisoned for the most part, minus a few stragglers that were left behind, such as Galyn. All those people got to live again because of what *I did.* I was lightheaded, overwhelmed by the thought of what would've happened had I stuck with my original choice. I almost cried with relief that I didn't have to carry that weight.

Rose ran with me back to the grounds of Yggdrasil, where I saw a small community of elves and witches gathering around Elliot's floating body in the gazebo. I rushed up to the witches and screamed if he was alright, only to be stopped from continuing by a few elves.

"His wounds are healed, but his mind is broken," they said simultaneously.

"What does that—"

"Coma," Rose interjected.

The elves would not let me pass, saying they needed to concentrate on finding the source of his broken mind. Losing Barrea was hard enough, and while Elliot and I had a rickety relationship, this wasn't how I wanted to see him.

The Witches of Yggdrasil were confident he'd be okay; confident he'd live. However, there was more bad news. His comatose state was due to undertones of magic, something Lorraine had hidden in her spell to keep him this way. This is what they had to cure, and when I asked how long, they told me it could be months. The success of this was completely up to me from here on out.

Once again, I found it hard to control my breathing. My fingers couldn't even control their movements as I ran my fingers through my hair and dug my nails into my scalp. Amilyana said it better than anyone, this was too much to deal with at once, and I was starting to crack under the pressure.

"Look up, lass." Fristlyn's voice sang to me, so I listened and looked up and straight ahead, toward the exit to the river that was just beyond the Coven's grounds. He stood there, just as I saw Amilyana dart down the path that led to the riverbank. *"Breathe with me, I know you can feel it."* As he communicated with me, I could hear his exhale and inhale, slow and deep breaths. I matched it best I could, and each breath I took was better than the previous. *"Just because the decisions are yours doesn't mean you have to do it alone. Remember that I love you, so let's get going."* I didn't say it, but, "I love you, too," was at large in my mind. I had hoped he heard it.

Just as Rose was tugging for me to get going, another hand rested on my shoulder, and I was blessed by a woman with short, jet black hair and deep-set eyes. Theadalla, who Amilyana said was quite the revered healer, arrived to help Elliot's broken state.

"Go on," she smiled. "I'll take care of him, I promise."

Rose yanked on me one more time, but this time I cooperated and raced through the grounds and down the road that exited Yggdrasil.

CHAPTER 43

It took longer than I care to admit to see Amilyana and Fristlyn working together, combining their magic at the riverbank. My attention was elsewhere.

Across the wide, calming river were the dreadful woods that almost took my life away, the same ones that took Barrea's. The woods of danger, death, and decay that beat me down until I was ready to give up, lacking the will to continue. Though something was different on a grand scale.

The dead trees that I had learned to fear, the trees who didn't protect me from the outside but worked hard to trap me inside, were now lush. Full of dancing leaves and blooming flora. The island was dead without magic; it couldn't live without it. Once again, I was given another example of the good I had done while stressing over the bad.

These were reminders I needed; the last thing I wanted was to regret the decision that brought life not only to trees but to actual living people as well. I had to remember these facts, as it was all that was keeping me grounded right now.

Rose marveled at the restored forest, as well; her home had finally come back. It was the first time I saw a genuine smile on her face, and the red irises of her black eyes sparkled as she gave a silent greeting to every leaf, every flower, and every brush of life.

Our infatuation was cut short by Amilyana's shouting. Fristlyn's voice tried to calm her down, but she dismissed it. I looked to see what the commotion was about and saw that Tara had arrived, from seemingly nowhere, as was her way.

"I'm just here to help," I heard Tara explain.

"No one *asked* for your help," Amilyana fired back just as I approached.

"If asking for her help was an option, I would've," I leered. Ami was not fond of my new sense of leadership, but even I could admit she was out of line. "We're going against a witch who isn't thinking clearly; her mind is erratic. I don't know much about magic, but I can only assume an erratic mind has erratic results. We need all the help we can get." Getting a week's worth of sailing done in just a few hours was going to take all the magic we could get, and Tara demonstrated her power was supercharged. Her being here was good. Ami's vendetta, though none of my business, would have to wait.

"Well, why can't she just teleport you there, then?" Amilyana fired back. "She's proven she can do it!"

"I wanted to," Tara explained, as calmly as she could, though I heard her rising irritation. "I even asked; big daddy boss man of mine said no."

My fingers lifted to my lips to cover a laugh as did Fristlyn's, though Amilyana was not amused.

"Sounds like *Eden*," she seethed. "Your superiors were always up to something."

"Trust me," Tara explained. "Different kind of boss."

"Ladies," I groaned. "This is not working for me. My people, which includes a little girl I'm responsible for, are about to face a problem their worst nightmares couldn't comprehend. This feud will have to wait."

If looks could kill, then the one I got from Amilyana would've obliterated me. "You don't know what she is capable of."

"You do," Tara chimed. "So I'd take my help as a win."

"Enough," I shouted, putting the argument to rest. "You said you had a boat, I've yet to see it."

"Come, lass," Fristlyn said, pulling Ami by her upper arm; she lifted it with a fist, toward me, as if ready to turn the tables. Fristlyn succeeded in diverting the High Priestess's attention back toward the river, and Rose departed to stand next to her king as he held Amilyana's hand, focusing on the water.

Tara gave a sheepish look toward me, now scared I knew she had something to hide. It didn't matter to me at the moment; all my mind thought about was getting back to Metsa and stopping Lorraine from hurting Marla, Soen, or any of the other residents. Even Doc and his tavern came to mind. So, I just mouthed a, "Thank you," because Tara didn't have to be here at all.

A blue light enveloped Amilyana while a gold one hugged Fristlyn. The consistency of colors was something I began to notice. Whenever either of them used magic, those colors were present, just like how Tara's was a shimmery silver, and Lorraine's was black. Whether or not it was personalized to them, or their method of magic was a question for another day.

As the colored mists grew more intense, I saw the water of the river begin to bubble. Not boil, exactly, just a bubbling ripple that grew larger as they both focused. It wasn't long before I saw a sail emerge from the depths of the river, followed by a deck, and then a whole ship was lifted from the water and set afloat, neat and balanced as water poured from any orifice and back into the river.

I wasn't sure if they realized it, but I did. They both used excessive magic back at the tomb and showed no signs of tiring. The release of magic had put a temporary overcharge on their abilities, and I intended to take full advantage of that, as well.

"Is teleporting us on the boat at least something you can do?" I gave Tara a side-eye, and she hit back with a grin and nodded.

"I should be able to swing that," she confirmed. "Who all is coming? Just us?"

"I should stay back, maybe get a head start on rebuilding the colony," Rose's voice interjected. She moved away from Fristlyn and met me, but this wasn't an option.

"Rose...I could really use you there," I pleaded. "We'll get you back; I promise."

"You haven't really needed my help so far..."

"I do, though. Trust me, I do."

Rose nodded, and I turned to Tara and nodded. At the click of her tongue, she waved her hand, and all of us were enveloped by her silver smoke, which blinded me for just a moment. When my vision cleared, I stood atop the main deck of the freshly risen ship. I was a tad disoriented, but it passed not long after.

I was quick to get to work; positioning Fristlyn and Ami on the quarter deck and placing Tara just behind the bowsprit. I wasn't sure if positions mattered, but I didn't want to risk it.

The river acted as a channel, cutting the Coven Isle in half with both ends feeding into the sea. Amilyana and Fristlyn would have to combine their abilities to push, and Tara would steer. Rose and I both stabilized ourselves by holding tight onto the mainsails beam, preparing for an uneasy ride.

"Let's go," I shouted. "Push."

The boat jerked forward as Fristlyn and Amilyana held hands once more and shot the boat out to sea.

I was thrilled to finally be going home yet feared the state it would be in by the time I got there.

CHAPTER 44

FRISTLYN'S PREDICTION WAS CORRECT, AND I WAS GLAD WE PLANNED ahead. As Tara forced the ship to turn out of the channel between the Coven Isle, and we sailed past and away from the island, the first thing we saw was our ruined boat, wrecked out at sea. Lorraine tried really hard not to give us a chance of stopping her. Too bad I wasn't as dumb as she thought because she just might've gotten away with it otherwise.

My brain was split in two, in two different places. One was concerned about Elliot; the hag's magic was strong enough that just healing his wounds wouldn't wake him up, and he was left there with a bunch of elves, or witches, whom I didn't have time to get acquainted with. As my hands gripped the beam of the mainsail, I said a silent prayer over and over again, wishing for his recovery. Never mind my feelings toward him or lack thereof, he was still a close friend.

The other half of my brain reached out to Marla. When I told her I would be coming back, I didn't intend for it to be to save her life. She was a child and she wouldn't be able to comprehend the power of an unpredictable witch, dead set on bringing a legendary person back from the dead. Marla, along with Soen and all of Metsa, was in danger to an extent even I couldn't fathom.

We'd make it, though. I know we would.

The telekinetic strength between Fristlyn, Amilyana, and Tara was immense and the ship was hurling through the sea. Faster than any pirate or military captain could help to achieve; it wasn't long before I saw the cloud of smoke out in the distance. Metsa's own beacon that told sailors where they were.

Getting this close panicked me; I had put on a brave face but now that we were closer, an hour and some minutes away from what I assumed was going to be an intense battle, I couldn't help but bite at my nails. Of course, Fristlyn noticed. As observant as ever.

"We have your back, lass. We'll be prepared this time."

Whenever he talked to me that way, through telepathy, I got more and more frustrated because I didn't know how to communicate it back. So all I could do was just look in his direction. His eyes were narrowed, his face red as veins fought for freedom against his skin. Amilyana didn't look any better.

"I'll teach you how to properly do this another time, lass. For now, just whisper the words out loud. I'll hear them."

I started to do just that, but before I could say anything, Amilyana collapsed, crippling to her knees as she cried out in exhaustion. The ship came to a crashing halt, and Rose and I fell flat on our faces while Tara was knocked off the forecastle deck, though she at least landed gracefully on her feet.

Fucking show off, I joked with myself.

Everyone was fast to get collected and rushed up to Amilyana, who was desperately breathing for air.

"I've...I've used too much magic today," she said, although Fristlyn was encouraging her to talk less and focus on breathing.

"We both have, lass," he assured her, and I noticed his breathing was heavy, as well. I didn't need to hear it to know, I could feel my chest tighten as he exerted a lot of his own power.

I turned to Tara, who looked lost as to what she should do or say. She and Ami weren't on good terms, by any means. Tara was silenced and unsure how to proceed.

"You've only had to turn the ship once, really," I pointed out. "Do you have enough energy to carry us all the way? Give these two a rest?"

After a single nod, Tara became a babbling fool. "Well, I don't-I mean, I never exactly...You see it's different, 'cuz-yeah, yeah I have enough." Now she and I shared an awkward exchange. All I needed was a yes or no, and I was getting sick of how dodgy she was becoming the more I got to know her.

"All right, position yourself here, and I'll get these two on the main deck to relax a bit." Rose and I helped Amilyana up to her feet, walked her down from the quarter-deck, and sat her up against the closed railings of the ship. I directed Fristlyn to sit next to her, and just relax the rest of the way. Both of them soon started to groan whilst rubbing their temples. Magic happened in the mind, and while normally I could just imagine how bad they hurt, I was blessed with feeling Fristlyn's and I started to get queasy, as well.

Seemed it wasn't just me, as after we stopped for a while, Rose took the chance to hurl out her insides over the side of the boat. She may think she's just a spider with an ability to turn human, but she became more mundane the longer she was in her two-legged form.

I contemplated following her example. Fristlyn's headache was growing to be unbearable, but Tara approached as she manifested a small white bottle of sorts in her hand. She handed it out to me, offering me whatever was in the contents.

"Aspirin?" she offered.

"What...what the hell is an 'aspirin'?" I asked her, not wanting to take the unknown bottle with unknown whatever was inside.

"Drugs. Would you like some drugs?" She reworded, paired with an immature snicker. I shook my head, and the bottle was gone at the wave of her finger. "Let me know if you change your mind. You totally should, but whatever floats your boat." My eyes were wide and perplexed. I understood the words she was using, but she kept using them in ways I didn't understand. When she admitted defeat, she simply shook her head and muttered "Damn Relica, I swear," as she made her way back to the quarter-deck.

Once Tara was repositioned, she called down to us to let us know the downside of her taking over.

"We're going to move just a *little bit,* and I cannot stress that enough, a teensy tiny bit slower than before. I need to," she paused to let out a small, mockery of a giggle, *"'conserve my energy,'"* she finished, using her fingers as air quotes.

Just as Tara was preparing to push the ship onward again, I heard her voice, Lorraine's voice, echo in my head.

"Being a leader means you must make unsavory decisions. Are you prepared to make such choices?"

I whispered a "yes," but I don't think that worked, either. It may work with Fristlyn, but I didn't have the bond with Lorraine that I did with him. However, I was confident that I could. Sylvestra herself had faith in me; I was prepared to do what needed to be done. Regardless, the hag continued:

"Enemies to friends is always a touching story—but reverse those two words, and it's now a sad truth. Let us see how you fare against such a change."

My entire world stopped, and the air became stiller than Sylvestra's corpse. My eyes darted to Fristlyn, then to Amilyana, up toward Tara, and then down to Rose. What was Lorraine planning? What spell was she about to do?

I unholstered my crossbow and took several steps away from all of them, panicked, and told everyone to stay back.

"Lass," Fristlyn exclaimed, confused and his hands now up in the air. "What's wrong? Why are you pointing that at me?"

"I'm not sure what's about to happen," I shouted.

Rose finally stopped emptying her guts out into the sea and turned to face the commotion.

"Lorraine…she's talking to me, something about friends becoming enemies, I don't—I—" My chest tightened even more from my own panic, on top of what I already felt from Fristlyn's exertion.

"Princess, think this through," Rose's voice groaned as she tried to collect herself. She put a hand up and started to approach me. I know I was scaring them, but I was petrified as to who Lorraine was going to turn against me. "RoGoria," Rose called me, stern and forceful, her voice shook my bones and I was taken aback when her monotone demeanor faded; she was actually trying. "Lower the bow; she's not strong enough to take any of our minds. I promise we're fine."

My breathing picked up, and only got faster the closer Rose got. As I panicked, I went to turn my bow on her, but she was far quicker than I.

She whipped my hands with spider silk, in a similar fashion I'd seen Fristlyn use his, and knocked my bow from my hands.

I whimpered at the thought of being defenseless and struggled to unholster my gun. When I finally got a good grip on it, Fristlyn's arms were already around me and we both fell to our knees.

"*I love you,*" he spoke, privately. The words were meant for me, and me only. "*I love you. I love you. I love you.*"

Wasn't helping; now, I just felt like scum.

Lorraine knew how to use her enemies as weapons; using their traits to figure out how she should attack, and she knew everything about me. Fristlyn, Amilyana, Rose, Tara. Lorraine knew I wouldn't be able to do this without them, and that was her biggest weapon against me.

I pulled away from Fristlyn, but he pressed his forehead to mine. "Breathe with me, lass."

Half a breath in and the boat shifted, rocking with a force that knocked everyone down on asses. We all panicked now and tried to stand, but it happened once more, and we were all down again. Amilyana shouted out of frustration; I was beginning to see how small a temper she had. Tara hadn't fallen with grace to land on her feet this time, she was knocked clear off the quarter deck and fell flat on her back.

Next was music. I heard a haunting tune from the depths of the ocean, which caused my heart to stop the war drumbeat it had been playing since Lorraine spoke to me. I'd heard the tune before, though something was different. Last I heard it, it made me feel safe. I knew I was plundering through the darkest depths of the sea when I heard it last, but it promised rescue. While the melody was the same, the pitch, the key, it was all different. It promised death.

"Lass…" Fristlyn started. "Who else have you made friends with?"

The water crashed around us, a thunderous roar as the waves were mutilated by an ascending serpent's tail. Onyx black with green spiked dorsal fins lining the top of the tail. I saw the fins at the end, appearing right above us on the port side of the ship. The tail extended down under the water, under the boat, and back up to a four-armed creature on the starboard side. I knew her. I'd met her before. The onyx eyes, the webbed hands, though now there were four of them, and the narrow, spiky teeth. She was three times the size she was before. I was warned of all of this; while Galyn was still alive after the imprisonment of magic, she was diluted. I released it all, and she reverted to the bloodthirsty monster mermaids were said to be.

The friend I made was gone, but I realized the one favor she granted me: she tried to stay away.

As she continued to sing her song, and while I stared at the dorsal fin that went from her head all the way down her back, I whispered Galyn's name. The song faded and turned into a chilling screech. It was that screech that snapped me out of it, destroying the fear that Lorraine intended to infect me with. This wasn't my friend; my friend wasn't a bloodthirsty sea beast.

No, this would, in fact, be easy.

I stood to my feet and picked up my crossbow, holstering it, and, instead, equipped my gun and saber to my hands. My blade crackled and sparked with lightning still from Lorraine's attack back at the tomb. Tara noticed it, gave me a grin, and nodded, and I realized there was something about my new sword she had failed to mention. I was eager to discover what it could do.

I looked to Fristlyn, who now had his polearm in his hand and his sharp finger armor pieces at the ready. He'd need to use limited magic. Amilyana readied her hands, too, ready to throw what little she had left at the monster.

Rose was already in spider form when I looked, and Tara had her white and gold quarter-staff ready.

"Attack," I ordered in a low, tired growl.

Fristlyn was the first to move, using minimal spider silk from his free hand, gliding up the mainsail in a trapeze artist-like motion. He flew and tried to claw at Galyn, but the sea beast moved out of the way only for Fristlyn to wrap around and soar back to the main deck, landing on his feet.

Galyn wailed once more and tried to slam her entire body into the main deck, but a light blue forcefield emanated with each blow the mermaid threw at us. Amilyana.

I turned to her to see a glowing ball of blue between her hands, as she chanted *"Protect us folk of the faer, be it by the Hourglass."*

Over and over again, she repeated the incantation, keeping anything from coming in, but allowing us to go out. She had very little energy left, and just keeping the barrier up was causing her to be winded. We'd have to make this quick.

"What can you do?" I asked Tara, who was looking a little stressed.

"My boss isn't answering me, I—"

"Then, there are no rules until they tell you otherwise."

"You don't understand, my boss is—"

"*There are no rules. Until they tell you otherwise,*" I repeated, leering at the mysterious witch.

Tara shrugged, finally, and said, "I mean, I guess!" Her shimmery smoke enveloped her though it turned gold near the end and focused into a ball of pure light in front of her. Her eyes rolled back into her head, leaving only the whites and red veins showing. She unleashed the ball at Galyn, and it exploded, blinding the mermaid. Rose took this chance and launched herself out, biting the mermaid and injecting venom in different spots in her back and chest.

Good. Get the venom as close to the heart as possible.

Galyn jerked around and about, and the blood-curdling scream from Fristlyn came as soon as Rose was thrown in the deep dark depths of the sea. I filled with inner rage, though not my own, not entirely, anyway, as Fristlyn cursed at the humanoid sea serpent.

I felt the bubbling boil of blood to the point where it started to be too much for me to handle, and as I tried to get Fristlyn to focus. I realized he was busy. I watched as my friend's mouth unhinged from his jaw, stretching down to almost the center of his chest. An echoing crack of a shout emanated from within his throat, followed by hundreds, no, *thousands* of small spiders pouring from his mouth. I stepped back as the eight-legged critters infested the main deck, and started to glow with his identical gold, magical essence. Fristlyn's eyes turned gold themselves, a glowing beacon that was intended to lead the mermaid to death.

"*Call of the spider,*" was all he said in a voice so low, and it had an echo that wasn't of this world. Almost as if the wind, the water, and Relica itself spoke the words. All the spiders launched themselves at Galyn, and Fristlyn's spell activated, sizing the arachnids up till they were about the size he was when we had first met.

At the drop of a hat, he created an army, though it was all he had left. He crippled down to the floor of the deck, just as Galyn was pushed back down to the sea under the weight of a thousand oversized spiders. Amilyana was crippled, too, and the barrier was put to rest. Tara, who showed no signs of being tired, put her own right back up as I tended to Fristlyn.

"Please, lass," he begged me. "She needs to be okay," his eyes started to well up, and mine did, too, in unison, feeling his fear, his pain, and his despair all at once. "I need to make sure she's okay!"

"You need to stay right here," I ordered him, running my fingers through his golden hair. I kissed his forehead and stood straight up. "I'll finish this." At everyone's protest, I ran to the side of the boat where Galyn had fallen, where Rose was thrown and took the privilege of thinking about my next move away from me.

If I stopped to think about it, I wouldn't do it.

Fristlyn shouted for me in the same horrified tone he did toward Rose as I threw myself off the side and vanished into the deep depths of the sea.

The moment I entered the sea, panic sunk in. Though sunlight illuminated the way, the awareness of being in the dark, eerie depths of the sea made my blood run cold, freezing my heart as it pumped pure anxiety through my veins. My arms and legs moved with minds of their own, causing me to lose air as I struggled to remind myself what the hell my plan was.

Everything stopped once I saw things floating up around me. Spider carcasses, and soon all I could do was stare at them and hope one of them wasn't Rose. I examined each one, distracted by them, which only made it worse when something rammed into my side and yanked me far from the boat.

I saw the mermaid's tail; several scales were cracked and in disarray from the army of spiders that clung to her, biting away at whatever flesh they could find. Galyn was interested in me, though; human, ripe with flesh to feed her mindless hunger. I was looking into her onyx eyes, mad at myself that I refused to see the animal she was all this time.

Her mouth opened, and I was threatened by those familiar teeth; thin, skinny spikes protruding from her gums. Her jaw unhinged, and the gums popped and jutted out and amidst my fear, I recognized the opening she provided. Even in the water, my sword sparked with ethereal electricity, which whispered to me as Galyn moved closer to take a bite out of my face.

With a heavy grunt, I heaved my arm toward her, blade pointing right into the cavity that would consume me, and jammed it through the roof of her mouth.

Galyn began to twitch and jolt around, and lightning enveloped her body and caused the few spiders that remained to let go and release her. Every so often, her body would glow, and I could see her skeleton in quick, single-second flashes. I watched as her skin began to fry and boil from inside out. Soon, her grip on me released, and I held on to her as her body floated up to the surface.

I removed my sword from her jaw and pulled myself up out of the water, using her corpse as a raft. The ship approached by the time I was up, and the surviving spiders began to crawl up the side to the main deck. It was only when the biggest one of them all, a large black spider with a red Hourglass on her belly, approached me and extended a single hairy leg out to me, did I know we were all safe. I grabbed Rose's "hand" and swung around to her abdomen and clung on tighter than I'd ever held Fristlyn as she carried me to the main deck of the ship.

I wasted no time cowering in a corner, trying as hard as I could to collect my composure.

Fristlyn scolded me, with love, and ordered me to stop throwing myself off boats. As this was, indeed, the second time I'd done that.

"Yum," I heard Tara say as she gazed over the boat, examining Galyn's corpse. "Hey, who wants to grab a nice fish platter when this is over? I have a sudden craving for seafood."

When Tara's eyes met mine, she took one step back when she realized I was glaring at her with the force of a thousand winds.

"You know, if I had known this was enchanted," I started, irritated and presenting the sword which still zapped the occasional bolt, "I might've been able to save us *a lot* of hassle."

She clicked her tongue and shrugged. "One, I doubt that. Two, you need to stop thinking I'm going to be convenient. It's kind of my whole shtick." She let out a chortle, dismissing the fact I was genuine with my aggravation. She held out a hand and helped me up to my feet, and retreated to the quarterdeck, ready to resume moving the ship.

I offered Fristlyn a hug, but he was hugging Rose and shed a few tears, relieved she was okay. I stepped back and gave her a hug, as well. Still in spider form, her little hairs poked and itched my skin, but I didn't mind. Everyone was still safe, and I wasn't ready to lose anyone else. Fristlyn pulled me in, and Rose retreated to her human state, and we all hugged each other.

I offered for Ami to join, but she was still catching her breath from all the power she had used.

I hoped an hour was enough for both her and Fristlyn to regain some strength.

Tara moved the boat forward, and we would soon be arriving at Metsa's docks.

331

CHAPTER 45

THE STEAM AND SMOKE THAT SURROUNDED THE TOWN OF METSA weren't as thick as I remembered. The iconic symphony of spinning gears, clanking metal, and incomprehensible chatter was missing; there was nothing but silence when the ship docked, and I began to fear the worst.

We had little time to waste here; I couldn't spend my time looking for Soen to figure out what was going on. The sudden hiding of Metsa's people worked in our favor, though, as we would be able to handle our foreseeable showdown with Lorraine with little distractions. The only hindrance I was caused was a small panic over Marla, and wherever she was. I just hoped Soen had her somewhere safe.

Tara didn't waste any time, either, using her seemingly limitless pool of magic to tie ropes to posts, roll up the sails, and open the ramp for us to exit onto the docks. I asked her if she planned on staying around to help, and she informed me she got special permission from her superiors to do so. I made it clear how thankful I was as the stillness of Metsa caused me to feel unsettled and having someone of her caliber put some of that to rest.

We all charged up the wooden stairs, creating our own little war march as our boots awoke the old wood; each step creaked under every stomp.

We sprinted through the Lower City, into the market district, and stopped when we reached the iconic fountain with faerie centerpiece, which no longer fit well with what I knew about the Faer Folk—the Settlers of Old.

"How are you two doing?" I asked both Amilyana and Fristlyn, bouncing a finger back and forth between them.

"Not anywhere near fully rejuvenated, lass," Fristlyn answered first. "But I regained some fight. Only silk magic, for now, it seems."

"That's fine," I said, nodding back to the ship. Several of his summoned spiders remained, and I suggested that he order the colony to be out here. "What about you, Ami?"

"I can resort to basics," she explained. "I won't be able to conjure any demons, though. That could kill me if I'm not careful."

"What about…" I trailed off, nodding left to right while I tried to find the right words.

"Necromancy, yes, is still in working order," she said. "None of us used any magic, that's not the problem. Telekinesis is a science, but my mind feels as if it's burning."

"That's fine," I interjected. "Stick to basics, then; barriers, telekinesis, whatever you can do. I want you and Tara to stay here."

The two cringed at the thought, but I shushed them both before they could say anything. "Your past isn't of my concern right now; work together, please."

They nodded, though both were still far from thrilled.

"All right," I continued. "Rose, you and I will storm the hag's house."

"Lass—" Fristlyn tried to interject.

"Fristlyn, I trust you to find Marla. Make sure she's safe, keep her safe if she isn't." He tried to argue further, but I wouldn't have it. "You can feel when something goes wrong. You'll know if I'm in trouble. That does us no good if you're right next to me; it kills your element of surprise."

"I can't lose both of my girls, lass," the Spider King explained. I knew where his stress was, I did, but I couldn't have it jeopardize everything.

Rose rested an arm on my shoulder and looked at her longtime companion with minimal compassion and emotion; though, it was the most I'd ever seen on her. "We'll be fine, my king. I'll watch her back."

"And I, hers," I reiterated. "Just, please, make sure my little girl is safe."

Fristlyn finally nodded, though it was heavy with hesitance. He lifted his arm and snapped his fingers three times, and after a minute I saw about twenty spiders enter the city from the docks.

I nodded to everyone, solidifying the plan, but before I left, Tara stepped in and removed my sword from its scabbard. I watched as it sparked with jolts of lightning, and she pointed at one of the rose-shaped pieces on the handguard. It illuminated ethereal indigo; I hadn't noticed it before.

"The dimmer it gets, the less of that magic it has," she started to explain. I was shocked; I wasn't expecting an explanation at all, as was her way. "The blade absorbs and borrows power; it doesn't keep it. Try blocking any spells she throws at you to get some new toys to attack and defend with."

"Thank you," I said, "for finally giving me details." I paired that last bit with a laugh, which she returned.

Tara placed a hand on my shoulder and leaned into my ear. "You got this," she whispered. "You're ready."

And I sure hoped she was right.

ROSE KICKED the door down to Lorraine's abandoned house, something I promised was fun to do. She agreed and let out what I think was her version of a laugh.

We both stormed the house, though I had no plans of how to find Lorraine in there or if she'd be there at all. The house wasn't exactly big; the first floor was a living room, a small kitchen, and the entry foyer. Upstairs was a barren attic.

Both of these elements were unchanged; the house looked just as it did the last time I was here.

"Are you sure she's here?" Rose asked me from the kitchen. I heard the roaches scatter and cringed when I heard her let out a, "Damn, roaches sound delectable right now." *Not a human with a spider form,* I told myself. *Spider with a human form.*

"No," I answered. "I'm hoping for just a clue, though." I had no reason to believe she was here besides the fact that this was where she squatted up until we left for the Coven Isle. There had to be some belongings of hers that might point us in the right direction. I planned for the worst, however. If she was here, this fight would find its way outside.

We checked the upstairs, but it was left in the same disarray as it was before; the knocked-over furniture, the damaged frames, and paintings, Fristlyn's old webbing. Nothing was new.

After scouring both floors of the house, I finally grew frustrated and leaned onto the extravagant fireplace in the living area and cursed out my misfortune. Rose tried to be supportive and gave me a pat on my shoulder with less than no compassion behind it. It made me chortle; someone of her emotionless void trying to offer comfort. She became more human the longer she acted like one.

"Where did you first see her?" Rose asked. I guess trying to retrace steps couldn't hurt.

"I'm not sure; she had to have been hiding *somewhere.* I went to leave the house and she charged at me from nowhere, attacking me by the front door."

At the very drop of air from my words, the scene replayed in my head. I met Fristlyn, walked down the stairs, almost left the house, and the brittle old woman pounced on me from behind. She wasn't in the kitchen; the light from the door saw to that. She wasn't upstairs. I had my first conversation with Fristlyn, that same day, up there and it provided nowhere for her to hide. She came from somewhere, and the whereabouts of which became crystal clear.

Before she pounced, I remembered hearing the sound of scraping metal, like a grate being gently dragged. I looked down into the large fireplace, and sure enough, there was a massive grate on the floor underneath soot, blending it with the rest.

"You must be joking," Rose groaned. I doubt she got much reading done in her life as a spider to recognize how problematic this situation usually was; she had to have gone through this before.

"I'm afraid not," I groaned back. "Give me a hand, I guess."

We stuck our fingers through the opening of the grate and lifted it to reveal a ladder that went deep underneath the stone walls of Metsa. Rose and I stepped back, gagging at a putrid stench of rot and decay.

"By the Hourglass!" Rose exclaimed, though now keeping her voice in a whisper as she clamped her hands over her nose.

"When I first saw her, she was dragging a bloodied sack," I explained, also accompanied by a gag. "I guess the smell doesn't bother her."

Rose and I both stared at the opening leading down to who knew where. Neither of us wanted to go in there, but we both knew we had to. We found ourselves playing the game of who was going to go first.

I took a few steps closer to it, and even just doing that made the stench twice as awful. My nose stung, no matter how hard I held it shut, from the smell of pure rot. Climbing down there would be worse.

I approached closer, anyway, looking down to see a ladder, making it easy access. I almost hoped there wasn't one there. It would've been nice to be sent back through no fault of our own, but we both didn't have an excuse now.

So, I went first. Sitting on my rear, I slid myself until my feet were able to touch the ladder then used my one free hand to descend down. Rose followed, and we were soon engulfed by the darkness.

The ladder seemed to go on forever, as we descended deeper and deeper; the smell growing more pungent as we got closer to the floor. It took all my strength not to vomit; I kept telling myself that seeing the ripped-up pieces of Barrea was worse than this. I could handle this.

My foot slipped on one of the iron poles of the ladder, and I let out a small whimper as I almost fell to my death, presumably, but managed to keep myself stable.

Soon, there was a floor. It was a lumpy, unbalanced floor, but a floor. I hopped down and assisted Rose in finding her footing, but even the spider whose entire movement was based on balance couldn't find it here.

The floor was uneven to an extreme. One step had a slight elevation, another had random decline which felt like pure stonework. The parts that didn't feel like rock felt soft, which only then did I realize what we were walking on.

Corpses. Deteriorated flesh and bone, none of which were proportioned to look like humans.

As I was about to throw up from *that* realization, my eyes pinpointed a flash of red light, then green, then yellow. The light brought brief moments of clarity and revealed that Rose and I were in a narrow, dark corridor. It was also clear where the stench was coming from.

I was relieved to not see human corpses; the rot and decay were large fish and some animals. This actually brought a bit of joy; while the fishy stench was death-inducing, this told me that

Lorraine was, in fact, fragile enough to break through to. She hadn't murdered anyone, not yet.

We made our way to the end of the corridor where we saw a doorless entryway, where the light was coming from. I withdrew my sword and gun and was ready to storm through and stop whatever spell Lorraine was about to cast, but Fristlyn's voice appeared and added a new sense of uneasiness in my gut. *"Lass. I think they're going to kill me."*

I froze. I hadn't been taught how to do this yet, how to communicate back to him, and if I spoke out loud, I risked the chance of Lorraine hearing me.

"They're all here, lass. I don't know how it's possible."

Who? Who was there? Who else was an enemy besides Lorraine right now? What was going on?

Who, Fristlyn? Who is it?

"Is everything okay?" Rose whispered, and I put a finger up and shushed her. She didn't like that, so I tried mouthing "I think Fristlyn is in trouble." Whether or not she understood me would be an answer I'd never receive.

"Marla is safe, but she..."

But she what? What is happening? A wave of nausea hit me, and it hit Rose, as well. Fristlyn never answered me back, and now he wouldn't have a chance to. I recognized this feeling; I felt it when Tara put us on the boat. Only now, when it passed, we were past the doorway and found ourselves in Lorraine's chamber.

The chamber looked as I would've predicted; dark, with various desks, and workstation tables with alchemy supplies tossed around. The stone walls glimmered to the few lanterns that were around, hanging on menacing sconces throughout.

In front of us was a large altar, in which Sylvestra's rotten corpse was laid with respect. It was haunting, her mouth forced open by nature; loose and leathery flesh completed the look. Her dress, however, was still intact and left undisturbed. Even in death, her carcass told you a master was there.

"Do you care to see the final product?" Lorraine's voice could be heard, but she was out of sight at first. She rose up from behind the altar, placing several spherical gems around the high priestess's body.

What was I supposed to say? I wanted to get through to her, but I didn't know her well enough. Her pains, her past, nothing. I had no ammo to use on her except the ones that would harm her; maybe even kill her. But not killing her was a request I intended to meet.

"I'm impressed," she continued. "Dumbfounded, even, that you took on a mermaid and lived to speak of it. I can't think of another human who has done that..." Lorraine wasn't impressed. I felt as if she was talking just to fill the silence. "You really are a persistent little pest; you'd make a fine witch if you applied yourself."

"I have no interest," I snapped. The thought of using magic made me furious, and it was right then when I made a vow to myself that I never would. Enchanted weapons are one thing, but the actual practice of witchcraft ceased to have any drive for me. Nothing to do with my faith in God, but everything to do with not trusting myself to have the discipline, let alone the power to control it.

"Oh, well," Lorraine said. "It's not for everyone."

Her tone, her demeanor shifted. I almost got a tone of relief as if this spell she was about to cast would fulfill her wildest dreams.

It hit me. Harder than Galyn had when she rammed into me; everything became crystal clear, and I realized exactly how she was feeling. Her endgame. Her true motive.

I've felt what she was feeling before.

"Lorraine—"

"No." She waved a hand, and I felt my mouth close shut; I lacked the ability to open it on my own accord. "I really do not want to hear it; anything you have to say, that is. I've waited far too long. Been mad, damn near insane, for far too long. Once more, I'll be whole."

I knew what she meant. I knew what she wanted. *I knew it all.*

I struggled and tried to scream as Lorraine took in a deep breath; I assumed to start her incantation, though she didn't speak. I was muffled, though; my lips glued shut, and there was nothing I could do about it. I looked to Rose, who was still frozen, but when her eyes met mine, she knew it was up to her.

She attempted to move, but she couldn't. I watched her body twitch and she even went as far as to extract eight, skinny black legs out of her back as Fristlyn did with his own. They were able to move in and out, but nothing else after that. Lorraine's magical hold pressurized us without us feeling anything. Paralyzed by the horrific art of witchcraft.

Lorraine drew in another deep breath, lifting her arms as she did so, and I braced myself for what I was sure to be a loud, aggressive chant.

But she said nothing. She seemingly...*danced.*

Her feet never moved, but her arms flailed. She first touched her fingers together, making a triangle between her thumbs and pointers. After which, she arched her back and broke her arms free, drawing in deep breaths as she moved. Lorraine then leaned her whole upper body to one side, extended her arm overhead, and touched her fingers just below the wrist of the other as her cheek pressed against the shoulder. She drew those fingers down her arm, but as she did so, a blue, shimmering strand of light tangled itself in her arm hairs.

When her hand met the bridge of her nose, she whipped that same hand to the other side, and the blue strand of light cracked in the air. With those same fingers, she drew a circle—a blue circle—in the air, cutting it into quarters using the light strand attached to her hand as almost a pen of sorts. Once the circle was completed, ethereal nuts, bolts, and cogs appeared within, and she turned each cog to the left. My muscles spasmed as I could hear the cranking locks and keys turning within the magical circle of blue, blinding light.

Finally, she spoke. "Stygian Knight; Faer of Life and Death."

Stygian. There was no way it was the same. It couldn't have been. I shot an alarmed look to Rose, who did everything in her power to avoid making eye contact. It *was* the same name.

Black and white balls of light circled her as she spoke, the spell officially starting to be cast. I hadn't failed yet; there had to be something I could do. Soon, the urge, the need, to pick at my skin, scratch my arm, play and tug with my hair, all hit me at once. Being forbidden to move caused me pure agony and torture, so my breathing went out of control. I wanted to collapse, but I couldn't.

I couldn't move a damn thing, so all I told myself was, *I hadn't failed, yet* over and over.

Lorraine stood, staring puzzled into the circle, before startling us both with a deep, sharp inhale. We watched in peril as the pupils of her eyes grew four times their size, overshadowing her inhuman golden irises. Her wrists slammed into the surface of the altar, and said, "Release Sylvestra, bring her home. Release her, bring her home." With each time she said it, the pacing picked up until there was no space between the words. No chance to even take a breath.

An intense wind arrived, yet there were no windows down there, no broken cavity that led to the outside. This was pure magic, and it was creating a storm.

"Release her! Bring her home!" she shrieked once more, and finally Rose started to break. Her eyes welled up and it looked as though she was filled with remorse. If she was close to Fristlyn, then she met Stygian before. I didn't need her to confirm that she blamed herself for his abilities being misused in such a fashion.

Finally, Lorraine began to growl at the wind, and the cut quarters of her magic circle opened to reveal darkness behind the flaps of each piece.

Then, it just stopped. Dead in the wind, everything just vanished, but what followed was the most harrowing voice I had ever heard. While not menacing by tone, it still demanded respect. It had power, and it knew it.

"You are a damn fool, Lorraine."

Black essence swirled around the altar, and even Lorraine was overwhelmed by the power, stepping away from Sylvestra's carcass. The black mist was using the altar as a conduit, giving it a black glow as it siphoned into the dead priestess's body. Lorraine let out a hysterical laugh, though it lacked a maniacal feel; it wasn't as if she was going mad, just unhinged, like the sudden relief she had been craving for years was finally hitting her.

The candles on the sconces which decorated the walls blew out, leaving us in the dark. Random glass vials and loose parchments flew about in a frenzy, and then Rose and I both crippled down, gasping for air and gaining mobility once more. Lorraine had stopped focusing her magic on us, and we were free.

"Distract her!" I yelled to Rose through the magical storm, and she was up and running around the altar, where I saw her land a swift punch onto Lorraine's jaw.

Rose herself had become unhinged, fighting with a primal aggression as she grabbed the witch by her dress straps and shoved her away from everything.

The witch landed next to me, so I crawled over and locked her neck with my arm.

Then, the smoke dissipated, and the blue circle of magic ceased its presence.

Lorraine struggled under my weight to stand, and I felt magic push against my stomach and hurl me off her. I landed on the stone steps which led to the corridor from before, slamming my head into the rock.

I heard Rose call my name, though she was soon thrown on top of me. My vision was blurred, and I was dazed in general. The only bit I could make out was Sylvestra's body; still rotted, still decayed. Only now, it was upright, and it stared right at us.

CHAPTER 46

"It's not perfect, but it's working," Lorraine's voice trembled as she staggered to the awoken, undead witch. Her hand was placed on her heart and shook with overpowering emotions. "I...I can almost feel you," she gasped, now at eye level with the coherent corpse.

Sylvestra wasn't back. I don't get how Lorraine thought she was because that wasn't the high priestess I met when I was being drowned. Her body became a coffin of its own right, filled with whatever essence had just been put into her. Her eyes were still missing, now replaced by a sunset-colored glow. The flesh remained molten, flaking onto the ground as she moved. Sylvestra had been dead for four thousand years; it was remarkable she had any flesh, to begin with.

Lorraine placed her hands on the bony cheeks of her reawakened friend.

I heard a slight weep which rang into my ears from the pulsating pain in my head. I felt a wetness trickle down my face, soaking my brow and staining my own cheeks. Blood. I must've split my head open on contact.

Rose helped me to my feet, though as dizzy as I was, I relied on her for stability.

"We need to leave," she ordered me, but I shrugged her off.

"I need...to..." I fell back, leaning onto Rose as she tried to pull me away. I had her release me, and I limped toward Lorraine. "That's not...that's not her, and you know it."

Lorraine's head jerked toward me, and I jumped at the sight of her dilated pupils, leaving no trace of her iconic golden irises. The witch seethed at me, and the sheer sight of her left me feeling hollow. "You know nothing, *Princess*," a hiss of a voice came from her mouth. "You know nothing of my priestess, and you'd—"

Lorraine was interrupted by the harrowing screech of Sylvestra. The undead witch opened her skinless jaw, let out a banshee's cry, and went feral as she dismounted the altar. She rushed me, dug her bony fingers into my gut as she threw me back on a wall.

Rose tried to assist, but Lorraine grabbed her from afar and shoved her to the opposing side. Sylvestra ran into the corridor, with Lorraine chasing after her and laughing as I heard them climb up the ladder, slamming the grate to the abandoned house down. At the sound of the metal hitting stone, we dropped to the floor, and my vision went black.

I wasn't unconscious, but the blackness helped ease my headache.

"Take all the time you need, lass. There's a fun surprise waiting for you," Fristlyn's voice radiated in my brain. Soon, in the blackness that I blessed myself with, his face was all I pictured. His green and purple eyes, his golden hair, the high heeled boots I noticed him run in with no problems, all of it. My mind was cleared for him, and only him, so I thought I would give it one more try.

"Are you still in danger?" I thought.

"Fuckin' fuck! You did it!" I heard him laugh in excitement at my words. *"I'm fine, for now. Might get quite the beating later, but that's okay. I have a debt to repay."*

"What are you talking about?"

"You'll see when you get out here. I believe help is on the way."

Just as the words were spoken, I heard the metal grate open and close, and I heard a deep, familiar voice complain about the stench. A deep feminine voice followed, childlike but gruff. The voices got louder, and I heard Rose let out a "Shit..." as the two voices entered. I knew the man's voice to be Soen, but the girl's voice didn't ring any bells.

I opened my eyes to see the Mayor of Metsa, still as well-dressed as usual, flashing me his annoyingly perfect smile. I was happy to see it. His darkened sepia skin was what really told me I was back home and that I was safe. Damn near iconic-looking, he promised safety for his people.

"Good to see you again, Princess," he sighed, helping me up to my feet as the unknown companion tended to Rose. "Not happy to see you like this, but you survived the dangerous part."

"Mama!" I heard the gruff girl's voice call to me. She ran up and gave me a hug, though I was shocked by how she had changed. Her skin faded from the gorgeous light brown that it was and became a grayish-green color. Her bottom teeth were long and sharp; her honey eyes were now a vibrant red.

"I don't...what happened?"

"You happened," Rose said as she joined our group. "You released magic, and you seemed to have restored the people here."

"Exactly," Soen agreed. "The Orcs of Metsa are forever in your debt; you brought them back. Little Marla here, even."

"I'm guessing her parents never left her; they were killed in the genocide?" I asked.

"Oh, no, they really did," Soen said. "Just big fat up and left her here for reasons I'm unsure. But it seems to be okay. That's why you're here."

I looked at Marla, who was smiling so endearingly at me. Though her new smile was something I would have to get used to.

It was clear why Fristlyn felt he was in danger; the whole city would probably turn on him once this was settled. I'd have to plead his case, though the orcs had every right to be furious.

"We should get moving," I said, being polite as I rejected Rose's offer to hold me. My head was still killing me, but my vision was becoming less dazed. I wiped the blood from my face and walked toward the door with all of them following me.

"It's a battlefield out there," Soen informed me. "Do you have a plan?"

"I need everyone who isn't me to focus on Sylvestra. Leave Lorraine for me."

"You sure you'll be able to take her on by yourself?" Rose asked.

"Of course not," I chortled. "But a fight to the death is not my goal. I just need to get her to hear me out."

That would be easier said than done, but Lorraine had already given me a hand in fighting her. She was foolish with her words. "Know your enemy," she had said.

Well, Lorraine. I think I know you pretty well.

CHAPTER 47

We stormed out of the abandoned house. Well, Rose, Soen, and Marla stormed; I just limped to see the warzone the Lower City of Metsa had become.

Orcs fought the carcass that was Sylvestra, who was wailing with each spell she cast. Zombies alone were terrifying, but ones that could wield magic were just pure evil.

I noted where both Amilyana and Fristlyn were; Ami was helping the citizens fend off Sylvestra while Fristlyn fought Lorraine. He used little Ani'Mas magic to fight her and relied on his acrobatics. He had to be using some power for it, though. I watched as he jumped from the flat ground of the lower city, spun around, and passed one of the Upper City bridges, landed with grace, and then either charged her with his polearm or his armored claws.

Tara was tending to Lanstrid, the drunken crop vendor whom I had to steal food from. Now a thin, moss-colored orc, I only recognized him as he shouted drunken obscurities from his wounds.

Amilyana was taking the fight head-on, facing the corpse of her mother as if she was her arch enemy. Paired with spiritual allies, whom she had summoned herself, and the spiders that Fristlyn created, Sylvestra's malevolent corpse was outnumbered. Good, now I only had Lorraine to worry about.

"They're dying…" I spoke. "Your people are dying."

"Our people," Soen corrected me, placing a hand on my shoulder. "And no one is dead yet; you're a princess, how do you want to help your people?"

"People need to stop calling me that," I ordered. I looked at Soen and Rose, both of who were guilty of referring to me by my old title, the one that was no longer mine to own. "All throughout my journey, I always thought, 'I'm a princess, not a fighter.' I think it's about time I switched those words."

"What are your orders?" Rose asked.

My orders. I was in charge.

"You three join the citizens in fending off the priestess's corpse. I have a feeling there is no way to kill her; Lorraine will have to willingly release her hold."

"You think you can get her to do that?" Soen inquired, doubting my abilities. I doubted them too, but I wouldn't be alone.

"I'll have Fristlyn; he and I will take her on together. Defend our city, please."

"You heard the lady, let's move!" Soen ushered Rose and Marla down to the Lower City, but he stopped once more to speak to me. "Tea when this is over?"

I gagged. "At least make mine sweet."

That damn smile again. "Anything to keep you around, my fighter." He then ran to the steps that led to Lower City.

Still injured, I hid my limp the best I could, as well as my pulsating headache while I walked across the bridge closest to the docks. Fristlyn had pushed Lorraine back this far from the rest of the people, and I could see it was taking its toll on him. His chaotic enjoyment of the fight faded, and his acrobatics grew less impressive as he stumbled with each time he landed.

Maybe if you weren't in damn heels.

349

As I positioned myself right above them, Fristlyn began to glow in a golden light and revealed his Spider King form to give him a small boost.

I took a deep breath and cleared my mind until it was just him. His face; his iconic eyes became my anchor for communicating to him. My way of focusing on my bond.

"If I jump on her, do you think I'll die?"

I smiled at the cackle that echoed in my mind, and as I looked down, I saw he was smiling, too.

Lorraine threw an abundance of fire at him, though he dodged it and gave a swift hit with his whip, knocking her to just below me.

"Try it, lass! We'll know if you die. I might even cry about it."

No, he most certainly would cry about it. I've already seen what the aftermath looks like when someone with this type of bond dies.

I stepped back and prepared myself. The pulsating pain of my head refusing to go away, which wasn't a complete loss; the pain was fueling me. I ran and launched myself off the bridge and dropped down. Lorraine was right below me. If I were to miss, there might be a question of underestimated intellect on my part.

I grabbed her shoulders as I fell, tearing her down to the ground. I was up in less than a moment, withdrawing my sword only for her to push it far from my reach with the use of magic.

"Are you *fucking mad?*" Lorraine asked.

"Quite," I said. "So be careful."

That got a heavy laugh from Fristlyn; his wit was rubbing off on me.

Lorraine began to boil. Just like she said, I had to know my enemy for combat, use what I knew against her. Sparks of lightning zapped in one hand, while fire burned the other. I was much closer to her this time as she cast spells, seeing the true effects. Magic was based on payment and exchange of some kind, be it physical or mental. Something as trivial as the head trauma

Fristlyn and Amilyana felt, or something as extensive as what I saw now.

Her hand of fire was incredibly blistered and burned, and as she summoned spells, I noted the twitch in her eyes as she fought to ignore the pain. The lightning created sores and open wounds; physical spells required physical payment. So, the more elemental magic she used, the more she put herself in pain.

Physical elemental magic was her specialty. As she launched her attack, she moved her hands together and combined the elements. She fired the electric flame directly at me, but I'd learned that physical spells require physical defenses. I barrel-rolled out of harm's way, dodging the spell completely. I wasted no time in charging her and gave a good right hook, connecting with her chin. I was more agile than her; she relied too much on her magic to bulk up her physical capabilities, so I continued with a swift roundhouse kick to the gut and staggered her back quite a bit.

"Lookit you, lass!" Fristlyn exclaimed as appeared behind her, grabbing her with two of his thick brown spider legs and tossing her back toward the fountain. The former hag tossed and rolled, her back hit the fountain with ferocious impact.

"Careful; we don't want to kill her." I reminded him.

"No, lass—you don't want to kill her."

"No, lad," I retorted, with a friendly mockery. *"Sylvestra doesn't want us to kill her."*

Another laugh from the elf as I bolted toward the witch. I felt a grip around my waist as Lorraine tossed her hand out; I was lifted and slammed back down into the ground and heard a crack as my arm connected to the stone. I roared in pain, knowing it had been broken and would really affect how I would use weapons; my dominant arm was busted.

As I tossed from the agony, I watched Fristlyn as he gave a hard kick, the heel of his boots crushed into Lorraine's stomach, and she spat up blood from the attack. I pushed myself up with one arm and charged her once more. I succeeded with slamming my entire body into her, crippling her back down once again.

Lorraine vanished in a cloud of smoke, then reappeared behind Fristlyn.

I kept my right arm elevated by my chest, still burning from my bone breaking.

"Lass, hold out your other hand."

I did so and was blessed by the return of my sword, placing itself like a glove on my hand. As the blade still sparked, and I began to cut at the air, random sharp blades of lightning released themselves and flew at the witch. The ones she couldn't dodge she would block with a yellow barrier. I screamed as I slammed my blade down to the ground, and trenches of electricity dispersed and ravaged the witch's bare feet.

The sparks around my blade vanished, taking all that was left of the enchantment. I was desperate to find a solution now that my ranged attacks had been put on hold. Luckily, Fristlyn also worked at brainstorming an idea.

"Block this, lass," Fristlyn ordered once more. I faced him as a whip of spider silk came plundering toward me, and I held up my sword to see his magic siphon itself into the blade. The rose-shaped metal that was once blue with lightning was now gold as Fristlyn recharged the weapon. The sharp steel of the blade then fell limp once I activated its ability, hanging down like a whip. I maneuvered the flexible blade around to get a feel for its fluidity. Helpful, but dangerous, as I now had to make sure I wouldn't bisect Lorraine on accident.

I twirled the blade around and stabbed at the air; the blade reached all the way across and pierced her chest, right where her lung would be. I released the hilt and the blade retracted itself, slamming the handguard into her breast.

Lorraine fell to her knees, the sword sticking from her pierced lung was enveloped by green smoke. Healing magic, which was good. I knew a simple stab, though fatal to anyone else, wouldn't have killed her.

I staggered toward her, arm aching an unforgiving pain, as she gasped for air and scowled at me.

Her black eyes retreated, blessing me with the beauty of her golden eyes.

"Now that I have your god damn attention, might I have a word?"

CHAPTER 48

"I HAVE NOTHING TO SAY TO YOU, *PRINCESS*," LORRAINE SNEERED. The cries of Metsa's citizens filled the air as Sylvestra's reanimated corpse continued to cast spell after spell, weakening a barrier both Amilyana and Tara were fighting to keep up. Amilyana was running low on energy as Sylvestra killed off her remaining spirits. The carcasses of Fristlyn's eight-legged companions decorated the ground around the zombified witch.

All who remained on the battlefield was Rose, who combined her acrobatics with her ability to go from human to black widow behemoth whenever she chose.

I glared back at Lorraine. "Then, you can listen," I said. My tone was calm, cool, and smooth as the words brushed against my lips. I knelt on one knee, marrying my eyes with hers. All my life, and throughout this entire journey, everyone dominated me with their eyes; their gazes that fell on me, and I hated it. I hated feeling like a naive fool of a girl for not understanding a concept I only just learned about half a month prior. It was my turn, and I was starting with the witch who gave me problems from the beginning.

"Heal my arm," I ordered before I got started. "I know you can do it. Heal my arm."

She scowled at me as was typical of her. Her golden eyes were piercing, almost threatening as she narrowed. "I owe you *noth—*"

With the only usable arm I had left, I grabbed her by her cheeks, yanking her closer to me. Our noses touched, and I noted the pleasant smell of hibiscus on her. Not the scent I would've associated with her, but that only proved my suspicions as to who she was.

My leer was deadly; I stared her down, and damn near growled my next words. "You owe me *everything*. I have a friend in a magic-induced comatose state because of you. That friend lost his wife because of you."

"I did not kill the cook!" Lorraine shouted. I felt a wisp of magical energy push into me, but I did not move. Her power was dwindling; the rush she had been feeling was fading. Her own inner flame died out, and the excessive use of magic was catching up to her.

"No, you just caused the events that led to her demise," I reminded her. "Because of you, I was the only one there to protect her, yet she ended up dying to make sure I was all right. *You* did that, Lorraine. *You* brought about my hallucination. *You* summoned the flesh fiends. *You* separated us. Barrea died because of *your* actions. *You* took control of Amilyana's banshee guardian. You did it all. So, allow me to reiterate; heal. My. Fucking. Arm."

I expected to feel a cooling flow of magic, followed by the feeling of my bone being locked back in place and healing. Instead, I felt a stinging feeling in my head as black smoke enveloped her hand, which preceded four familiar voices. All the voices called my name, so I turned behind me to see Fildra, Prince Darien, Rolan, and Barrea behind me.

A cheap illusion, as if I would be unable to get Lorraine's symbolism behind how they were presented. Fildra and Rolan both had bullet wounds to the head; blood-stained Fildra's white hair, while Rolan's blood crusted over his face. Prince Darien had it flowing from his eye, which I had popped like a grape.

Then, there was Barrea standing there, even though her muscles, ligaments, and cartilage had been ripped from her body. Her skin was in ribbons, and there was no evidence of a throat ever being there. Her blood was still fresh, the last death I had witnessed.

All four of them talked as if I were at fault for their deaths. Though it was true for Prince Darien, which I felt no remorse for, it wasn't true for the others. Fildra was a wild, mad woman; she didn't even know what was happening, just that the man who robbed her of luxury was walking down her street. Rolan chose to help me more than I had asked. I was grateful, and he did, in fact, die for me, but that wasn't my fault. That was Father's. Barrea knew I wasn't at fault for her death; her situation would've played out the same whether I was there or not.

I turned back to lost witch once again and narrowed my eyes at her poor attempt to hurt my mental being. "'The biggest enemy to an Illusion is awareness,'" I quoted. "You'll be surprised to hear, I learned that from you."

Lorraine's eyes widened, and confusion possessed her face as they did so.

"That's why I want to have this chat, Lorraine. I know what kind of person you were; the ghost of your past-self haunts Yggdrasil to this day, and she helped me against your tricks."

"Shut your mouth," she roared and unleashed a quick jolt of lightning, but it snapped back and blew out before she could cast the spell. Her power was running out, and it didn't help that she kept up a continuous healing magic spell to keep her lung from collapsing.

"I know what you're feeling, Lorraine."

"You know nothing of what I feel!" she shouted. She then tried once more to attack me with a flaming fist, but it shorted out once more. Lorraine's dwindling strength was only hurting her as the fire burned more sores and wounds on her hand. Her healing magic recovered those wounds right away, causing her to push harder to stay alive, to keep her lung from collapsing under the penetration of my blade. She screamed out of frustration, not being able to hurt me anymore. The witch had been tamed.

Lorraine grunted from pure rage but was immobilized as she lashed out with just her words. "You are nothing more than a naive princess who knows less than the basics of the world you only just discovered. Sylvestra was my sister, my closest companion during the Witch's Wars. We could've won! Yet, she sacrificed herself and took away the one thing that made me feel whole. Ever since that day, I've been a shell, no different than what you see over there," she jerked her head to the fight between Sylvestra and Rose, hinting at the former high priestess herself.

Rose flipped around and evaded what the corpse had to offer, but even she knew she was only extending the lives of Metsa citizens by mere minutes.

"She and I were one. And now she's nothing but dust and bones, and you can't begin to imagine what that does to a person. You'll never know what I—"

"You feel numb," I interjected, growing tired of her monologue.

Lorraine's eyes grew twice their size, and she hiccupped a gasp at the sound of my understanding.

"You forget, I've been through the Ritual of Imprintation myself. Thank you, by the way, for making that nothing more than a waste of time."

"That's a little harsh, don't ya think, lass?" Fristlyn chimed in just for me with a chuckle.

Ignoring it, I continued. "I know how overwhelming the bond is between two people who engage in that together. I do. There's no level of love, marriage, friendship, or intimacy can overshadow it." I watched as her sunset eyes gleamed through the buildup of tears. I was breaking through, just as I had hoped.

"I'd be lost if Fristlyn died. The numbness I felt can't compare to that, or to you. But I've felt it. I've felt the endless void and the desperation to feel something, *anything*, for even just a fraction of time. I kissed Fristlyn, whom I wanted nothing to do with at the time due to his past monstrosities." I know bringing that up hurt him, I felt the sting in my chest as my words scarred his. I couldn't look at him, though; feeling it was bad enough. "What do you feel now? I'm eager to know how this solved your problem. I know you feel something; you said it back in your lair. Tell me, is it everything you hoped?"

Lorraine began to stifle a cry as she looked at that ravenous zombie who attacked the barrier, which contradicted everything I knew about the legendary hero. Amilyana was up and face-to-face with the undead priestess now, doing an arrangement of movements similar to what I saw Lorraine doing. When she finished, an ethereal chain bound the corpse to Amilyana, and it stood with stasis no longer having its own control to move. Ami told me she had energy for one last spell, and she used it to bind herself to her mother's corpse. It only now hit me that Amilyana and Lorraine had a past of their own; if Lorraine was as close to Sylvestra as she claimed, then this whole situation must've been brutal for Ami to endure.

As I turned back to Lorraine, I noted how she couldn't keep her fingers still, and how she bit at her lip and tore it till it bled. Her own ticks, similar to my picking at my nails and pulling at my hair. Lorraine and I had so much in common; two sides of a similar coin.

"You know that's not her, lass," Fristlyn added as he approached, and knelt to her. He placed a hand on her back, which I expected her to reject. Though I was wrong, she accepted his comfort. "You were her closest companion; you know she and I didn't get along, yet even I know that isn't her in there. Some angry specter that is a mere shred of the woman she used to be."

"Not her..." she whispered. "It's not her I feel."

"I suggest you go fucking fix it," I whispered as I grasped the hilt of my saber and pulled it out of her chest. I watched the magic work and close her wounds before darting over to the rage-filled corpse.

She wailed as she did so, screaming, "It's not her," over and over again until she placed her hands on the undead beast. Grasping her shoulders, in front of everyone, she screeched the word, *"Release,"* causing blue light to explode from Sylvestra's body.

As the body crippled back down, reverting to the soulless husk it should've been, Tara released the cracked barrier and dropped to her knees, now fatigued herself. Amilyana laid on her back screaming, applying pressure to her head. She had already drained so much of her power and fought hard to protect Metsa.

Lorraine, to my own mixture of empathy yet pleasantry, was toppled over Sylvestra's body. She wailed into the rotted bones, apologizing profusely for desecrating her grave.

Amilyana, though screaming in pain from the mass amounts of energy she channeled during the day, saw this and roared with anger. The fiery priestess moved to attack, but a whip of Fristlyn's web, as well as my enchanted sword, shut her down. The brief distraction reminded her of the anguish in her head, and she was down.

I started to approach the distraught witch, but Fristlyn stopped me for just a moment. With what little energy he had left, he wrapped my arm in his healing silk and complained about his own headache afterward, though it was not as intense as Ami's.

I stood over Lorraine, accompanied by Fristlyn, Tara, Soen, and Rose, who had just helped Amilyana up and held the warlock's arm over her shoulder.

I extended my own to Lorraine, who stopped crying when she saw my mercy.

She rejected it, but not out of bitterness. She explained the aftereffects of her magic, and the number of electric-based spells she used would fry my remaining good hand. All she asked was that I would allow her to recharge, and she would be on her way.

Soen, being the mayor, granted her request, though she would be under constant supervision for as long as she'd be in the city.

I just congratulated her for feeling her own feelings for the first time in thousands of years, something she didn't even realize she was doing.

CHAPTER 49

I WAS SURPRISED MY BED DIDN'T BREAK FROM THE FORCE OF MY body falling onto it. While not as cushioned or luxurious as the beds at Yggdrasil, nothing was as comfortable as the bed of my own house; the pain of my broken arm was shadowed by the feeling of being home.

Both Marla and Soen decorated the house while I had been gone. Absent of the worn wooden dressers, bedframe, and rusted sconces; everything was replaced with Metsa's iconic brass work. Repaired windowsills and hardwood flooring completed the apartment.

I grinned as I heard Marla's reborn gruff, orcish voice offer every scrap of food to Lorraine, who was chained to my table downstairs. Even though Lorraine had been an enemy, Marla's golden white heart wanted her to feel safe. I was so warmed by Marla's generosity that I sat up to try and listen in, smiling at the young orc naming dish after dish she could provide for the witch.

Upon sitting up, my eyes detected a wardrobe that my bedroom lacked before. It wasn't brass like all the other decor and furniture; this was dark oak with a gleaming finish to it. A lovely piece such as this would've cost Soen a fortune, and I knew he had paid out of his own pocket for it.

Trying not to strain my healing arm, I stumbled out of bed, and moved toward it and gave a soft graze at its smooth, sanded feel. A ruby gem acted as the knob; the mayor really spared no expense on this piece or the set of clothes inside.

When I opened it, I was blessed with a beautiful suede coat. Evergreen silk, with an extravagant curled collar, full of blood-colored feathers. My eyes welled up as I ran my fingers down the gold stitching, with matching lining on the rims.

The open door contained a full-length mirror, so I removed the coat from its hangings and threw my burgundy jacket onto my bed.

Wearing the green coat didn't make me feel like a princess, or a queen, for that matter. Though it made me feel powerful like I was a woman of respected importance.

"Not for everyday wear, but I hope you like it," Soen's voice startled me, breaking me from my trance as I adored how I looked in the coat.

As he leaned against the doorframe of my room, I returned his perfect smile with my own, though I showed no teeth as I hated how inferior my own were.

"No, it certainly is not," I agreed. "Why such a lavish gift?"

"We are entering a new world, RoGoria," he informed me as he stepped into my quarters and stared out one of the two windows. "If you thought Relica's politics were messy now, imagine what it's like to have magic in the mix. I'm a mayor, and my people need me here. I have little time to spend on overseeing the decisions that will come this way."

I rolled my eyes. "Please, don't dodge my question. You said you'd stop doing that once I returned."

He laughed and looked at me, followed by stepping toward me. As he brushed my new coat, he continued. "When you and I spoke at Yggdrasil, I told you there may be a change in position for you.

You're too much of a natural born leader to be a mere guard. Your rise to power after Elliot's injuries, as well as your method of handling Lorraine have proven that. Your previous teachings as a princess would make being a captain a waste."

"So, what are you suggesting?" I asked, eager to know what he had in store for me.

"I want you to represent Metsa; I'd like to offer you the position of ambassador and take a seat as Metsa's Representative of the Relican Senate. In the time between you releasing magic and coming home, Mazz'Ra, Farlara, Sune'Sun, and Haven Call have already started planning laws and regulations that will be in place. We plan on getting the others on board soon. Amilyana is getting ready to sail soon; she's already asked if your companion, Mr. Everleef, will help her in reestablishing the High Court."

I was washed with a sudden feeling of being overwhelmed. Seeing the Elves of Yggdrasil made it clear how drastic we had changed Relica; and how many lives, cultures, and communities we restored. "The Relican Senate, the High Court...all concepts from the before ages, I'm guessing?"

"Established during the Age of the Hourglass, when magic was normalized, yes." He nodded. "Are you interested?"

I bit my lip as I pondered Soen's proposal. It was clear I wouldn't have time to think it over, so I'd have to give him an answer now. I poked at his arm and offered a smirk. "Do I get my own office?"

Soen laughed, though I wasn't joking. "Yes, across the hall from my own. It was a storage area, but we plan on expanding Metsa, and I've already ordered to have it cleared for you. It will have a view of the garden, just outside the Barracks."

"Regardless, I will greatly accept," I confirmed, and I held out my hand for him to grasp.

He was gentle as he did so, lifting my hand near his face so that he may press his soft lips against my skin. My entire body got warm as he did so, and it only then occurred to me that, as a mayor, he could be what I had been avoiding all these years, a potential suitor, and a beautiful specimen at that.

"Let's have tea later tonight if you aren't too busy," he continued. "First, Mr. Everleef has requested you. He's at the docks, getting ready to depart."

"Depart?" I asked, now feeling a sudden sadness wash over me, which caused ignorance toward his request for tea.

"Yes, he's not exactly welcome here, not by me. I have no quarrel with the elf, but the orcs…"

"Right, of course. Besides, this isn't his home," I said, even though it had been his home for quite some time. His true home was back on the Coven Isle, which was reborn as one of the most welcoming places in all of Relica now that magic had been restored. "I'll see him off, then."

I DIDN'T RUN to the docks to see Fristlyn depart, though the thought crossed my mind many a time. Not like my decision would have mattered; walking through the Lower Streets of Metsa made me a target for the overwhelming amount of "thank you"s. I would barely get a few steps in before an orc would stop me, shake my hand like a mad person, and profess his or her or their undying gratitude.

One of those orcs was Doc, whom I met at the local tavern that he owned. I thought he was big as a human, but orc Doc could squish him. His skin was on the greener side, and just one of those fat fingers was the size of my face. He expressed how happy and thankful he was for my saving his people, and he had a big, happy smile. I assumed it was happy, anyway; the teeth of an orc were sharp, curved, and all-around menacing to look at. This would be something I would have to get used to, more so with Marla.

A lot of the orcs told me how they reclaimed their heritage. Beau and Theresa, two of the guards who worked right alongside

Elliot, were now named Bourn and Taliti. Marla remembered her orcish name, Makar'Iik, though, she said people could keep calling her Marla, claiming she loved the new name more. I was supportive and let her know as long as that was her decision and she wasn't doing it for anyone else, including me, though I admit learning to pronounce her given name was a task I was happy to avoid.

Fristlyn called to me as he saw me approach Amilyana's ship at the docks, and as I became just an arm's length away, he teased me by singing, "Someone has a crush on the mayor," while doing a little dance. I shushed him and asked him to be quiet, but he repeated it over and over again while doing his little off-beat dance. I hit him hard in the arm, as friendly as I could, and he acted as though I murdered him before busting out in a laugh.

Fristlyn's happiness was genuine; I could feel it growing, though it was still tainted by despair. He was still shameful about his past, and being around the orcs, whom he wronged, wasn't helping things. It's why he thought he was going to die when Rose and I were in Lorraine's hidden chambers. He thought the orcs would be seeking their revenge, but the brutish race seemed to just be happy to be restored. However, if they were happy with how things were, and Fristlyn was feeling remorse, it just added to his humility. I wasn't going to disregard that.

There was more to it, though. Fristlyn opened up to me about his previous marriage, and while he cracked open the door just a little bit, others threw it wide open. Seeing Amilyana use that spectral scythe hurt him. I had felt that, too. Plus, hearing his late husband's name be used in an incantation by Lorraine really opened my eyes. Was Fristlyn married to an Old One? A Faer of Death? I knew those were answers I wouldn't get, at least not from him while the wounds were still fresh after thousands of years.

I watched as the chaotic elf kept up his dance and smiled,

happy regardless of his past pain that he was able to find some scrap of happiness.

"I hear you're leaving," I finally said, my words soaked in somber.

He stopped his dance and gave a fake frown. "Aye, lass," he confirmed. "Not exactly welcome here; felt I should leave while they're distracted."

"You should reach out, apologize."

"That's what *I* said," Rose chimed in from behind him, helping Amilyana load a large, body-length box onto the ship. I shouldn't have been so surprised. No way Amilyana was keeping the corpse of her mother here. "Slip in the apology while they're happy, higher chance for the results we want."

"I don't want results, my queen," Fristlyn stated. He was bold in his words and stood by them. That much I could tell. "And I did apologize. When you all were in the abandoned house. They acknowledged it, but I'm not to step foot into Metsa per their wishes."

I felt the grin be birthed on my face as it transitioned to grin from idle. "With all due respect, I agree. I'm not an orc, so I really don't, nor can't, have an opinion. These people—"

"*Your* people," Fristlyn interjected. "This is your home now, lass. These are your people." He had no idea just how true his words were. For now, I would work right under Soen and lead these people.

"Well, then," I continued. "As my first declaration, I have to demand that you hold yourself accountable for your actions."

Fristlyn gave me a gentleman's bow. "As you command it," he paused, flashing me a wink, "*Ambassador.*" The Spider King gave me a hug and whispered a heartfelt goodbye before retreating onto the ship just as Amilyana approached me. The high priestess held out her hand, and I grasped it, giving one, firm shake.

"I'm not sure if I like you," she informed me. "You're naive, and you seem to just react blindly to danger, not thinking about the best course of action, yet your heart is in the purest of places. I think that is what's keeping me from having a sheer distaste."

I chuckled. "Well, you're arrogant, boastful about your arts, yet I saw not a lick of Necromancy or Demonology from you. I suppose I could say the same about yourself."

We shared a chuckle, and then Amilyana boarded the ship with Fristlyn.

Next was Rose, but all she offered was an awkward face and a punch to my arm. She saluted me, and I offered a hug which she was hesitant to accept. "These people are in good hands with you," she said. "Keep them safe."

Rose was the first one to wave at me from the ship as it departed Metsa's docks. Followed by Fristlyn, though he kept saying he'd miss me over and over again in a little voice in my head. I prayed distance wouldn't be an issue; I would always want to talk to him.

I stayed until the ship was far enough out that I couldn't see them anymore, saddened by their leaving now. I tried to be strong, but the bond with Fristlyn was immense and pure. Not just because of his mark on me, his Imprintation, but because I knew there was no ulterior motive there. Rose didn't talk much, but I was fond of her, as well. Whether or not that was a mutual feeling, I didn't know; she was monotone in speech but I knew she at least didn't mind me.

The high priestess and I clashed, but Amilyana was still a powerful ally to have. If I had to kiss ass to keep her around, so be it. I knew Elliot was in good hands with her and her wife.

My ears picked up the sound of crunching sand behind me, which then turned to faint steps on the wood of the docks. A pleasant, light pitter-patter; this wasn't the sound of someone who was wearing boots like most of Metsa adorned, myself included. These steps were bare, and I realized I had one more person to see off.

CHAPTER 50

I FACED LORRAINE, AND FOR THE FIRST TIME, THERE WAS NO HATRED between us. Uncertainty and lack of trust maybe. But no anger. No hate. Just by the way she stood, with one hand rubbing the opposite arm, the shuffling of her bare feet; she was telling me she wasn't an enemy anymore.

In fact, as we stared at each other, her body language was deeper than just that. Her eyes were wide and darted around as she tried to center her attention on me. She was shy, near sheepish because of the interaction, and it hadn't even started yet. I watched her lips twitch as she searched for the words to say, and how to say them.

I decided I'd put her out of her misery. "Is this goodbye, then?"

Lorraine's eyes went still, centered, focused on me as the relief of no longer having to start the conversation possessed her. "You are really going to just trust me to be on my own? After everything I've done?"

"Who said a damn thing about trusting you," I asked her, making sure to reveal a small grin to establish that I was joking. "I just have nothing to offer. I can make you a prisoner, wallow in pity inside a cell. Doesn't seem to be a productive choice though."

"Even after the chef..." she trailed off at the mention of Barrea, but I shook my head.

"You didn't kill her. Granted, you separated us, which wasn't helpful. However, it was the island that killed her."

Lorraine had nothing to say to my retort, gazing out to the open sea instead. I had a list of questions for her now that she had somewhat collected herself. Knowing what I know now, though, my brain was putting the pieces together. Amilyana never mentioned Lorraine or told me about her, though it was clear they knew one another. I would've even expected Lorraine to be an auntie of sorts while the warlock was growing up. Yet, Ami kept that from me. Everyone had taken turns keeping information from me. It was beyond irritating and made this whole mission harder. It was clear to me now, that they remained unbiased for my benefit, so I could make decisions for myself. Sylvestra told me my life was tethered to the choices I made, and everyone took turns making sure I wasn't swayed one way or another. In a way, Lorraine did this too.

Maybe if I had known how she was feeling from the beginning, I would've supported her decision. She, along with several others, loved pointing out how naïve I was. I could've been manipulated by her this whole time, but that just wasn't in her nature. Lorraine was so numb that she was bad at being the bad guy.

A strong gust of wind hurled from the bay, and the witch's long, decorated braid glided gloriously in the wind as she shot me an awkward glance. "I guess I should be off."

"Where will you go?" I asked her.

"I'm not sure yet. Far from here. Besides, I'd rather you not know my whereabouts. I...I need to handle this on my own. Like the Spider King, I need to stew in my choices."

I chortled. "You were there, weren't you? To save the orcs that day."

She nodded. "Sylvestra, Amilyana, Alsyn, and I each took our own battalion. We dropped the orcs off here, and I guess they got to work and made it the city it is today." Lorraine took a few steps near the edge of the docks. She turned and was about to speak, say something that seemed important given the look on her face. Remaining silent, unbiased, she caught herself. And with another breeze, she bid me farewell and vanished into black smoke, tussled and torn by the wind.

SOEN ALLOWED me to take the next few days just to relax and get reacquainted with home life. I took the mayor up on this, except I kept one hour of my day blocked for Tara. The mysterious witch informed me that her superiors, though she chose to use the words, "Big daddy boss man," much to my dismay, had ordered her to stick around. For one hour a day, Tara and I would engage in combat training. Some days would be hand-to-hand combat, and others would be melee. Ranged training I took from the Guards of Metsa, who were honored to assist.

Marla and I spent most days together. Metsa wasn't home to a lot of children, so there wasn't an outstanding education system. I'd go over some tutoring every once in a while, though as the days went by, she reclaimed more and more of her orcish ways. Orcs age at a different pace. Similar to Elves, they could live for thousands of years, so their maturity accelerated. An eleven-year-old orc, such as herself, had more in common with that of a fifteen-year-old human, so teaching her to read was really all that I could do.

The restoration of the orc made me question her parents' abandonment further, but Marla still didn't fully understand herself. She was born in this era, so she didn't live through what a lot of the other orcs did. Her being abandoned was the only hardship she really faced, but she assured me she was happy the way things are now. The emotional endurance of such a young girl was astounding. It was like she didn't care her parents left her and was content with living with a stranger. I supposed that was all I had to know about the relationship she had with her family.

I started taking her to my combat training with Tara. If she was going to be a part of my life, I might as well find some ways for her to help. Besides, Marla had some aggression to let out if my theory was correct.

When my days off came to a close, Soen himself walked me from my home to City Hall, where he showed me my new office. He spared no expense; a gorgeous, finished mahogany desk with a glass top adorned with fake flowers, a personal request, greeted anyone who entered the room. I hoped this would make me seem approachable.

The desk was littered with papers, files, and books, though organized, at least. The books went over basic laws of magic; not how to use it, just how to understand it. The different areas of magical study, the prices that came with them, and subcategories. Things I would need to learn if I were to be a representative in the Relican Senate.

The neat stack of parchments was from other leaders, some of whom had just been reborn from the freeing of magic and were ready to get back to work. Such as the Coven of Lovely, Farlara, or the Shamans of Sune'Sun. One was a letter from Amilyana Lo'Ren, the High Priestess of Yggdrasil, which claimed she was getting ready to reestablish the High Court, the prestigious circle of magic-users that reigned supreme of magical politics, each representative was head of another coven. Soen said I would have to respond to these acknowledgments so that I could get acquainted.

I sat at my desk and looked over the files. They detailed all the World Leaders who would be having a seat at the senate meetings, which would take place every four months. Havencall, Linlecross, Mang'Coal, Que, every single one. When I reached the last file, I gripped it hard and crinkled the papers inside. Lord Luke of

Sheol, Mazz'Ra. It seemed my efforts to avoid him had failed as now I would be in direct contact with him from here on out.

My anxiety toward this was only spurred on by the haunting thought of what my father was up to. He had driven Sheol into the ground to search for Sylvestra's Tears, and this file made it clear of his awareness of magic being released. He wanted the Tears for something, and I could only assume he was a step closer to achieving whatever his goal might be.

I knew I would have to keep a watchful eye over him and keep him from achieving his goal, at all costs. This world is new to us both, and we each represented the two sides of the coin; the one who is ready to help the world be a safe place for all, and the one who is committed to bending it to their will.

ACKNOWLEDGMENTS

I have been dreading this page because it requires me to...just get all up in my feelings, which I hate; it's too crowded in there. I guess I'll just dive on in, here. I do want to start by giving a shout-out to Christina Kaye, my author mom. Finding you on TikTok was the best thing that happened to me in getting my dream started. I found a mentor, friend, and boss all rolled into one. Speaking of bosses, Justin H. gets some of the spotlight, too. Thank you for providing me a safe space to come in and write when I didn't have a computer of my own and showing me that good bosses do, indeed, exist. Other work peeps, such as Sylvia M., Sam D., Darius W., Traci Z., Antonio V., and Sam "Chuck" V., you all were super supportive in this endeavor, and I'm forever grateful. Jacob Holt, my fiancé, my truest of true loves, my Prince Charming, the Nimue to my Merlin, the Stygian to my Fristlyn, the Captain Hook to my Emma Swan, the Tara McClay to my Willow Rosenburg, and the Vision to my Wanda, I love you so much, and I'm forever thankful you took my hand on this path from our very first date. My Queen Beebs, Breeanna Graham... you had my back from the second you trained me as a cashier, and you've never left my life since. You're the Shaggy to my Scooby, and I wouldn't have it any other way. Riana, love, you've been with me since I was a WEE little Wattpad writer with a dream. Now you get to walk with me as it comes to fruition, thanks to your support. My Illinois Crew, Emma DeVries, Welcing, Jacob (lol), Kris Gullang, Ashley Scott, Dominic Cichocki, and Austin Welch. All people I knew in high school, and I would not have expected to have you in my life as an adult, let alone supporting me in my dream. I thank and love each and every one of you. All my TikTok supporters, you all get the spotlight, too! Be it current or future, thank you for showing interest and being a big part of what motivated me. FLORIDA FAM! Joey Rivieccio, Jerry Bishop, Keoni Grabowski, David Benoit, Cassidy Cameron, Alex Grisham, Kenzie Smith, y'all were essential in my growth during this journey. I'll never forget you guys. Some other important names, before I dive into the craziness that is my Family: Karen Davis, Phylis Cheiro, Jean Garner-Steele, Ellen Oldenburg, Karen Lowe, Nick Lowe, Don Lowe, Matt Lowe, and of course, Kim Lowe. Thank you all so much for the unconditional love and support from you all. My family, I need to start with my mom; you saved me, adopted me, had no obligation to step up to the plate, but you did and were taking names as you did so. I couldn't have written a story about a strong, stable woman if I weren't raised by one. Rick, my brother. We've never been super close in our adult age, but I'm blessed that the black sheep of the family came as a package deal with the two of us. Sibling drama sure doesn't stop there! A big shout-out to my sister, Ashley Goodner. Thank you for not only supporting me but also finding me after thirteen years. I'm so thankful we got to reconnect and that I got to meet your family. Grandma Jeanne, Grandpa Mick, Uncle Mike along with his wife and kids, and Auntie Kristy, Uncle James, and all four of their amazing little kids. Grandma and Grandpa Stafiej, Uncle Don, lil' Linda, Logan, and my Aunt Colleen... thank all of you for helping me along the way and showing excitement for me when I told you I was releasing my first ever fantasy novel. On my fiancé's side, Crystal, Alan, Lee, Tonya, Hunter, Tia, of course, little Niya, Grandma and Grandpa Crew, Grandpa Dwaine and Grandma Sherry, Tiffany King and her kids, Tyler, Emily, Hayden, and Haylee, thank all of you for accepting me into the family and supporting my dream.

Thank you all so much for giving me a reason to write and follow my dream.

With Love to you all.

ABOUT THE AUTHOR

Kota Kai Lovett is a fantasy author, native to the Chicago suburbs. Growing up with a love for storytelling, he knew early on he wanted to be an author. He grew up immersed in fantasy media, watching shows like *Buffy the Vampire Slayer* and the 1998 miniseries *Merlin* when he was only seven. This was only the beginning of his love for fantasy and science fiction stories.

Kota lives in Illinois with his fiancé and their cat and dog.